About t

USA Today bestselling author **Kat Cantrell** read her first Mills & Boon novel in third grade and has been scribbling in notebooks since she learned to spell. What else would she write but romance? When she's not writing about characters on the journey to happily ever after, she can be found at a taekwondo tournament, watching *The Big Bang Theory* or dancing with her kids to Duran Duran and Red Hot Chili Peppers. Kat, her husband and their two boys live in North Texas. She is a former Mills & Boon So You Think You Can Write winner and a former *RWA*® Golden Heart® finalist for best unpublished series contemporary manuscript. Visit Kat online at katcantrell.com

New York Times and *USA Today* bestselling author **Cathryn Fox** is a wife, mum, sister, daughter, aunt and friend. She loves dogs, sunny weather, anything chocolate – she never says no to a brownie – pizza and red wine. Cathryn lives in beautiful Nova Scotia with her husband, who is convinced he can turn her into a mixed martial arts fan. When not writing, Cathryn can be found Skyping with her son, who lives in Seattle – could he have moved any further away? – shopping with her daughter in the city, watching a big action flick with her husband, or hanging out and laughing with friends.

Annie West has devoted her life to an intensive study of charismatic heroes who cause the best kind of trouble in the lives of their heroines. As a sideline she researches locations for romance, from vibrant cities to desert encampments and fairytale castles. Annie lives in eastern Australia with her hero husband, between sandy beaches and gorgeous wine country. She finds writing the perfect excuse to postpone housework. To contact her or join her newsletter, visit annie-west.com

Opposites Attract Collection

Opposites Attract:

Love In Paradise

KAT CANTRELL

CATHRYN FOX

ANNIE WEST

MILLS & BOON

First Published in Great Britain 2025
by Mills & Boon, an imprint of HarperCollins*Publishers* Ltd
1 London Bridge Street, London, SE1 9GF

www.harpercollins.co.uk

HarperCollins*Publishers*
Macken House, 39/40 Mayor Street Upper,
Dublin 1, D01 C9W8, Ireland

ISBN: 978-0-263-41719-7

PREGNANT BY MORNING

KAT CANTRELL

To my sister. Our trip to Italy remains
one of my most cherished memories.

One

Matthew Wheeler stepped into the fray of Carnevale not to eat, drink or be merry, but to become someone else.

Venice attracted people from all over the globe for its beauty, history or any number of other reasons, but he doubted any of the revelers thronging Piazza San Marco had come for the same reason he had.

Matthew adjusted the tight mask covering the upper half of his face. It was uncomfortable, but necessary. Everyone wore costumes, some clad in tuxedos and simple masks like Matthew, and many in elaborate Marie Antoinette–style dresses and feathered headpieces. Everyone also wore smiles, but that was the one thing he couldn't summon.

"Come, my friend." Vincenzo Mantovani, his next-door-neighbor, clapped Matthew on the shoulder. "We join the party at Caffe Florian."

"*Va bene*," Matthew replied, earning a grin from the Italian who had appointed himself Matthew's Carnevale guide this evening. Vincenzo appointed himself to a lot of things, as long as they were fun, reckless and ill-advised, which made him the appropriate companion for a man who wanted to find all of the above but had no clue how to accomplish it.

Actually, Matthew would be happy if he could just forget about Amber for a few hours, but the ghost of his wife followed him everywhere, even to Italy, thousands of miles from her grave.

Vincenzo chattered in accented English as he and Matthew pushed through the crowd along the edges of Piazza San Marco and squeezed into Caffe Florian, where it was too loud to converse. Which suited Matthew. He had the right companion, but he wasn't sure Vincenzo did.

Like most Venetians, the man had never met a stranger and had immediately latched onto the American living by himself in the big, lonely palazzo next door. Vincenzo's description, not Matthew's, though he couldn't deny it had some truth. He'd outbid an Arab prince by the skin of his teeth to buy the palazzo overlooking the Grand Canal as a wedding gift to Amber, but they'd never made it to Italy in the eleven months after the wedding. He'd been too busy working.

Then it was too late.

Matthew sipped the cappuccino his new friend had magically produced and summoned up a shred of merriment. If he planned to think about something other than Amber, dwelling on her wasn't going to work. She would hate him like this, would want him to move on, and he was trying. His sole goal this evening was to be someone who wasn't grieving, someone who didn't have the weight of responsibility and his family's expectations on his shoulders. Someone who fit into this fantastical, hedonistic Carnevale atmosphere.

It was hard to be someone else when he'd been a Wheeler since birth.

Matthew, along with his brother, father and grandfather, comprised the foundation of Wheeler Family Partners, a multimillion-dollar commercial real estate firm that had been brokering property deals in North Texas for over a century. Matthew had firmly believed in the power of family and tradition, until he lost first his wife, then his grand-father. Grief had so paralyzed him the only solution had been to leave.

He was a runaway from life, pure and simple. He had to find a way to get back to Dallas, back to the man he'd been.

The beaches of Mexico had failed to produce an answer. Machu Picchu had just exhausted him. The names of the other places he'd been had started to blur, and he had to do something different.

A month ago, he'd ended up in Venice. Until real life felt doable again, this was where he'd be.

Near eleven o'clock, Vincenzo herded a hundred of his closest friends—and Matthew—the few blocks to his house for a masked ball. The narrow streets allowed for only a few partygoers to pass simultaneously, so by the time Matthew arrived at the tail end of the group, the palazzo next door to his was already ablaze with lights and people. In marked contrast, Matthew's house was dark.

He turned his back on it and went up the stone steps to Vincenzo's back entrance. The sounds of Carnevale blasted from the palazzo, drowning out the quiet lap of the canal against the water entrance at the front.

Inside, a costumed attendant took his cloak. An ornate antique table in the hall blocked Matthew's path to the main area, an oddity with its large glass bowl in the center full of cell phones.

"It's a phone party."

The gravelly voice came from behind him, and he turned to find the owner.

A woman. Masked, of course, and wearing a delicate em-broidered dress in pale blue and white with miles of skirts. The neckline wasn't as low cut as almost every other fe-male's, but in combination with so much dress, her softly mounded breasts drew his eye. Whimsical silver butterfly wings sprouted from her back.

"Was my confusion that obvious?" he asked, his gaze firmly on her face.

She smiled. "You're American."

"Is that the explanation for why I don't know what a phone party is?"

"No, that's because you have more maturity than most of the people here."

So she must know the guests, then. Except for Vincenzo, who had disappeared, Matthew knew no one. This little butterfly was an interesting first encounter.

Most of her face was covered, with the exception of a full mouth painted pink. Caramel-colored hair hung in loose curls around her bare shoulders. Stunning. But her voice…it was sultry and deep, with a strange ragged edge that caught him in the gut.

He'd been looking for a distraction. Perhaps he'd found one.

"Now I'm curious. Care to enlighten me?" he asked.

She shrugged with a tiny lift of her shoulders. "Women drop their phone into the bowl. Men pick one out. Voila. Instant hookup."

His eyebrows rose. Vincenzo partied much differently than Matthew had been expecting. "I honestly have no good response."

"So you won't be fishing one out at the end of the evening?"

A tricky question. The old Matthew would say absolutely not. He'd never had a one-night stand in his life, never even considered it. This kind of thing had his brother, Lucas, written all over it. Lucas might have pulled out two phones and somehow convinced both women they'd been looking for a threesome all along. Well, once upon a time he would have, but in a bizarre turn of events, his brother was happily married now, with a baby on the way.

Matthew did not share his brother's talent when it came to women. He knew how to broker a million-dollar deal for a downtown Dallas high-rise and knew how to navigate the privilege of his social circle but nothing else, especially not how to be a widower at the age of thirty-two.

When Matthew left Dallas, intent on finding a way to move on after Amber's death, he'd had a vague notion of becoming like Lucas had been before marrying his wife, Cia. Lucas always had fun and never worried about consequences. Matthew, like his father and grandfather before him, had willingly carried the weight of duty and family and tradition on his shoulders, eagerly anticipating the day his wife would give birth to the first of a new generation of Wheelers. Only to have it all collapse.

Becoming more like Lucas was better than being Matthew, and nothing else had worked to pull him out of this dead-inside funk. And he had to pull out of it so he could go home and pick up his life again.

So what would Lucas do?

"Depends." Matthew nodded to the bowl. "Is yours in there?"

With a throaty laugh, she shook her head. "Not my style."

Strangely, he was relieved and disappointed at the same time. "Not mine, either. Though I might have made an exception in this one case."

Her smile widened and she drew closer, rustling her wings. The front of her dress brushed his chest as she leaned in to whisper in her odd, smoky voice, "Me, too."

Then she was gone.

He watched her as she swept into the main room of Vincenzo's palazzo and was swallowed by the crush. It was intriguing to be so instantly fascinated by a woman because of her voice. Should he follow her? How could he not follow her after such a clear indication of interest?

Maybe she'd been flirting and it hadn't meant anything. He cursed under his breath. It had been far too long since he'd dated to remember the rules. Actually, he'd never understood the rules, even then, which was saying something for a guy who thrived on rules. But this was Venice, not Dallas, and he was someone else.

There were no rules.

Matthew followed Butterfly Woman into the crowd.

Electronic music clashed with old-world costumes, but no one seemed to notice. Dancers dominated the floor space on the lower level of the palazzo. But none of the women had wings.

Along the edges of the dance floor, partygoers tried their luck at roulette and vingt-et-un, but he didn't bother to look for his mystery woman there. Gambling was for those who knew nothing about odds, logic or common sense, and if she fell into that category, he'd rather find a different distraction.

A flash of silver caught his eye, and he glimpsed the very tips of her wings as she disappeared into another room.

"Excuse me." Matthew waded through the dancers as politely as he could and chased after the only thing he could recall being interested in for eighteen very long, very cold months.

When he paused under a grand arch between the two rooms, he saw her. She stood at the edge of a group of people engrossed in something he couldn't see. And he had the distinct impression she felt as alone in the crowd as he did.

Tarot junkies crowded around Madam Wong as if she held the winning lottery numbers. Evangeline La Fleur was neither a junkie nor one to buy lottery tickets, but people were always amusing. Madam Wong turned over another card and the crowd gasped and murmured. Evangeline rolled her eyes.

Her neck prickled and she sensed someone watching her. The guy from the hall.

They locked gazes across the room, and she gave herself a half second to let the shiver go all the way down. Delicious. There'd been something about the way he talked to her, as if truly interested in what she had to say. About Vincenzo's stupid phone party, no less.

Lately, no one was interested in what she said, unless it was to answer the question, *"What are you going to do now that you can't sing anymore?"* They might as well ask what she'd do after they nailed the coffin shut.

Hall guy's suit was well-cut, promising what lay underneath it might be worth a peek or two, his lips below the black velvet mask were strong and full and his hands looked…capable. The man trifecta.

The music faded into the background as he strode purposefully toward her without so much as glancing at what he passed. Every bit of his taut focus was on her, and it had a powerful effect, way down low in places usually reserved for men she'd known far longer.

Boldly, she watched him approach, her gaze equally as fixed on him.

Bring it, Tall, Blond and Gorgeous.

The mystery of his masked face somehow made him more attractive. That and the fact he couldn't possibly know who she was behind her mask. This…pull was all about anonymity, and she'd have called anyone a dirty liar who said she'd like it. But she did. When was the last time she'd been within a forty-foot radius of someone who wasn't aware of how her career had crashed and burned? Or the number of Grammys she'd won, for that matter.

For a time, she'd dwelled in the upper echelon of entertainers—so successful she didn't require a last name. The world knew her simply as Eva.

Then she was cast aside, adrift and alone, with no voice.

"There you are," he murmured, as if afraid to be overheard and determined to keep things between them very private. "I'd started to think you'd flown away."

She laughed, surprising herself. Laughter didn't come easily, not lately. "The wings only work after midnight."

"I'd better move fast, then." The eyes on her were beautiful, an almost colorless, crystalline blue that contrasted with the black border of the mask. "My name is—"

"No." She touched a finger to his lips. "No names. Not yet."

As he looked very much like he wanted to suck her fingertip into his mouth, she dropped it before she let him. This stranger was exciting, no doubt, but she had a healthy survival instinct. Vincenzo's friends were a little on the wild side. Even for her.

Yet she'd been following Vincenzo around Europe for a couple of months and couldn't seem to find anything better to do. She wanted to. Oh, how she wanted to. But what?

"Are you seeking your fortune, then?" He nodded to Madam Wong and the crowd parted.

Madam Wong shuffled her cards. "Come. Sit."

Tall, Blond and Gorgeous pulled the brocade chair away from the draped table. Evangeline couldn't see a way to gracefully refuse without drawing unwanted attention, so she sat, extremely aware of the capable hand resting on the back of the chair inches from her neck.

When Madam Wong shoved the deck across the table, Evangeline cut it about a third of the way down and let the fortune-teller restack the cards.

After that quack doctor butchered her vocal cords, Evangeline had spent three months searching for a cure, eventually landing on the doorstep of every Romanian gypsy, every Asian acupuncturist and every Nepalese faith healer she could find.

No one had a way to restore her damaged voice. Or her damaged soul. In short, this wasn't her first tarot reading, and she had little hope it would be any more helpful than all the other mumbo jumbo.

The only positive from the nightmare of the past six months came from winning the lawsuit against the quack doctor, who no longer had a license to practice medicine, thanks to her.

The costumed crowd pressed closer as Madam Wong began laying out the spread. Her brow furrowed. "You have a great conflict, yes?"

Oh, however did you guess? Evangeline waited for the rest of the hokey wisdom.

The withered old woman twirled one of the many rings on her fingers as she contemplated the cards. "You have been cut deeply and lost something precious."

The capable hand of the masked stranger brushed her hair. Evangeline sat up straighter and frowned.

Cut.

She had been, in more ways than one.

"This card…" Madam Wong tapped it. "It confuses me. Are you trying to conceive?"

"A baby?" Evangeline spit out the phrase on a heavy exhale and took another breath to calm her racing pulse. "Not even close."

"Conception comes in many forms and is simply a beginning. It is the step after inspiration. You have been inspired. Now you must go forth and shape something from it."

Inspiration. That was in short supply. Evangeline's throat convulsed unexpectedly. The music in her veins had been abruptly silenced and she hadn't been inspired to write one single note since the surgery from hell.

Madam Wong swept the cards into a pile and began shuffling. "I must do a second spread."

Speechless and frozen, Evangeline tried to shake her head. Her eyes began to burn, a sure sign she'd start bawling uncontrollably very soon. It was the wrong time of the month for this sort of emotional roller coaster.

She needed a code word to get her out of this situation. Her manager had always given her one, so if the press asked a sensitive question, she'd say it and he'd rescue her.

Except she had no manager and no code word. She had nothing. She'd been rejected by everyone—music, the industry, fans. Her father.

"I believe you promised me a dance."

Tall, Blond and Gorgeous clasped her hand and pulled her out of the chair in one graceful move.

"Thank you," he said to Madam Wong, "but we've taken enough of your time. Good evening."

And like that, he whirled her away from the table, away from the prying eyes.

By the time he stopped in an alcove between the main dance floor and the back room, her pulse had slowed. She blinked away the worst of the burn and stared up at her savior. "How did you know?"

He didn't pretend to misunderstand. "You were so tense, the chair was vibrating. I take it you don't care for tarot."

"Not especially. Thanks." After a beat, when it became apparent he wasn't going to ask any questions—which almost made her weep in gratitude—she made a show of scouting around for a nonexistent waiter. "I could go for a glass of champagne. You?"

The thought of alcohol almost made her nauseous, but she needed a minute alone.

"Sure. Unless you'd rather dance?"

"Not right now."

Actually, she was thinking seriously about ditching the party and going to her room. A headache had bloomed behind her eyes. Except her room was right above the dance floor and Vincenzo's other guests had taken the rest of the rooms.

"Be right back. Stay here." Her stranger vanished into the crowd.

Maybe she could quietly gather her things and check into Hotel Danieli, with no one the wiser.... She groaned. As if. She had a better chance of finding solid gold bars on the street than an empty hotel room in Venice during Carnevale.

The stranger returned quickly with two champagne flutes, and she smiled brightly, clinking her rim to his in a false show of bravado. Yes, he was gorgeous and intuitive, but she wasn't going to be good company tonight. She nursed the drink and tried to think of an exit strategy when over his shoulder, she caught sight of her worst nightmare.

It was Rory. With Sara Lear.

Of course he was with Sara Lear. Sara's debut album full of bubblegum pop and saccharine love songs had burned up the charts and was still solidly at number one. The little upstart hadn't worn a mask, preferring to bask in the glow of stardom. Rory was also unmasked, no doubt to make doubly sure everyone knew who was with Sara. He was nothing if not savvy about his own career and his band Reaper made few bones about their desire to headline one of the major summer concert series. Hitching his wagon to a star was an old pattern.

Evangeline had flushed his engagement ring down the toilet after he dumped her and gladly told him to go to hell when he asked for it back.

Rory and Sara strolled through the main room as if they owned it, and why wouldn't they? Both of them had functional vocal cords and long, vital careers ahead of them. Six months ago, Evangeline would have been on Rory Cartman's arm, blissfully in love, blissfully at the top of her career and still blind to the cruelty of a world that loved a success but shunned a has-been.

The headache slammed her again.

She knocked back the champagne in one swallow and tried to figure out how to get past Rory and Sara without being recognized. Sara, she wasn't so worried about; they'd never officially met. But her ex-fiancé would out her in a New York minute without a single qualm. A mask only went so far with someone who knew her intimately.

She couldn't take the questions or the pitying looks or the eyes watching her navigate a very public meeting with the guy who'd shattered her heart and the woman who'd replaced her in his bed. And on the charts.

"More champagne?" her companion asked.

Rory and his new Pop Princess girlfriend stopped a few yards from the shadowy alcove where she stood with the masked stranger. She couldn't step out into the light and couldn't risk standing there with no shield.

Desperate times, desperate measures.

Praying she'd read him right, she plucked the half-empty flute from her savior's hand, set both glasses on the ledge behind her and grasped the lapels of his tux. With a yank, she hauled him into a kiss.

The moment their lips connected, the name Rory Cartman ceased to have any meaning whatsoever.

Two

Matthew had only a moment to register her intent. It wasn't long enough. When the winged woman pressed her lips to his, his body lit up and flooded with heat. She was like a conduit to a nuclear reactor, and the shocking sensation of her warm mouth on his threatened to bring on full meltdown.

He knew precisely what Lucas would do in this situation.

Cupping her face with both palms, Matthew tilted her head to slant his mouth against hers at a deeper angle. Her lips parted on a sigh, and the hands holding his lapels tightened, drawing him closer.

Nearly groaning, he kissed this nameless butterfly until he couldn't think, couldn't stop, almost couldn't stand. The shock of awareness and incendiary carnal lust picked up where his brain failed.

Shocking. And yet familiar. As if they'd done this before, exactly this way, pressed against each other in the shadows. Their lips fit, their bodies slid together with ease. He was kissing a stranger—a nameless stranger—and it should feel wrong, or at least odd.

It was so very right.

This woman was not at all his type—too glittery, too sensual, too beautiful. He couldn't imagine introducing her to his mother or taking her to a museum opening where they'd rub shoulders with the elite of Dallas.

But he didn't care.

For the first time since Amber died, he felt alive. His heart beat in his chest and blood flowed through his veins and a woman was kissing him. He reveled in these small clues that he hadn't been buried alongside his wife.

After an eternity passed in a blink, she broke away and stared up at him, her breath coming in short gasps. "I'm sorry."

"For what?"

He hadn't kissed a woman other than Amber in five years and as a reintroduction to the art, it was off the map. Surely she'd felt some of the same heat.

"I shouldn't have done that," she said.

"Yes, you absolutely should have."

He might be out of practice, but she was still firmly in his arms, and a woman who hadn't just had her world shaken to the foundation would have stepped away by now.

She inhaled sharply, her chest pushing against his and stroking the flame higher. "Not under false pretenses. I have to come clean. My ex is here, and that was a poor attempt to hide from him."

"I beg to differ. As attempts go, I thought it was pretty good."

A quavery laugh slipped out from her kiss-reddened lips and then she did step away, out of his embrace. But not too far.

"Just so you know, I don't go around kissing random men."

"There's an easy way to fix that. I'd be happy to introduce myself and thus eliminate the randomness."

"That would be awesome because I'm pretty sure I'm going to kiss you again."

She *had* felt it.

The thrill swept all the way to the soles of his feet. Tonight, he was someone else, and as it seemed to be working out well so far, why screw around with it?

"Matt. My name is Matt."

It flowed from his mouth effortlessly, though he'd never been Matt in his life. But right here, right now, he liked Matt a hell of lot. Matt wasn't bogged down in inertia and terrified he'd never find his way out. Matt hadn't walked away from all his responsibilities at home or lain awake at night, eaten with guilt over it. Matt hadn't drifted around the world in search of something he suspected didn't exist, only to land in Venice holed up in a cold, lonely palazzo.

Matt had fun and kissed costumed women at parties and maybe got to second base before the end of the night.

She smiled. "Nice to meet you, Matt. You can call me Angie."

Angie. It was too harsh, too common for such a delicate and ethereal woman. The careful phrasing tipped him off that it wasn't her real name, but since he'd similarly hedged, he couldn't exactly complain.

"Which one is your ex? So we can steer clear."

Since she'd been trying to hide, he assumed the breakup had been nasty and not Angie's choice.

Surreptitiously, she glanced behind her, then faced him again. Her soft brown eyes bored into his, luminous with appreciation. "He's over there, on the couch with the little blonde."

Matthew located what had to be the couple she meant. They were locked in a torrid embrace, and the guy's hands were down the blonde's dress. Ouch. Not only was her ex at the same party but also not much for public decency.

"They didn't get the memo? This is a masked ball."

"I like you," she said with a decisive nod.

He grinned. "I like you, too."

"That's good, because I intend to thoroughly use you. I hope you won't be offended."

Matthew's eyebrow shot up. "That depends, I suppose, on what you plan to use me for. And I really hope it's in the same vein as kissing me to hide from lover boy over there."

Apparently Matt knew how to flirt, too. There was no other explanation for such blatant come-ons.

Her tongue wet her lips, and the way she did it—while eyeing his lips at the same time—clamped down hard on his lower half. "You just became my new boyfriend."

"Excellent. I didn't realize I'd applied, but I'm gratified to have survived the rigorous selection process."

She laughed, and that gravelly timbre sliced through his gut anew. "Just for tonight. I can't stand the thought of anyone feeling sorry for me because I'm here alone. Pretend we're together, and I'll buy you breakfast."

Breakfast? He might be in for an evening with a little more action than he'd envisioned.

Was that what he wanted?

"I'm not the slightest bit offended. Unless I'm the backup choice. Is your real boyfriend otherwise engaged?"

"Very nicely done. But unnecessary. You don't have to be all casual-like if you want to know whether I'm available. Just ask."

Dang, he *was* out of practice. But dating had felt like such a betrayal. For so long, he couldn't, and when he finally deemed himself ready, no one appealed to him. Even if he'd dated every one of the sophisticated, demure women in Dallas angling for an invitation to dinner, none of them had wings.

He swallowed and dived in. "Angie, are you seeing anyone?"

"Yeah, this guy named Matt." She stood on tiptoe to whisper in his ear, like she'd done in the hall when they first met. It was becoming something he enjoyed thoroughly. "And he's really hot, too."

"Really?" No one had ever referred to him as hot. At least not to his face. The notion buzzed through his heightened senses and settled in nicely. "I must know more about this guy."

"I'd like to, as well. Vincenzo's got a great balcony on the second floor. Grab a couple of glasses of champagne and meet me there."

She turned and threw a saucy glance over her shoulder as she swayed in the direction of the stone staircase beyond the roulette tables.

He couldn't comply fast enough. Lucas would definitely see what this sexy little butterfly had in mind, and Matt was pretty curious, too. This was one night where anything might happen, and for once, he was looking forward to the possibilities.

The balcony overlooked a closed-off side courtyard that had fallen into disrepair. The small space above was poorly lit and cold, but had the bonus of being Rory and Sara free.

Evangeline was confident Matt wouldn't recognize Rory, as her new friend didn't seem the type to listen to punk rock, but her ex-fiancé's picture did end up next to hers with alarming frequency, even six months later. She couldn't be too careful.

Vincenzo's entertainment system vibrated the stone below her feet. In the distance, the revelry at San Marco drifted along the streets, wrapping the city in festive noise. Singing, instruments, the pop of what might be fireworks, all of it blended into the mystique that was Carnevale. And, for a moment, she was by herself at the world's largest party.

She didn't have to wait long for Matt. Her masked companion came through the unlocked French door with two champagne flutes balanced expertly in one capable hand. It was February in Venice, but the shiver that twisted her back had nothing to do with the temperature.

Thank God she hadn't ditched him. If she had, she'd have

run smack into Rory and missed the single most perfect kiss in the history of time. As stand-in boyfriends went, Matt had it going on. And he'd kissed her headache away, too.

She could find worse company to stave off the perpetual loneliness. Especially among Vincenzo's friends.

Matt handed her a glass and clinked the rims in an echo of their first toast. "This balcony is very difficult to find. How did you know it was here?"

Without the muddle of loud music, his voice was nice—clear, with a hint of the South running through it.

"I'm staying with Vincenzo. My room is down the hall."

"Oh? How do you know Vincenzo, Angie?"

Only her mother called her Angie, so it had seemed safe enough to use the name, though she regretted the necessity. Matt was a genuinely nice human being, someone she'd probably never have connected with under normal circumstances.

"Friend of a friend. You?"

As he was well-spoken and had far more class than Vincenzo's typical wealthy, spoiled buddies, she'd pegged him as a casual acquaintance.

"I'm staying next door."

Well, that made sense. Here on business and renting for the duration, most likely.

"Will you be in Venice long?"

Below the mask, his mouth turned down. "I'm not sure."

As she knew exactly the tone one used to say *back off*, she didn't press him, though now she was curious what his business in Venice might be. Shipping, maybe. She'd never dated a businessman and rarely interacted with people in that realm unless it involved contracts.

Whatever his livelihood, it was to remain a secret for the time being, and since she had secrets of her own, that was fine. She tossed back some champagne, let the bubbles fizz across her tongue and contemplated this very intriguing stand-in boyfriend.

Of course, if they stayed on this balcony, she didn't really need a companion, coerced or otherwise, as a shield from questions and ex-fiancés. So maybe she needed him for something else entirely.

She was alone in the most romantic city in the world, and Matt represented a golden opportunity to change that for one magical evening, then leave before he realized who she was. Loneliness went hand in hand with the fresh scars of rejection that kept reminding her not to let anyone get too close.

But an anonymous encounter—that was a horse of a different color. If he didn't know who she was, he couldn't reject *her*.

The direction of her thoughts heated her up fast despite the chill in the air. But who could blame her for going there when the man's mouth made her blood boil?

There was this strange awareness between them, which she'd felt the moment he'd turned to face her in the foyer. It was almost a recognition, as if she'd seen him many times, but had never quite caught up with him to start a conversation.

Yet he'd never removed his mask. She knew he had a chiseled jaw to match his well-defined mouth and a solid chest under his lapels, but that was it. The rest of his face remained hidden, like his body, his hopes, his disappointments…the mystery of it whet her appetite for more.

"Ever been on a speed date?" she asked him.

He took a sip of champagne and shook his head. "Can't say that I have."

She doubted he'd ever have a need to resort to such a thing. Dating as a whole never worked for her. Men usually fell into three categories: starstruck, unavailable or opportunist.

Rory was firmly in the last category. His rejection had been crushing, especially after losing her voice. She'd thought of all people, he'd understand and would sympathize. That he'd be there for her during the worst crisis of her life. Instead, he couldn't dump her fast enough. On the bright side, he'd cured her of any desire to have a man in her life permanently.

Which made her masked friend exactly what the doctor ordered.

"I haven't either, but I always wanted to. It seems like fun."

"I'm always up for fun. What does it entail?"

She loved the way he talked, like it never occurred to him that normal people's vocabulary didn't usually include words like *entail*. And like it never occurred to him that she hadn't gone to college. He treated her as if she possessed intelligence. That was potent.

"Well, to the best of my knowledge, there's a time limit. We have to get to know each other as quickly as possible before the bell rings. It's designed so you can figure out if you're compatible in a short period of time."

He cocked his head, lips pursed. "I already know I like you. Why do we need to have a speed date to figure that out?"

She shook her head, gaze glued to his. A part of her wanted to take this instant attraction to its natural conclusion as fast as possible. But no smart girl jumped into the pool without at least some clue how deep it was.

"Consider it part of the application process. There's a spark here, and I'm curious to see what happens if we fan it."

His irises flared. "Just so I'm clear, how does the time limit factor in?"

"Ask as many questions as you want, as fast as you can, and when the timer on my phone goes off, you're going to kiss me."

His palm cupped her face, tilting it up to almost meet his. "What if we skip the timer and I kiss you right now?"

"That's no fun." She firmly removed his hand from her chin, only to lose it to her hair as he threaded his fingers through the loose curls not caught up in her feather head-piece.

His warm thumb rested in the hollow behind her ear, brushing it lightly. "Clearly you need a refresher on how good my lips feel on yours."

The shiver went deeper this time, and a nice little hum zipped along her skin, tightening all her erogenous zones into an ache she'd not experienced in a long time. Apparently the speed date was unnecessary to fan the spark.

"Where's your sense of adventure? Five minutes."

She pulled her phone from the clutch tied to a string at her waist and tapped up the timer. She set it on the stone ledge behind Matt, then locked onto the ice-blue of his eyes. Anticipation was one of her favorite parts, and she'd happily drag it out as long as she could.

"I'll go first," he said. "How many times have you seduced a man on a balcony?"

She couldn't help but laugh. Was that what she was doing? "Never. I'm making all sorts of exceptions for you."

"How many times have you seduced a man period?"

"Once or twice. I'm not one to apologize for having a healthy sex drive. Should I?"

"Not to me. Maybe to all the other men down there who are missing out. Your turn."

"I'm naked. What do you do first?"

"Fall down on my knees and weep with joy. Did you really mean to ask what I'd do second?"

Oh, yeah, she really did like Matt. There was something to be said for a guy who could make her laugh with such regularity. "That is what I meant, and before you get all smart-alecky with me, go ahead and hit me with third, fourth and fifth."

"Did I buy you dinner first?"

"Who cares? I'm naked or did you forget?"

"Oh, no, my gorgeous little butterfly, I did not forget. I

asked because I'm trying to get a solid picture in my head of the scene."

His hand pressed on her nape, oh-so-slightly, and her head fell back. His lips grazed the corner of her mouth, not quite touching, but close enough to send a frisson of sparkling heat all the way down to her core.

Well, she hadn't intended for this speed date to descend into foreplay, but okay. It was *sizzling*. And personal information, like their secret professions, or lack thereof in her case, wasn't likely to come up.

"Are you naked on a bed after I've undressed you?" he murmured against her jaw, breath fanning the uncovered part her of face and making her ache to turn into those lips to complete the connection. "Or naked in the shower and have no idea I'm about to join you? Naked, but asleep and I'm going to awaken you slowly?"

Her lungs hitched. "Cheater. You've played this game before."

She felt his mouth turn up against her cheek. "Let's assume I'm a quick study. Your answer? I believe that was three questions."

"It was?"

Who was seducing whom here? And how far did she want this to go? Never had she contemplated such a dangerous liaison with a mysterious man she'd only just met but who touched her on so many levels.

"Bed, shower or asleep? I must know in order to tell you what I plan to do. Or perhaps you'd prefer I show you?"

Yes, yes she would. Except she couldn't speak, as he slid an arm around her waist, drawing her taut against his warm body. She clutched his shoulders and they were amazing and strong underneath his jacket. "There's no shower on this balcony."

"So true," he murmured. "The alarm's going off."

It wasn't. She didn't care.

He covered her mouth with his and turned her into liquid

mercury for the second time. The man was a master, hot and forceful, and her lips fell open under the divine pressure. He plunged in, tongue skimming against hers, deliciously rough and tasting of champagne.

She moaned and changed the angle, inviting him deeper, urging him forward with small tugs of her hands against his shoulders. *More*, she needed more, needed to quench the thirst raging in her veins with this extremely arousing man.

Judging by the full-fledged blaze between them, he felt the same. About *her*, not Eva. How great was that, to be with a man who hadn't already made a bunch of snap judgments?

"Touch me," she commanded hoarsely, her damaged voice even more raw with desire.

Almost hesitantly, he palmed her breast through the thick bodice of the dress, and she nearly growled in frustration. Forget that. She reached down and gathered up the hem of the ridiculously full skirt and tucked it under the sash at her waist. She guided his hand through the opening, straight to her bottom.

It was his turn to groan as he flattened his palm against her bare cheek. "A thong? That is unbelievably sexy."

"Not nearly as sexy as your hand on it while I'm still fully dressed." He explored the uncovered flesh and traced the strings into her crevice and back out again. Her knees almost buckled. "Don't stop. Keep going."

He took her mouth again, ravenous and greedy, as his fingers nudged underneath the silk. Just far enough to steal her breath for a long second. Blatantly, she circled her pelvis, silently begging him to go deeper.

Whether she'd planned to go this far or not, her body wasn't holding back. She was about to come apart under his capable hands.

Instead, he withdrew entirely and blew out a heavy breath, smoothing her skirts down with a confusing finality. "Angie, I have to confess something."

"You're married." Disappointment swamped her so quick

and so fast she nearly convulsed. The ache, which had moments ago been a vortex of desire, cooled. She should have known.

"No." He shook his head in vehement denial. "I'm completely unattached. It's just…I don't…"

"You're not attracted to me." But his impressive length had ground hard against her, evident even through the monstrosity of fabric at her waist.

He swallowed hard. "How could you possibly think that? I've never been so turned on in my life. There's this one small problem. I've never seduced a woman on a balcony, so I'm ah…unprepared."

Oh. "You don't have a condom."

The giggle slipped out before she could stop it. He was just so flustered and so cute, running a hand over his dark blond hair with evident frustration. It caught her quite unexpectedly in a soft, warm place inside. Talk about being unprepared.

Was he ever going to stop being so unexpected and amazing? God, she hoped not.

Three

"I'm glad you find my lack of preparation amusing." Matthew certainly didn't. He'd never been so mad at himself and so happy she wasn't angry, all at the same time.

And he had never been in quite so much physical pain. Yes, the women in his social circle were sophisticated and demure, rightly so, but lukewarm in their approach to everything.

He never realized how truly hot it could be with someone so uninhibited.

"It's not funny. Trust me, it's not." She pulled him down by the lapels and kissed him sweetly. "That's for not having a condom."

"What?"

She shrugged with a delicate one-shoulder move. "I've been around my share of dogs. It's nice to find someone who isn't always thinking with what's in his pants. Besides, this isn't the dark ages. You can easily be mad at me for not having one."

"I take it that means you don't."

She shook her head. "And I can't do birth control. Everything gives me headaches. But we're in luck because it's

Carnevale. I bet we can score a boxful of very festive condoms from Vincenzo's room."

So now Matt had been reduced to stealing condoms. Brilliant. Condoms were not first and foremost on his mind, yet he'd gladly jumped into her wicked game without hesitation.

What was he doing on this balcony?

"Maybe it's a sign."

"A sign? Like what, we're not supposed to hook up tonight?"

Hook up. Matthew Wheeler did not *hook up*. He'd been happily married to the perfect woman and would still be if an aneurism hadn't killed her. Commitment made him tick.

Angie might discount the idea of signs, but he couldn't. This wasn't meant to happen and probably for a very good reason. Did he really want a one-night stand with some woman he'd met at a party? It just wasn't his style.

The empty palazzo next door called his name, offering a place to retreat and lick his wounds. Where he would go to bed alone, dream about Amber and wake in a cold sweat. If he slept. Sometimes he lay awake, racked with remorse over leaving his family in the lurch.

That was his real life. This interlude with a winged woman at a masked ball was nothing but a fantasy born of desperation and loneliness. It wasn't fair to use Angie to appease either.

But God Almighty, it was difficult to walk away from her. When she'd been in his arms, pliant and sizzling, he heard the distinct sound of his soul waking up.

Angie's kiss-stung lips and luminous brown eyes nearly did him in. She'd asked him to be her fake boyfriend at this party, a role he'd stepped into with ease and enthusiasm, but without really considering what enormous pain must have driven her to ask.

He couldn't abandon her.

Matthew might not hook up, but neither did he have to listen to Matt, who despite Angie's belief, was very much thinking with the bulge in his pants. He needed to cool down and evaluate his goal here before he got carried away by the fantasy.

So he'd split the difference.

"Let's dance."

Wary surprise wrinkled her mouth. "At the party?"

"Sure. Why not? You haven't had a chance to throw your new boyfriend in lover boy's face yet." Neither of them had done much spelling-it-out and some clarity might be in order. "And I'd like to take a step back. Make sure we're both headed in the same direction."

"I hear you. The balcony *is* cold and I do like to dance," she mused. "How about this? I'll dart into Vincenzo's room and stuff my clutch with as many condoms as it'll hold. We'll dance. If you move to music like you do on a speed date, we'll be headed in the same direction all right—back upstairs and into my bed."

His pants grew tighter. Exactly how many times did she envision having sex? He shook his head to clear the erotic images she'd sprung loose in his brain. It didn't work.

"I'll consider myself warned."

She smiled and it was a whole lot wicked.

Matthew took her hand and led her toward what promised to be a provocative round of dancing. At least in a room full of people, the temptation to dive under Angie's skirt would be lessened.

If he did that again, he'd like to be much more clear-headed about it.

Unbelievably, more people had gathered in the rooms downstairs, filling the dance floor to overflowing. Couples swayed and dipped to the slow song. Matthew drew Angie into the sea of dancers, carefully navigating to protect her wings. He hadn't danced in a long time but the ballroom classes he'd let Amber drag him to came back in a rush.

He positioned his arms and prepared to try some semblance of a modified waltz, or at least do the best he could in such a crowd. Angie melted against him, undulating her hips against his in a hypnotic, sensual rhythm. A hot lick of need coursed through his gut. She hadn't attended the same classes. Obviously.

He held her close, mimicking her moves. All he could think about was the scrap of silk underneath her skirt. And the foil packets rounding the sides of her clutch. He wasn't doing a very good job of splitting the difference.

Angie's ear was right by his mouth, and he had the most insane urge to nibble on it. Instead, he cleared his throat to ease the knot of sexual tension that had stiffened everything in his body.

"What if we continue our speed date but take it down a notch?"

She repositioned her head so it was lying in the hollow of his shoulder. The feathers anchored in her hair brushed across his neck. "I'm listening."

"What's your favorite color?"

"That's more like forty-seven notches. I don't have a favorite color. I like the rainbow." Someone bumped into her, shoving them closer together, not that he minded. "What's yours?"

The smell of her hair weakened his knees. Outside, it hadn't been so noticeable, but in the close, heated confines of the room, the exotic scent curled through his nose. Even her shampoo was unearthly, as if he needed another reminder they came from different worlds.

"Black. It goes with everything."

"How practical. I like that in a man. Where were you born?"

"Dallas. And please don't ask me if I've met J. R. Ewing. I've never been to Southfork, and I don't watch the TV show." That was one constant about Europe. Everyone knew Dallas from either reruns of the old drama or the reboot version on cable. "What about you?"

"Toronto. My mom moved to Detroit when I was a baby and became a U.S. citizen. That's where I grew up."

So maybe their worlds weren't as far apart as he'd assumed. "You're American?"

The silence stretched long enough for Matthew to wonder if he'd said something to offend her. But she had to know her ragged voice didn't carry a discernible accent and was unusual enough to warrant such a question.

"I'm nothing and everything," she said with a laugh that wasn't a laugh. "Usually I tell people I'm French Canadian. But I haven't been to Toronto in years. Or Detroit for that matter."

"Is your mom still in Detroit?"

"She lives in Minneapolis, for now, working on her fourth marriage. I have fam—other people in Detroit."

Other people? He didn't ask. The undercurrent of pain in her voice had been strong, and if she'd wanted him to know, she'd have said.

"Your home is in Europe then?"

"Or wherever the wind takes me." She injected a note of levity, but he wasn't fooled. Nowhere felt like home and it bothered her. "Do you still live in Dallas?"

"No." Lack of a home was something they shared. He'd sold his house, his car, everything. The only possessions he had to his name were the clothes in the closet at the palazzo and a few childhood mementos stored in his parents' extra bedroom. "I'm going where the wind takes me, too."

At least until he found the way home.

She stopped dancing and collided with the next couple, earning a dirty look from them. Impatiently, she pushed Matthew off the dance floor toward the side wall and peered up through her mask, eyes liquid with sympathy. "I'm sorry."

"For?"

"For whatever happened."

She didn't question him,, though she could obviously read between the lines as well as he could.

A wave of understanding rippled between them. Both of them were searching. Both of them carried secrets full of pain and misery and loneliness.

They weren't different at all.

She whispered, "I'm glad the wind blew us to the same place."

All pretense of speed dating evaporated. Something much more significant was happening.

"Me, too."

Amber's death had broken his heart, nearly broken him entirely, and he couldn't fathom feeling that strongly about anyone else. For months and months, he'd despaired of ever feeling *anything* again, and like a foghorn echoing through the mist of his grief, this gravelly-voiced fantasy had appeared.

She was a gift, one he wasn't ready to give back.

No, he didn't want a one-night stand with some random woman, but he couldn't resist exploring what two damaged souls might become to each other.

With his brain firmly in command, he drew her hand into his and smiled.

"Instead of directions upstairs, I have a better idea. Come home with me."

Home. Evangeline liked the sound of it. She'd never had a home.

She'd had new stepfathers every few years. A half sister, Lisa, whom their father had obviously preferred since he'd married Lisa's mother. Plenty of hotel rooms and airplanes—all of that, she'd had.

She wished she could indulge in something so simple, so achingly honest as *home.* But imagine if she took off her mask and Matt turned out to be a reporter. Or worse.

At Vincenzo's, masks were part of the ambience, the anonymity. Masks kept things surface level. Masks kept a man at arm's length and promised nothing more than one night, a brief, sizzling interruption of loneliness. Masks prevented rejection. And scars. She'd had enough of both, thanks.

And there was no doubt Matt had a couple of his own scars.

With a light laugh, she blinked at him coquettishly. "What are you proposing?"

"A continuation. No exes. No crowds. No rules. Just me and you and whatever feels right."

Oh. That might be okay. "What if I wanted to keep our masks on? What would you say?"

"No rules. For anything."

Her insides shuddered deliciously. "That's a little open-ended. How do I know you aren't into some very naughty things?"

"You don't. We're both taking a leap of faith."

The wicked gleam in his eye didn't reassure her, but it certainly piqued her interest. "I might be into naughty things."

"I'm counting on it." He tugged her hand as the music switched to another electronic number. The crowd went crazy, pressing in on them from all sides. "Come on."

To her left, she glimpsed Sara Lear posing for a picture with two men in drag. Rory was nowhere in sight, but he might pop up again at any moment. That decided it. The last thing she wanted was to be at this party alone, constantly reminded of how she wasn't Sara.

Matt was clearly lonely, too. She'd head in his direction and see where it led.

"Let's go. Right now."

He kept her hand in his and led her out of Vincenzo's palazzo via a side entrance. They crossed a moonlit court-yard and climbed an ornate outer staircase to the second floor. Matt held the door for her to enter ahead of him. Lights flashed.

"Welcome to Palazzo D'Inverno," he said.

Evangeline's breath stalled in her throat. Relief frescos lined the walls and extended to the ceiling, where the colors exploded into Renaissance-style art of unparalleled beauty. Modern terrazzo floors studded with chips of marble and granite spread underneath her feet and met three sets of glassed French-doors leading to what appeared to be a marble balcony overlooking the Grand Canal.

Three long leather sofas in sea-foam green formed a U in the center of the living room, and all three afforded an amazing view of Venice, lit for Carnevale with breathtaking splendor.

"This is unbelievable." There were no other words. Vincenzo's palazzo had been in his family since the time of the Medici but it couldn't hold a candle to this one. "I had no idea anything like this still existed in Venice."

Matt's mouth twisted into a semblance of a smile. "Keeps the rain out."

"Whoever owns this place hit the jackpot. You're lucky they agreed to rent it out. It's amazing."

He shot her a quizzical look. "I'll be sure to pass on the compliment."

"Do you have all three floors, or just the *piano nobile*?"

"Top two. The bottom floor isn't restored. The bedrooms are upstairs. Would you like to see them?"

"Was that a line?" She grinned at his chagrined expression. He was endearing in a way that shouldn't be possible in conjunction with his forceful, compelling personality. "If so, I must say it worked extraordinarily well. I not only want to see the rest of the house, purely for aesthetic reasons of course, but I want to get out of this dress in the worst way."

She took a step toward the twisting staircase, but he tugged her back and pierced her with his beautiful crystalline eyes, capturing her gaze with his and refusing to let her go.

"Angie, I didn't invite you here solely to get you naked.

When I said no rules, I meant no expectations. If nothing happens, that's all right. I don't mind if we talk until dawn. Whatever feels right. Remember that."

"Matt—" The rest froze in her throat.

He was nothing like the people in her world. He carried a hint of vulnerability, a depth that pulled at her. And his restraint—that she couldn't fathom. All the men she knew took what they wanted, when they wanted it.

Not this one. He was very clearly telling her she still had choices, regardless of how brazenly she'd thrown herself at him all night. He didn't just see her as an outlet to slake his thirst but as a valued companion. That was powerful. And seductive.

She whispered his name again. "I don't mind if we talk, either."

She never talked. Talking sucked, especially when the sound of her own voice made her cringe. But they both deserved to have choices.

"Is that what you want?"

She craved the attention of this man, who seemed to understand exactly what she needed, when she needed it. To understand the weight of loss and the pain of being adrift, desperate for an anchor.

Something momentous swelled in her chest. "I just want to be with you."

"You've got me. For however long you'd like. I'm not going anywhere." As if to prove it, he lowered the lights, creating a romantic ambience instantly. He sat on the couch and spread his hands. "Think of me as a smorgasbord."

She laughed, and it blew away all the thick implications of the moment.

"Now that's something I've never had before. By the way, I wasn't kidding about getting out of this dress. I can hardly breathe, and it's heavy."

"Would you like a T-shirt?"

"Um, not really. What I'd really like is your help." She

stepped out of her heels, crossed the room and sat on the couch facing away from him. "The laces in the back are too hard to reach."

"What would you have done if we hadn't connected? Slept in it?"

Connected. That hit her in all the soft, warm places again. This was a connection, a greater one than she'd been looking for, or had expected, and far more precious—thanks to the custom of wearing masks for Carnevale. She'd never have let her guard down otherwise.

"I would have figured out something," she murmured as he gently lifted her curls and swept them up over her shoulder. Her skin prickled as she felt his gaze on the bare expanse from her hairline to the strapless bodice.

His hands skimmed down her back on either side of the wings, stoking the fire he'd built on the balcony, which hadn't extinguished at all. Those strong fingers pulled on the threads, unknotting them and drawing them through the grommets with deliberate, aching leisure.

She kept expecting to feel his lips on her shoulder, on the column of her neck, or at the place where fabric met her skin. But the longer he held back, and the longer her skin burned for his touch, the crazier it drove her.

Yes, he was a master at this anticipation game. Among other things. When she finally got him naked and under her, she'd show him a thing or two.

Except she still wasn't sure they were headed for the bedroom. It was disorienting to have her temporary, surface-level liaison morph into something undefinable. Something so much more than a quick fix for loneliness.

So what was it?

Finally, after an eternity, the laces pulled free from the bodice, loosening the corset and spilling her breasts partially over the neckline of the dress, and he still hadn't made a move.

"It, uh, has to come over my head," she said without turning around. She raised her arms. "Can you…?"

He grasped the bodice but she was sitting on the skirt, so she wiggled and he pulled, until the yards and yards of lace tulle eased past her waist. The mask popped up onto her forehead, but she repositioned it before the skirt fully came off.

Then she was naked except for her thong. And the mask. What would he do first? The way he'd answered that question back on the balcony had been maddeningly vague.

He draped her dress over the back of the couch. She faced the canal, away from Matt, and he had yet to say a word. Screaming sexual tension whipped through all her nerves until she thought she'd pass out.

"So. What did you want to talk about?"

His soft laugh settled inside her. "I'm wondering about this."

He traced the trail of eight notes tattooed in a string at the small of her back. The smooth touch unleashed a tremor she couldn't control. "It's a tattoo."

"The notes are all the colors of the rainbow. I like it."

No one had ever noticed that before. "Music is important to me."

It was more than she'd meant to say and communicated none of the shock of pure grief the words had unearthed. She shoved the grief back, like she always did, shoved back the longing for a voice to express the pain. If she had a voice, she'd have no pain to express. It was a cruel, vicious circle she couldn't escape.

Except this was one night she didn't have to face the darkness alone. "Matt."

"Angie."

The smile in his voice warmed her. "Just making sure you're still there. Are we going to talk some more or is there something you'd like to do instead?"

"Was that a line?"

"Yes. It was." The ache at her core spread, and only the man behind her could ease it. She'd never wanted to be with someone more. What did she have to do to get him to make a move? "Obviously not a good one since you're still sitting there like yo—"

"Stand up and turn around, Angie."

She did slowly.

His hooded gaze swept her from head to toe, lingering along the way and unleashing a delicious tingle in all the places his eyes touched.

"You are the most beautiful woman alive. Come here."

He grasped both her hands and stood to meet her. In one breath, he drew her into his arms and kissed her.

Flames exploded at their joined mouths, between their bodies, crackling down the length of her bare skin where the soft fabric of his suit brushed it. Oh, how wrong she'd been. He *was* a man who took what he wanted. And he wanted to consume her whole.

She wanted to let him.

They *connected*. On every level.

When he tilted her head back to access her throat with his firm, gorgeous mouth, their masks caught at the corners. Patiently, he disentangled them and glanced down into her eyes, suddenly still. "No expectations. Does this feel right?"

Without warning, he skated a hand down her spine and fanned it at the small of her back, cradling the tattooed music notes in his capable hand as if he knew he held her very center.

Her eyelids fell closed and she moaned. "More right than anything I've ever felt. Please don't say you're really in the mood to talk."

He laughed against her throat, and she felt the caress of his lips clear to her toes. "I'm not. But I would be happy to talk, if that's what you wanted."

She shook her head almost imperceptibly, terrified she'd dislodge his mouth from her skin. "I want you."

"Good. Because I'm about to make love to you."

Yes, she wanted that, too. To be filled by this very different man, to the brim. To connect, bodies and minds. Souls.

He threaded a hand through the hair at her neck, his fingers solid and firm against it. "Angie," he murmured, almost reverently.

"Stop." Tears stung the corners of her eyes. Baffling, irrepressible tears because she wanted something else from him, something she'd resisted all evening. "Just stop."

"Okay." His hands withdrew and the sudden lack of support buckled her knees.

"No! Don't stop touching me. Stop calling me Angie." Before her subconscious could come up with one of the hundreds of reasons it was a dangerous idea, she reached up and yanked off her mask. "My name is Evangeline. Make love to *me*, not the mask."

Four

"Evangeline."

It flowed from Matthew's mouth like a prayer. Yes. *That* fit this angelic, winged woman who had bared herself to him in more ways than one.

He drank in her face, and it jolted something inside, as if his soul had done a double take and said, *There you are.*

"Angie is a nickname. Evangeline is who I am."

A nameless emotion tightened his throat. "I'm honored you trusted me with it."

She'd done far more than simply remove her mask. The significance of it sent a flood of guilt through him. Guilt because he could shed his physical mask—but not his internal one.

And still he drew off his mask and dropped it to the floor. "Allow me to reciprocate."

For a long while, she fixated on his face. His neck heated. Who would have thought taking off a mask could provoke such intensity?

"God, you're gorgeous."

"Most people call me by my given name, but if you want to address me as God, I won't argue."

She laughed, pushing her firm breasts into his chest. "Way to defuse the moment. That's a rare talent."

He'd intended to diffuse his own embarrassment at her frank admiration, which even Amber had expressed infrequently. But if Evangeline chose to believe he had superpowers, so much the better.

"Are we finished with the revelations?" he asked.

"Not even close. Now that I've seen what's under that mask, I'm dying to peel away this suit—" she flicked his bow tie "—and get a look at the rest of the goods."

"I hope it meets with your expectations." His voice dropped. Nerves. Of all things.

Before fully internalizing the implications, he swept Evangeline into his arms and carried her up the stairs to the bedroom.

"Any man who can do that without having to catch his breath most definitely has a body that'll meet my expectations," she said as he laid her on the bed. "Oh, wow. That's quite a fresco."

Matthew glanced up at the ceiling, where stucco divided sixteen individual paintings last touched by a brush during the Renaissance. "It's my favorite."

"I like it, too. I'll lie here and look at it while you fetch the condoms out of my clutch. Which is downstairs." She flipped him a cheeky grin as he cursed.

He cursed some more as he tromped back down the narrow stairs in search of the errant bag. It was still attached to her dress, but instead of pulling out a couple of condoms—because who was he to question how many they'd need—he untied it and brought the whole thing.

The bulging sides of Evangeline's clutch induced a healthy dose of reality. He was about to have sex with a virtual stranger, one whose face he'd seen for the first time less than ten minutes ago. Halfway up the stairs, he paused.

Was he really going to go through with this?

It was one night. One night in which he had an opportunity to turn the tide of his grief and rejoin the living by spending time with a beautiful woman who made him feel ten feet tall—feel being the operative word. One night when he could act recklessly with no one the wiser. He was in the most romantic city in the world, perhaps on purpose, and he wanted all that Venice had to offer.

Evangeline was draped across the cream-colored comforter when he strode through the bedroom door. She studied the ceiling with pursed lips, hair spread out underneath her and breasts freely on display. That lack of inhibition—it staggered him. Excited him.

His body hardened in anticipation, and his fingers tingled as he recalled the smoothness of her bare skin. This one night was a rare offer from the universe, and he was incredibly lucky to get it.

She glanced over with a sultry smile. "You. Come here."

Only a fool would pass up what was clearly fate.

With one hand, he got rid of his shoes and socks as he crossed the room. He tossed her clutch on a pillow and stared at her gorgeous form, flawless in the lamplight. "Hold on a minute."

He pulled a book of matches from his bedside drawer and lit the candles lining ornate sconces on each side of the bed, then clicked off the light.

"Nice. You could have gotten me here a lot faster if you'd said that was the first thing you'd do once I'm naked." She sat up and grasped his lapels, drawing off his jacket with a quick yank. "And you have on too many clothes. I'm feeling self-conscious here."

He let the jacket fall to the floor. "I can't imagine why. You're beautiful."

Flames flickered over her skin and threw honey highlights into her curls.

Her hands, which had been busy with his tie, rested flat on his chest, and she rose up on her knees to meet his gaze.

A hundred emotions poured from her expression, passing between them in silent communication.

"You know why," she said.

He did. In her eyes, he saw the same things she no doubt saw in his. They had an understanding, nonverbal and mystifying, but very real. He'd felt it from the first moment in the hall. He felt it now.

She was self-conscious not because of her nakedness, but because she'd removed her mask and feared learning she'd made a mistake in trusting him.

This night was about two damaged people seeking a port in the storm. He was going through with it because he wanted to live up to her trust. Wanted to fall into a woman so different from any he'd ever met, one so wrong for a real estate broker from Dallas, but perfect for a man who didn't know who he was or how to live his life anymore.

He wanted to see what happened if he let go of all the rules. It couldn't be worse than the purgatory of the past eighteen months.

If he did it right, it would be spectacular. Meaningful. And Matthew did *everything* right.

"I'm not going to disappoint you," he said hoarsely.

"I know. I wouldn't be here otherwise." Her voice had grown impossibly huskier as well, skating across his skin, burrowing its gravelly hooks into his center. "I've just never done anything like this before. Never wanted to."

Well, that made two of them. Hopefully they could figure it out together. "No expectations. No rules."

"I remember. Except I have this one rule." She made short work of removing his bow tie and began slipping his shirt's buttons free with deliberate care as she peeked up from under her lashes. "I get to explore first. You have to wait your turn."

He went so hard, his spine curved. Had a woman ever undressed him so provocatively?

"That's a pretty unfair rule. Why can't we do it at the same time?"

"Because I said."

The last button popped from its mooring, and she slid blazing fingertips across his bare chest on her way to his shoulders. His shirt came off in her hands and she yanked it halfway down his arms, trapping them against his side.

"Actually," she added, "the rule states I get to explore twice, once with my eyes and another time with my mouth."

Said eyes roamed over his exposed skin as she pulled him closer with the grip she had on his shirt. Without warning, she spun him and tied his hands behind his back with the fabric.

"Oh, now that's *really* not fair."

"All's fair in love and war." Still on her knees, she turned him back around to graze a fingertip down his chest and into the waistband of his pants. "I'll let you go when I'm done exploring."

She drew him closer and dropped his pants and briefs to the floor, ravishing his erection with her eyes, as promised.

He kicked his pants away. "I can easily break out of this you know."

"You won't." Her light tone fooled him not in the least.

This was love *and* war. And holy cow, did that get his juices flowing in a way he'd never have guessed. He'd play along, but she better believe he'd be dishing it out when he got the chance.

With a soft sigh, she twirled her finger. "Turn around. I want to see it all."

He faced the wall opposite the bed, slightly uncomfortable and enormously turned on by the notion of her eyes traveling up and down his naked body.

"When does the mouth exploration start?" he called over his shoulder.

Her answer came with a soft touch at the base of his

spine. Hair brushed his skin as she nibbled upward and his long-neglected body erupted with heat.

By the time she reached his neck, her tongue had joined the party. He groaned at the wicked swipe of wet heat against his earlobe, and allowed her to spin him slowly as she followed the line of his jaw with her lips.

Then there was no more talking as she kissed him.

He wanted to drag her into his arms and respond in kind. But he couldn't. His honor forced him to stay constrained as she did her best to drive him mad. He spiraled closer to the edge as she tilted his head in her palms to take the kiss deeper, teasing her nipples across his chest in a tantalizing back-and-forth dance.

Evangeline broke the kiss, arching her back sensuously. The silk of her thong brushed his length, and he nearly came apart right then and there.

No. He breathed heavily through his nose and clamped down on his reaction.

"Matt," she breathed into his ear, and the low croak was the sexiest thing he'd ever heard. "When I first saw you, I noticed those capable hands. I want them on my body. Now."

She reached around to pull the knot of his sleeves apart, but he'd already yanked his wrists free.

His mouth was on hers instantly as he slid both palms down the heat of her back to cup her bottom. Smooth. Arousing. He crushed her against his erection and plunged into sensation, freely allowing his body to revel in the impressions, the awareness. Finally, he felt something other than frozen and disoriented.

As he dipped underneath the triangle of silk at her thighs, she moaned and strained forward, seeking his fingers, throwing her head back in pleasure.

That was as arousing as the feel of her skin.

She was nothing like Amber.

He willed away the comparison—ghosts had no place here. But the thought circled and grew. Amber had been sophisticated, elegant. Beautiful in the way of a glass swan with special handling requirements.

He'd always held her in slight reverence as the future mother of his children, and they'd shared a strong relationship anchored by common interests and goals. Their love life had blossomed into something wonderful and good. But conducted in the dark, under the sheets, which Matthew never minded.

This was something else, something erotic and animalistic and wicked. Evangeline wasn't Amber. And there were no rules tonight.

He wanted to bury himself in this woman and be resurrected a new man.

Evangeline enfolded Matt with her arms and willed him to hurry. But there was no rushing the man she'd been goading with tied hands for the past few minutes.

His fingers wrapped her in a veil of pleasure as they slowly traveled across her skin, spinning magic through her center as he touched her everywhere—inside and out.

Yes. Exactly what she needed—to be filled, valued, appreciated. Accepted.

With incredible restraint, he lowered her to the mattress and drew off her underwear, then crawled up the length of her body, laving every inch of skin as he went. He reached her throat and tilted her head back to taste with hard suction. Simultaneously, his thigh separated hers, relentless against her sensitized flesh and setting off pyrotechnics behind her eyes.

She'd never dropped into such heavy desire so quickly, never been so hot and ready to explode. Usually it took a while. But then, they'd been engaged in foreplay in one form or another since their first meeting in the hall.

Was it any wonder Matt was about to take her under with only his thigh?

His tongue circled her breasts, then treated her to the

same intense suction he'd used on her throat. Her back came off the bed, arching, as her feminine parts contracted. She gasped.

"Now, Matt."

It was supposed to be a demand, not a plea. But the words left her lips on a broken sob, and she no longer cared that a man had reduced her to begging.

He extracted a condom and fingered it on. It took an eternity but then he was back between her thighs, sliding into her. Watching her as they became one and their gazes locked. Something powerful, divine even, swelled between them and her heart thumped in time with the throb in the air.

No, she'd never done this before because she had no idea what *this* was.

It certainly wasn't a random hookup. But neither was it safe. The deeper the connection, the deeper the eventual pain.

She'd taken off the mask in a calculated gamble, and Matt hadn't recognized her. It should have allowed her to simply revel in this one night where a man couldn't hurt her because he didn't really know her. It should have been freeing. Not confusing.

Desperately, she cast about for a way to eliminate the swirling mass of vulnerability this man evoked by simply looking at her. Through her.

"Not this way." She wiggled and he rolled to his side, confusion evident.

"Too soon?"

"Too missionary." Waggling her brows, she knelt on the bed and glanced back at him. "Try this on for size."

He grinned and instantly heated her back with his torso, mouth to her neck as he filled her again from behind. Much better. Now she couldn't see all that depth of emotion. And vice versa. They'd pleasure each other and stave off the loneliness for a night and go on.

His fingers teased her flesh. Clearly this was not his first rodeo. She let her senses flood with Matt and moaned as he lit her up expertly. His name fell from her lips and too late she realized it didn't matter if she could see his face. His touch conveyed more depth than she'd dreamed possible.

Tears pricked her eyelids. She wanted that touch to mean everything she sensed it did. But was terrified to admit it. How could she convince herself this was nothing but a brief divergence if he kept touching her that way?

The orgasm, quick, powerful and amazing, swallowed her whole long about his second thrust, and he exploded with his third.

She collapsed, chest to the bed, and he spooned her into his arms, both of them still shuddering. He held her tightly and she curled into him, shocked at how natural it felt, how right, when normally she preferred not to be touched as her body cooled.

"I have never come so fast in my life," she gasped. "I think that's my new favorite position."

Though somehow, it hadn't been quite the cure for her confusion that she'd envisioned. And lying here in his arms with his thumb tenderly stroking the curve of her waist wasn't helping. The powerful flames of desire he fanned weren't sexual. She wanted Matt to be different. Special.

She should get dressed and leave. Right now, before she found out he wasn't.

But if she left, what then? Spend the rest of the night alone, huddled in the dark, listening to Vincenzo's guests party till dawn?

"It's definitely my new favorite position." He cleared his throat. "Though I'm willing to try a couple of others to verify. In a few minutes. I know we have all these condoms, but you're not an easy woman to recover from."

She had to smile at that. Nice to know it had been staggering on both sides.

A part of her had prepared to be kicked out. Maybe hoped she would be—it was safer that way. Not all men liked a woman hanging around afterward. Finding out Matt didn't fall in that category thrilled her. Dangerously.

"What if we just talk?"

Where had that come from? She never stayed.

She nearly took it back, but her soul ached, and Matt inexplicably salved it. Morning was soon enough to escape. For now, she wanted one whole night of fantasy, where nothing mattered but being with a man who liked her and wanted her around.

His lips curved up against her temple. "A continuation of our speed date?"

The chilly palazzo air raised goose bumps on her arms. "Well, I'm not sure how we could find any more levels of compatibility. But okay."

He laughed. "Yeah, we gel. At least in bed, which is fantastic. It's been a while."

"Really? How long?"

Rolling her gently to the side, he pulled the covers free and nestled her back in his arms underneath them, like he'd read her mind. "A year and a half. Or so."

Oh, God. "Are you like, religious or something? Did I make you break vows?"

"No." He was quiet for a long time. "That's when my wife died."

Something hot exploded in her chest. His pain—she'd seen it, knew it was there, but never would have guessed its roots went so deep.

"Oh, Matt. I'm so sorry."

She rolled and took his lips with hers in a long kiss of sympathy. Why, she didn't know. It wasn't like she could fix anything or erase his agony, not with a million kisses.

"Thanks," he whispered against her lips. "It was a long time ago."

Her heart hurt for him and furiously demanded she find a way to salve his soul in return. "There's no statute of limitations on being sorry that someone you loved is gone."

"I guess not." His smile flipped her stomach. "When you said *talk,* that's probably not what you meant. But I thought you should know."

Because there was something more here than either of them had expected. He felt it, too.

"That's why you're drifting. To find some sort of closure." His nod confirmed what she'd guessed. "You're not in Venice on business, are you?"

"I wish it was that simple. If only there was a way to close the deal on grief, I'd be all set."

Matt was a widower. It felt weird. "People our age shouldn't die."

People their age shouldn't lose a career over botched surgery either, but crappy things happened with no rhyme or reason.

He smoothed a curl away from her face, his expression unreadable, and she waited for a demand that she slice open a vein in kind, share her personal pain with him. She wouldn't. Couldn't. And it wasn't fair to Matt that he'd hooked up with someone nowhere near as willing to be vulnerable.

But he didn't hand her a scalpel.

"Are we the same age? Wait, am I allowed to ask that? Isn't there a rule about asking women their age?"

A laugh slipped out. "No rules, remember? I'm twenty-seven."

"Thirty-two." He grinned. "Not nearly old enough to need *that* long to recover."

She let him change the subject by kissing her breathless and rolling on top of her, bracing himself on his strong forearms. He met her gaze, his eyes full of her, not pain. They'd connected over their mutual search for a way to combat the darkness, and it was working.

For one magical night, they had each other.

Five

When Evangeline awoke, Matt was watching her, cheek to his pillow. The drapes were flung apart, and sunlight spilled into the room, across the bed. With strong features and those amazing blue eyes, he was more gorgeous by morning light than he was by candlelight.

"Hey there." He smiled and laced their fingers, bringing hers to his lips.

She smiled back. "If you're always this cheerful in the morning, you might want to keep sharp objects under lock and key."

With a laugh, he tucked a curl of her hair behind her shoulder. "I'm not this cheerful ever. You have the unique effect of being a good influence."

Or the unique effect of breaking his dry spell with women. The sunlight had returned her cynicism, apparently.

"Are you watching me for a reason or auditioning to be my stalker once the boyfriend job is over?"

"For a reason. But you'll think it's weird."

Her eyes narrowed. "Weirder than watching me while I sleep?"

"I like your face." He shrugged. "It was covered most of the night, and I haven't seen it nearly enough yet."

"There's nothing special about my face." Other than how famous it was. She sat up and threw off the covers, intending to flee before the discussion went in a direction she didn't like.

Besides, it was morning. She'd stayed long enough.

His hand shot out from under the sheet to grab her wrist and tug her back. "I could look at you for hours."

"I'm naked. Of course you could." *Men.* But his eyes weren't on her uncovered body.

She was trying so hard to assign typical male qualities to Matt, and he wasn't letting her.

"You still have feathers in your hair."

"I do?" Her hand flew to her hair and sure enough, a mess of pins still held part of her headpiece in place. Wonderful. Her hair must resemble a bird's nest after a monsoon.

"Let me."

He rose up from the cocoon of sheets, which fell from his body in a slow waterfall, and her belly contracted. There was very little typical about Matt, and his prime physique was no exception.

He scooted up behind her, but not close enough to touch. It didn't matter. His heat radiated outward, stroking her skin with delicious fingers of warmth. With aching gentleness, he plucked a pin from her hair, then another, his breath fanning her scalp as he worked.

Awareness prickled her skin and ignited a slow burn in her center.

"That was the last pin."

But his fingers stayed in her hair, combing it lightly, patiently untangling the snarls. Then his fingers drifted to her shoulders in a caress. He lifted her curls and touched the back of her neck with his warm, talented lips, unleashing an unexpected shiver.

She shouldn't stay. Her one magical night was over, and

morning light put a damper of reality over everything. In fact, she should have left before he woke up. Why hadn't she?

"Matt."

The lips paused in their trek across her nape. "Are you about to tell me you have somewhere to be? Nice knowing you, but party's over?"

Was she that easy to read? "I don't have anywhere to be."

Well, that was a stupid thing to admit. Now she had no exit strategy if she decided she needed one.

"Then don't go."

His hands gripped her arms, drawing her backward into him, supporting her with his chest as he ravished whatever he could reach with his mouth. Her insides erupted.

She wasn't going anywhere, not yet. But she also wasn't doing this backward. Not this time.

She spun in his arms and wrapped her legs around his waist. The delight playing with the corners of his mouth sent a shaft of heat through her. "Just try and get rid of me, cowboy."

His laugh rumbled against her flesh. "Not everyone from Texas rides horses."

"Who's talking about riding horses?" She shoved his chest and knocked him back against the comforter, moving onto her knees over him. "Giddyap."

Now there was a sight. Gorgeous, masculine magnificence spread underneath her thighs. Matt was hard all over, had a nicely defined torso and a wicked smile. She'd won the man sweepstakes and had been daft enough to miss out on watching him last night.

Eyes stormy with dark desire, he lifted his chin. "Your turn to fetch the condoms."

She stretched to pull one off the bedside table and ripped it open with her teeth. "Done."

"Then saddle up, sweetheart." He shoved his hands under

his head with a mischievous wink. "You don't have to tie me up this time."

Which she'd only done to ratchet down the emotion of the moment. It had failed miserably.

"Liked that, did you?"

The flippant response almost caught in her throat. Because she didn't want to be flippant. Didn't want fun and games. She wanted the tender, profound Matt of last night who made her feel cherished.

When had she turned into such a *girl*? Five minutes ago, she was halfway out the door—mentally, at least—and here she was wishing for the opposite. Matt had her completely messed up.

"I have yet to discover something about you I don't like," he said.

"I've got you good and fooled then."

He pierced her with the force of all that depth behind his eyes. "I don't think so."

She looked away, letting the condom fall to the bed. "You don't know me. Not really."

No one did—by design. How much worse would rejection hurt if someone dug through all the protective layers and exposed her core? Well, she already knew. It would feel an awful lot like when her dad hadn't wanted her.

"That's not true." He sat up, resettled her against his thighs and cupped her chin. "I recognized you as soon as you took off your mask."

Her heart plunged to the floor and tried to keep going. "You did?"

Why hadn't he said anything? Duh. He hadn't because he'd wanted to score with Eva. Of course. Disappointment nearly wrenched a sob from her frozen chest. He wasn't special. Big surprise.

"Something inside me did, as if I'd always known you." He shook his head with a half laugh. "Sorry. I'm no good at this, and to top it off I sound like a starry-eyed teenager. They must put romance in the water here."

"What are you saying?"

He huffed out a frustrated breath. "I don't know. I mean, it wasn't like, hey didn't we go to the same high school? It was an elemental recognition. Inside. Nothing like that has ever happened to me before." Matt's fathomless eyes begged her to understand, but she couldn't sort through the panic in her abdomen to put definition around his words. "I thought you felt it, too."

He meant that indefinable swirl between them. The *connection*.

Cautiously, slowly, her heart started beating again.

"The first time I kissed you. It didn't feel like the first time. Is that what you mean?"

He lit up, zinging her in the stomach. "Yes. That's it exactly. Everything between us…it's just right. We're sitting here naked having a conversation, and it's not strange."

The smile cracked before she registered that he'd pulled it from her. "Feels pretty good to me."

"Me, too. I know as much about you as I need to. You're my butterfly."

His lips claimed hers in a kiss full of promise. And like that, he turned the tables on her again, making her yearn for things she shouldn't, such as another night of absolving her loneliness in the arms of a man who wasn't eager to get rid of her. A man who made her feel valued.

If she stayed, how long could that possibly last?

The sooner she left, the sooner that yearning could dry up and blow away. But the second she walked out the door, she'd be back in the real world, lost and alone, with only the thin layer of Eva for protection—and that didn't go very far anymore.

Rock. Hard place.

With Matt, she was simply an anonymous woman enjoying the uncomplicated company of a man, and it gave her room to breathe she hadn't known she needed. One night hadn't been enough. But if she stayed, it was like giving Matt permission to get closer. That couldn't go well.

She stared into the depths of those almost-colorless-blue eyes.

A small voice in the back of her mind insisted she was selling this completely atypical man short.

Matthew palmed Evangeline's chin and kissed her until his brain sizzled. She was naked in his lap, legs around his waist, and the position was so sensually erotic, he was one rub of her flesh away from going off like a bottle rocket.

Last night had been a fantasy. This morning—still pretty unreal. He'd awoken with a start, afraid Evangeline had evaporated like so much mist in the sunlight. But there she was, hair draped over the pillow, breathing deeply in sleep, beautiful against his sheets. The way she filled his bed was so very nice.

Their one night was over. It wasn't enough, and he wasn't ready to say *ciao*.

Her hands cupped his butt, urging him closer and he was already almost inside her. One quick thrust and he would be. His thighs strained. He groaned against her mouth, blindly seeking the condom wrapper with clumsy fingers before it was too late.

His fingers closed around it, and he eased back a bit to roll it on, still kissing her because he couldn't stop.

Finally, it was in place. He lifted her bottom and slid in, all the way, and she breathed his name as he situated her flush against him.

His eyelids slammed closed as Evangeline washed through him, blasting away all the cobwebs until that incredible light of hers flooded the darkness inside. They moved together, heightening the pleasure, heightening the sense of completion until they both exploded simultaneously.

He wrapped his arms around her and held her tight

against his torso as the ripples went on and on. As they faded away, they left the warmest glow in their wake. His lips rested on her temple, and he couldn't have moved if his life depended on it.

"I like that position pretty well, too," she murmured, and he grinned.

"It has its merits." Her cheek rubbed his, bristling his morning stubble. As decadent as it was to still be in bed, they had to get up sometime. "Are you hungry? I'll make you breakfast."

It probably sounded as much like a stall tactic to her as it did to him. He didn't care. Too many things in his life had ended prematurely, and if she left, he'd probably never see her again. That would be a true shame.

"Do you mind if I take a shower first?" She made a noise. "I forgot, I don't have any of my stuff. Does the offer of a T-shirt still stand?"

"Sure. Give me a minute in the bathroom and then it's all yours." He eased her off his thighs and took shameless delight in watching his uninhibited butterfly roll onto her back, still breathing heavily.

Matthew pulled a T-shirt from the dresser and tossed it next to her on the bed. He bent down to kiss her thoroughly because he could, then whistled as he dressed and went downstairs to scare up some breakfast.

Whistled.

He'd be shocked, except his ability to be shocked had disappeared right around the time Evangeline had presented her naked backside and told him to hop on board. She was the most exciting woman he'd ever met, and under normal circumstances, real-estate mogul Matthew Wheeler would bore her instantly.

But this was Venice, and he was a guy who could keep up with Evangeline and talk about spiritual connections without flinching because there were no rules. Being Matt was liberating.

The updated plumbing in Palazzo D'Inverno only went so far, and when Evangeline turned on the shower upstairs, pipes rattled inside the kitchen walls. It was like music. His cold, lonely house was filled with Evangeline, and he liked it. A lot.

When she came downstairs clad in only his T-shirt, bare legs on display and wet hair dark against her shoulders, every drop of saliva in his mouth dried up.

"How do you make cotton look so good?"

He handed her a glass of orange juice.

"One of my natural talents."

She stood on her tiptoes to kiss him as if they were a couple comfortable in the kitchen dance from having performed it so many times. Sipping the juice, she perched on one of two stools at the center island and watched him at the stove.

"I hope eggs and toast are okay." He glanced over his shoulder and nearly dropped the spatula at the sight of such a tousled, stunning woman in his kitchen. "I guess I should have asked."

"It's fine. I don't do whacked-out diets or lament about animal rights. I just eat."

"I like that in a woman."

"I like a man who cooks."

They traded scorching hot glances until the scent of toast filled the air. He pulled it from the toaster and plated everything, then sat next to her at the island.

This was the first time he'd eaten a meal with a woman in…too long to recall. He'd missed the simple pleasure of awaking to warm female, of sharing a bathroom. Laughing and making love whenever the mood struck.

He missed being married, more than he'd realized. No amount of wishing, cursing, grieving or wandering could bring Amber back, though he'd irrationally tried it all. He could only embrace what *was* possible.

"So," he said after swallowing a bite of toast. "Do you have plans for the weekend?"

"It's Wednesday. The weekend is a long way off."

At home, his calendar filled months in advance and he lived by his schedule. In Venice, he'd learned calendars were a dirty word, which he still hadn't adjusted to. "I'd like to see you again. Maybe go on a date."

He definitely wasn't done with what Evangeline made him feel.

She put her fork down with all the fanfare of a royal announcement. "I'm not so big on dating."

"Oh." The brush-off. Apparently he was rustier at this than he'd realized, because he'd have sworn they had something going on here. "What are you big on?"

Her gravelly laugh surprised him. "You."

"Uh, okay." To stall, he shoveled food into his mouth and chewed slowly. His wits did not gather. "Can I assume you *are* that into me then?"

"Matt." She sighed, and it didn't reassure him. "You're the best thing that's happened to me in a long, long time. But—"

"Why does there have to be a *but?* I'm the best thing. Roll with that." He encouraged her with a finger twirl, unable to keep the grin off his face.

Negotiation time—his best skill. She was in for a surprise if she thought there was a chance in hell he was letting her get away.

Shoulders slumped, she stared at her plate for a long time. "What if I said I'd like to see you again too, but here? At your house?"

Her body language told him volumes about the importance of his answer.

He shrugged. "The last time I dated, dinosaurs roamed the earth. I'm not so big on it, either. I just want to see you. When? Pick a day that works for your life."

A firm commitment would settle the uneasiness prickling his spine quite well.

When she looked up from her plate, tears had gathered

and one slid down her face. A giant fist clenched his gut as she wiped away the tear.

"I don't have a life," she whispered.

"Evangeline…" What was he supposed to do? Say? Feel?

Instinctively, he slid from the stool, gathered her into his arms and held her, mystified, but happy to be doing *something*. She melted into him, her hands clutching his shoulders as if she couldn't get close enough, and he ached over her unidentified agony.

"I'm sorry. I don't usually fall apart in the middle of being asked out on a date." Her watery chuckle gave him hope things hadn't gone entirely to hell.

"I'm not asking you out on a date. No, ma'am. I have it on good authority you aren't big on dates. I'm asking you to my house for…dinner?" he offered, praying that would get a thumbs-up. "I'll cook."

"Dinner would be nice," she said into his shoulder. "Tonight. Tomorrow night. Any night."

"Tonight. In fact, just stay," he said, voicing the invitation he should have issued from the outset. This place needed her light. *He* needed it. "Unless you're sick of me or need to go hang out with Vincenzo since you're his guest."

"Vincenzo is probably sleeping off his hangover and won't notice if I'm there or not."

The forlorn note clinched it. Unless he'd completely lost his marbles, she wasn't ready to say *ciao,* either.

"I'll definitely notice if you're here or not. Italian TV leaves a lot to be desired, and I'd rather be with you. Spend another night, or better yet, through the weekend." The words rushed out before he'd hardly formed the thought, but the relevance of it, the weight of what he asked, was already there, inside him. He'd finally woken up from an eighteen-month stupor, and there was no way he'd let it end. "Will you stay?"

She hesitated, lids closed in apparent indecision. When

she opened her eyes, the flicker in their depths warned him something he might not like was about to happen.

"Why haven't you asked me about my voice?"

He blinked. "Was I supposed to?"

"It's damaged. Aren't you curious? You can't tell me you haven't noticed."

Damaged? It hadn't always been that way? "You noticed my hands and I noticed your voice. I love your voice. It's one of the sexiest things about you."

"It's not sexy. It's horrific, like a sixty-year old with a four-pack-a-day habit."

He laughed, but it didn't sound like he was amused. Because he wasn't. "That's ridiculous. Your voice is unusual. That's what makes it special. When you say my name, it latches onto me, right here." He grasped her hand and slapped it to his stomach. "I love that. I love that you can affect me by speaking."

She pulled her hand free. "You're being deliberately obtuse."

Frustrated, he shoved fingers through his hair. He'd invited her to draw out their one night, not solve world hunger—couldn't it be a simple yes or no?

"Fine. Evangeline, what happened to your voice?"

"When you sing a lot, polyps grow on your vocal cords. Sometimes they rupture. It requires a special expertise to perform the surgery to fix it. Adele had a good doctor. I didn't."

His brain nearly curdled at the lightning-fast subject change. "What's a lot? Like you sang professionally, you mean?"

"Yeah. Professionally. A lot." Her eyes searched his, hesitating, evaluating, and he got the impression she was feeling him out. They were still very much in the throes of negotiation, and he couldn't stumble now.

"No false pretenses," she said. "If I stay, I need you to know. When I sang, it was by another name. Eva."

"Eva."

The name flashed an image in his mind of the woman before him, but transformed into a lush, heavily made-up singer on stage in a tiny gold dress, with a hundred dancers weaving around behind her.

"Eva-who-performed-at-the-Super Bowl-Eva?"

She nodded, expression graveyard still as she waited for his reaction.

"Is that supposed to scare me?"

"I don't know what it's supposed to do. I just couldn't stand it being between us."

Matthew went cold. "Are you disappointed I didn't recognize you?"

When she'd removed her mask, he'd thought the jolt of recognition was uncanny. Had his subconscious simply remembered her from a halftime show?

The disappointment sharpened and stuck in his gut. Then faded abruptly. He'd felt something between them long before he saw her face.

"No, relieved." She clutched his hand. "My fame doesn't bother you? I have a lot of money. Does it change anything?"

"Not in the slightest."

She wasn't just wrong for Matthew Wheeler; she was in a whole other stratosphere of incompatibility, with a life full of limos, designer drugs and glittery celebrities. Hell, she *was* a glittery celebrity and glittery didn't gel with the blue bloods in his circles. But he'd realized they were wrong for each other five minutes after meeting, and though he desperately wanted to find a way to get back home, that wasn't happening today.

This was a finite Venetian affair, and Matt didn't care who she was. She made him feel alive for the first time in eighteen months, and that made her perfect for right this minute.

"Since we're going full bore on disclosures, I have money, too. I bought this palazzo as a wedding gift to Amber, my wife. In Dallas, I was a partner in a multimillion dollar real estate firm and drove an Escalade. Then I dumped all my responsibilities and jumped on a plane. I have little to offer anyone right now. Should I have told you that before we got involved? Does it change things for you?"

If it did, he wouldn't blame her. He was a bad bet emotionally.

"Is that what we are? Involved?" Some snap crept back into her eyes.

"Yeah. Wasn't looking for it, wasn't planning on it. I left Dallas to regain my sanity after my wife died, and I finally feel like that's possible, thanks to you." He slid a thumb down her jaw. "Stay."

"Matt," she whispered, and her palms came up to frame his face. "This is crazy. We just met."

"Tell me you're ready to walk away and I'll show you to the door."

She shook her head. Hard. "But you don't want to be seen in public with me. Someone always recognizes me. Then the harassment starts, rehashing how my career is over." Her eyes filled again. "It's not a lot of fun."

There was the source of all that anguish he'd sensed. This amazing, beautiful butterfly had been damaged beyond repair, and the public refused to let her forget. A fierce, protective instinct tightened his arms around her, filling him with a heavy impulse to do something to fix it for her, to help her.

They'd both lost something, and perhaps she needed him as much as he needed her, though she seemed much less willing to admit it.

In order to get her to stay—to give them *both* the peace they desperately sought—the terms might have to be less structured than he would like.

"Good. I don't want to go out. I don't want to share you." He gestured toward the room at large. "Inside these walls, we can block out the rest of the world and just be together. I need that. If you do too, then go to Vincenzo's, get your stuff and stay here for as long as that's true. When it's not, leave. No rules. No expectations."

It *was* crazy. And rash. So unlike a guy who missed his wife and valued commitment. That was the reason it worked, why he and Evangeline gelled, because he wasn't that guy right now.

Crazy was what made it great.

Six

Evangeline sneaked into Vincenzo's without stumbling over any passed-out revelers.

Once in her room, she threw on a sweater over Matt's T-shirt and stabbed her legs into jeans. Then she packed her suitcases in preparation for either the biggest mistake of her life or the smartest thing she'd ever done.

Jury was still out on which one Matt was. But she was willing to see what unfolded as they blocked out the world for a few days, especially with the caveat of his consent to leave whenever things got too stifling.

Roots weren't possible for someone like her, who fed from new experiences and new destinations. Who knew the dangers of staying in one place too long and allowing someone to matter. Being with a man who got that was huge.

So was the fact that he wasn't in a hurry to get rid of her.

When he'd asked her to stay, he still had no idea who she was—she could tell. And somehow, that had been the clincher. Eva ceased to have any relevance. Actually, it hadn't been a factor between them all along and she'd never had that. What started as a short-term anonymous encounter had accidentally turned into something else.

It was scary to be just Evangeline, scary to be so exposed, but deep inside, she yearned for someone to see beneath the layers and value *her*.

As soon as she found out Matt wasn't that someone, she'd be out the door.

In record time, she shut the lid on her second suitcase and zipped it. She had packing down to a science.

As she carried the suitcases down the marble staircase to Vincenzo's first floor, one of his buddies who'd passed out on the couch stirred. Franco. Or maybe it was Fabricio. He sat up and blearily evaluated her as he scrubbed his jaw.

"Eva. Didn't know you were here." A night of hard drinking slurred his accented English almost unintelligibly. He zeroed in on the suitcases. "Leaving already?"

"Yeah. Tell Vincenzo I said later."

"Wait. Do my show this week." He lifted his chin. "*Milano Sera* will treat you well."

She took in his too-handsome face and two-hundred-dollar haircut that not even a night of couch surfing could ruin. Now she remembered him. Franco Buonotti. He was the host of a late-night talk show on an Italian network. He'd bugged her a couple of times before to do an exclusive with him.

"I don't think so."

"Aww. Not even for me?" He batted his eyelashes, and she almost snorted.

Italian playboys were so not her type—she was more into blue-eyed blonds Regardless, she hadn't broken her silence on the botched surgery in six months and didn't see a reason to change that now.

"Not even."

She escaped to the haven her blue-eyed blond had offered.

Upstairs in Matt's bedroom, she unpacked her clothes and arranged them in the empty spots he'd cleared for her in the closet and dresser. Unable to resist, she opened a drawer to finger his shirts. Very few of his items lay folded inside or hanging in the closet. He traveled as light as she did. But then, neither of them had a permanent home.

Oddly, seeing their clothes mixed felt very permanent. It shouldn't have put a smile on her face.

Matt ordered lunch to be delivered, and the soup grew cold because they were too busy talking to eat. He was transparent and genuine, and his willingness to share covered her tendency not to. He never ran out of stories, and she forgot to be wary by the middle of the afternoon.

That's when *Milano Sera's* host intruded on her haven. Matt answered a knock at the door, and she glimpsed the too-handsome face of Vincenzo's friend through the crack.

"I'll take care of it," she told Matt and shooed him away from the door. "I already said no."

"*Cara*, no one says no to me."

He'd cleaned up and squeezed his impressive build into tight Dolce & Gabbana jeans and a distressed T-shirt. That kind of sexy might work on tittering schoolgirls, but Evangeline couldn't titter to save her life.

"Yet I did. This is a private home. Please respect that."

She shut the door in his face and turned to see Matt watching her.

"Sales guy?" he asked with raised eyebrows. "What was he selling? Ice to Eskimos?"

And somehow he pulled a smile from her. Matt's talents were amazing. "He hosts a talk show on an Italian network and wants me to do an interview."

"Badly, I guess, to chase you here."

"I'm sorry he bothered us." She sighed. "It was a nice idea, to block out the world. Unfortunately, the world tends to camp out on my doorstep."

With it came the intrusion of Eva…and a reminder of all the reasons she'd latched onto the suggestion of a place to hide. If she knew the answers to the questions, interviews might not be so hard.

Her phone beeped, as if to underscore the point. Like an

idiot, she checked it to see an apology text from Vincenzo. Well, that was something, at least.

Matt took the phone from her fingers and tossed it on the credenza to his left without checking his aim.

"Hey, the world may come to you, but you don't have to answer to it." He swept her hand into his, holding it tight. "No rules at Palazzo D'Inverno. You don't have to do anything you don't want to."

"Thanks." It was therapeutic to have someone validate her choices.

He pulled her to the couch and settled them both into it comfortably. The sun was low enough in the sky to cast a glow over the whitewashed building opposite the palazzo.

His fingers tangled in her hair, and she experienced the deepest sense of harmony she'd experienced in a long while. Maybe the deepest ever.

"You drove an Escalade?" she asked in a blatant attempt to change the subject. "Really?"

It seemed too domestic for a guy who liked to throw rules out the window.

Matt chuckled. "Yeah. But I sold it, along with everything else. Seemed easier, since I had no idea where I was going or when I was coming back. Sometimes it feels like that part of my life was a dream, and I have a hard time remembering who that guy was."

So he hadn't really fit into that suburban existence. Venice was more his speed, and he'd obviously taken to the laid-back lifestyle. She wondered if she would have given him a second glance if they'd met at a party in the States.

"Did you end up in Venice because it reminds you of your wife? You said you bought this palazzo for her."

The fingers in her hair stilled. "Amber. Yeah, I did buy it for her. But she died not too long after we got married. She never got the chance to visit."

"That's a shame."

His wife had never seen this beautiful place Matt had

given her. But Evangeline couldn't quite squelch the thrill of knowing she was the only woman who had slept in Matt's bed, who had lain with him on this couch and eaten at his table.

"The lack of ghosts is the most attractive thing about Palazzo D'Inverno. You know what that means in English? Winter Palace. Seemed appropriate to come here. My soul felt pretty frozen."

Her heart ached for him. He wandered in search of a cure for his grief. Maybe he'd found one—her.

Silly. Probably a recipe for disaster to imagine herself a healer. But the notion was still there, pinging around inside her.

"The Italian who built this palazzo called it that because he came here during the winter from someplace colder. So did you."

"True." The expression on his face caught her right in her aching heart. "But it's only warmer because you're in it. I wouldn't have come to Venice if Amber had stayed here. I sold the house in Dallas we'd bought together. I can't be around things with memories. I get too attached."

Of course he did. Anyone with Matt's depth would be shattered by the loss of someone he'd obviously loved. He and his wife had shared a house and a life and a level of commitment she couldn't comprehend.

He was staring out the window blindly when she glanced at him. "Is it hard to talk about her?"

"Yeah." He didn't elaborate, and the hard set of his mouth said he wasn't going to.

For a guy who had easily told stories at lunch about his college days, closing off must mean it was a very taboo subject. She had an extra store of mercy for that kind of pain, especially for someone who'd been so very nice about Franco's invasion.

Maybe she'd stayed in the worst sort of foolish gamble—

betting that Matt wouldn't hurt her because he empathized with her pain.

Through the glass, she watched a bird pecking at the marble balcony. "When I was in an interview and the reporter asked a question I didn't want to answer, I'd use a code word. My manager would smoothly and quickly rescue me. We'll have one, too. Whenever one of us touches on a sensitive subject, the code word is sacred. It means 'get me out of this. No more questions.'"

That melted the stone from his expression. "What kind of code word?"

"You pick. Make it silly. That way, we can lighten the mood at the same time."

"Armadillo," he suggested immediately. "They walk funny."

The way he said it, all serious about the assignment, made her giggle. "See? It works. So do you want to call *armadillo* about Amber?"

His mouth twitched. "Maybe. And maybe I'm starting to get through it. I can say her name out loud without flinching. Progress."

Because of her? Maybe she hadn't given herself enough credit in the healing department.

Then he tipped up her chin and pierced her with those pale blue eyes. "I'll be your manager. In the interview."

Her lungs seized. "What are you talking about? I'm not doing the interview."

He didn't get it at all. Had she lost her gamble already?

"But if you wanted to, I'd stay right there with you. Say the word and I'll rescue you." He smiled and it was so gentle, she almost smiled back. "Nothing wrong with both of us making progress."

So, he'd obviously drawn a few of his own conclusions about her reasons for saying no.

She shook her head. "I don't want to do the interview."

"Okay."

And like that, he dropped the subject in favor of launching into a discussion about what she might like for dinner. She responded, but most of her attention was back on Matt's offer to be with her during the interview.

If he'd pushed, her heels would have dug in. But he never forced her to explain herself—backing her into an emotional corner was the fastest way to irritate her. It was almost like he knew.

"Matt?" He didn't even comment about how she'd interrupted him. "You'd do that for me? Rescue me if I say *armadillo?*"

"Sure." His brows wrinkled in confusion as he squeezed her hand. "I said I would. Does that mean you're going to do the interview?"

Patiently, he waited her out, his silence nothing more than encouragement to go on if she chose. Or not, if she chose, which was usually the path she took. "I don't know. I've had a strict no-interviews policy since the surgery."

"Do you get stage fright in front of all those cameras or something? Just picture them in their underwear."

The mental image of cameras wearing a pink, lacy bra-and-panty set made her giggle. "That's not the problem. I just don't like the questions."

"Well, no offense, but that guy doesn't strike me as a hard-hitting news journalist. If he asks you about anything more strenuous than where you shop, I'll fall over in a dead shock." He brushed a thumb across her cheek. "If I was going to jump back in the water, I'd get my feet wet with a small-time Italian talk show first."

"I'll think about it."

She'd think of nothing but. Because his point was valid.

He gave her plenty of space by bounding up immediately to cook dinner. She trailed him to the kitchen to watch him beat the raw ingredients into submission, which she thoroughly enjoyed.

"While you're sitting there," Matt said as he pulled covered platters from the refrigerator. "You should start thinking of the proper way to thank me for this fantastic dinner."

She returned his wicked grin. "Exactly how good of a cook are you?"

"My mama taught me well. Though I believe she intended for me to feed myself. Not use my culinary skills to seduce women."

"But you're so good at both. She should be proud."

They laughed and traded banter, and dinner was everything she'd anticipated when he'd asked her to stay—a low-key, enjoyable evening with a man who liked her.

Matt wasn't the only one who needed to heal. She got that. But he had a prayer of getting there one day, especially if she truly helped him along. Unfortunately, there wasn't anything he could do in return to fix her vocal cords. She was permanently scarred, and at best, this Venice interlude was a distraction from the rest of her life and what she would do with it.

For ten years, she'd worked hard, so hard, to climb the charts. Nothing had been handed to her. Only by tapping into her emotions and feeding her muse with the next greatest adventure had she found success. Being aimless and idle grated on her almost as much as having no voice. She wanted—needed—meaning again, but what if she invested in something and it kicked her to the curb like music had?

The public's hostile clamoring for a piece of her just increased the difficulty in answering the questions. But how long could she go on ignoring the fact that the person who really needed that answer was Evangeline?

Milano Sera was a benign compromise, and the addition of Matt's strength made it somehow seem a lot safer. She should do it, if for no other reason than to gain some progress toward the answers. If Franco put her back against the wall and demanded an explanation of who she was going to be from now on, all she had to do was say *armadillo*.

* * *

Evangeline's former publicist agreed to work with *Milano Sera*'s team to arrange an interview, with two important stipulations—Matt must be given free rein on the set, and Franco had to tape the show remotely from Vincenzo's house.

No one argued. Two days after Evangeline tucked her belongings into Matt's dresser, the taping was a go.

She checked her makeup one last time in the framed mirror above the marble double-sink vanity. A remote taping meant limited resources, so she'd handled her own clothes and hair in the ensuite bathroom she'd been sharing with Matt. No change from regular life; the days of stylists and three dedicated makeup artists were long over. She didn't mind. The activity gave her a chance to calm her nerves.

Eva stared back at her from the mirror. Whatever happened today was happening to Eva. She had to remember that.

When she and Matt entered Vincenzo's palazzo, the buzz of activity stopped as if a plug had been pulled. A statuesque, authoritative woman in her forties barreled over to pump Evangeline's hand and escort her to the makeshift set, introducing herself as the show's producer.

Gingerly, Evangeline perched in the tall, canvas chair the producer had indicated and smoothed her fuchsia skirt as the camera director lined up the shot, fiddled with the lighting and barked orders at the stressed assistants. Matt watched it all without comment from the edge of the camera zone, one hand shoved in his back pocket. It was a deceptively casual stance, but his keen blue eyes missed nothing.

So far, so good. The anchor of Matt's presence went a long way.

Franco strolled over to take the other chair, appropriately slick in his Armani suit and practiced smile.

"Eva, I'm happy you changed your mind."

Sure he was. The ratings boost would likely make his year.

An assistant clipped the small microphone inside Evangeline's strappy top, which she'd specifically chosen because its design allowed for the microphone to be completely hidden.

"I enjoy watching *Milano Sera* so I'm happy to be here, as well."

Franco nodded, though he surely didn't believe either falsehood. Another assistant dashed over and frowned over Evangeline's microphone as Franco murmured to the statuesque director.

"There's a small difficulty, *signorina*." The assistant unclipped the microphone and dashed away to return with another one. "Speak to Franco now."

"Thank you for having me, Mr. Buonotti," she said obediently.

Franco shook his head and tapped his earpiece. "It's no good."

The producer and another man whispered to each other furiously as assistants milled around.

"What's the problem?" she asked Franco. Foreboding settled in her chest at his blank expression.

"Your voice, *cara*. It's not working well with this remote equipment," he explained, not the least bit apologetic, as if the equipment wasn't to blame, but *she* was. "Too low. They can't get it to register."

Her cheeks heated. Rejected by the taping equipment.

"Try again. Speak directly into the microphone." Franco cleared his throat. "Tell me, Eva. What is your life like now that your voice has been so tragically altered?"

A cold, clammy sweat broke out across her neck. Slicked her palms. Eva. He was talking about Eva's voice. Not hers.

"Um." She shook her head as her brain shut down.

Matt was wrong. The interview hadn't even started yet, and already Franco was probing her wounds with inflammatory phrasing. Fashion tips, she could handle. Why had she naively believed Matt that shopping would be Franco's focus?

Armadillo.

Her throat clamped closed and she couldn't get the word out. Couldn't make any sound at all.

This wasn't happening to Eva, it was happening to *her*.

But then Matt was there, leading her from the chair and tersely informing the producer that Eva did not deign to give interviews to second-rate talk shows without proper equipment.

"Nice," she said when she could speak again, which happened right around the time she crossed the threshold of Matt's house. "You're the best manager I've ever had."

"I'm sorry I suggested that."

He was still bristling, his expression hard and unyielding. And maybe a little frightening.

"It's not your fault."

"It is. I had no idea he'd be so insensitive."

He muttered a particularly inventive slur on Franco's paternity and heritage simultaneously.

Amazing how Matt could still make her smile in the midst of emotional uproar.

"If it makes you feel better, you made up for it, like by quadruple."

It hadn't been merely a rescue, but an expert extraction completed without letting on to her distress *and* giving *Milano Sera*'s team the impression they'd upset her diva personality. A miraculous feat in her opinion.

"It does not make me feel better." He flipped on the lights to dispel the February gloom. Instantly, she cheered. This *was* still a haven. "You told me exactly what would happen. But I was so sure I knew what would help."

Clearly frustrated, he heaved a sigh.

She tucked herself into his embrace and laid her head on his shoulder, right at the hollow she'd first discovered while they were dancing. "You've given me exactly what I needed. A place to block all that out."

His arms tightened, drawing her into his body deliciously. "I'm glad, sweetheart. Palazzo D'Inverno is available to you as long as you want it."

Not the house. You.

He helped, in so many intangible ways. In his arms, nothing seemed as bad.

She didn't say it.

If nothing else, Franco had shown her the protection Eva had provided in the past had all but vanished. She had nothing left to be rejected but the deepest part of herself, and that was something she refused to risk.

No matter how much she wished Matt held some sort of magic key to her future, he couldn't be anything more than a brief distraction. There was no question their Venice affair was going to be hot, fantastic…and short-lived.

She refused to become dependent on a man—not just a man, but one with his own demons—to fill the gap music had left behind, and she could see it happening as if Matt's beautiful eyes had turned into a crystal ball. Worse, it would be all take and no give, because her store of trust was in short supply. That was totally unfair.

How much longer did it really make sense for her to stay?

Seven

Matthew blinked and it was somehow Saturday already.

Evangeline filled his house, exactly as he'd envisioned, and blinded him to everything else. They didn't go out, more through his insistence than hers. He'd set up an account at both the local pharmacy and the grocery store so Evangeline could order whatever she needed to be delivered. The creative thank-you she'd given him for his thoughtfulness still ranked as one of the highlights of the week.

And there had been a lot of highlights, especially the gradual lightening of the shadows in her eyes, which he'd only made worse with his meddling. He was gratified she'd stayed long enough to let him undo the hurt he'd caused.

He'd never had a relationship with no promises past breakfast. Certainly never thought he'd have suggested it. Every morning, he expected—braced—to find she'd left in the middle of the night.

It was getting old. But the terms were too necessary to change.

The wanderlust in her eyes was unmistakable. When she talked about performing in Budapest or Moscow, her expression reminded him of when he was inside her. Rapturous.

She couldn't sing, but she still liked roaming. Eventually, she'd move on and leave him behind.

Which was good. This thing between them was amazing, but he couldn't keep it up, not long term.

He glanced at his phone. With the time difference, Mama should be at one of her Saturday-morning fundraisers right about now. The perfect time to call. He dialed and waited for voice mail to pick up.

"You've reached Fran Wheeler. I'm busy saving the world with style and grace. Leave a message."

His mother's voice poured alcohol on the exposed wound of guilt in his gut, which was approximately half the size of Texas. "It's me, Mama. Just checking in to let you know I'm still alive. Talk to you later."

He wouldn't, because he never called when she might actually answer.

What would he say? *Sorry about taking off. No, still not coming home. Still not capable of being the Wheeler you raised me to be.*

He had to go home and pick up his responsibilities with Wheeler Family Partners.

But he'd left because he couldn't do it any longer, couldn't see his grandfather's empty desk every day. Couldn't attend fundraisers and ribbon cuttings without Amber. Couldn't watch Lucas and Cia sneak off during the boring parts of events and return with all that love and affection dripping from their faces.

It was too hard.

So he'd live in the present and wring every bit of pleasure out of it.

He sat at the kitchen island and watched Evangeline wash lunch dishes in the sink. He cooked and she washed dishes. Worked for him—the view was very enjoyable from his stool.

"What do you want to do now?" he asked. She flashed

a naughty smile over her shoulder. "Twice this morning wasn't enough for you?"

"Never enough. I like you too much."

Yeah. He liked her, too. Everything was fun. Showers. Dishes. Long talks in the afternoon. "The weather is supposed to be unseasonably warm today. What if we have dinner on the roof?"

"There's a rooftop patio?" Her gravelly voice was hopeful as she dried the last dish and put it away.

That voice. It still dug in, sharp and hot inside no matter how many times he heard it. It was the first thing he wanted to hear in the morning and the last thing he wanted to hear before he went to sleep.

"Did I forget to mention that?"

"Never mind dinner. Show it to me right now."

"Sure." He took her hand and led her outside.

The breeze from the canal was chilly, but bearable, as they climbed the outside stairs to the roof. Venice unfolded as they walked out onto the patio.

Evangeline gasped. "Oh, Matt. I could live here. Right here in this spot. The view is amazing."

"I know. It's one of the reasons I bought this palazzo."

Several of the plants lined up in clay planters against the railing had withered and died, but a few remained green, fresh against the backdrop of browns, terra-cotta and white from the surrounding buildings.

Millions of dollars of real estate stretched on either side of the canal. Once, he'd have taken in the structures with a critical eye, evaluated the resale value, calculated the square footage. Mapped the location and noted the neighborhood features automatically.

None of that could compare to the gorgeous vision standing next to him. The look on her face—he'd move a mountain with a teaspoon if it put that expression of awe and appreciation there.

"You can see the spires of San Marco. And Santa Maria

della Salute. Isn't it beautiful?" She pointed, but he was busy looking at her. Her loose curls blew against her cheek and her eyes were luminous and his gut tightened. His reaction to her was so physical, so elemental. Would he ever get tired of that?

"Yeah. Beautiful." His fingers ached to sink into her hair. Among other things.

That was the beauty of their arrangement. They did whatever they wanted, when they wanted to do it. And he wanted her, wanted to make her feel as good as she made him feel. Right now.

"Let's go back inside."

"What? Why?" She flicked him a puzzled glance and turned her attention back to Venice.

"Because," he said hoarsely, and the unexpected catch in his throat swallowed the rest of the words.

With obvious concern, she eyed him. "Are you okay?"

No. Not hardly. He tugged on her hand. "Come back downstairs. Please. I want to be with you."

"You *are* with me." Her gaze traveled over him. Finally, she caught on to his urgency and grinned. Wickedly. "Oh. Well, I've got news for you. My girl parts work the same whether I'm inside or outside."

Attention firmly on him, she leaned in and teased him with a butterfly kiss while her hands wandered underneath his shirt. He was already half-aroused, and her fiery touch drained heat south instantly.

"Evangeline." He groaned as her fingers dipped into the waistband of his jeans to cup his bare butt. "We're on the roof."

"Uh-huh," she murmured against his mouth. "If you want me, take me, cowboy."

The kiss turned carnal as her tongue crashed with his and they drank from each other. She stole his reason, transformed his desire into crushing need, drew him out of time and place.

He was totally hooked on it.

Tilting her head, he changed the angle, went deeper, fed his senses with the feast of Evangeline.

Their hips aligned, seeking the heat, the promise of completion just beneath their clothes.

He nearly lost his balance as his shirt came over his head, gripped tight in her fists. She threw it to the concrete. Before he could protest, she had his zipper down and her warm hands stroked his flesh, coaxing him out from behind the fabric of his underwear.

They were on the roof. And he was on display.

Then she knelt. Her mouth closed over his length, and conscious thought escaped him as his knees weakened. Running on pure carnal instinct, he pushed deeper until the licks of fire spread through his blood like an inferno, tightening into a knot at his center. He couldn't keep from coming another second.

"Hold up, sweetheart."

He eased from her mouth and in a flash, dropped to the ground and pulled her into his lap. The breeze cooled his fevered skin. Street sounds wafted from below. And he didn't care. She encouraged him to do new things, things he'd never do under normal circumstances, and somehow it made sense.

In moments, her clothes landed in a heap and her mouth landed on his, legs wrapped around his waist, exactly the way he liked.

Yes. He fed the flames as he slid into her. Eyes closed, he froze, sustaining the perfect pleasure of being inside her sweet body, reveling in the physical, carnal hunger that drove him to join with her.

He'd left Dallas desperate to feel again. She'd burrowed underneath the ice-covered inertia and sensitized him. To the limit.

She moaned his name and rolled her hips, drawing him deeper than should have been possible. The roof, the air,

Evangeline—*something*—heightened the sensations, spiraling him toward oblivion faster, stronger, fiercer than ever before.

Her gaze captured his, and the morning sunlight refracted inside her eyes, brightening them. The ache of near release bled upward, into his chest, his throat.

Lids fluttering, she surrendered to an exceptionally strong climax. It rippled down his length and detonated his own release. The blast echoed in his head, blacking out his vision.

He held her slumped form, dragging oxygen into his lungs. That had been…different. And in a relationship full of different, how could there be so many shades yet undiscovered?

How could he crave still more when they'd delved so deeply already?

When she shifted, resettling in his lap, clarity blew away the awe of the moment.

"Evangeline. We forgot to use a condom."

"It's okay," she mumbled against his shoulder. "It's the wrong time of the month."

Women and their bodies—that was a mystery he'd yet to solve even after being with Amber for years. He heaved out a shudder of a breath.

"Sure?"

"Well, either way, too late now." She smiled up at him. "And it was worth it. I don't know how you do that to me. It was unbelievable. Even for us."

"Yeah. It was."

She'd noticed the difference too, but attributed it to the lack of a barrier. Which he didn't believe for a second. Sure the sensation was mind-altering. He'd do it again in a heartbeat if given a safe opportunity. But there was more to it than forgetting a condom, and he feared it had everything to do with Evangeline. With who he was around her. Because of her.

"We'll be extra careful from now on." She wagged her finger at him. "You have to stop being so adorable and sexy."

"Me?" That he could never get used to. It was disturbing when she told him how much he turned her on, which she did frequently. Disturbing because he liked it, and didn't understand what about her was so compelling, when she and Amber were such polar opposites. "You're the one who was all gorgeous with the hair in your face."

"You've got it bad and you might as well admit it."

His pulse stuttered. "Got what bad?"

A crush? Feelings? Was she staring down the barrel of their relationship and seeing things that weren't there?

Or was he making excuses for things he didn't want to examine too closely?

"An addiction to inventive positions," she explained with a wicked laugh. "And locations, apparently."

His muscles relaxed, and he eased her up to help her get dressed, then stepped into his own clothes. "That's all you, honey. I'm just here for the food."

Her laugh uncurled across his skin with gravelly teeth and stayed there. She affected him in so many ways. And not all of them were good.

A dose of guilt wormed into his consciousness. He'd found a temporary cure for his ills, but how fair was it to keep using Evangeline?

"Hey." He caught her hand and brought it to his lips. "You know I don't have much to offer. Emotionally. Right?"

She nodded, gaze searching his quizzically. "I'm not confused about what's going on between us. We're keeping the demons at bay until it doesn't work any longer. Were *you* confused?"

"No. Just checking."

Keeping the demons at bay. Yeah, that was exactly what they were doing. She knew he wasn't capable of anything more right now.

They meandered downstairs to do absolutely nothing except be together.

It shouldn't have been so easy. They should get on each other's nerves. Or complain about socks on the floor, dishes in the sink. Argue about something.

They didn't.

The longer he spent in Evangeline's company, the less he recognized himself. He hadn't put on a suit since the masked ball; he hadn't ironed a shirt or balanced his checkbook. T-shirts and spending money recklessly felt far too comfortable. As comfortable as Evangeline.

He hadn't dwelled on Amber in days. Wasn't that the point of all this? Why did it feel so strange?

Venice provided a much-needed break from real life as he searched for a way to get back to Dallas, to the responsible, centered, married man he'd been. When he'd understood his place in the world and woke up happy every morning.

He didn't know what would work to turn back time, or if what he sought existed. But he was starting to wonder—if he'd known what to look for, what would he have found instead of glittery, wrong-for-Matthew-Wheeler Evangeline?

And would he recognize it, now that Evangeline had so filled him he couldn't see around her?

Late one afternoon, Evangeline's phone buzzed. She retrieved it and flopped on the couch next to Matt, then glanced up from the text message to catch his gaze.

"Vincenzo's cousin, Nicola, is throwing a small dinner party," she said. "Tonight. Do you want to go? It's casual. He assures me the guest list is well vetted."

They hadn't left the house in a week. Self-preservation warred with the gypsy part of her soul that liked parties and people and experiences. All of her parts liked Matt, so it wasn't a hardship to wake up in his bed every morning.

"Sounds fun. As long as you're okay with it."

And that was why. He was amazing and intuitive and

never crowded her. Gradually, she'd stopped practicing her exit strategy and just enjoyed hanging out with him. Plus, she'd grown rather fond of starring in Matt's rodeo. The man shattered her with those eyes alone.

Was she okay with going out? It was dinner at Nicola's house, not a public flogging. She hesitated.

"Nicola lives on the other end of the Grand Canal. How should we get there?"

With silent, reassuring strength, he covered Evangeline's hand with his. "Private water taxi. Put on a big hat and a scarf. It'll be dark. No one will know it's you."

"Done." She accepted the invitation and deleted the other text message she'd received from her half sister, Lisa, without reading it, then spent an hour getting ready. Which gave her plenty of time to get worked up about her sister.

Lisa was seventeen. And her parents had been married. The anger, the sheer resentment was embedded deep. Their father had chosen a life with one daughter over the other— Evangeline would never forgive that. She sent Lisa extravagant Christmas gifts in a petty attempt to show her father there were no hard feelings. And maybe to quietly announce that hey, no dad needed for her to be a huge success.

Evangeline hadn't spoken to her sister since the botched surgery. How many texts did she have to ignore for Lisa to give up? It wasn't like they were real family.

Putting it out of her mind, she vowed not to let unpleasant history ruin the fun evening she and Matt had planned.

When Evangeline returned downstairs, Matt was waiting for her, dressed in dark jeans and a sweater. His eyebrows rose.

A floppy hat covered her pinned-up hair, a scarf hid the lower half of her face and giant sunglasses completed the disguise.

"Perfect." Matt shot her a playful grin. "Except maybe lose the glasses. It is nighttime."

She slipped them off and returned his smile. "Happy?"

"Always."

That thrilled her to no end, to be responsible for Matt's happiness. That was part of the reason she stayed. It was powerful to watch him slowly heal.

The taxi picked them up at Palazzo D'Inverno's water entrance and motored away from the dock. The driver steered under the Ponte dell'Accademia and up the canal to Vincenzo's cousin's house. Twinkling stars competed with the twinkle of Venice, both lit for the night with stunning brilliance.

They arrived a few minutes later. Once inside, Evangeline started to introduce Matt and realized with no small amount of mortification that she didn't know his last name. It hadn't seemed important, until now.

With a quick grin that said he'd read Evangeline's mind, he stuck out his hand to Nicola Mantovani, their hostess. "Matt Wheeler."

He repeated it to Nicola's boyfriend, Angelo. Vincenzo shook Matt's hand and introduced his lady friend for the evening, whose name Evangeline promptly forgot. He never called his dates again anyway.

Nicola lifted an unobtrusive finger toward a uniformed servant, who sprang forward to pass out wineglasses full of deep red Chianti. The tiny, dark-haired Italian raised her glass. "A toast. To new friends."

Expertly, Nicola finessed everyone to the lushly appointed salon where they took seats and chatted politely.

When Vincenzo launched into an impassioned review of the performance he'd seen at Teatro alla Scala the prior weekend, Evangeline leaned in to whisper in Matt's ear. "Wheeler. That's a nice last name."

Matt grinned. "We haven't formally introduced ourselves, have we?"

"Evangeline La Fleur." She stuck her hand out in mock solemnity. "Nice to meet you, Matt Wheeler."

Vincenzo paused long enough to drain his glass and motioned for a refill.

In the silence, Angelo asked Matt, "What do you do?"

"I'm a partner at a commercial real estate firm in Dallas, Texas."

No hesitation. No dodging the question. It was clearly how he defined himself or the answer wouldn't have come so quickly. It put an odd barb in her stomach because she wouldn't have been so quick with her own answer.

"Oh, do you know J. R. Ewing?" Angelo snickered at his own joke. Evangeline rolled her eyes, but Matt just laughed.

He was such a good guy to spend time with her friends and not call them out for being lame. But here she could relax and just be herself, without the pressure of Eva.

"Real estate." Nicola wrinkled her nose. "Houses?"

"No, we haven't delved into residential. We sell office buildings. Downtown high-rises." When he warmed to the subject, the pang in her stomach poked a little harder. He loved his job. It was all over his expression. "Land for development. That sort of thing."

We. Not *I*. An interesting choice of phrasing. Who was the *we*?

"High-rises. That sounds impressive." Nicola's nose unwrinkled and she leaned forward, suddenly a bit more interested in Evangeline's companion now that she scented money.

"Matt's very successful," Evangeline threw in, though she didn't know much about the ins and outs of the life he'd left behind. Neither last names nor pre-Venice activities had ranked very high on the priority list of their discussions. She'd always assumed it was by design, since Matt's wife was a taboo piece of that past.

But really, of course he was successful. Look at him.

He squeezed her hand. "Evangeline's being kind. I've been on an extended vacation. Wheeler Family Partners was the top-selling firm in Texas last year, but its current success is due to my brother. Not me."

"You work for a family business?" Nicola asked, and Matt nodded, explaining how the other partners were his dad and brother and the firm had been in his family for over a hundred years.

No one else seemed to notice the catch in his voice, but it sliced at her.

Family meant nothing to her, was almost a foreign word. But to Matt, it seemed as if it had been the cornerstone of his existence before Venice. He'd communicated far more than the simple logistics of a job—he'd belonged to a unit.

He wandered in search of answers now, but did he eventually want to return to his roots? She didn't want to ask. Didn't want it to matter. But the barb in her stomach was also due to realizing they were less alike than she'd assumed.

She waited until after dinner, when they'd settled into the water taxi to return to Matt's house, to bring it up again. "Tell me more about your life in Dallas."

With a laugh, he kissed her sweetly. "Why? Do you need to take a nap? That would be so boring you'd nod off in a second."

Her lips curved. "Boring? You? There's no way the guy who put his hand under my dress on a balcony could ever be boring."

"I drove a sports utility vehicle, Evangeline."

"But you left it all behind." His wife's death had turned him into a drifter. Like her. They'd both been honed by tragedy but had yet to recognize their new shape. She desperately wanted to feel that kinship with him again after learning they'd come from such different places. "So it doesn't matter now, right?"

"It matters. I walked away from a legacy. The name of the firm is Wheeler Family Partners. That pretty much en-

capsulates it. Family is everything. And I abandoned them."
His voice never wavered as he listed his sins.

Strength. He had it in spades and it pulled at her. The men
in her life were weak. Spineless. Matt regretted his actions
but took full responsibility for what he'd done.

"I didn't mean to poke at scars. Armadillo?" she offered.

"Yeah. It's not a great subject." He curled her palm
against his. "What was your life like when you were singing?"

"Busy. Lonely." The hand holding hers tightened. Encouraging her to go on. He was so easy to be with—maybe
she could open up, just a little. "The guy from Vincenzo's
party, Rory, he was supposed to be the cure for that. We
were so similar, both with careers in the industry. Both
happy being nomads. He had some bad habits, but I stepped
over the empty Jack Daniel's bottles because I was in love
with him. Turns out he wasn't content to be saddled with
a has-been."

"I'm sorry."

"I'm not. Longevity isn't one of my gifts." She'd have
tried, for Rory. And probably would have bungled it all up.
"That's what made being an in-demand vocalist so great. I
sang all over the world, was constantly on the move."

She'd loved it, loved having a new destination, new experiences.

And that was the gist of it, wasn't it? She and Matt had
a kinship born of shared pain, but it was tenuous at best. A
successful, solid real estate broker who valued family had
nothing in common with a music business has-been who
sported a giant albatross called Lack of a Career around
her neck.

Besides, his heart still belonged to his wife, would always belong to his family. Hers had been cut from her chest
by the same blade that destroyed her career. Maybe even
before that.

She'd shared this time with Matt because they were both slaying their demons.

How much longer would it take for this refuge to crumble around her?

Eight

Evangeline rolled over and pulled the sheets up around her neck. Cold. And still dark. Though her brain languished in the fog of semiconsciousness, she could tell Matt wasn't asleep. His breathing was too even.

Two weeks and four days into it and she could already gauge his state of consciousness. She also knew his favorite foods, the exact rhythm to move her hips to make him explode, how to get that blinding, sincere smile out of him that shivered her insides.

And if he was awake, she knew she'd never go back to sleep.

They were becoming dangerously entangled for two ships who were supposed to be passing in the night.

Supposed to be. But she was still here.

She kept looking for a reason to leave. Kept waiting for claustrophobia to set in or for Matt's true colors to shine through. The longer she spent with him, the more convinced she became that he was the real deal and she could trust him. He was a genuine guy who wasn't looking for the quickest way to get rid of her. Who treated her like he'd stumbled upon a rare treasure.

Instead of scouting for the exit, she stayed. The longer she stayed, the more obstacles she saw to keeping this Venice bubble afloat.

Why couldn't she have met Matt in six months? A year? At any point in the future when she'd figured out who she was going to be and could give Matt what he deserved—someone a lot more together, at a different place in her life.

She scooted across the cool sheets and nestled into his arms. "You need a glass of warm milk?"

He kissed her temple. "Did I wake you up? Sorry."

"You didn't."

But maybe on some level, he had.

That instantaneous spiritual bond hadn't dimmed in the slightest. Sometimes, he finished her sentences, and sometimes, she didn't have to speak at all. It was more than gelling and she puzzled over the indescribable, powerful nature of their relationship.

It should feel weird. Suffocating. It didn't.

"I'll go downstairs so you can sleep."

Something was bothering him. Matt's ghosts continually haunted him and lots of great sex hadn't produced quite the exorcism she'd have wished.

She snaked an arm over his chest to hold him in place. "Don't you dare. Talk to me."

"It's not a middle-of-the-night subject. But thanks." His hand wandered over to stroke her breast and as lovely as that was, his touch carried a hint of preoccupation.

"Anything is a middle-of-the-night subject. It's dark. Sleepy. What better environment is there to lay it all out?" Unless he was about to call it off. That froze her pulse. She didn't want it to be over.

She'd thought they were both happy to live in the here and now. Both happy to see what unfolded. The lack of boundaries made it easier for her to stay but also made it easier—for either of them—to walk away.

Should she have checked in with him before now?

The hand on her breast stilled, but didn't move away. "You wouldn't rather go back to sleep?"

"I'd rather you weren't upset. Tell me, and let me make it all better. That's what I'm here for, right? To beat back the demons." Which was a two-way street, and he did his part well. "But unlike other forms of self-medication, I don't come with a hangover."

"You don't pull any punches, do you?" A deep breath lifted his chest. "I was thinking I should be over Amber by now."

"What? Why would you think *that*?"

Oh, that was such a better subject than calling it off. He hardly ever mentioned his wife, and she respected his privacy. But curiosity pricked at her, naturally. What had Amber been like? What was so special about her to have shattered Matt into so many pieces?

"It's been a year and a half. How can I still be so messed up?"

"You can't put a time frame to grief. Life doesn't have checklists."

"We weren't married a whole year. She's been dead longer than the length of our marriage."

"So? You loved her." Obviously a lot, more than Evangeline had ever loved anyone, or could even imagine. She could, however, *easily* imagine how it would feel to be the object of such unending devotion.

Especially Matt's.

That put a hitch in her lungs. She suddenly, unreasonably wished for something impossible—the hope that she might one day take Amber's place in his heart. Impossible, because she'd have to open herself up in return and trust Matt with her deepest layer. Impossible, because he was still hung up on his wife. That was the biggest obstacle of all.

Apparently dark-and-sleepy was a good environment for her conscience to spill confessions, as well. As long as she didn't start doing it out loud...

Matt shifted restlessly. "Am I doomed to suffer for the rest of my life because I fell in love with someone? It's not fair."

He was destroyed. No one should have to bear that much of a burden without relief.

"I don't have all the answers." She rested her palm on his heart, which beat strongly despite her suspicion it was badly broken. "The only thing I know for sure is life sucks and then it gets better until it gets worse again. Sometimes I think God likes to see what happens when the carpet is pulled out from under you."

After a long minute of silence, he said, "It doesn't bother you that I'm moping around over another woman?"

Well, now that you mention it...

"I didn't say that." Boy, he'd taken her no-subject-off-limits-in-the-middle-of-the-night seriously, hadn't he? Despite asking, she didn't think he'd actually appreciate knowing about the burning-in-the-gut jealousy of Amber she'd just discovered. "But we're cool. I understand. Of all people, trust me. I understand."

Probably too much. Other women wouldn't put up with being a form of self-medication. But Matt wasn't presenting her with a buffet of choices. What would she pick if he did?

The question bounced around inside her with no answer.

"The pastor at Amber's funeral said something that's stuck with me. The valleys of life are impartial and temporary. If that's true, I should get over it already, right?"

"Is *that* why you're beating yourself up? That's total crap!" Evangeline's vision grayed for a furious moment. Pastors should soothe people in their time of grief—not spew lies. "The valleys of life are anything but impartial. Or temporary. Both of us had the center of our existence ripped from our fingers. No warning. That's as personal as it gets, and I refuse to accept that we don't have the right to be pissed off about it because it's gone forever."

His arms tightened around her, holding her close, calming her. *He* was calming *her*. "Is that what happened? You had the center of your existence ripped away?"

"Yeah. I did." Her chin trembled.

"You don't talk about it."

Just like he didn't talk about Amber. "No voice. It kind of puts a crimp in the talking thing."

"That's a cop-out. Especially with me. Should I tell you again how sexy I think your voice is?"

She sighed. Transparency was one of the many things she couldn't avoid with Matt. It went hand in hand with the vibe between them. And it went both ways. He'd veered away from Amber on purpose, maybe to avoid talking about her. Or maybe to find some straw he could grasp from her own experiences. They were *both* fighting their way out of the valley.

He was so compassionate and decent and didn't want anything from her but her company. She should honor that.

"I lost everything." She shut her eyes. "Not just my career. I sang my whole life, from as early as I can remember. Back then, my voice was the one thing that belonged to me and no one else. Singing was a coping mechanism."

"What were you coping with?" he asked gently.

"You know, stuff. My home life." She hadn't thought about it in years. But that had been the genesis of using her voice to express all the things going on inside.

"My dad, he was a hockey player for Detroit. A seagull who swooped in, got my mom pregnant and never called her again. She tracked him down, got child support. She moved to the U.S. so he could know his daughter. Guess how many times I heard from him?"

"Evangeline…" Matt nearly pulled her on top of him in a fierce hug, lips buried in her hair.

"It's fine. I'm over it."

"I don't think so," he murmured and softened the contradiction with a light kiss. "You started to say you had family in Detroit. When we were dancing."

God, she had. How did he remember that? "He's not my family. He lost that chance. But, I…have a…sister."

"Are you and your sister close?"

Evangeline laughed but it came out broken. "She worships me. Not like in a million-screaming-fans way. Because she wants to sing."

Lisa texted her all the time asking for career advice. Evangeline still didn't know why she'd ever answered. No one had helped her. But before the surgery, she hadn't been able to stop herself from pathetically responding each and every time. Once, she flew Lisa and three friends to London for a concert for Lisa's fifteenth birthday. It was the last time she'd seen her sister.

After the surgery, Evangeline went into a hole and stopped responding to the texts. One of these days, Lisa's name on her caller-ID wasn't going to cause such deep-seated anguish. She hoped. It wasn't Lisa's fault their father was a bastard.

"Is she any good?" Matt asked.

She shrugged. "I've never heard her sing. Too busy, I guess."

"You've got time now," he pointed out quietly, but his words reverberated in her head like the boom of a cannon.

"Yeah. I should call her." She wouldn't. What would she say? They had no relationship, had only ever connected over their mutual interest in singing. Now they had nothing in common other than a few strands of DNA. "Armadillo."

She was done with midnight confessions. Lisa was a corner she couldn't stand being backed into.

"I should call my brother. I haven't talked to him in a month." Matt rolled away and she missed his warmth. Had she hurt his feelings?

A sick niggle in her stomach unearthed the realization that she'd set up the code word as a way for him get out of difficult subjects, but only she used it.

"Is a month a long time?" she asked.

"We saw each other every day. His office was next to mine. We went to the same college, played basketball with some guys once a week. And you know. He's my brother. It's my job to make sure he stays out of trouble."

"You miss him."

It wasn't a question. She could hear it in his voice and didn't have to ask if they were close. Could Evangeline have a similar relationship with Lisa if she tried harder?

No. Evangeline wasn't cut out for family relationships. Didn't want to be. It hurt too much.

"That was before. When Amber was alive. After, I drifted through everything, disengaging until everyone stopped trying. I kept thinking something would happen to snap me out of it. Then my grandfather died and I realized. *I* had to snap me out of it. So I dumped my entire life in Lucas's lap and left." He chuckled derisively. "I even sold him my house. He's in *my* house with a wife he's gaga over, making new memories, about to deliver my parents their first grandchild. I should be there, living that life."

There. Not here. Venice was a temporary fix. She knew that. So why did it make her so sad?

"Are you jealous that your brother is happy?"

At least they had that in common.

"No. Not really. Maybe a little." He sounded defeated all at once. "Mostly I'm glad. I never thought he'd get married. He was kind of a screwup. But he met this woman who transformed him into a guy I didn't recognize. He's responsible. Committed. Expecting a baby who will be the first of the next generation of Wheelers. That was my role. A role I couldn't do any longer. And I need to figure out how to do it again."

He had more demons than she'd realized. "You're not just trying to get over Amber. You're trying to fit back into the life you had with her."

A life that included lineages. Babies. Roots and new

branches on the family tree. Concepts so alien she barely knew how to label them.

He huffed out a breath. "I can't. I know that. But for as long as I can remember, I've done the right thing. I ran Wheeler Family Partners, and I was good at selling real estate. Successful. Amber was a part of that. She had connections, came from a distinguished family. There were five hundred guests at our wedding. CEOs of Fortune 500 companies. A former U.S. president. The governor. We were happy being a power couple. People could depend on me. I want that back."

Her stomach dropped. No wonder he hadn't cared about her celebrity status or her money. He had his own social clout, in a world far removed from hers.

A cleft, one she hadn't realized was there, widened.

He hadn't embraced the wanderlust—he'd been desperate to find the magic formula for curing his grief so he could pick up the broken pieces of a life he'd abandoned, but yearned to return to.

Unlike her, he *could* go back. And would. Not only did neither of them have a whole heart to give to anyone else, they came from different places and were going different places.

She kissed his cheek. "I depend on you. Right now, you're my entire world."

How pathetic did that sound? He had a career waiting for him. A family. Both would welcome him back with open arms, she had no doubt. No mother who took the time to teach her son to cook would turn her back on him.

"Right now, I'm pretty happy being your entire world."

Shock flashed behind her rib cage. "Really? I thought you were heading toward the big breakup."

He *should* be heading toward the breakup. She should, too.

"What, you mean of us?" He laughed and shifted suddenly, rolling her against him, tight. "You're the best thing that's happened to me in a long time. Why would I give that up?"

"Isn't that what we've been talking about? You want to go home." Home to a place she couldn't follow. Her gypsy soul would wither and die in the suburbs. "This is…our Venice bubble. It's not going to last."

Quiet settled over them, and she waited for him to agree.

But he said, "I don't know if I *can* go home. My family— the obligations. It feels so oppressive. Like it's too much for me to handle. I want to be me again, but at the same time I want to keep hiding." He chuckled darkly. "God Almighty, I sound like the biggest pansy."

No, he sounded like a man in incredible turmoil. For once, she'd stayed. She'd done it as an attempt to block out the future, but instead, quite by accident, she'd discovered this sensitive, wonderful person. What a juxtaposition. She ached to salve his wounds, knowing the moment she did, he'd leave her.

Rock. Hard place.

"I want to sing. I can't. We're both stuck in a rut we can't get out of."

Matthew listened to the sound of Evangeline's heart against his and threaded fingers through her hair.

"Rut. Valley. Same difference."

There was nothing quantifiable about the grieving process. It had stages, or so he'd read. But they weren't easily identifiable so he had no idea if he'd gone through them all, remained immobilized in one, or had stumbled his way back to the beginning to run through them a second time.

He'd been stuck in the valley for far too long. And he was sick of it.

Her lips grazed his throat and stayed there. They'd both lost so much. Did she find it as comforting as he did to be in the arms of someone who understood? She not only understood, she'd given him permission to be mad.

That was powerful.

Because he *was* mad. And felt guilty about being mad. Evangeline somehow made it okay to let all that out, let it flow, and the anger cleansed as it burned through his blood.

"I was part of something," he said. "In Dallas. Some sons rebel against the family business, but I couldn't wait to be on the team. My parents were proud of me, and I thrived on that. Thrived on being married and looked forward to starting a family. Then it was gone and I couldn't function. I don't know how to get that back."

The sheer pressure of life without Amber had nearly suffocated him. But it was more than missing her. They'd been like cogs in a complex machine, complementing each other. He didn't know how to be successful without her.

"I admire you," she said quietly.

He snorted. "For what, disappointing everyone?"

That was at least half his onus—how did he face everyone again, knowing he'd abandoned them? Knowing they were eyeing him with apprehension, waiting for him to freak out again?

"For recognizing that you needed time away to get your head on straight. It was brave."

"Cowardly, you mean," he corrected. "People deal with pressure gracefully all the time. I cracked. It wasn't pretty."

"But you changed things. You left your comfort zone and struck out to fix it, without any idea how or where that would occur. That's sheer courage in my book."

He started to tell her she should reread that book but closed his mouth. She saw him differently. But that didn't mean she needed glasses. Perhaps he did.

"Thanks. That's nice to hear."

"You had a choice and made it." The unspoken *I didn't* wrenched his heart.

"Have you ever noticed the stuff people say when you're grieving makes no sense?" That was another gripe he'd been carrying around since the funeral.

"What like, 'Sorry for your loss'?"

"Yeah. My favorite is, 'But think of all you do have.'" He struggled to voice the anxiety whipping through him. Struggled to phrase it in a way that didn't sound self-centered. And gave up. This was Evangeline. He didn't have to pull punches. "It's meaningless. Thanks for pointing out I still have a mom and a dad. That makes it *all* better. And oh, yeah, I have my health. The fact that I'm still breathing is supposed to get me through the valley?"

"I got an, 'At least you still have all the money'. Don't get me wrong. I'm grateful I can afford to eat. A lot of people can't after losing their job. But money doesn't make up for losing who you were."

"Exactly." It was like she peered down his throat and read the words in his heart, expressing for him what he couldn't formulate. "Singing was your purpose. So what do you do now that it's gone, right?"

She laughed without humor. "Isn't that the million-dollar question?"

He'd meant it rhetorically, but something in her tone tugged at him. "Is it?"

She didn't answer, and he lightly bumped her head with his chest. "Middle-of-the-night. Nothing is sacred."

Don't call armadillo. His senses tingled. This was critically important, he could tell.

Her soft sigh drifted across his skin. "I don't know what to do now. That's my demon."

"The one I'm here to beat back for you?" The phantoms in her eyes weren't just from losing her voice. How could he have missed that? Because he'd been wallowing around in his own problems instead of tending to hers.

"Singing is all I'm good at. My only talent."

"Not hardly."

"Being good in bed isn't a talent." The eye-roll came through loud and clear.

He bit back a chuckle and the accompanying comment—
it is the way you do it.

"You're good at making me cheerful. That's something
no one else could accomplish, so don't knock it. But I was
going to say the music industry can't be easy to crack or
everyone would do it. Persistence is a talent. You worked
hard to achieve success."

"Yeah. Hard work." Her voice fractured. "There was a
lot of that."

There was more, something else she wasn't saying, and
she was hurting. The inability to fix it crawled around in
his chest. But this middle-of-the-night was exactly what
he'd asked for—the exploration of what two damaged souls
could become to each other.

Dang it if he'd fail at being what she needed.

"Hey." He brought her hand to his cheek and held it there,
reminding them both he wasn't going anywhere. "This
demon of yours, what does he look like? Big and scary?
Small and quick with a sharp stick? I'll do a much better job
of keeping him away if I have an idea what I'm looking for."

She laughed, low and easy, drawing a smile from him.
"Big. With claws. And he doesn't shut up. Ever."

"What does he sound like? James Earl Jones or more
Al Pacino?"

"Dan Rather."

Ah. "So your demon moonlights as a reporter who asks
you questions you don't like." And he'd bet the demon answered to the name *armadillo.*

"Yeah."

The single syllable quaked through her damaged vocal
cords and snapped something behind his rib cage.

"Like what?" he whispered, his voice nearly as raw as
hers.

"It's not the questions." She shifted and wet pooled into
the hollow of his shoulder right about where her eye had
been. Tears. "It's the lack of answers. Bad stuff happens.

They were just vocal cords. Why don't I know what to do next?"

"Because," he countered fiercely. "You're not out of the valley yet. Once you clear it, then you'll see where to go."

He had to believe that was true, had to believe it was possible. He wanted out of that valley—for himself, but also to show her the way.

"Music was a part of my soul." More tears dripped onto his chest, but he didn't wipe them away. Didn't move at all for fear of stemming the tide of her grief. "And I thought it always would be or I wouldn't have inked eighth notes on my body permanently. How do you find a new direction when something so ingrained is gone?"

Silently, he held her, suddenly furious that he didn't have the answers. Her anguish vibrated through him and wedged into a place he'd thought was dead and buried.

"I could have the tattoo removed," she continued brokenly. "Turned into something else. But what? Who am I going to be for the rest of my life?"

Yes. *That* was the million-dollar question. Evangeline voiced things he could hardly define, let alone articulate. They gelled because she struggled in exactly the same ways he did.

And perhaps they'd solve it together.

"Is there no way to keep a hand in music? Do you play an instrument?"

"Piano." She sniffed. "I wrote all my songs."

An odd sense of pride filled him with the admission. She'd produced something from nothing, using a creative energy he couldn't fathom.

"That's amazing. I thought other people wrote songs for recording artists."

A tune filled his head instantly. Hers. She'd written the notes, sang them. He wished he could have heard her live. Wished he could ask her to sing for him, here in the dark.

His gut split in two over the loss of something he'd never dreamed he'd want.

"Other people do write songs, when the artist is just a voice. Like Sara Lear." She growled. "I hate how catty that sounds. But geez, I could trip and fall into a piano and accidentally write a better song than the ones she sings."

Was her ability to connect dots broken or was she too close to see the obvious? "Then do it. Write one for her."

She shook her head against his shoulder. "I can't."

"Can't, or don't want to?" he countered softly.

"The words…they've all dried up."

"They'll come. You're an artist who isn't just a voice." He stroked her hair. "You'll figure it out. We'll both figure it out, and in the meantime, we'll hold each other in the dark and lay it all out there."

"Matt?" More snuffling. "I'm glad I stayed. I don't stay as a rule. No rules is nice for once."

Finally, he breathed a little easier. The conversation could have veered into something ugly. But he'd navigated it pretty well—he hoped—despite a distinct lack of experience with damaged souls, his or anyone else's. His relationship with Amber had been straightforward and undemanding. Safe.

He'd certainly never experienced quite so many highs and lows when she'd been alive.

"It can't last. This thing between us," he clarified. Evangeline was merely passing time with him until she figured out her next steps. She'd said as much. It shouldn't hollow him out—wasn't that what they were *both* doing here?

"I know that," he added, "but I can't stand to be in the valley alone. Please don't think less of me for selfishly dragging it out."

"I don't think you're selfish."

She wouldn't. Evangeline was the single most nonjudgmental person he'd come across. He could tell her anything. Had told her things he'd never said out loud. He didn't worry about disappointing her with his failures. Ironically, because he'd set out to be someone else with her, his internal censor-switch had shut off. He had the freedom to pour out the angst and fear he'd carried for months.

He wished he had more to give her in return and was suddenly sorry they'd met while they were both still stuck in the valley.

Nine

"Let's go out," Evangeline announced late one afternoon as they watched a movie, snuggled together on the couch.

Convinced he'd misheard, Matthew hit the volume, almost dropping the remote. "Out? As in out in public?"

Other than an occasional rooftop visit, they hadn't crossed the threshold of Palazzo D'Inverno since the dinner party a couple of weeks ago. He was on a first name basis with the grocery store delivery guy, who delighted in correcting Matthew's poor Italian.

"Yeah." She shrugged. "Take me on a date tonight."

"You hate dating."

"But I like you." She fluttered her lashes, coquettishly. "So I'm willing to make sacrifices. I might even let you talk my clothes off after."

"What's going on? Cabin fever?"

It was certainly starting to get to him. As much fun as Evangeline was—and really, was there such a thing as too much sex?—a slight sense of restlessness wouldn't go away, no matter what he did.

"I don't know. Maybe. I haven't worn makeup in forever. I'd like you to see me in something other than one of your T-shirts."

"I like you in my T-shirts. I like you best in nothing at all," he threw in. "But I could go for some dinner with a beautiful woman."

"Dinner and maybe a show." She leaped off the couch, suddenly animated. "Ooh, I have the perfect dress. I haven't worn it yet. I'm going to hog the bathroom. Do you need anything out of it?"

"Nah." He grinned at her enthusiasm and flipped the channel to a cable news station since the movie clearly wasn't of interest any longer. "I'll be here. Waiting. For a long time, I suspect."

An hour later, he'd donned a button-up shirt and ironed some pants, the most effort he'd expended to get dressed in ages. Evangeline still hadn't emerged from the bathroom so he flopped on the couch to amuse himself by flipping through the channels.

She called his name from the stairs.

He glanced at her and his heart locked up.

Evangeline La Fleur had put on yet another mask. She'd transformed into a fantastical vision in a clingy blue dress, honey-brown curls loose around her shoulders, sultry eyes full of mystery and promise, legs shaped by spiked heels that made his mouth water. And he'd kissed every inch of that gorgeous body.

How could she still punch him so hard without a word when they had few secrets between them any longer?

A button-up and kakis were far too casual to have *that* on his arm. Actually, the man in the clothes left a lot to be desired, as well. The glittery superstar walking down his stairs had nothing in common with Matthew Wheeler.

"Ready?" she asked, her gravelly voice raw and thrilling. Like always. It jump-started his lungs again as he stood to meet her. She was still the same person underneath the mask.

"I'm not sure. I think you've stolen my ability to walk. You're...I don't know what to call you. *Beautiful* is too simple a word. You're exquisite." Flustered, he straightened his belt and smoothed his hair. "Sure you want to be seen with me?"

She laughed, throatily, with her head thrown back. It was genuine and elemental, and he hardened in an instant.

"I'll ask you that same question in a little while, when we've drawn a lot of unwanted attention. I thought about playing it down, trying to blend. But it would be pointless. Anyway, I wanted to look nice. For you."

"For me?" That pleased him, enormously, and he yanked her into his arms, careful not to muss this gorgeous creature. "Thanks. It is a pretty good hit for my ego. And I will thoroughly enjoy looking at you all evening as I imagine what I'll say to talk your clothes off."

Her fingers walked down his chest and dipped into his pants to lightly graze his swollen flesh. "It'll have to be good. Maybe with some begging."

He groaned. "We're not going to make it out the door if you keep that up."

Withdrawing her hand, she smiled with a mischievous curve to her lips. "I'll save it for later then."

Eyes still crossed, he helped her into a coat and slipped on his own. Lacing their fingers, he led her outside into the night. Carnevale was long over and the cool March air held a hint of the Italian spring to come.

"Walk or water taxi?" he asked. "I thought we'd go to this little out-of-the-way place I found, instead of somewhere trendy. I hope that's okay. It's only a few blocks."

"Walk. I haven't seen nearly enough of Venice. There's a different feel when you're on the street, in the middle of it all. The view from your living room, or the roof even, is amazing. But removed. You know?"

Yes, he did. He'd been removed from everything for so long. Tonight, he was fully in the land of the living, with

Evangeline, and it did feel different. As if he'd emerged from a dark tunnel and the world had burst open around him.

As they strolled, other couples nodded or called "*Ciao*" upon passing. Streetside shops blazed with light behind glass, wares on display in the window. The pace of life in Venice ebbed and flowed with the canal waters, tranquil and slowed. Peaceful. History—the heartbreak, the triumphs—radiated from the very cobblestones and dripped from the stucco veneer of the ancient buildings.

People had lived and died in this city for centuries before Matthew's Northern European ancestors had jumped the pond to America. Life would continue on after Matthew was long gone. It was the here and now that counted.

He squeezed Evangeline's hand, and she glanced over at him through those soft brown eyes that he liked waking up to every morning. Not for the first time, he wondered if there was a way to stop dragging this thing out and do something crazy, like put a stake in the ground and hash out a plan to make it work long term.

Except he'd been searching for a way to move on after Amber's death, never realizing a step in that process might include falling in love with someone new.

It felt disloyal to Amber to think something like that.

This thing couldn't last. Not because he and Evangeline wouldn't work in real life. That was true, but surface level. Deep down, he wasn't sure he could do it again, give his whole being to someone else. Love someone else. Have a household, a baby, a life with someone else.

He'd created the temporary nature of his relationship with Evangeline to make her more comfortable with staying, but it was really an excuse. He'd latched onto it to avoid the truth—he wasn't ready to move on.

They found the restaurant easily. The maître d' showed them to their table, and Matthew ordered a bottle of Chianti, which the efficient staff brought immediately.

"Well. Here we are." Evangeline raised her glass and they clinked rims. "Our first date."

In a manner of speaking. Seemed strange to be on a first date with a woman he'd made squirm under his tongue as he knelt before her in the shower that morning. "Guess we did things out of order."

"That's okay. I'm not big on tradition."

"Like marriage?" Why in the world had he picked that rock to kick? He already knew her stance on commitment.

She wrinkled her nose. "Well, doesn't seem like it works out for many people, does it?"

It had for his parents and grandparents. Seemed to work tremendously well for Lucas and Cia, what little of their relationship he'd been around to witness.

His own marriage had been perfect. With Amber, he'd done things in the exact right order. They'd gone to the opera for their first date. Amber had worn gloves and left them in his car. On purpose, he knew, so she'd have an excuse to call him. Which she had done, two days later.

After three dates, he kissed her and three months to the day, he surprised her with a suite at the Fairmont, where they'd made love for the first time, in a nice evening full of potential. That's when he'd known he would propose, but he held off until they'd been together over a year, then, for Christmas, he'd given Amber a white-gold Tiffany engagement ring that had belonged to his grandmother. Everything safely unfolded according to plan.

For all the good it had done him.

Voices from the front of the restaurant interrupted his musing. Evangeline's face froze as a couple of sharply dressed teenage boys argued with the maître d', pointing at her.

"Sorry, they followed us in here," she said. "They noticed me on the street, but I figured they'd move on."

"What are you apologizing for?"

"Because it's invasive. Or it will be." She pasted on a

smile as the waiter came up behind her to whisper in her ear. She nodded, and the teenagers rushed over to babble incoherently in a mixture of Italian and English, shoving pieces of paper at Evangeline for her to sign. One of the boys handed her a Sharpie and brazenly lifted his shirt. She scrawled "EVA" in flowery script across his pectoral muscle.

Really? Matthew looked away as something black and sharp flared deep inside. These kids had no sense of decorum whatsoever.

And he absolutely did not want to admit the pain in his stomach had to do with Evangeline's palm on the guy's chest. Jealousy. As if she belonged to Matthew and he had a right to expect he'd be the only man she touched.

Evangeline was a good sport through it all. She posed with the boys for at least a dozen pictures, hastily snapped on their phones by the beleaguered waiter. When she was "on," her otherworldliness intensified, sharpening her beauty but making her seem almost untouchable.

She hadn't put on a mask—but taken one off. Eva was an extension of her essence.

Finally, the teenagers drifted out the door, leaving a tense silence draped over them both.

"My fans mean a lot to me." She flicked her nail across the tines of her fork without looking at him. "The ones I still have anyway. But it can be a bit much for someone not used to it. I knew better. I shouldn't have asked you to take me out."

"It's okay." Her biggest concern had been inconveniencing him or upsetting him, but he got that her celebrity went part and parcel with the rest. He reached out to cover her hand. "It's a small price to pay. You're worth it."

Her eyes grew shiny. "Thanks. We're lucky they weren't reporters."

They ate dinner without any more interruptions. When they left the restaurant, bright flashes halted them in their tracks, and he got a glimpse of the reason for her earlier concerns.

Two media-hounds lounged a few feet away, easily identifiable by their professional cameras and lack of interest in capturing the Venetian splendor all around them. Their sharp gazes were on Evangeline as she stepped into Matthew's side, snugging up against his ribs closely. Too closely. Seeking what? Protection?

A prickle of warning went down his spine.

The men blocked their path, crowding them with their solid builds and flat eyes. Not guys who looked eager to be reasonable.

"Eva," the shorter one on the left—American—called out. "Mind if we ask you a few questions?"

Matthew was about to calmly suggest it would be in their best interests to let them pass. But Evangeline's sharp intake of breath tripped something in his blood.

"I mind," Matthew said, and stepped in front of Evangeline, shielding her from the men.

"Who are you?" The one on the right zeroed in on Matthew. "*You* got time for a few questions? I'll be sure to spell your name right."

"No comment," Evangeline said and earned both men's pointed attention.

"Is that what your voice sounds like now?" The short one whistled. Nastily. "Like a cement mixer with boulders inside. Can I tape it?"

She was trembling against Matthew's back as she pulled on his arm. "We'll go the long way home."

Home. Not to a show, which she'd chattered about endlessly during dinner. If the reporter had latched onto anything else except her voice, Matthew would have let it slide.

These two idiots weren't ruining their night out. "Back off. We're of no interest to you."

"You're with Eva, you're news, buddy." The taller one

snapped off a few photographs, blinding Matthew with the flash.

"You want to get that camera out of our faces before I do it for you?" Matthew blinked hard in an attempt to clear the white starburst from his retinas.

"Are you threatening me, pretty boy?"

"Obviously not well enough if you have to ask. So I'll be clearer." Matthew nodded to both men curtly, tamping down his fury. "Stop harassing us or you'll be examining the ceiling of an Italian jail cell shortly. Or the ceiling of a hospital room. Your choice."

The men glanced at each other, smiling cruelly. "You gonna take on both of us? Over *her*?"

Her. As if she was worthless because she'd lost her voice. The fury welled up again, traveling through his veins, curling his hands into fists.

Walk away. Now. Before you do something you'll regret.

He pivoted and grabbed Evangeline's hand to escape in the opposite direction. They'd only taken a couple of steps when the men skirted them, blocking their path again.

"Hey, what's your hurry?" the short one asked and leered at Evangeline, his gaze on her legs. "We're just doing our job."

If the smarmy little rat didn't get his dirty mind out of the gutter, Matthew would remove it from his skull. Through his nose. "Insulting people who are trying to walk down the street is not your job."

"No, satisfying the public's curiosity is. And we're all curious. What's Eva up to now? Who's the mysterious man escorting her around Venice?" The taller one shoved a small recorder at Matthew, nearly chipping a tooth. "You tell us. We leave. Easy."

"We already said—" Matthew backhanded the recorder away "—no comment."

He shrugged. "Then we'll write our own story. Eva does Venice with an American schoolteacher on holiday. Eva's new beau—disinherited playboy after her money? Eva sleeps her way into a modeling contra—"

Matthew's fist connected with the reporter's smug mouth. He reeled backward, smashing into the other reporter.

God, that had felt good. He shook out his throbbing knuckles.

The man regained his balance, touched his bleeding lip and glanced at his fingers. "I'm pressing charges."

"See you in court. Until then, stay away from us."

He spun and herded Evangeline through the throng of wide-eyed onlookers and down a side street free of people. They didn't talk, but she grasped his tingling hand tightly.

His heart rate still in the upper stratosphere, he paused in a dark alcove. "You okay?"

"Are *you*?" She touched his face, tentatively. "I've never seen you like that."

"Never been like that." He'd never punched anyone in his life. Not even Lucas, though his brother had surely asked for it on many an occasion. Matthew handled conflict with his brain. Usually. Nothing with Evangeline worked like usual. "The things they were saying were hurtful. No one has the right to treat you that way."

She melted into his arms. "Thank you," she murmured against his shoulder. "I can't tell you what that meant to me."

It had been pure reaction. No thought to consequences. No reason involved. Just a ferocious drive to protect Evangeline from being hurt.

He held her close and his pulse shuddered anew. Amber would have been horrified. Not grateful. Amber didn't let much affect her and would have blown off reporters with some practiced sound bite. He'd never had a reason to protect her. A reason to be jealous. A reason to feel like he was dancing across a high wire with no net and not only craved the danger but kept asking for more.

Amber was gone.

And if he didn't disentangle himself from Evangeline soon, the man Amber had married would be gone, too. Then who would he be?

The next afternoon, Evangeline stretched out on the couch with Matt's iPad and downloaded a fluffy beach-read novel to entertain her while he took a shower. She needed a distraction from the slimy swirl those reporters had put in her stomach. The media had been a part of her life for a long time, and they'd never bothered her until after the surgery.

Now they just made her sick—physically, deep inside.

When Matt came downstairs, hair still a little damp and darkly golden, she forgot about the story on the page and watched him cross the room. Delicious. He still made her shiver despite the fact that she knew exactly what was underneath that waffle-print shirt and jeans. Maybe because she knew.

But it wasn't the body that got her going.

Matt had jarred something loose the moment he smashed that reporter in the face. It was far more than what he'd done with *Milano Sera*'s people. That had been simply an extraction. The incident with the reporters—something else entirely. She'd never felt anything like it, the rush of release, the empowerment of knowing he valued her enough to stand up to the evils of the world.

He had her back. No one ever had before.

"Busy?" he asked.

"Nope." She laid the tablet on the coffee table.

What could possibly compete with his attention? She loved being his focal point, morning, noon and night. Sure these were extraordinary circumstances, but no doubt he operated the same in real life, with his full commitment on whatever was in front of him. Matt did everything wholeheartedly.

"Do you know if Vincenzo is home today?"

She shrugged. "I think so. I saw him come home early

this morning when I was washing the breakfast dishes. I doubt he's even awake yet. Why?"

"I'm having something delivered. A surprise. Call him and ask if you can hang out over there for an hour. No peeking, either." With a mischievous smile, he snagged her hand and crossed her heart for her.

The area under her fingertip lurched sweetly. "A surprise? For me? What is it?"

He shook his head and mimed zipping his lips. "You'll see soon enough. Call."

Mystified and with no small amount of curiosity, she woke Vincenzo from his postdebauchery sleep and announced she was coming over.

Vincenzo answered the door with a bad case of bedhead and a worse attitude. She flounced past him into the living room and perched on the sofa. "You don't have to entertain me. Go back to bed."

Their friendship went back a couple of years, hinging on a mutual love of parties and a glittering social scene, but it had never been deep and meaningful. Like most of her relationships. Except one.

He eyed her. "Trouble in paradise, *cara*?"

"What, you mean between me and Matt?" She flicked off his concern with a wave. "He's surprising me with something."

She'd told Vincenzo very little about her relationship with Matt. On purpose. It didn't have the same transcendence when explained to an outsider.

Vincenzo jiggled his dark brows. "An engagement ring?"

Automatically, she started to deny it. But what if it was? No. Surely not. Venice was a temporary arrangement.

"He'd stick that in his pocket. Wouldn't he?"

She glanced at her hand, bare of jewelry since she'd ripped off Rory's ring and flushed it. Matt wasn't proposing. No way. He was looking for a way home, not a new wife. There were too many ghosts flitting through his heart for that.

"I am not an expert in matters of marriage." Vincenzo lifted one shoulder and shuffled in the direction of the marble staircase to the second floor, calling out, "Lock the door when you leave."

Alone, she contemplated what she'd say if Matt did get down on one knee and claimed he'd gotten over Amber....

He couldn't. If he did, she'd have to say no, and their affair would be over. Marriage—she couldn't imagine anything she'd be more ill-suited for.

She fretted about it until he texted her to come home.

When she burst in the door of Palazzo D'Inverno, the surprise nearly knocked her off her feet.

"Oh, my God."

A shiny, ebony grand piano stood in the corner of the living room, overlooking the Grand Canal. Matt sat on the bench, quietly watching her, and the two together put a glitch in her lungs she couldn't breathe through.

"Presumptuous of me, I realize," he said. "But I thought you might enjoy having it to play since going out isn't so fun."

Her fingers curled spontaneously. She hadn't touched piano keys since the surgery. Hadn't wanted to. Didn't want to now.

"Thanks. It's…nice."

His eyebrows rose. "You're welcome, and you seem a little underwhelmed. Did I screw up?"

Vehemently, she shook her head. "It's the most thoughtful gift anyone's ever given me."

"Okay. I'll take that." He slid off the bench and engulfed her in his warm, safe arms. "But there's more. Do you want to tell me, or is the piano now the armadillo in the room?"

The laugh slipped out. "How did you know I was going to call armadillo?"

"You get this closed-in face whenever you're about to say it."

"I don't want to play." It fell out of her mouth. Maybe on accident, or maybe because she couldn't bear for him to be so understanding and not get anything for it.

"You don't have to. I can send it back." He hugged her tighter and then released her. "I'll call the delivery company right now."

"No." That had definitely been said on purpose. She was safe with Matt. She knew that. "*Want* is the wrong word. I can't play."

"Like you've forgotten how?"

"Like the music is a razor blade." *Cut*, Madam Wong had said. The music had been cut from her throat and it cut when she heard it and it cut when she played.

"*Screw up* would be too kind a phrase, then," he said. "I'm sorry. I didn't know it was hard for you to play. I envisioned you gaining something…I don't know, peaceful from it."

Her eyelids shut in sudden memory. The piano had been her refuge in a lonely house growing up, the one thing her mother had given her. Because it was the path to fame and fortune, foremost, but Evangeline turned it into something else. A means of expression she'd channeled in conjunction with her voice. Always together.

The piano still had the music inside. She didn't. But in Palazzo D'Inverno, there were no rules, and the two didn't have to coexist. They could have value individually.

"I'd like to find some peace," she admitted. "I don't know why it's so hard."

"Peace is elusive."

She'd meant playing the piano was hard. He'd cut through the outer layer and exposed the raw truth. But not the whole truth. "Not when I'm with you."

With a smile, he captured her hand and pulled her toward the piano. "Then let's do it together."

"What? You don't play."

But he situated himself on the bench and drew her between his spread legs, placing her fingers on the keys under his own. "Teach me. I've been listening to music my whole life. How hard can it be?"

She snorted out a giggle and leaned back against the solid chest supporting her, his breath teasing her ear and his heart thumping her spine.

Safe. Matt was her anchor in a sea of anxiety.

"Move your hands. That's not how you learn. Here, listen."

Slowly, she picked out the notes to "Twinkle, Twinkle Little Star." The keys sank under her fingers with measured float, producing rich tones from under the raised lid. This was easily a hundred-thousand-dollar piano. And Matt had given it to her because he wanted her to experience peace by gently prodding her toward something she could still do.

She didn't mind that kind of push so much.

"A little elementary of a song choice, don't you think?" he said into her ear, and she elbowed him.

"Try it, smart guy. Go ahead." She nodded to the keys.

He plunked out a few scraggly notes that sounded more like he was dragging a screaming flamingo down the street than playing a song. But he got about half of them right—a hundred percent more than she was expecting.

"Not bad. Practice makes perfect."

"Show me another one." He nudged her with his chin, peering over her shoulder intently at the spread of white and black keys. "Something that takes both hands."

Without prompting, her fingers spread, arranging themselves around middle C and the melody trickled out. Then gained strength as her muscles remembered how to stretch and fly.

Matt's hand crept across her stomach and he held her tight as she played, never once flinching if her elbow caught him. He'd held her through a lot of difficult stuff. Had since the very first moments in the alcove at Vincenzo's party.

When the last notes faded, she slumped, drained.

"One of yours?" he asked softly.

"The first one I ever recorded." But on a synthesizer and with a faster tempo, when she'd had the energy of a burgeoning career to fuel her performance. "My fingers are tired."

His lips rested against her temple. "You don't have to play anymore. Though I enjoyed every second of it."

"It's a good kind of tired. Thanks for playing with me. It helped." The armadillos were having a throw-down in her stomach, but after last night, the exposure of being Eva again and sitting here at the piano, it was too much to keep from bubbling over. "It more than helped. I'm reminded again of what music means to me."

Reminded again of the peace of simple expression, which had been impossible, until lately.

"What does it mean?"

Escape, she thought. Music had been an escape. It could be again, in a far different way. She could separate music from Eva, peel back that layer and see what was underneath. Eva was gone. Evangeline could be herself.

"It means I have choices."

"You did a brave thing by playing the piano again." It was a gentle echo of what she'd said to him during the middle-of-the-night, nothing-is-sacred conversation. "It was hard, but you did it. Choose to do something else difficult. Write a song for Sara Lear."

"I'll think about it."

"Good." It was all he'd say. Somehow, that encouraged her to fill the silence.

"The music industry…" She cleared her raspy throat— a wasted effort. "It'll rob you of everything you'd hoped to gain. The fame, the money…I readily admit I loved that part. But there's a price. You lose a sense of yourself and who you are without all the costume changes. People don't see you anymore. Not the fans. Not the execs. Both put you on a pedestal but watch to see if you teeter just a tiny bit. Then the new song doesn't climb the charts as fast as the last one. The fans are fickle, and the producers mutter about profits."

It was a no-win catch-22. Everyone wanted a piece of her until they were done with her. Rory. The industry. And everyone eventually rejected her, even people who should love her no matter what.

"I see you," he murmured.

She nodded. "That's why I'm still here."

Matt made it safe to ditch the mask and be herself. He was the one man on earth she could trust with the deepest part of herself and not be braced for a rejection because she wasn't good enough.

He was the only one who could get her to stay because for the first time in her life, staying was better than leaving.

Ten

Moonlight poured through the panes of glass in the bedroom. Evangeline eased out from under Matt's arm and pulled the covers over his gorgeously muscled torso. He shifted but didn't wake up.

She watched him breathe, unable to tear her eyes away. Sooty lashes brushed his cheeks, and underneath those lids lay the most amazing depths. No matter how many mornings she woke wound up in his long limbs, it wouldn't be enough. She could stand here forever and bask in his presence.

But the words were flowing, calling her with their siren song, begging her to commit the emotion to paper. She couldn't ignore the first stirring of inspiration.

The piano had unwound something inside her, and Matt patiently drew it out, helping her examine it in his clearheaded, logical way.

Downstairs, she plopped onto the couch with the back of a take-out menu and a pen. Fifteen minutes later, lyrics covered every blank space on the menu. Good lyrics. For the first time in *months*, she'd tapped into her center and captured the music.

She rummaged around for more paper and came up empty-handed. Matt's iPad sat on the coffee table and though under normal circumstances she'd never use a digital page, she couldn't lose momentum.

When she hit the power button, one of the squares with the logo WFP caught her attention. It hadn't been there before.

She touched it and the website popped up. Wheeler Family Partners. The header contained the profiles of four men and she recognized Matt's instantly. The chiseled good-looking face next to Matt must be his brother, Lucas. A total player. She could see the look in his eye a mile away and hoped his wife kept that one on a short leash.

The other men must be their dad and grandfather. Andrew and Robert, according to the About page. Matt favored his grandfather. They both had the same piercing gaze and straightforwardness. She could tell neither of them would ever lie, cheat or steal.

Her eye wandered down the paragraph. Geez. Wheeler Family Partners had done eighty million dollars of business in the last quarter of the previous year alone, largely owing to the sale of a communications complex in North Dallas.

And Matt had been the spearhead of his firm. Like she'd assumed, he'd been successful at everything he'd tried. Business. Marriage. Getting her to stay.

He was far more special than she'd imagined.

She tapped the website closed and brought up a free-text application, more than a little concerned she'd stemmed the fountain of words with her side foray into Matt's domain.

A blank page materialized. It didn't scare her.

But the words she typed did. She couldn't stop, didn't even pause as the song fell from her fingers, fully formed. Whereas the first round had taken shape in bits and pieces, this one had structure. Order. And it would be a guaranteed hit. She knew it. All four of her Grammys had been for songwriting, not singing.

The piano hovered in the corner of her peripheral vision, and she glanced up at it, then up the stairs to where Matt lay sleeping. No piano this time. She didn't want to wake him.

The fortune teller had predicted she'd conceive. And this felt like birth, like the beginning of something wonderful and amazing. A metamorphosis.

As the last word appeared, she finally removed her fingers from the screen and read over the song again, hearing the tune in her head as she internalized the words. With the right voice, like Sara Lear's, it would climb the charts instantly.

She saved the file to her cloud account and powered off the tablet, staring out the window at the quiet canal.

The right voice. It wouldn't be hers. She wasn't ready to let the song go to another home, but for the first time, it didn't sting so badly to envision it. Thanks to Matt.

Here in the dark, it didn't seem so frightening to admit she was falling for him. He was so genuine and real, and her stupid heart hungrily latched onto those qualities. She knew better. Knew that nothing could crumble the monument to Amber in his chest. But her heart had its fingers in its ears, refusing to hear the message from her brain.

Matt was a heartbreak waiting to happen.

She should go before it was too late. Nicola had a place in Monte Carlo. Vincenzo had been making noises about shoving off in that direction in a few days and had texted her the address with an open invitation to join the group. Her stomach rolled. It had been off since the reporter incident.

Matt still needed her. His turmoil churned below the surface, popping up in his faraway gaze at odd moments. She'd give anything to ease that note of sheer anguish in his voice when he talked about his family and the life he'd lost.

She didn't want to leave.

Her head fell back against the couch cushion. The riot of colors splashed across the ceiling was dim with only the outside canal lights to illuminate it. The paintings depicted domestic vignettes; men and women sleeping, eating, playing with children. This had been someone's refuge, built to escape a harsh climate.

She and Matt had both done the same. And despite what she told herself about the reasons she stayed, she needed him as much as he needed her. How much longer could they hide away here before Venice became a stumbling block to healing instead of a sanctuary?

Matt's gentle hands in her hair woke her. Daylight streamed through the panes leading to the balcony and beyond the glass, Venice was awash with the morning.

"You okay?" Matt asked from behind her. "Why didn't you come back to bed?"

"Meant to. But I fell asleep." She yawned. The mist of sleep would not clear her mind, like she'd dunked her head in a vat of Jell-O.

"I'll make you some breakfast."

Food did not sound appealing in the least. "You go ahead. I'm going to take a shower. I'll grab something later."

He leaned to plant an upside-down kiss on her lips. "Want me to scrub your back?"

Which was code for Very-Little-Bathing-To-Occur. "Normally I'd be all over that. But I'm just wiped out. The shower is to wake me up." She smiled to soften the blow.

"If you're sure." He brushed a thumb tenderly across her temple and disappeared into the kitchen. Thumps of cabinets opening and dishes clinking drifted out. Comforting sounds. Sounds of home.

How would she know? She'd never had the kind of home the noises had evoked. Never wanted one.

Until now.

Oh, God, where had that come from? This wasn't her home. It wasn't even Matt's home. Home was for people who wanted to stay together, who implicitly trusted each other and never spent all their energy looking for the exit.

She didn't do the domestic thing for a reason. And her subconscious argued that the reason was because she hadn't done it with the right person yet.

Heavy with fatigue, she wandered upstairs to take a long hot shower and get dressed. Somewhere along the way, she began to feel human again. By the time she returned to the lower level, Matt was watching cable news with the crinkle in his forehead that meant he was bored.

When he caught sight of her, he lit up, his expression radiant, and he was absolutely the most gorgeous man on earth. Her heart squished. Out of nowhere, lines of a new song popped into her head. A sappy, sugary love song.

She wasn't just falling for him, she'd splatted flat on the ground and then a giant cupid had stepped on her.

"Feeling better?" he asked.

"Define *better*," she mumbled, eyes closed in case her stupid, inadvisable feelings were beaming from her insides. "I'm awake, if that's what you mean."

He leaped off the couch and hustled her into the kitchen so he could ply her with food, though the thought of putting anything in her mouth made her slightly nauseous.

Idiot reporters. Those creeps were still upsetting her. She didn't say anything. There was no point in Matt being upset, too.

Gulping orange juice, she took a seat at the island and watched Matt move around the kitchen. Poetry in motion. He was never content to shove a couple of pieces of bread in the toaster and call it breakfast. His idea of cooking involved creativity usually reserved for master chefs.

Today, he was making an egg-white omelet with pro-sciutto and sun-dried tomatoes, and a half-moon of cantaloupe on the side. He placed the plate in front of her with a flourish and refilled her empty orange juice glass.

She forked a bite into her mouth and swallowed. It stayed down. "Delicious. As always. You should open a restaurant."

"Nah. I just throw some stuff together and pray it turns out." He waved it off with a pleased smile. "Cooking is fun."

"I'm glad one of us thinks so." Her idea of fun was paying someone else to cook. And clean up the kitchen. Matt had never met a pan unworthy of his olive oil or chicken stock. But he made such fantastic dishes, she really didn't mind cleaning up.

"Well, I never used to." He shrugged. "But I like cooking for you."

"Why, because I'm so inventive with how I show my appreciation?" She waggled her brows.

He laughed. "That is one of the perks. But mostly because you let me. Amber…she was kind of a Gordon Ramsay about her kitchen. I stayed out of it."

The omelet took on a whole new significance. "You never cooked for Amber?"

"Sure, when we were dating. But then, I don't know. She loved to cook and prided herself on it, so I just didn't anymore." He stared out the window at the joint courtyard Palazzo D'Inverno shared with Vincenzo's house, his gaze faraway and dejected. "I paid through the nose to upgrade the kitchen in this place. For her. I didn't expect to be the one who would actually use it. Honestly, I probably never would have started cooking again if you hadn't stayed."

That put a lump the size of a grapefruit in her throat. She couldn't swallow. "Thanks for resurrecting your spatula for me."

He shot her a grin. Lately, it didn't take long at all for him to snap out of his Amber mood, which, if she had her way, he'd get out of permanently.

"You eat too much takeout. Or you used to. You were practically wasted away to nothing when I got ahold of you. At least this way, I know you're putting something healthy into your body."

"Oh, I see. You cook for me because you're concerned about my health," she joked back.

And then it sank in. It wasn't a joke. He'd been taking care of her. All along. Maybe subconsciously she'd known that and hence had begun to equate kitchen sounds with a sense of home.

Matt communicated in subtle, baffling ways she'd never experienced—probably because she never stayed long enough to allow it. What was he trying to tell her with food? That he might have deeper and more lasting feelings for her then she'd thought?

Wishful thinking at its worst.

Her eyes burned with the sudden prick of tears.

The omelet turned to mush in her mouth, and she shoved the plate away. "I didn't get much sleep last night. Think I'll go back to bed."

"Are you coming down with something?" He skirted the island and cupped her chin with both palms to peer into her eyes, concern practically dripping from his touch.

"I'm fine. Just tired."

Narrowed blue eyes locked onto hers. The deflection didn't fool him, but he chose not to call her on it.

Upstairs, she threw herself onto the bed, but it smelled like Matt and that wasn't conducive to sleep, unless she wanted to have red-hot dreams about the way that man's mouth felt on her body. She'd rather be experiencing the real thing, but with something far stronger than desire in his gaze.

She wanted Amber's place in his heart. It was a really inadvisable thing to long for. But that didn't make the longing magically disappear.

Matt had cooked for her. He'd been taking care of her in a way he never had with Amber.

Maybe he just needed more time to get over her. Maybe being here, in the house he'd bought his wife, prevented Matt from fully healing. Was Evangeline falling down on her job by dragging out their Venice bubble?

She rolled over and buried her face in the pillow, exhausted but unable to shut off the hamsters turning the wheel in her brain. She'd never been so tired in her life, probably because she'd rendered herself completely inactive. This was the longest she'd stayed in one place.

Monte Carlo beckoned. The words—the music—flowed again after a long, painful hiatus. If she stayed, all that lovely inspiration might dry up again. The wind had always guided her well enough before.

But if she moved on, Matt might lose all the progress he'd made. Worse, they'd never find out what might be possible between them. He couldn't go home yet; that much he'd made clear in more than one conversation.

What if they moved on together?

A daring question. But what if it worked?

If she said the idea of being loved by Matt didn't thrill her, she'd be lying. A solid, committed man like Matt would never fail her, and in turn, she'd never fail him. They had an unparalleled measure of trust in each other, an understanding. That was the way love was supposed to work. She wanted that, for once in her life.

But what if she asked and he said no? He'd been drifting in search of a way to get his old life back. Just because he wasn't ready to go home this minute didn't mean that goal had changed. Could she really risk Matt's rejection?

After mulling it over for a long time, sleep finally claimed her.

Matthew's slight restless feeling graduated into a full-blown itch to do something productive. He settled for getting out of the house.

He took his laptop to the rooftop patio and sat in the sun. The Venetian spring was unbelievable, still cool in the mornings, but a warm breeze wafted from the Adriatic Sea, laden with the pungent scent of marine life.

He wished Evangeline had come up to enjoy it with him,

but she was taking an afternoon nap for the third time in a week.

Something was up, and he suspected she slept to avoid him. Because she was leaving. He could feel her winding down, becoming less talkative.

Honestly, he was avoiding "the talk," too. It didn't feel finished, this thing between them, but only because he didn't want it to be. For once, the idea of no commitment seemed like a blessing. There would be no broken heart in his future when she took off.

The organ in question gave a quick, painful tug at the thought of Evangeline leaving, and he shut his eyes until it started beating normally again. *No more of that, now.*

Since he had an afternoon to himself, Matthew poked around in his stock accounts, balanced his checkbook and generally killed time with stuff that had no promise of holding his interest.

He logged onto WFP, curious to see if anything new was going on. Lucas had posted a few sales, but nothing major and certainly not at the same clip as his brother had performed last quarter. First quarter historically saw the best sales as companies began the year with clean budgets.

The numbers should be better.

Strategies, marketing, building specs—all of it scrolled into his head and he latched on greedily, gratified both the knowledge and the drive was still there.

They could easily gain visibility by—

Stay out of it.

Lucas was handling it, as he had been. What good could Matthew possibly do from halfway around the world?

Renewed guilt gnawed on his insides.

Real estate was in his blood, and he'd missed the negotiations, the deals, the art of reading a potential seller. But the restlessness was more than lack of a job; it was a lack of setting goals and working to achieve them. Feeling successful and knowing his effort would be rewarded tangibly.

He wanted to be dependable, responsible Matthew Wheeler again, not a grieving, guilt-ridden widower.

Maybe he could check in, casually, without throwing his weight around. That might work. He was still a partner, regardless of whether he'd been acting like one, and there was no time like the present to start making amends.

Evangeline had played the piano. Maybe he could take a step out of the valley, too.

A baby step. The top of the mountain would grow closer with each one.

Before he thought better of it, he fished out his phone and sent Lucas a text message.

The response came instantly. You're alive?

Matthew flinched. Yeah, he deserved that. He shot back: Still have a pulse last time I checked. What's going on with WFP? 1st Q looks like a train wreck.

What do you care?

I care. I'll send flowers to soothe your bruised feelings later. 1st Q?

Lucas's answer took almost five minutes, during which Matthew sweated through some very unpleasant possibilities, like Lucas had fallen off the responsibility wagon or something had happened to their father.

Richards Group opened shop in Dallas.

Matthew swore. That had never crossed his mind.

Saul Richards owned the Houston real-estate market and the Wheelers owned North Texas. It was understood that Richards stayed on his turf and the Wheelers stayed on theirs. The shift wasn't a mystery—Richards had scented Wheeler blood with Matthew out of the picture.

Matthew shouldn't be out of the picture. Lucas had been

handling it. Now he needed help. Wheeler Family Partners had been in business for over a century, and Matthew refused to be the one who let it fail.

It was time to go home.

The thought didn't fill him with dread like he'd expected. His life in Dallas had been inescapably intertwined with Amber, with the expectations of creating a family and upholding traditions. But she was gone and as he'd flippantly, but accurately, told Lucas, he still had a pulse. Lucas had married a wife who helped him succeed, and they were happily working on the continuation of the Wheeler line.

There was no pressure for Matthew to fill his old role until he was ready.

The healing had happened so gradually, he hadn't realized it.

Evangeline called his name, and he glanced up to see her waltzing across the patio from the stairs. Sunlight beamed across her face, and she smiled. It slid down his throat with a jagged edge and sliced something in his gut.

God Almighty, she was almost ethereal. But sexy. Strong. Luminous.

Fingers numb, he dropped his phone to the concrete and pulled her into his lap to kiss her thoroughly. She smelled like sleep and Evangeline and everything good in the world. She'd helped him heal. Brightened up his house. His soul.

As the familiar lightning-fast rush of heat filled him, it suddenly occurred to him that if he went home, he'd have to end things with Evangeline.

Then he had the most dangerous thought—what if she came home with him?

No. He couldn't fathom issuing such an invitation. An invitation for what? To hide away in some lover's nest while he stormed the gates of Saul Richards's blockade on the Dallas real-estate market? She would grow bored with Dallas in about five minutes. She'd grow bored with Matthew Wheeler in four.

He could imagine going home for the first time in a long time. But he could not imagine Evangeline there, fitting into Amber's role as the woman behind the Wheeler. Mostly because bright, glittery Evangeline could never blend into the background the way Amber had, quietly providing support and encouragement, organizing get-togethers and charity events with his mother. The women in his world were beige.

Evangeline shifted in his lap, straddling him, her tongue finding creative ways to tease him. Yeah, she was as far from beige as Venice was from Dallas, and he forgot about everything but the warm breeze on his face and the hot woman in his arms.

She drew back, breathing heavily, with a businesslike glint in her eye. "I came to talk. Stop distracting me."

Talk. That sounded bad.

He scooted her back an inch, off his blazing erection, in deference to the directive. "Hey, I'm not the one looking all sexy and disheveled and climbing all over you."

"Can't help myself," she murmured and sighed, thrusting her chest into his. "You're so tempting."

She wasn't wearing a bra and talking was pretty much the last thing he wanted to do.

"What did you want to talk about?" he asked, and snaked a hand under her T-shirt, which was actually his, and hell if that wasn't the most arousing thing ever. He fanned a palm across her bare back, gradually working it around to the front where her breast fell into his eager fingers.

She moaned and arched against him. "Monte Carlo."

He paused, thumb and forefinger wrapped firmly around her nipple. "What about it?"

The end of things now had definition. She was going to Monte Carlo, and he did not want to think about all the implications.

"There's a party." She gasped. "Don't stop. Whatever you're doing, it feels amazing."

"You mean this?" Tweaking her nipple again, he shoved

her up against his erection because maybe they were going to talk *and* have sex. It would be the first time in several days they'd connected outside of bed.

"Yes. That." She writhed against him, igniting his flesh. His eyes crossed. "I didn't bring a condom. Fair warning."

"Well, now. That sounds like a challenge. Hmm. What can I do that doesn't require a condom?" He yanked the T-shirt up and closed a nipple between his lips, sucking for all he was worth. Her warm skin felt like velvet in his mouth and she moaned his name, bucking against him.

He loved her responses, loved that *he* could do that to her.

He slipped a thumb down her shorts and inside her panties to circle her trigger-point, and relentlessly pleasured her until she came apart. Beautiful. He could watch that over and over.

Boneless, she slumped against him, and he breathed through his nose until his erection subsided to merely painful instead of excruciating.

"You were telling me about a party?" he prompted when her breathing slowed.

This was it. She was taking off. Maybe later today. This might be their last time together.

He did not want to give her up.

"I was?" She rolled her head to nuzzle his neck, nearly sending him off the edge of the chair.

"In Monte Carlo. Talk fast because we're finishing this in about four seconds downstairs." He stood with her in his arms, sad it was over.

No, not sad. Devastated.

"Um…" She met his gaze and smiled, but it never reached her eyes. "Never mind. We can talk about it later. Take me downstairs."

Swallowing, he nodded. She didn't want to ruin their last time together with unpleasant reminders of what was about to happen. Neither did he.

Evangeline was the best thing that had ever happened to

him, enlivening him, encouraging him—but also encouraging him to keep hiding. To keep being a runaway.

It was best to go their separate ways, like they'd always planned. Lucas needed him, and the sting of reentering his old life without Amber had mellowed. When he went home, Matt would disappear forever, and there'd be no more wild and crazy, totally-un-Matthew-like Venetian affairs. He'd have his identity back. A plan. Security.

Evangeline would be free to fly off wherever she chose to go next, chasing the wind to the ends of the Earth.

The thought should have made him happier.

Venice was a transitory interlude, and now it was done. He only wished that truth eased the tightness in his lungs. And in his heart.

If only….well, life didn't give anyone the luxury of "if only."

When he picked up his phone to follow Evangeline back to the lower level, he saw another text from Lucas.

I'm handling Richards. Don't worry your pretty little head about it.

Eleven

Evangeline stared at the half-packed suitcase blindly and gnawed on a fingernail. Not one of her previously mani-cured-within-an-inch-of-their-lives fingernails remained.

Matt had gone for a walk. By himself. She didn't blame him for dealing with reality in his own way. Venice, the temporary fix, was over. It just didn't feel like it should be, and if things went the way she hoped, it wouldn't have to be.

She'd almost asked him to go to Monte Carlo. It had been right there on the tip of her tongue, but at the last mo-ment, she couldn't chance a "no," not after he so cleverly steered her away from talking about it. He didn't *want* to talk about it.

But she had a hunch they'd be doing nothing but talking by the time he came back from his walk, because something huge and frightening and momentous might have happened and it sat right in the middle of her consciousness, scream-ing its presence. All she had to do was verify it.

The doorbell chimed.

Evangeline bolted downstairs and grabbed the package from the delivery guy, slammed the door in his face and only remembered she'd forgotten to tip him after she locked herself in the bathroom.

Hands shaking, she pulled the pregnancy test from the brown wrapper. It was pretty much a formality. Icing on a cake that had already been baking for over a month, since the no-condom roof incident. The fatigue, the slight nausea, the way she sometimes couldn't get enough of Matt's hands on her overly sensitized body and other times, couldn't stand for him to touch her at all—it meant something much more weighty than a need to move on.

This morning, she'd done the math, then called the pharmacy the second Matt went for his walk. Bless him for his foresight in setting up a delivery account, though she doubted either of them could have envisioned it would prevent unwanted photographs of Eva buying a pregnancy test.

Two minutes passed in a blur, and her life changed forever when the little plus sign appeared as expected.

A sob bubbled from her throat, but it was half shaky excitement and half disbelief. Madam Wong's prediction that she'd conceive had encompassed more than songs.

A baby. She was going to have a baby. Matt's baby.

It would be a girl, with Matt's beautiful blue eyes and her voice. Her heart fluttered. Of course. This baby could be the answer to her future. She couldn't sing, but she could learn to be a mom.

And Matt would be a dad, father to their baby. She'd be giving him the one thing Amber never could—the family he wanted. He'd forget about his wife in a heartbeat, like she never existed, and come with Evangeline to Monte Carlo.

Before, she and Matt didn't make sense long term. Now they did. The baby would clinch it. He'd never reject his own flesh and blood. She and Matt would be happy, deliriously in love, with the proof of Matt's devotion strapped into a baby-carrier on his back.

They'd *both* have a family. Together.

Okay, she was getting ahead of herself. She had to tell

him first. But there was no doubt this would be the cata-
lyst to keep them together. No doubt he'd be thrilled. He'd
drifted into her life for a reason—to heal, surely, but also
to move on with the next phase of life.

Evangeline was his next phase.

When his key rattled in the lock, she jumped up from the
couch to greet the father of her child. A powerful twist of
emotion welled up, like she'd never felt before. She tried to
emblazon it in her memory so she could get it into a song
as soon as possible.

"Hey," he said. "I'm glad you're still here. I got you something."

"Funny. I have something for you, too." Did she sound
giddy?

His grin arrowed straight to her heart. "You do? What
is it?"

She shook her head. "You first."

Pulling a wrapped box from a bag, he dropped it into her
cupped hands. "To remember me by."

Wait until she told him he'd already given her the greatest memento possible.

The wrapping paper hit the floor. Jewelry. She flipped
the hinged velvet lid and gasped.

"Wow. That was not what I was expecting. I love it."

It was a white enameled Carnevale mask, painted with
delicate brush strokes in a rainbow of colors. Teardrop diamonds spilled from the eyes. She pinned it to her shirt,
over her heart.

He grazed the mask with a fingertip and glanced up. "I'm
glad. I wanted you to have something unusual but easily
carried. Since you move around a lot."

That nearly knocked her to the floor. "Thanks. It means
a lot that you understand me."

"I'm trying to." He cocked his head. "What did you
get me?"

"My gift is unusual but easily carried, too. I hope you'll like it as much."

She hadn't wrapped hers. Fishing it from her pocket, she handed over the pregnancy test.

"What is it?" He took it with a puzzled expression.

Then his whole body stiffened. His expression, his eyes, everything went absolutely still.

"You're pregnant?" he asked hoarsely, gaze flitting back and forth between her and the plus sign. "The naps. Drinking orange juice like it's going out of style. You're pregnant."

"And you're going to be a father." She couldn't keep the smile off her face. "Congratulations."

Matt sank onto the couch as if he hadn't heard her, still staring at the piece of plastic in his hands. "So I assume this means you're keeping it."

Horrified, she glared at him. "As if there was a possibility I might not? Of course I'm keeping it."

"Okay." He blew out a breath and rubbed his forehead absently, not looking at her. "Okay. I just wanted to make sure I understood. That's the right decision. But I'll support you no matter what."

"I never had a doubt."

Matt wasn't like her father. He was solid, capable. Not weak. Matt was a forever kind of guy and somehow, she'd been lucky enough to find him. A baby changed everything. It gave him more than enough reason to move on. With her.

"It was that time on the roof. Wasn't it? When we forgot the condoms." He looked a little green around the edges. "You said it was the wrong time of the month."

"I thought it was. I miscalculated. But it was already too late, and honestly, I'm glad. We're having a baby and I'm looking forward to being a mom. How do you feel about being a dad?"

Matt shut his eyes. "You've had a little more time to process than me. Give me a minute. Can I get you a drink? Crackers?" He shoved both hands behind his neck, like he was trying to hold his head in place. "I don't even know what to do for a pregnant woman. Be right back."

She watched him flee, breath rattling in her throat, cutting off all her oxygen as she reevaluated his reaction. It never occurred to her that he wouldn't welcome the news. He'd always wanted a family, hadn't he?

Well, he'd said he needed a minute. She had no choice but to give it to him. When he came back, he'd be ready to talk about the future, and then they could make plans to go to Monte Carlo.

Everything was going to be great.

Matthew escaped to the kitchen, formerly his haven. The place where he went to create, feel productive.

Hands spread wide, he leaned on the counter, head down. There still didn't seem to be any blood circulating in his brain. The walls were too close together and the gap between them narrowed.

Pregnant.

Evangeline was *pregnant*.

He wasn't ready to think about being with Evangeline forever, wasn't prepared to examine why they still gelled when they shouldn't. Couldn't get past the fear that suddenly not one, but two people could easily become the center of his existence. Only to be ripped away.

This was his reward for flagrantly disregarding the rules and living in the moment with no thought to consequences. This was what running away from life had gotten him.

Automatically, he filled a glass full of water and downed it without coming up for air once.

From here on out, he'd have to do the right thing. Ironically, if he'd been doing the right thing all along, this never would have happened. But he was a Wheeler, first and foremost, and it was far past time to start acting like one.

What was he going to do? Evangeline would never fit

into his life in Dallas. But she had to. Because he had to. Neither of them had a choice any longer.

Something rushed through his heart. *Relief.* They didn't have a choice but to make it work, whether he was ready to think about forever or not. Forever had started the moment she spoke to him in Vincenzo's hall. Venice was over, but they could still be together.

He returned to the living room, calm and in control. He hoped.

He sat on the couch next to Evangeline. "I'm sorry. I'm one hundred percent here now."

But minus a drink for her. Maybe he was more like ninety percent here.

"I'm glad." Her eyes were enormous and shiny. Red. She'd been crying and it wrenched his heart. No matter what he was going through, it hardly compared to an emotional *and* physical wallop, like what had happened to her.

Stop thinking about yourself, Wheeler.

"Hey," he said softly and took her hand. "It's going to be okay. Did I make you cry? I didn't mean to."

She shook her head. "I'm all emotional. From hormones, I guess. I've never been pregnant before."

"It'll be fine. I'll be here for you. Take you to the doctor and—" he swallowed against the sudden burn in his throat "—be in the delivery room to cut the umbilical cord."

All things he'd looked forward to doing with Amber. Seeing his wife rounded with their child. Lacing fingers as they watched the image in the sonogram. Never had he imagined it happening with someone else, and *never* would he have anticipated the spike of unadulterated elation at the thought of doing it with Evangeline.

Ruthlessly, he shut off the emotions careening through his chest. Becoming emotional would not help this situation.

"So we're going to be together?" she asked tentatively, and her grip on his hand tightened. "You want to be a part of the baby's life?"

The baby's life. He shook his head, to clear it, to whack something loose that made sense. How would anything make sense ever again?

There was so much more to consider than the pregnancy. The next eight months were only the beginning. He and Evangeline were going to be parents, of a kid who would eventually walk and talk and learn to ride a bike.

A baby. He was going to be a dad. Panic nearly blinded him—but the clearest sense of awe fought its way to the forefront.

"We'll raise it together. Of course we will."

The baby would be a Wheeler, entitled to everything Matthew could and would provide. The circumstances weren't ideal, and this curveball certainly jerked him back to reality.

Venice was *definitely* over. They needed to make plans, decisions. Find a place to live. Insurance. A car with a baby seat. His head spun. He didn't own a car anymore.

Evangeline gave him a watery smile. She was so thrilled, and he hated to squelch her enthusiasm, but they both needed to get real, really fast. Their relationship was now permanent. Two people who had almost nothing in common other than enormously painful events in their pasts were going to be parents.

"Together," she repeated. "I like the sound of that. There was something about you, from the very first, that called to me. The fortune-teller even predicted it. That we'd conceive. Remember?"

What he remembered was chasing down a beautiful butterfly for the sole purpose of feeling something again, and tripping headlong into an affair he'd believed would help him get back home. All he'd wished for was a sign that he'd make it back to his old self. That he might heal.

Instead, one passionate round of rooftop sex had bound him to this woman permanently. A woman who was so different from every woman he'd ever met and with whom *he* had to be different to even keep up.

As stakes in the ground went, she'd presented him with a doozy. A baby. The panic rose again, thick in his throat. He pushed it down.

They'd be together. They'd have a family. It was a blessing, no matter what.

"We can get married quietly." If they didn't have any guests, the date of their wedding didn't have to be publicized. They might be able to hide the fact that the baby was conceived out of wedlock. Anything to avoid causing his parents public embarrassment.

His back teeth clacked together. But he wouldn't lie to his parents—they'd have to know the truth. The vision he had in his head of sitting with Amber on his parent's sofa and gleefully telling them about the coming grandchild shattered. Of course, it had shattered long ago.

"Married? What are you talking about?"

"You're pregnant. We're getting married." Out of order. Once again.

She laughed. "Matt, we don't have to be married to be together. Love isn't dependent on a piece of paper."

Love? Did she think he was in love with her? Was she in love with *him*?

Evangeline made him crazy. She provoked sensual— okay, downright erotic—impulses from him. Pulled his soul from the deep freeze and made it okay to say whatever he wanted. Feel whatever he wanted. He couldn't do that forever. His life—his real life—had order and structure. No surprises. He had to get that back.

And he didn't want to be in love.

Never again. If he was doomed to suffer forever for falling in love with Amber, he certainly didn't want to repeat that mistake. Especially not with Evangeline, who made him feel so much. Especially not now.

How much harder would it be to love his child's mother and lose her?

The thought of losing either the mother or the child squeezed his chest so hard, he couldn't breathe. He cursed—was it already too late?

"A baby isn't dependent on love, either," he said. Harsh. But true. Neither of them could afford to keep up the fantasy they'd been living, and he needed to internalize that fact as much as she did. Real life wasn't about mystical connections and Venetian love affairs between incompatible people.

"We're getting married," he repeated.

Her eyebrows came together. "Who said I wanted to get married? You didn't even ask me."

He dismissed her words with a wave. "That's just a formality. Marriage will be good for you."

Her career was over—but she could be a wife and a mother. He had to make her see that. There was so much more to consider than whether he'd *asked* or not.

She recoiled as if he'd slapped her. "A formality? I deserve to be asked. With a ring. And you know, something along the lines of 'I love you and want to be with you the rest of my life.' Try it and then I'll give you my answer."

She was right. He'd gone about proposing the wrong way, but God Almighty, who could blame him? This humdinger of a development had flipped him inside out.

"I don't have a ring. As far as I knew, we were kissing each other goodbye today. I'm sorry." He took a deep breath and slid her palm to his mouth, kissing it in silent apology before he released it. "Let's figure out the next steps together."

She smiled. "The first step is to remember we're going to be happy."

Happy. Happiness had been a sheer impossibility when he left Dallas. But Evangeline had changed that.

They could be happy outside of Venice. Evangeline was amazing, strong, resilient. Look at how she'd walked into the lion's den of that horrific interview. Faced down the reporters. Played the piano. She could adapt to the role of Mrs. Wheeler and enjoy a life with roots. After all, they'd have a baby and a household to keep her busy and content.

She'd been searching for the next steps, and he'd give them to her. Being his wife would keep her demons away permanently, and she'd definitely become less…glittery. Then they'd gel in Dallas as well as they did here in Venice.

He returned her smile, and somehow it relaxed him. "Well, at least we already know we can live together without killing each other."

He didn't have to give her up. It was easier to picture her in Dallas if he forgot about all the reasons he and Evangeline wouldn't work and instead focused on what would be great.

"I'll let you cook. All the time. I have no problem with a man in my kitchen. It turns me on."

Her thumb smoothed over his and for the first time since he'd walked into the hornets' nest, he actually felt in control again.

Evangeline tucked her feet up under her and leaned into Matt's warm chest. Finally, things had clicked into place, and he'd lost that panicked edge, poor guy. She got that it was a little rough to have something so life-changing dropped on you out of the blue. The adjustment was still messing with her, too.

Marriage—of course he'd want that, and she was still contemplating it. If he came up with a really good proposal, she might actually say yes.

There was a shock. She'd thought Rory had crushed the desire for marriage out of her forever. But Matt wasn't like other men, and to him she was so much more than a broken voice.

"There's a lot to discuss," he said, and she nodded against his shoulder.

"First off, I'd like to talk about Monte Carlo." Thankfully, she hadn't brought it up yet. This way, it was practically a foregone conclusion. "The party is already in full swing but if we leave by Thurs—"

"What?" Matt tilted her head up to pierce her with a puzzled gaze. "We can't go to Monte Carlo. Especially not to a party."

"That's where all my friends are. We can tell everyone the news, and of course I can't drink any champagne, but you can have a glass for me."

It would be a fantastic way to celebrate. Not exactly the kind of party Vincenzo and his crowd were used to, but fun all the same. Maybe someone would volunteer to throw her a baby shower.

"We don't have to stay long," she added. "A week, tops. Then I suppose we can come back to Venice until the tourist season star—"

"There's no more Venice." His lips curved up in a half smile, maybe in apology for cutting her off *again*, but the rest of his face was pure confusion. "Surely you've realized that. We'll be flying to the States. We can leave as soon as you're ready. Somewhere along the way, I'll buy a ring and we'll get married at my parents' house."

A little discombobulated, she frowned. "I thought we already talked about the marriage proposal. And there still hasn't been one. Plus, I don't want to go to America. I hate it there. You think the press is bad in Italy, wait until you've dealt with the gossip websites."

"I don't want to deal with the press at all. Unfortunately we don't have that choice because America is where Dallas is and that's where we're going."

"Dallas? You want to go back to Dallas?" The harsh consonants rang in her ears. She'd always known that was his goal, but things had changed. *He* had changed. And he'd said more than once he didn't think he could go back yet. Monte Carlo was an opportunity to continue healing. "What's in Dallas for you?"

"Dallas is where my family is, my job," he explained, and his tone implied she should have already figured this out. "And that's where I have to live in order to do it. Also, my mother is there. She'll help you with the baby."

"I have a mother."

In a manner of speaking—she'd rather eat Brussels sprouts than ask her mom for parenting advice, and honestly, she might not mention the baby to her mother at all. Evangeline hadn't darkened the door of her mother's in a year or two. It wouldn't be out of the realm of possibility to keep the pregnancy from her.

"Your mother is welcome to come and stay for as long as you want her to," Matt offered, and she tried not to gag at the thought. "But my mother will be involved. I want her to have a relationship with her grandchild."

"There's an app for that. It's called Skype."

"That's ridiculous." He flicked off her suggestion as if she hadn't spoken. "I'll probably buy a house close to my parents. There's a good private school in their neighborhood. How early is too early to get on the waiting list, do you think?"

"Matt." He was babbling about something called Hockaday. It was like they were speaking two totally different languages. She tugged on his shirt. "Matt. I'm not moving to Dallas."

Dallas would be the *worst* place for Matt. He seemed to think he was ready, but it was too soon. He needed more time to heal, more time with her.

"Sure you are. There's a really great arts district, and my mom knows a lot of people. She can introduce you to other moms your age. You'll like it."

The first tendrils of alarm unfolded in her stomach. "*You* don't even like Dallas. You said it was oppressive. Do you really think you can go back to real estate, like you're still the same person you used to be?"

The look on his face when he'd been telling Nicola and

Angelo about his family firm—well, he might love his job, but it wasn't going to be the same. He'd walked away because he needed something else.

He needed her.

"I have to be that person. That's the real me. This?" He pointed at the frescoed ceiling. "This is not me. This is some other guy who'd lost his way. Dallas is where I was always trying to get back to. I have you to thank for getting me on the right track."

"Dallas isn't the right track. You're talking about shoehorning both of us, and a *baby*, into something that doesn't exist anymore. Monte Carlo is the best option for us. We're moving on together. Don't you see?" Desperation laced her words, because it was clear he *didn't* see.

"Monte Carlo is not a place for the mother of my child." His lips firmed into a no-nonsense line she'd never seen before.

"It is when I'm the mother."

Their gazes locked, and the frozen blue of his irises nearly took her breath. All of Matt's incredible depth—the quality she'd always treasured the most—had vanished.

"I don't want you around those kind of people," he said.

"*Those* kind of people?" Her spine stiffened in shock. "And what kind of people would those be, Matt?"

He had the gall to glare at her. "Alcoholics. Like your ex. People who stumble home after a night of who knows what, like Vincenzo, and throw phone parties."

Eyes wide, she snickered to cover her rising distress. "Would you like a stepladder to see over that double standard you just threw up? May I remind you where we met?"

"That's irrelevant. You're not going to Monte Carlo."

Who was this man talking to her out of Matt's mouth and watching her from his eyes, but who clearly was *not* Matt? It was like he'd put on another mask, but this one scared her.

"Are we really on such opposite sides of this? How can that be?" She looked for some glimmer of the empathy they'd always had. It wasn't there, as if the link between them had been severed. The tendril of panic exploded. "I don't understand what's going on."

"We're having a baby. A baby that will be raised in Dallas, where it will have the best care and the best opportunities." The corner he was pushing her into grew sharp against her back. He *never* pushed. Why now? "Where we can have a good life and be happy. Like you said."

Dallas was his idea of a good life? "What, exactly, do you envision me doing in Dallas? Tea parties with your mother?"

He shrugged. "Sure. If you want to. Or volunteer. My sister-in-law runs a women's shelter. Maybe that would appeal to you. It'll take a while to get back in the swing of things, even for me, but I usually get invitations to at least one or two social events a week. Charity balls and the like. When the baby comes, you can take it easy and focus on being a mother."

"Charity balls?" Her voice squeaked. Which would be unremarkable except it was the highest tone she'd accomplished in a very long time. "Have we actually met? Hi, I'm Evangeline La Fleur, and I live in Europe. I'd like for the father of my child to live in Europe with me."

"Or?"

The challenge snaked through her.

"Or don't. But you're talking about a life in Dallas that I can't do." If she put down roots in Dallas, what would happen to her if it didn't work out? If he decided he didn't want her to stay after all?

"Can't? Or won't?" His tone sliced through her, and tears burned at the corners of her eyes.

"Can't." She took a deep, calming breath, but it shuddered in her chest. "Matt, have you listened to me at all? I'd die in that environment. Die, as in wither up into a dried bit of nothing and blow away."

They *both* would. Why was he being so stubborn?

"You'll be with me. I'll keep you entertained." His wolf-ish smile unleashed a nauseous wave in her abdomen.

"Is that all I am to you?"

"No. Of course not." He shook his head, sobering, and every fiber of her being wished for him to follow that with, *I love you.* "I want you to be my wife."

That's when it all snapped into place. The sick churning in her stomach sped up.

"You haven't been trying to get over Amber. That's why it's taking so long. What you've been searching for isn't a cure—you've been looking for a *replacement*. The whole time. And you found one."

"No one can replace Amber." A lethal edge to his expression whipped out and knifed her in a tender place deep inside. "I would never attempt to try."

"Of course. My mistake." One of many. But she couldn't let it go, couldn't stop from ensuring they both heard the brutal truth. "I've been falling in love with you. All along. Tell me that's one-sided."

The harsh lines of his face softened. "I'm sorry. I'm not trying to hurt you."

"But you're going to anyway."

Her heart froze in disbelief. She'd put it out there, only to have it slapped down. It had never occurred to her that she wouldn't be successful at healing him. That the baby wouldn't be the answer. That her feelings wouldn't be returned.

But Matt was honest to a fault, and he'd never lie to her. He didn't love her.

He couldn't, because she wasn't Amber. She'd never be able to fill the empty place in his heart, and she'd been a fool to think that demon could ever be slayed.

Her whole life had been shaped by rejection at the hands of people who didn't love her because she wasn't someone else. She wasn't Lisa. She wasn't Sara Lear. And she *wasn't Amber.*

"Evangeline…" He sighed, and deep lines appeared around his eyes, aging him. "I've never made you any promises. I don't make promises I don't intend to keep. And I'm not ready to be in love again. Might never be."

Brutal. She'd had no idea how severe the truth could really be. "So you're proposing we get married and raise a kid. But as roommates?"

"We've been living together without being in love. Why does being married have to be any different? It'll be like Venice, but permanent. If you don't want to volunteer, then do something else, maybe related to music. Give private singing lessons."

"I can't sing," she choked out, and the final stitch holding her heart together snapped. The organ fell into two pieces somewhere in the vicinity of her womb, where the child she thought they'd love as a couple grew.

"Piano lessons then." He took her hand, squeezing, as if nothing was wrong. As if everything was going to work out fine. "If you taught me, you can teach anyone. It doesn't matter to me as long as the baby is taken care of."

It doesn't matter to me.

She was nothing more than a warm oven for his offspring. Not someone to love and cherish. It was the ultimate rejection of everything she'd imagined their relationship to be.

She yanked her hand out of his grasp.

She'd invented a connection—one that didn't actually exist—out of her own loneliness and fear of an empty future. In the end, Matt wanted something from her far more damaging, and far more heartbreaking, than she could have ever predicted. He wanted her to sacrifice everything that made her who she was, and in return, he vowed to *never* love her the way he loved Amber.

Maybe he wasn't capable of loving anyone other than Amber.

Why hadn't she realized that sooner?

"Oh, the baby will be taken care of. *My* baby," she corrected fiercely. This was one time when she'd be doing the rejecting. "I don't actually need your help, in case that wasn't clear. I'm not a wide-eyed sixteen-year-old, terrified and penniless. I've got a net worth in the eight figures. The baby will have every opportunity available under the sun. You go back to Dallas and attend some stuck-up snobby rich people's charity event. I'll be in Monte Carlo living the life that makes sense for me. *You* can have a relationship with your child through the internet."

She fled up the stairs, tears streaming, and locked herself in the bedroom to finish packing.

Twelve

"Evangeline." Matthew banged on the door again, barely resisting the urge to kick it in. "Open the door. We're not finished, not by a long shot."

What in the name of all that was holy had just happened? Somehow, Evangeline had broken up with him, like they were a real couple.

But weren't they? He was going to marry her. He *wanted* to marry her.

He'd invested considerable energy into figuring out the next steps—marriage, a house, a stake in the ground—and Evangeline was *throwing it back in his face*.

This was killing him. His insides tossed and turned faster than a shoreline in a hurricane.

"Oh, we're finished," she called, and slammed something—a drawer. "A good lawyer will help us work out the visitation rights."

Visitation rights. Lawyers. If this was a nightmare, it was not ending fast enough.

"Lawyers are not the answer."

"Why, don't you have one?"

He rolled his eyes at her scathing tone. "I *am* one.

Granted, not well-versed in the ins and outs of international custody law. But I'm pretty sure I could hold my own given time to acclimate."

Some shuffling. The door flung open to reveal Evangeline's ravaged face. He hated it when she cried. Hated being the reason.

"You're a *lawyer*?" She spit it out like he'd admitted to being a member of the Black Panthers.

But at least she was talking to him again. He had to get this situation back under control before she took off to Monte Carlo and he never heard from her again.

"I passed the bar. Is that really important in light of the other really important thing we should be discussing? The baby?" he prompted.

She crossed her arms. "Well, we're full of disclosures today, aren't we? No wonder you're so sanctimonious. Anything else you forgot to tell me?"

"It's not like I hid it on purpose to make you mad. It just never came up."

"But it perfectly illustrates the point. I *trusted* you." She was so worked up, she bristled. "I've never been anything but honest about who I am yet I don't know you at all."

Direct hit. He had worn his mask far longer than she had.

Punching photographers. Sex on the roof. Midnight confessionals. None of that was really him, and she was calling him on it. This was all his fault.

A doozy of a headache landed right behind his eyeballs.

"I didn't set out to deceive you."

All at once, she deflated. "I thought…well, it doesn't matter now."

"It does matter. Evangeline—" He pressed a fingertip to both eyelids, willing the headache to disappear. It didn't. "I don't want to deal with custody and visitation through lawyers. The baby belongs with both parents."

Evangeline and the baby belonged with him, in Dallas.

Their choices about the future had been taken from them, and he'd think about why that made him so happy later.

"Then come to Monte Carlo with me." Her soft brown eyes beseeched him, pulling at him. Unearthing the confusing, unnatural reaction he had to her. "Prove that you're the man I think you are. More hinges on it than what's going to happen with the baby. You came to me broken. I want you to be whole again. Let me heal you."

"But you've already done that." He couldn't help it. He pulled her into his arms, and the feel of her, the warmth, the familiar scent of her hair, knocked his equilibrium loose, nearly putting him on the ground. "That's why I can go back to Dallas and pick up the reins of who I was. Because you made me feel alive again."

Alive. Yes. And without her, what would he be?

"No." She buried her face in his neck. "You're not healed. If you were, you would be able to love me."

That was the kicker. They had different definitions of *healed*.

"I didn't lie to you. I told you I didn't have anything to give. I'm sorry, but a baby doesn't change that."

She nodded. "I understand. And it doesn't change the fact that I can't marry you. If we were in love, I…well, it doesn't matter, does it?"

She'd sliced through everything, right to the heart of it. She wanted him to love her. And he couldn't.

The purgatory of loss was too painful. He wasn't willing to risk backsliding into a hole of depression again. Not even for her.

Especially for her. She made him feel too much.

This was not the opportune time to figure out all this. He'd been searching for a way to get back on track, not searching for someone like Evangeline.

"No compromise?" He had a sick feeling in his gut that he already knew the answer.

"Oh, Matt." She kissed him, lightly, and her lips lifted

too quickly. "Sure I'd compromise. London. Madrid. Pick a place. Monte Carlo isn't nearly as important as what it represents. You won't fully heal until you accept that your old life is gone. You can't go back. Neither of us can. All we can do is move forward. If that's what you want, Monte Carlo is the answer."

He couldn't chase her around the globe like a teenager with a trust fund and no responsibilities.

"Not for me."

It wasn't the right answer for her, either. She'd never find the next steps in Monte Carlo, and the anguish would swallow her whole if he wasn't around. How in the world did she think she'd survive without him?

The baby belonged with him. *She* belonged with him. He wanted to howl with the injustice of it, that he couldn't make her see the logic.

She stepped out of his embrace, dry-eyed. "Then, this is goodbye."

Matthew called a cab instead of Lucas, though he knew his brother would pick him up from the airport. Family would always be there for him, regardless of the grief he'd put them through for the past eighteen months. But he couldn't face anyone.

Not yet. Not when he still couldn't process that he'd left Evangeline in Venice.

The mother of his child. And he'd had to let her go.

After several more arguments, a bucket of tears—not all hers—and a bunch of slammed doors, he'd finally given up trying to reason with her. Stubborn woman. She refused to see what was best and actually threatened to disappear if he didn't accept her decision.

Ultimately, their connection was nothing but the magic of Venice, blowing smoke and illusion to cover the truth. They weren't meant to be together.

The cab pulled up at his parents' house. The driver hefted

the suitcases from the trunk, accepted the folded bill with a nod and drove off, leaving Matthew on the sidewalk in the middle of the suburban neighborhood he'd grown up in. The neighborhood he didn't recognize at all.

His mother had planted something flowery and purple in the side yard that he'd never seen before, and the house's wood trim had been painted. Maybe the brick had been power-washed. A car rushed by on the street behind him, likely only driving thirty miles an hour, but it felt more like a hundred. All of it lent to the sense of being somewhere unfamiliar.

There weren't any cars in Venice. Boats slipped by quietly in the canal or sometimes the cheerful call of a gondolier announced its presence. People strolled the streets and enjoyed a slower pace. He'd grown used to it. Preferred it.

The front door creaked, and his mother poked her blond head out. "Now there's a sight for sore eyes. Get in here, honey. You should have told me you were coming."

Matthew grinned at the break in her voice. "Hey, Mama. It was a surprise."

"It certainly is. Surprise me less or you'll give me a heart attack." She flew over the doorstep and into a fierce hug.

This, at least, felt very familiar. Very welcoming. He'd missed her.

Mama hustled him into the house and fluttered around, doing a bang-up job of ignoring Matthew's protests about staying in a hotel. To stem the tide, he carried his stuff to the extra bedroom upstairs. Arguing with Mama did not ever end well.

"Sit. Let me look at you." Mama sank onto the couch and he followed. She smoothed a lock of hair from his forehead. "Staying long?"

"Yeah." He knew what she was really asking. "I'm home for good."

That put weight on his shoulders. He'd thought he was

ready. He *was* ready. But it was so permanent. And so Evangeline-free.

Her sharp gaze swept him, twice, with a combination of disbelief and hope. "Did you find what you were looking for?"

The harsh laugh scraped at his throat. "Not really. But I figured out it's because I didn't actually know what I was looking for. I don't do well without a plan."

"You never have. So what's your plan now?"

"I'm going back to WFP. Lucas has managed to get himself into a hole, and I'm going to get him out." First time in a long time he had a sense of purpose. A goal. It felt good. Right.

Mama shot him a puzzled glance. "A hole? Did he tell you that?"

"I know about Richards Group. It's partly the reason I came home." The other part had everything to do with a singular desire to be dependable, straight-arrow Matthew Wheeler again. To do something he excelled at and had ultimate control over.

"I think you should talk to him. We'll have a big family dinner to celebrate you being home. Call your brother. Tell him to come early so you can get on the same page." She smiled. "Far be it from me to get in the middle of my boys, but honey, you left. Lucas has been handling things. I doubt he's going to take kindly to you sticking your nose into WFP and bossing him around. A word to the wise."

Matthew checked the eye-roll out of sheer respect for the woman who had birthed him. But it was hard.

"I'm not going to boss him around, Mama. I'm here to help."

She nodded. "Just you remember that. You're helping. Not in charge."

The transatlantic flight caught up to him then, and he cracked his jaw with a yawn. "I'm going to take a shower and maybe watch TV for a couple of mindless hours." Decompress. Be alone without his mother's shrewd gaze on him. He pulled her into a long hug. "Thanks. For letting me come home."

"Silly." She thumped his shoulder, her eyes shiny and full. "You're still my kid, no matter how big you get. I love you. You're always welcome here."

He almost spilled everything then, all the heartache of the past eighteen months, the depression, the disorientation. How he'd experienced it again tenfold on the flight home at the hands of a different woman. But the wounds of Evangeline were far too fresh and the wounds of Amber far too…faded.

He frowned. When had that happened?

"See you at dinner."

Dropping a kiss on his mother's cheek, he went upstairs to clear his mind with a hot shower, which didn't work.

When he'd last been in Dallas, the burden of grief had turned the sunniest of days dark. Amber was constantly on his mind, how he couldn't go on without her. How everything they'd planned was dashed. He'd expected coming home to bring all that back. It hadn't.

When he thought about Amber now, it was with a hazy sort of warm rush. The prongs of grief had lifted.

The skin he washed was the same. But the man inside wasn't. That's why the neighborhood and his mother's house had been unrecognizable. Despite all his yearning to slip back in time, to a place where he knew everything was safe and right, he couldn't. The only thing he could do was accept that he had changed.

Like Evangeline had said.

But if he accepted that his life was something different now, who would he be?

He called Lucas and then flipped on the TV to lose himself in the oblivion of sleep.

The door crashed against the wall, waking him. Groggily, he sat up and swung his legs off the edge of the bed. The empty bed.

He wasn't in Venice with Evangeline. He was in Dallas. Alone.

A fuzzy Lucas lounged against the door frame, hand in his pants' pocket and a smirk on his face.

"God Almighty, you look like roadkill in August." Lucas tsked.

"Thanks. That's exactly what I needed to hear. I was sleeping, by the way," Matthew groused and rubbed a hand across his eyes. His brother's form snapped into focus. "Though I appreciate that you were so eager to see me you couldn't wait."

Lucas snorted out a laugh. "I just didn't believe you were actually here. Had to see it for myself. You back?"

"Looks that way."

"All the way back?"

"Why does everyone keep asking me that? I'm here, aren't I?"

Lucas sat on the edge of the bed a couple feet away, dipping the mattress. "You were in bad shape. I'm concerned. Sue me."

Well, I am a sanctimonious lawyer.

Matthew's head dropped into his hands. It wasn't just jet lag crushing him. Evangeline—knowing he'd hurt her, being without her—weighed more than he could bear.

"Honestly, I don't know if 'all the way back' is possible."

"Amber's death nearly destroyed you. Don't let it finish the job," Lucas advised quietly. "You took some time away. Now rejoin life. I'm working on trouncing Richards Group. Another Wheeler on the job can't hurt."

Matthew nearly laughed. "If only Amber were the problem, I'd be all set. Unfortunately, I traded one impossible-to-solve issue for another."

Lucas nodded sagely. "This has to do with the very sexy lady you met. What happened?"

Matthew met his brother's sharp gaze. "How do you know about that?"

"Everyone knows about that. You photograph well, as it happens. So she figured out she's too good for you, huh? Am I going to be nursing you through a broken heart?"

Matthew growled. "Shut up. You don't know what you're talking about."

"Oh, poor baby. Did she make you cry?" Lucas thumped him on the arm, and Matthew shot him a glare.

"Back off. She's pregnant."

He hadn't meant to say anything. But it came out nonetheless, too huge to stay under wraps.

"Then what are you doing here without her?" His brother's eyes narrowed. "Oh. It's not yours."

Matthew's fist curled, and he almost let it fly, but curbed the impulse at the last second. Where had that anger come from? He wasn't in Venice, free to do whatever he wanted, when he wanted to.

"Of course it's mine. And God, it's a mess."

Lucas started laughing and didn't stop even when Matthew shoved him. Finally, Lucas wiped his eyes. "Oh, how the mighty have fallen."

"What's that supposed to mean?" His brother's face might actually be improved with a good slug to the jaw.

Still sniggering, Lucas crossed his arms. "May I remind you of what you said to me about Cia? I believe you accused me of getting a one-night stand pregnant and self-righteously informed me that accidents happen."

His stomach twisted as he vaguely recalled saying something asinine to that effect. "Is it too late to apologize?"

"Nah." Lucas grinned. "No apology needed. It's nice to know you're human like the rest of us. Where is she now? Did you have a fight or something?"

"Worse. She threw my marriage proposal back in my face and took off with her friends."

"That sucks." Lucas whistled in disbelief. "Women. Can't live with 'em, can't shoot 'em."

Matthew had made it sound like Evangeline was a flighty, irresponsible girl who didn't understand what she'd given up, which was completely unfair and not representative of how badly the whole thing had gone down.

"I guess I didn't actually propose."

Lucas's eyebrows rose. "What did you do then?"

"Told her we were getting married." Out loud, it sounded even worse than it did in his head. "It made sense, you know? You marry a woman you get pregnant. Instead, she's talking about lawyers and custody arrangements."

"Geez, are you that clueless?" Lucas huffed out a disgusted breath. "No wonder she dumped you. You don't have a romantic bone in your body, obviously. How in the world did *you* score with Eva?"

That bristled the hair on the back of Matthew's neck. "I didn't *score* with her. It wasn't like that. We had something—" *Special. Meaningful. Unexplainable.* "I don't know. Different."

"Different than what? Amber?"

Matthew's throat burned, and he almost used it as an excuse to clam up. But once, he and Lucas had been close. That their bond had deteriorated was totally his fault. He wanted it back. And the first step was being honest.

"Different than anything I've ever experienced. Amber fit me, fit my plans. Evangeline…doesn't."

But she fit Matt comfortably, like a second skin. Evangeline *was* different—sexy, arousing, provoking and flat-out frightening.

"So? Life is what happens when you're making other plans."

If only it was that easy.

"Since you're so smart, you tell me. If everything you thought you knew about yourself got flipped upside down, what would you do?" Yeah, asking *what would Lucas do* had gotten him into this mess. Why break tradition?

A perceptive light crept into his brother's eyes. "Well, now. That very thing happened, as a matter of fact. When it did, I looked to my older brother and said, *that's who I want to be*."

Matthew flinched. "Me? Which part of dumping all my responsibilities in your lap did you aim to replicate?"

"Nobody blames you for that. You needed a break. But I guess you forgot the rest of that conversation the afternoon Grandpa died. You said I could be you, and you were going to go be me. I took that seriously. I stepped up because I wanted to be as successful as you."

"I took it seriously, too." Matthew had to chuckle at the irony. "You want to know how I got Evangeline's attention? I pretended I was you. It worked."

Lucas grinned. "I've never seduced a pop star."

"Neither have I. I didn't know that's who she was at the time. All I wanted was to feel something again." And he'd done a stellar job. He felt stupid, frustrated and out of his element. "Then bam! There she was, like an answer to a prayer, only I hadn't prayed for *that*. I didn't have any idea what to do with her."

"Well, you must have had *some* idea since she's, you know, pregnant." Lucas ducked, but Matthew hadn't been planning to smack him. Not right this minute, anyway.

"Yeah, I'm not going to kiss and tell. Hope you get over your disappointment real soon." He flopped back against the pillow, exhausted. "Now she doesn't want anything to do with me, and my kid is going to be living in Europe while I'm here. Mama is going to be so disappointed."

"Mama? What about you? Aren't you disappointed in yourself?"

"I didn't need you to point that out."

Of course he was disappointed. He'd dreamed of a family for a long time. Instantly, the image of Evangeline holding his child, her beautiful face luminous as she smiled at the bundle, popped into his mind, and the sharp stab to the gut nearly doubled him over.

"I don't know what to do."

"You're going to figure it out." Lucas put a brotherly hand on Matthew's shoulder. "I've never seen you fail at something you put your heart into."

He eyed his little brother with new respect. Lucas had stepped into the role Matthew formerly occupied, and with more success than probably anyone had expected, thanks in no small part to Cia. Never underestimate the power of the right woman.

Lucas excused himself so Matthew could get ready for dinner.

When he arrived downstairs, everyone was already at the table. Conversation ground to a sudden halt—obviously because they'd been discussing him—when he came into view.

"Hey, son." His dad, who looked tan and fit, jumped up to give him a brief manly hug.

"Playing a lot of golf lately?"

His dad nodded. "Lucas is running the show at WFP, and I'm enjoying life. Care for a round?"

Matthew agreed without really intending to, but he was home. Home meant doing all the things he used to. Might as well reestablish the routine right away.

Cia glanced up at him and flicked her long, dark hair from her shoulder. "You'll forgive me if I don't get up." She pointed to her huge stomach, and he quickly averted his eyes. Pregnancy was a sore subject.

"Cia."

He kissed his sister-in-law's cheek and smiled at Mama, then proceeded to suffer through a long discussion about the strategies Lucas was working to drive Richards Group back to Houston where their competitor belonged. It was staggering to hear Lucas spit out such cogent, well-thought-out plans.

More than once, his attention wandered back to Venice, only to snap back to the present when someone said his name. *Matthew*. He'd been called that more times today alone than in all of the past few months.

It felt weird to answer to it.

Afterward, he flopped into one of the wicker chairs on Mama's porch, across from Lucas and Cia. They giggled and nuzzled each other until he thought he'd throw up.

"Get a room."

"Hey, just because you screwed things up with your woman doesn't mean I can't enjoy mine." Lucas ducked as Cia smacked him.

"Leave him alone," she said with a conciliatory kiss to her husband's jaw.

Matthew did a double take. His sister-in-law had never liked him. "Defending me? What is the world coming to?"

But she shot him a mellow smile instead of flaying him alive like she'd have done in the past. "You tell me. What has your world come to, Matthew?"

"Disaster," he muttered. Louder, he said, "Lucas spill all my beans?"

"No, the internet did. It was quite the discussion at the shelter for a week. Did you at least come home with an autograph or two?"

Yeah. Evangeline had taken a Sharpie to his insides all right.

Matthew grimaced. "I came home with nothing."

"I see your attitude hasn't improved. Shame." Cia clucked. "Now I owe Lucas something that's going to be very hard for me to do in my current state."

The smoldering glance she skewered his brother with said she'd figure out a way to pay up or die trying. They seemed blissfully happy, even almost a year into their marriage. Who would have thought?

"Did you lose a bet?"

"Yeah." Lucas answered for her. "The second she saw

the pictures of you and Eva, she swore you'd never come home. So I won."

Matthew shook his head. "I don't know how you could make such a bet over a picture."

Coolly, Cia evaluated him. "You haven't seen them. Have you?" Without waiting for his answer, she held out a hand to Lucas. "Phone, please."

When she got it, she tapped a few times and handed it to Matthew. Pulse hammering, he glanced at the photo taken in front of the restaurant in Venice, and zeroed in on Evangeline's beautiful, radiant face. The small resolution didn't diminish her light in the slightest. She burst from the screen, burst into his gut. The reporter he'd punched took a great picture.

"That picture is the first evidence I've seen that you have teeth. You have a nice smile," Cia said quietly.

He tore his gaze off the woman in the photo to look at the guy she was with. Him. But a version of Matthew Wheeler he'd never seen before.

"Before you left," Cia continued, "you had a permanent scowl. Kind of like now."

He certainly didn't have a scowl on his face in the picture. He looked happy. Blissful even, with his arm around Evangeline. They were close, so close, as if they couldn't bear to be apart for the few moments it took to reach the street. Her face turned up toward his, ignoring the iconic scenery around her. They looked like a couple. A real couple.

A couple so in love they only saw each other.

Whether he wanted it or not, it had happened. He'd been falling in love with Evangeline all along.

Lucas jumped in with a spectacular double-team. "That's the smile of a man who's a goner. If you're so miserable without her, why aren't you wherever she is, making it right?"

His brother—the relationship expert. Matthew almost rolled his eyes. "We're too different to make it work."

A lie. He was too afraid to make it work. He'd come home because running away was what he did. His eyelids slammed shut. Was that really who he'd become? A quitter?

"That's pure BS. You're not trying to make it work. You're here, and she's there. Trust me when I say pride won't keep you warm at night. Swallow yours. And watch a You Tube video on how to propose properly to a woman."

Maybe his brother *had* learned a thing or two about what it took. As he reevaluated Lucas with his arm around his pregnant wife, Matthew had a nasty epiphany. Lucas wasn't a screwup, or even much of a womanizer. In trying to be Lucas, he'd been chasing a shadow that didn't exist.

He hadn't been acting like his brother—he'd been Matthew Wheeler all along, but a better, braver, bolder version, who went by the name of Matt. Evangeline had tapped into his secret longings, ripped off his "Matthew" mask and enabled him to discover who he really was underneath the name.

The man Amber married had vanished and become someone else—a man in love with the mother of his child. An ocean separated them because he'd been blindly, self-ishly hanging on to slim threads of the past, too afraid of descending into depression again to realize he'd lost everything important.

He wanted to be that guy who kept up with Evangeline La Fleur and had sex on the roof and believed in the whims of fate that had seen fit to blow her into his path. He wanted to be with her and their child, regardless of whether it happened according to his plan.

The Screwup hat was firmly on Matthew's head. But the mistake hadn't been the accidental pregnancy—it had been letting Evangeline go.

How in the world could he make that right?

Thirteen

Evangeline lay on the bed and wiped her eyes for the forti-eth time. Morning sickness was worse than a slow death at the hands of sadistic monkeys. Crackers didn't help. Ginger ale didn't help. Cursing Matt didn't help and usually made her cry. Like now.

She craved his egg-white omelets with every pregnancy hormone in her body. All the other hormones craved him.

How could she still be so torn apart over a man who'd stripped her down to her base layer and then *rejected* her? She'd taken a huge leap of faith and trusted him enough to fall in love, only to be crushed. Again.

Really, she couldn't be angry with him. He hadn't lied to her. She'd been lying to herself about what he needed. He'd rather suffer than get over Amber.

But she *was* angry. And devastated. So much so, she couldn't stand to be around him any longer. The look on his face when she'd threatened to disappear had nearly killed her, but what else could she do?

Vincenzo's cousin, Nicola, knocked on the open door. "You need something, *cara*?"

"Thanks. I'm okay." She wasn't but Nicola didn't have

any magic capable of fixing her broken heart. Thank God she'd come to Monte Carlo, where people understood her.

"We go to a club soon. VIP lounge. No paparazzi. You join us?" The elfin woman raised a brow. "Maybe you meet someone new who helps you forget."

Ha. If only. "I better pass. I doubt someone new would care too much for me running to the bathroom every five minutes."

The effort required to simply get dressed was enough of a deterrent to a night out. Then there were the smoke machines, which probably pumped out fumes toxic to a baby. Flashing lights were guaranteed to give her a headache. Cocktails would flow—watered down most likely, but with enough alcohol to render them off-limits.

Of course all of that was just noise. She missed Matt, missed Venice, and nothing else held much appeal.

Nicola nodded and left her alone.

Evangeline bit back an urge to call after her, to beg her to come back and sit awhile. But Evangeline didn't want to be a burden on her nonpregnant friends. Which was all of them.

Still, Monte Carlo was beautiful. Outside the window of her room in Nicola's high-rise condo, the city unfolded in a myriad of lights, energy and people, generating an exciting vibe that spilled out into the Mediterranean via the hundreds of yachts lining the shore.

Alone time was good. She'd come here to feed her newly awakened muse. Now she had plenty of time to see what new brilliance flowed from her fingers.

But instead of reaching for the paper and pen on her bedside table—which had sat untouched for two days—she retrieved the printed page from under her pillow and unfolded the song she'd written in Venice the night she'd fallen asleep on the couch.

She'd probably read these words a hundred times now. The theme of connection ran through every line. Of course, because she craved it. Losing her voice had been devastating because it was the link between her and the listener.

But the song spoke to a different kind of connection. One between people, but deeper than the superficial link between a singer and a fan. It was about bonds, family. Things she'd never had at any point in her life, but somehow the right expression had come from her soul.

Because Matt's soul spilled over into hers with his strong sense of unity, goodness…and now she was crying again. How could she have gleaned so much from his depths when he'd closed himself off? It shouldn't be possible. But the evidence was on the page.

It was definitely a good thing she couldn't sing this. She'd never get through the whole thing without breaking down. Sara Lear would do the song justice, and it would be a nice hit for her already-stellar career.

Why couldn't she imagine Sara singing it? Professional jealousy? Probably.

She read the words again. She had to let go. This was part of moving on, something she must find the strength to do. Her voice was gone, but she had a baby on the way. One day, she'd like to look her child in the face and be able to say *I overcame a huge struggle. You can, too.*

One day, she'd like to tell Matt how he'd helped her realize she was more than just a voice, more than Eva. She still had something of value to give.

The song was proof.

All at once, she knew why she couldn't imagine Sara Lear singing this song. Sara didn't need a hit song writer—she had plenty of those barking at her door. Evangeline hadn't written this song for Sara, but for someone else entirely.

And now was the right time to give it away.

Before she could change her mind, she picked up her phone and dialed. "It's Evangeline. Your sister."

Family.

What had started as a simple phone call was actually much more profound. Her heart hadn't just been opened to Matt, but to a whole new world of connection. Even though he'd devastated her, he'd also introduced the wonders of permanence, longevity—all only possible if she allowed roots to grow.

"Hi." Lisa's surprise came through the line clearly in the one short word.

"Sorry to call you with no warning." How did you build a relationship from scratch? Start slowly or jump in with both feet? "I've been going through a tough time and I wanted to apologize for losing touch. Can we start over?"

Maybe somewhere in the middle, then.

"I'd like that. How are you? Your voice is different."

Evangeline chuckled. "The surgery messed it up. Listen, I wanted to ask you. Are you still singing?"

"Yeah. At school, we have a vocal group. I do that and karaoke on the weekends. Nothing that's going to get me noticed, but Dad said I can record some demos after graduation."

Dad. Her stomach twisted at the label Lisa so easily gave the man who'd done nothing more for Evangeline than donate sperm. But this was part of letting go too, and nurturing those fledgling roots instead of chopping them off at the source.

"I have a better idea. I wrote a song for you. I'd like to hear you sing it, and then if we both agree it's everything I hope, I'll book you a recording session with my former producer. He'll lay it down right."

"Omigod. Are you serious?" Half of Lisa's sentence came out a squeal. "You wrote a song for me? Why?"

A million different throwaway responses rose up, but this was about forging a new direction and exposing the deepest parts of herself. About living up to the bravery Matt had seen in her.

"I'm branching into a new career. As a songwriter. I expect I'll write quite a few songs. Who better to write for than family? If we work really hard and are fully committed, the partnership can launch both of our careers."

Committed. It had a nice ring to it. She'd had precious little commitment to anything and expected it to drop a weight on her chest. But instead, the idea of collaborating with her sister, long term, carried the most intense sense of peace.

Best of all, if someone asked her, *What are you going to do now that you can't sing anymore?*, she had an answer.

A new direction as a songwriter and a new direction with family. Timely, since she was going to have a family of her own when the baby was born.

A wave of guilt clogged her throat. She'd deliberately ensured that family would only consist of two—her and the baby.

That wasn't fair to Matt, Matt's family or the baby.

Evangeline surprised herself by saying, "I'm planning to be in the States soon. Would you mind if I dropped by Detroit so we can work this song face-to-face?"

"That would be killer. When?"

"I'm not sure exactly. I'll call you. I have a stop to make first. In Dallas."

Matt didn't love her—and she'd almost accepted that— but she didn't want her child to grow up without knowing its family. Her baby deserved to know his or her father. Grandparents. Uncle and aunts. Her child wouldn't have to suffer crushing loneliness its whole life. Like she had.

But none of that was going to happen if she hid in Europe forever.

Pregnancy hormones, or maybe just sheer disappointment in herself and in Matt for not being what she wanted, had driven her to make a rash decision she now regretted. What else had she categorically rejected before it could reject her?

She had to figure out a way to be a coparent with Matt, no matter how much he'd hurt her. Her baby needed her to be brave. She had to go to Dallas and forge a relationship with her child's family. She and Matt *were* getting a family together; it just wasn't going to happen the way she'd have liked. Somehow, she'd make it work, no matter where she ended up living.

The flight to Dallas was miserable. Two layovers, one delayed flight and a near-morning-sickness-mishap in the aisle of first class later, Evangeline plunked down in a cab and handed the driver Francis and Andrew Wheeler's address. When Matt had shoved it at her with instructions to mail any legal documents to his attention there, she'd never expected to use it personally.

When the cab stopped, her breath caught. The Wheelers' house was exactly what she'd envisioned. Welcoming. Homey. Located in a quiet, stately neighborhood she'd have no problem allowing the baby to run free through.

A pretty middle-aged woman answered her knock. Matt had inherited his mother's blue eyes and blond hair. The older woman's shocked gaze reminded her an awful lot of Matt's face when she'd handed him the pregnancy test.

"Hello," Evangeline said. "We haven't met but—"

"Matthew's not here."

"Oh. You recognize me." That had not been the greeting she'd expected. Actually, she hadn't known what to expect.

"Of course. You're the mother of my grandchild."

Not Eva. Not Evangeline. But something else entirely— part of a family. She took it as a sign that she'd made the right decision in coming here.

"I am."

Obviously Matt had told everyone about the baby.

Matt's mother blinked and her smile warmed. "And I'm terribly rude. I'm Fran. Please come in. You must be exhausted from your flight. May I call you Evangeline? I'm very happy to meet you."

Fran ushered her inside, chattering as if they'd met years

ago instead of minutes. The Wheeler household engulfed her
the moment she stepped into the foyer. Warm, rich creams
and teals tastefully accented the formal living room, but it
didn't feel stuffy. Framed photographs lined the mantel of
a large fireplace. All the pictures contained smiling people, clustered together as if they couldn't get close enough.

A family lived here.

"Your home is beautiful. I see where Matt gets his taste."

The older woman shot her a puzzled glance. "Thank you.
You call him Matt? And he lets you?"

"Is that unusual?" Evangeline perched on the edge of the
sofa and Fran joined her.

"He hates that nickname. Always has. Says it sounds
too much like a frat boy with a skateboard under his arm."
Fran patted her arm. "I like you already. Anyone who can
unstarch my son is a friend of mine."

Matt starched? Evangeline laughed involuntarily. If only
Fran knew how unstarched her son could truly be.

"I hope we can be friends. I'm actually glad Matt's not
here. I came to see you."

"You did?"

She had no idea how much Matt had told his parents, but
the relationship between her and Fran could and should last
a very long time.

"I did a selfish thing by taking off to Monte Carlo. Matt
hurt me, and I used that as an excuse to keep everyone away
from my baby. But I want you, and all of Matt's family, to
be a part of the baby's life. It's very important to me."

Fran's eyes lit up, just like Matt's did when he was happy.
"I'd like that, too. I'd like it better if my grandchild's parents were married. But I promise that's all I'll say to interfere with what my son has clearly informed me is not my
business."

So maybe he had told her everything. Having that kind
of bond with a mother—she couldn't fathom it. This woman
had shaped Matt, instilling in him many wonderful quali-

ties. And most of them were outside of the kitchen. His depth, his sense of commitment, his patience and kindness. All products of his relationship with his family.

Having roots allowed for magnificent things to grow. She wanted that for her baby, but recognized that *she* had to make it happen by sticking around and creating the connections. Maybe she'd open herself to being hurt. And maybe this family would welcome her.

"Marriage was one of the many areas where we disagreed," Evangeline admitted readily. "But I'm here because I realized I was wrong about a few of them. For example, I'm willing to reevaluate my stance on living in Europe."

"Well, that's a relief. It's a shame Matthew's not here so you can tell him personally. I think he'd be very interested in where else you might compromise. Ironically, you just missed him."

She should talk to Matt. No matter how hard it might be. They were going to be parents, whether she wished they could be more or not.

"Do you mind if I wait?"

Fran smiled. "You might be waiting a long time. He flew to Monte Carlo this morning."

Apparently Matthew *was* going to chase Evangeline around the globe.

He'd done everything short of walking up and down Rue Grimaldi yelling Evangeline's name in order to find her. Vincenzo hadn't realized she'd left Monte Carlo, and his cousin shook her head and said, "Sorry, *cara*. She said *ciao* and nothing else."

Frustrated and quite sick of airports, Matthew slumped against the seat of the final vehicle in a long series of shuttles from place to place to place—a water taxi. He needed to regroup, and what better place to figure out what the hell he was doing than Venice?

Palazzo D'Inverno provided the only bit of sanity he'd experienced in forever.

Matthew tipped the driver and clambered up the dock to the water entrance of his house. The palazzo was the only permanent thing in his life, the only thing he actually owned. Coming here had been a gamble. Evangeline had infiltrated this house, and the memories were likely to be vicious.

When he swung open the door, the quiet hush of peace washed over him. Everything was exactly as he'd left it. The piano stood silently in the corner, draped for protection against lack of use. The U of couches faced the balcony overlooking the Grand Canal. Frescos kept watch from the ceiling, the scenes frozen in time for eternity.

The sense of freedom, as if he could do or be anything he wanted was exactly the same, too.

But that probably had to do with the woman standing by the glass, framed by the grandeur of Venice.

"I was starting to think you'd never get here," Evangeline said, and smiled, punching him straight in the gut. Like always.

Evangeline was in Venice. Inside Palazzo D'Inverno, filling his house with her light. What did that smile mean? Was she buttering him up before she handed over the papers detailing the custody arrangement she hoped to talk him into?

"What are you doing here?"

It was far less than he'd like to say. But far more than his suddenly tight throat should have been able to voice.

"Vincenzo caught me at Heathrow. I changed my connecting flight and voila. Here I am."

Which told him not one blessed thing about her intentions. He hated not knowing exactly where she'd been, where she wanted to go, what she was planning, what she was feeling. Once, he would have known instinctively, would have gleaned a hundred nuances from the vibe between them without a word exchanged.

He missed it. He wanted it back.

"How did you know this was where I would end up?"

His voice broke. She was beautiful—radiant like the Madonna with child. Like Evangeline with his child. There was nothing in Dallas, nothing anywhere in the world worth more. Exactly how stupid was he for not realizing that before screwing up everything?

Was she still in love with him? Or had he ruined that, too?

His stomach pitched. Well, he'd just have to convince her to forgive him for being such a shortsighted moron. Negotiation was his best skill.

She shrugged and crossed the room, stopping short of invading his space, likely because he'd given no indication of whether he'd welcome her. "Lucky guess."

Or maybe something else had whispered his destination to her, something unexplainable and incomprehensible. But still real.

"I was coming to you. In Monte Carlo," he said.

"I know. Your mother told me."

Matthew shook his head. Evangeline scrambled his wits. "My mother?"

"I went to Dallas." Her eyes filled. "Matt, I don't want to cut our baby off from you. Or from your family. I was selfish and stupid. Apologies were in order, all the way around, starting with your mother. Ending with you. I'm sorry. I want you to have a relationship with our baby that's more than holidays and birthday cards once a year."

"Oh." Disappointment wrenched his battered heart. What had he expected, that she'd miraculously decided to give him another chance when he'd plainly told her he had nothing to give? "I'm the one who should apologize. I'm sorry, too. So how do you envision a relationship between me and the baby if you're living in Europe?"

"I'm not going to live in Europe. I called my sister. We talked, and she's going to record some songs that I wrote. I never liked the idea of giving my words to Sara Lear. But

Lisa, that's a different story. It'll be a great partnership. I'm going to stay in the States so we can work together."

Pride filled him. She'd found her way after all. "That's fantastic. Why did you fly all the way to Dallas to apologize in person?"

"Well, I was planning to go from Dallas to Detroit. It made sense in the mixed-up files of my pregnant brain."

He contemplated her slight form. "But you're here. Not Detroit."

"A funny thing happened when I got to Dallas. You weren't there. You went to Monte Carlo. I have to know why."

"Evangeline…" He hesitated, unsure how to undo all the damage he'd done the first time by trying to follow rules that made no sense for the man he'd become. But there were no rules in Palazzo D'Inverno. So he said what was in his heart.

"When I got to Dallas, it took about five minutes to know I was still in the valley. And when I looked up, I realized I couldn't get to the top of the mountain unless I had someone with wings to fly me there."

"Me?" she whispered.

He nodded. "Please, please forgive me for all the stupid things I said before. I can't be me without you. I love you."

Tears streamed down her face. "Really?"

"Really." He bridged the gap, drawing her into his arms, and she fell against him, clutching at his shoulders. Warm, light-filled Evangeline was in his arms. "I was the selfish one. Clinging to the past when I had the future right here the whole time."

"I don't understand. You said you weren't ready for that."

"I'm not." Who could ever be ready for someone uninhibited, wild and perfect like Evangeline? "To compensate, I refused to put myself in the position of letting my emotions get the better of me again. The problem with that, of course, is that it was too late. I was already in love with you."

The denial burst from her and he closed her lips with his fingertip.

"Shh. It's true. Amber was an integral part of my life for a long time, and when she died, it was like a car losing an engine. One can't function without the other. But I was never a car to you, and because of that, we fit differently. I couldn't see that until I went home and tried to be a car again."

"Are you saying you don't want to be a car anymore? Or are you trying to talk me into buying one?"

He laughed, shocked at the quaver in it. "I'm saying you were right. I can't pick up the reins of my old life and I don't want to. I want to find a new direction with you and our baby. Wherever the wind blows us. I went to Monte Carlo to tell you that."

Hope spread across her face.

"I want to believe you," she said cautiously. "But I trusted you, and you smashed my heart all to pieces. I can't be a replacement for your wife. How do I know you're really over her?"

"I don't want a replacement. Amber was only one color, and that was right for me before. You're all the colors of the rainbow. It's tattooed on you permanently because that's who you'll always be to me."

Her eyelids dropped for a beat, and when she opened them again, the soft brown sucked him under. "How do you always know the right thing to say?"

Because he'd learned that the right thing had context. The right thing wasn't always the same from day to day, and sometimes you had to do what was right for the person you were at that moment.

He grinned. "Several transatlantic flights in a row give you lots of time to think."

"What do you want? Did you come loaded down with a ring and a fancy marriage proposal?"

The pain in her voice tried and convicted him. He'd hurt

her, and saying the right thing wasn't nearly enough to make up for it.

"No." He'd gone against the very fiber of his being and come here empty-handed. "This time we're doing things according to your schedule. I'll follow you wherever you go, whether we've got a piece of paper calling us husband and wife or not. I will never again utter the word *marriage* until you flat out say that's what you want."

"Your mother will be upset."

Obviously Mama had treated Evangeline to an earful of the Fran Wheeler Sermon on the Merits of Marriage. Hopefully it hadn't stacked up Evangeline's disfavor against him any higher.

"She'll get over it. This is about us and what we want."

"And you don't want to marry me."

"On the contrary. Nothing would make me happier than to claim you as my wife before God and everybody. But it's your choice. Our relationship will be how you define it."

Amber had been his wife; that role fit her and what they'd shared. Evangeline was something else and fit the man he was now. The harder he tried to pin her down, the harder she'd flap her wings to escape. And he wanted her to be free to fly, as long as she waited for him to catch up.

A shrewd glint in her eye set off a frisson of nerves. "What if I wanted to live in Dallas? What would you say?"

"I'd say who are you, and what have you done with the woman I love?"

Her gravelly laugh clawed through his stomach with heat he'd missed. "My name is Evangeline La Fleur. And your name is?"

The best question of all and the easiest to answer. "Matt. My name is Matt."

"Nice to meet you, Matt." She shook his hand solemnly. "That's a nice name. I like it. You know the funny thing about names? They change. You think you're this person, the one the name refers to, and then all of a sudden, you have to redefine yourself."

"And with it comes a new name," he said.

That ripple of understanding passed between them, as strong as it had from the first. Finally, finally, the knot of tension at the base of his skull unwound, and he started to believe he'd leave the valley and crest the mountain with her by his side after all.

"So," he continued. "I'm getting a picture in my head of you living in Dallas. What else should I add to this picture? Will you be living by yourself? Or might I convince you to stay with me?"

A deep smile spread across her face. "You're pretty good at convincing me to stay. I'll give you that. If I stay with you, do I get my own room?"

"Nope. The baby gets his or her own room, but you have to share with me, whether we have a marriage license or not. See, I don't need a replacement wife, but I do need a lover. I seem to have an addiction to inventive positions. And locations, apparently, because I'm envisioning a very sturdy table in the kitchen. And maybe a screened-in porch. A large shower is a must, as well. Sound like something you might consider?"

Say yes. He'd be happy to throw in some begging if it turned the tide.

She shook her head. "You're crazy. I like that."

Crazy. Yes, he was. But only because he'd fallen in love with a woman who allowed him to be and feel and do whatever he wanted.

"Please tell me I haven't totally screwed up things between us. I'm open to discussion on how we'll raise the baby, and I don't care where we live. We can stay here in Venice if you want. I love you and want to be with you the rest of my life, wherever you are, whether we have a marriage license or not."

Her eyes grew misty. "That was the most romantic non-proposal I've ever heard."

"Is that a yes?"

"Not yet. I wasn't done with my apology. I'm sorry I was so stubborn. Before. I never should have tried to force you to heal my way or discounted the idea of living where you wanted to. I've been pretty selfish for a long time, excusing it because I'd lost something important. Important, but not crucial. I can't sing but I haven't lost my voice."

"Of course you haven't. You're *my* voice. You articulate the things in my soul far better than I could."

"Geez." Her lids flew closed and she swallowed heavily. When she met his gaze once more, the powerful connection swept through him again. "I was already going to say yes. But if you want to say some more romantic things, I'm all ears."

His heart took flight. "You were? What swayed you, the sturdy kitchen table or me finally gathering enough wits to tell you I love you?"

"The fact that you flew to Monte Carlo. The rest was nice to hear, though. I came to Venice to tell you I wasn't letting you go again, by the way."

He couldn't help but laugh. They'd chased each other around the globe. "I told you, I'll follow you anywhere."

"Then start walking." She turned and flounced up the stairs, hips swinging saucily. Halfway up, she called over her shoulder, "I'll be naked on the bed, thinking about how much I love you. I'm dying to see what you're going to do first."

Matt was pretty curious too and raced up the stairs to find out what two healed souls could become to each other.

Epilogue

Evangeline shoved the Murano glass bowl directly into the center of the art niche outside the baby's room. Much better. Decorating the home she and Matt had bought—together—down the street from his parents' turned out to be the most fun she'd ever had. Who knew?

Fran came out of the nursery. "Carlos tacked up the border. Do you want to check out the placement before I have him glue it down?"

Matt's mother had taken on the role of Contractor Supervisor and ruled the workers with an iron fist covered in lace. The two women became friends instantly, and Evangeline fell into the habit of consulting the older woman on just about everything. Fran knew color and style and had fantastic taste.

Since Evangeline had never created a home from scratch, the partnership worked beautifully—as long as neither of them mentioned the word *marriage*. She and Fran had politely agreed to disagree about the status of Evangeline's relationship with Matt.

"I'm sure the border is fine, but I do want to see it." Evangeline stepped into the explosion of red, white and blue, the color scheme she'd chosen for her son's room. The border looked perfect. Once the walls were finished, they could start arranging the room to welcome the highly anticipated arrival of Matthew Wheeler Jr., which frankly, couldn't occur fast enough.

She couldn't wait to see Matt's gorgeous eyes peeking out from her child's face. But she'd have to, because she wasn't due for twenty-two very long weeks. The ultrasound the doctor performed yesterday had confirmed both gender and delivery date. The little blob on the monitor was the most beautiful thing she'd ever seen.

"Andy's still out of town," Fran remarked after Evangeline had given Carlos the okay. "Would you like to have dinner with me and Cia? The boys can fend for themselves for once."

"Thanks, that would be lovely, but I have plans with Matt. Special plans."

"Next time then." Fran smiled and turned her Southern charm on Carlos to get his help with dragging the rocker into a corner.

The ladies spent a few hours in decorating heaven until Matt strolled through the door from work, his smile for Evangeline alone.

"I'll make myself scarce." Fran winked, clearly having interpreted the definition of "special plans" in her own way, and let herself out the door.

Evangeline forgot to be embarrassed as Matt folded her into his arms.

"Hey."

"Hey, yourself." God, he smelled good, like home. Home—simple and achingly honest, and she'd never loved something so much. Roots with Matt had grown strong and solid. "Sell anything?"

"Lucas closed the deal on the Watson property. Especially sweet since I yanked it out from under Richards Group without them realizing it." His grin fluttered her stomach.

He was so happy to be working with his brother again. And she was happy she'd agreed to live in Dallas so he could. Palazzo D'Inverno waited patiently for them to return, which they planned to do after the baby was born.

"I confirmed with Lisa," Evangeline said. "She'll be here next week to start learning the new songs I wrote."

"Great. I'm looking forward to seeing her again."

Evangeline had gone to Detroit twice already, Matt firmly by her side as she worked through reconciling with her dad. Family dynamics were still new and often frustrating, but she was trying. Matt assured her that was the important thing.

"You know what today is, right?" she asked.

A guarded expression leaped onto his face. "That sounds dangerous. Is this one of those rhetorical questions that I'm already supposed to know the answer to?"

She laughed. "I'll assume that means you don't. Four months ago today, I walked into Vincenzo's palazzo, praying that no one would recognize me. I even wore a mask to ensure it, but there was this guy in the hall blocking my way. If I'd arrived one minute later, he'd have already been gone."

Matt's arms tightened, smushing her softly rounded belly into his solid body. "Sounds like fate to me."

"Absolutely. How else would I have found the one person who recognized me with a mask on?"

She tilted her head up to kiss him lightly, and lost her train of thought as he cupped her jaw to deepen the kiss.

Fate. If she still had functioning vocal cords, they'd never have met. The center of her existence had been ripped from her fingers, but its loss had made room for this man and their family. Thank goodness the fire of tragedy had refined her into someone worthy of Matt's unending devotion.

With a squeak, she broke the kiss. Reluctantly. "Let's get back to that in a sec. I got you something to commemorate our anniversary."

"You did?" He lit up. "I like your presents. The last one will be hard to top, though."

His warm hand spread over their baby, safely tucked inside her womb. "Maybe. I gave it a shot. You'll have to tell me how I did. It's in the kitchen."

She clasped his hand and led him into the kitchen he'd designed from the ground up, with dark cabinets and top-of-the-line appliances. He never minded when she invaded his domain but threatened her daily that if she hung around while he was cooking, she'd better learn something. So far, nothing had sunk in because she was too busy watching the chef's butt as he moved between the stove and the prep area.

A small bag sat on the island. Snagging it, she handed it to him. "It's an armadillo."

"A what?" One eye narrowed. "You put an armadillo in this bag?"

"Yeah. There's this thing that I need to be rescued from. So I'm calling armadillo."

With a puzzled glance at her, Matt tipped the bag up and slid the contents into his hand. She plucked the box from his palm and cracked the hinged lid to reveal a platinum band inside.

"Rescue me from being single. Will you marry me?"

His eyes went so dark with pleasure, her heart fluttered. "Nothing would make me happier. What prompted this?"

"I find myself in need of another name change." Evangeline Wheeler—another role she had no idea how to perform but couldn't wait to figure out. "This time, I'd like it to be permanent. I can't risk letting that guy from the hall get away."

And he'd promised to never again push her into a corner and demand she do something she wasn't ready for. No rules. No expectations. The decision had to be hers. She loved that about him.

"Are you sure this is what you want?" His beautiful

crystalline-blue eyes sought hers and held, hope and love shining from their depths.

She nodded. "I thought I wandered in search of fulfillment, but I was really looking for you. I love you so much. Be my armadillo."

He grinned and pulled her into his firm, safe arms. "As funny as you've been walking lately, you should be the armadillo."

"Nice. You're the one who put me in this condition. I was busy trying to soak up the Venice view, but no. You had to go and look at me like you wanted to swallow me whole." Wicked heat sizzled through his expression and arrowed straight to her girl parts. She sighed, but it came out sounding happy and content. "Yeah. Like that. I love it when you get that look."

"And I love it that we do everything out of order. I'll buy you an engagement ring tomorrow," he promised.

And then he kissed her.

* * * * *

DEVOURED

CATHRYN FOX

This one is for you, Sylvie Howick. Thank you for all you do for me. You are a gem.

CHAPTER ONE

Peyton

"Where the heck is he?"

I mumble curses under my breath as I pace around my condo, weaving around packed boxes that are ready to be shipped to Malta first thing tomorrow morning, right before I jump on board my brother's Learjet and get flown to the island myself.

"You talking to me?" my best friend Carly asks.

I spin as she comes into the room with a glass of white wine and unceremoniously flops onto the buttery-yellow sofa. I'm going to miss Carly. I'm going to miss that sofa. Heck, I'm going to miss New York, too, but my dream job of teaching English to young students in Europe calls—and I'm eager to answer.

A bubble of excitement wells up inside me as I envision myself in the modern school located in the quiet community of St. Julian's, standing before a bevy of eager minds ready to learn a new language. Thank God, I studied Italian in college, as well as

Spanish, otherwise this opportunity never would have presented itself.

While I'm thrilled that I'm one of two candidates being considered for the full-time position, leaving my friends, my brother Cason and Londyn, his new wife, and everything else I love won't be easy. Leaving is never easy—that's something I know first-hand. But I'm only a flight away, and I'll have a place to come back to since Carly will be taking over the lease on my downtown condo while I'm in the Mediterranean for the next month, and hopefully longer. But that's going to depend on numerous things…

"No. I'm talking to myself. My 'husband'—" I pause to do air quotes around the word "—is not here yet. He's close to an hour late for our introductory date."

She crinkles her nose. "That's not a great way to start a marriage."

I snort at that. "You're right, it's not." Then again, having my brother choose a pretend husband for me, using the Penn Pals dating app he created when he was an undergraduate at Penn State, is no way to start a marriage, either. Not that we'll end up together in matrimonial bliss. Nope. Not happening. This girl is not setting herself up for that kind of disaster. If there's one thing I learned while being tossed around in the system, it's that I'm not a keeper. If I were, I probably wouldn't have lived in ten different foster homes in the span of five years. I just hope I'm compatible with whoever Cason chooses. We'll be living together in close quarters, and it'd be horrible if we didn't at least *like* each other.

"Is that what you're wearing to dinner?" Carly asks, her blue eyes tracking down my body as she cradles her wineglass like it's a treasured heirloom.

My pulse jumps as I glance at the snug black cocktail dress that's been sitting in the back of my closet for a year. I don't even remember the last time I had a need to wear it, but thought it would be perfect for tonight. "Why, what's wrong with it?"

She grins and twirls a strand of her hair around her finger. "Just that you look hot in that little number, and you don't want this guy to fall in love with you, do you?"

"Please," I say. "Tonight's dinner is so we can get to know each other and talk logistics. This arrangement isn't about love. It's about securing a full-time teaching job for me, and for him, it's about getting a big chunk of money for helping me get it."

I pull the tube of bright red lipstick that Londyn gave me from my purse and swipe the creamy, hydrating wax over my lips.

I turn to face Carly, anxiety welling up inside me when I check the clock for the millionth time. "What if he doesn't show? What if he changed his mind?"

"With the amount of money you're paying him, he'd be crazy not to show, and spending time with you..." She pauses to look me over again. "That's no hardship for any man, my friend." She snaps her fingers. "I also think you should exercise your matrimonial rights and get it, gurl."

I chuckle. "It won't be like that, Carly. We won't be having sex." Like I even know what sex is anymore…or ever. My days have been busy teaching at the local elementary school and I've been falling asleep at night while filling out forms for this new job. Truthfully, the last time I had sex was in college, and that fumbling experience left me cold and underwhelmed. I've pretty much blocked it from my mind and have been flying solo since.

There is, however, one thing—one man—I wish I could exorcise from my brain. But no, the kiss I shared with Roman Bianchi, my brother's best friend, still pings around inside my head like a runaway pinball, and that, my friends, is something I wish I could change. I try. Believe me, I try. But when I'm alone in my bed, my body stubbornly aware of how excruciatingly delicious it was to have his lips pressed against mine, a possessive claiming of my mouth that left me shaken and overly stimulated, I can't help but think back… Then he broke it off abruptly and laughed as he walked away. If his goal was to get me to hate him, he succeeded. He also succeeded in ripping my pride to shreds and reminding me I'm not lovable.

Stupid jerk.

"I need to call Cason," I say. "I pray my brother has a backup plan just in case the guy gets cold feet."

"I love that color lipstick on you, by the way," Carly says. "It goes nice with your auburn hair."

I grin. "Londyn gave it to me the night Cason proposed to her. She said it has aphrodisiac powers." A snicker full of disbelief rises up in my throat. "I seriously doubt that."

She glances at me over the top of her wineglass. "Hmm…"

"What?"

"You say you don't believe it, yet here you are applying a generous amount to your lips, anyway." Her grin is slow. "I wonder what Freud would say."

Seriously?

Could I subconsciously be hoping it works? Subconsciously hoping to entice my pretend husband, because I'd like to have one good sexual experience in my life?

Nah.

"You're a psychologist." I recap the lipstick, toss it into my purse and fish out my phone. "You think everything is a Freudian slip."

She reaches for the remote. "Probably because it is."

I laugh at that, and just as I'm about to call my brother, someone raps on the door. My heart jumps into my throat and I spin.

"He's here."

Why the heck am I suddenly so nervous? I give myself a once-over in the mirror and smooth my hand over my long auburn curls. Should I have put my hair up? Maybe spent a little more time styling it? God, what am I doing? This isn't a real date. This is just two people who are going to be spending time together, pretending to be married, getting the first meeting out of the way. During our flight tomorrow, we'll have lots of time to work out the kinks... I mean details. Yeah, details. That's what I mean, and *kink* was not a ridiculous Freudian slip. Not at all.

I don't think.

"Are you going to answer the door?" Carly asks, and I take in her grin. I have no idea why she thinks this is anything more than an arrangement. It's not.

I drop my phone back into my purse, and with a big smile on my face, I swing the door open. But as soon as I see the tall figure invading my front stoop, my jaw falls open, all pretense of happiness dissolving as I set eyes on none other than the big stupid jerk himself.

"What...what are you doing here, Roman?" I ask and try to glance around him, to see if my pretend husband is on his way, but his big, dumb body and impressive height fill my doorway and block everything else out—even the gigantic full moon.

"Well, hello to you, too, Peyton."

I take a fast breath, but my lungs are tight, constricted. "Why are you here?" I ask, and hate that I sound like a damn chipmunk jacked up on Red Bull.

His dark gaze moves over my face and slips lower to take in my dress, and goddammit, my traitorous body warms in all the wrong places. This is the man who kissed me and then laughed in my face. Sure, we were at Sebastian and Rylee's wedding, and the champagne had been flowing, but who does something like that? Who stares at me all night, turning my blood to molten lava, then plants the hottest, sexiest kiss on my lips, and walks away laughing?

A stupid jerk, that's who.

I give him a once-over. It's been a year since I set eyes on him, and I'm not sure how it's possible but this updated version of the man I hate is filling me with unwanted images—of him slipping between my thighs and bringing me to orgasm. My sex clenches, an impatient reminder that I crave being touched—properly, just once—and standing before me is a delicious specimen who undoubtedly knows his way around a woman's body.

You hate him, remember?

I shut down my overstimulated imagination and take in the tightness of his jaw, the rigid set of his muscles when he says, "I'm here to take you on a date and get to know you."

I stand there immobilized, my lungs void of air as his words sink into my rattled brain. "Surely to God you're not—"

"Your pretend husband?" He arches a brow. "Yeah, that's me, and I apologize for being late," he says, not looking one bit sorry at all. In fact, he looks completely pissed off, like he doesn't like this situation any more than I do. "There was an issue."

"An issue!" I say, my voice bordering on hysteria. "I'll say there's an issue."

"Well, this just became interesting," Carly mumbles under her breath as she turns the TV off and slips into the other room.

Interesting?

It's anything but interesting. It's a damn disaster. No way am I flying to Malta with Roman Bianchi and pretending to be married to him. I can't stand the man. In fact, I hate everything about him. Except his face. Yeah, I don't really hate that. And his body. That's pretty banging, too. But his tailor-made suit, yeah, I hate that. I just don't hate the way it highlights his broad shoulders and tight muscles, and reminds me my battery-operated boyfriend hasn't been cutting it for some time now.

Good lord, Peyton. Get it together.

I close my eyes tight, hoping when I open them again he'll be gone, his presence nothing but a figment of my imagination, but *nooooo*, when my lids snap open he's still standing there, his gaze latched on mine. I swear to God, in the nanosecond I had my eyes closed, the man grew taller, broader…hotter.

"I take it your brother never told you he asked me."

My gaze narrows on him. "This can't be happening."

I go for my phone again. "I need to call Cason. There must be a mix-up." I shake my head. "Why would he ask you?"

"Because I'm one of his best friends and he's completely overprotective of you," he says, something warm and personal in his voice as he speaks about my brother. "Trust doesn't come easily to Cason and he knows I'd never mess with his kid sister."

His words are combustible, like a spark to tinder, and it fuels the anger in my blood. "I'm a grown woman. I don't need my brother coddling me, and for God's sake I can mess with whoever I want."

"Are you saying you want to sleep with me, Peyton?"

"No," I say quickly, maybe too quickly, judging by the smirk on his face. "I don't even like you."

"Good, because I don't want to sleep with you, either." He scrubs his face, and I catch the flash of anguish in his eyes before he blinks it away. "In fact, I'm done with women," he mumbles under his breath. "Another reason Cason trusts me with you."

My body stiffens, and for one split second, my heart goes out to him, the hate inside me momentarily evaporating, making room for sorrow to fill the void. I might not like him, but that doesn't mean I don't have compassion or care about his well-being. Two years ago, his fiancée up and left weeks before the wedding. My heart squeezes. I can't imagine how awful, how excruciatingly painful, that was for him.

He kissed you, laughed and walked away, Peyton.

Anger flares bright at that brutal reminder, and I turn my focus to my phone. I'm about to punch in Cason's number when Roman's big hand closes over mine to stop me, his touch sending sparks of sensation through my body.

"He asked me to do this, so I'm doing it." He pauses, and I almost flinch at the seriousness in his face when he adds, "I'm not about to let him down."

No, I'm the only Harrison you don't mind letting down.

"We're doing this, Peyton," he says, his voice firm, businesslike.

I hate the tension in my body, the way it comes alive the second he's in the vicinity. My nipples tighten in betrayal, revealing my arousal, and I pray to God he can't see what he's doing to me.

"No, you obviously don't want to do this," I say through clenched teeth. "I'll get someone else." His thumb brushes the inside of my wrist, a gentle sweep that I'm not sure he's aware he's doing. Heated memories of the hungry kiss we shared come back in a sensual rush. As illicit images dance in my mind's eye, the visual caress teases and torments the needy spot between my legs.

"Whether I want to or not is not the point," he responds bluntly.

"I'll call Cason," I say, and squeeze my thighs together in an effort to subdue the heat in my body, but I'd have more luck stopping a runaway train with my pinkie finger. "We'll find someone else through the app. I'm sure there are plenty of other guys willing to help in exchange for cash."

"Maybe so, but Cason won't allow them." His head dips, and while his breath is soft against my face, it's like a tangible caress to my needy cleft. "You know I'm right. I'm all you got, Peyton, and we're doing this."

Anger and desire war with each other as I stare up at the man I hate. My traitorous body remains hot and achy from the way his hand is still holding mine, but I know there's one thing I'll never have to worry about with Roman Bianchi.

Him falling for me.

"Fine then." I snatch my purse from the hallway table. "Let's go to dinner and work out the kinks."

"Kinks?"

His brow arches and I give a fast shake of my head. "Details. I meant to say details."

Fuck my life.

CHAPTER TWO

Roman

"WE COULD HAVE taken Cason's plane," Peyton says, her lips turned down at the corners, a pouty little frown that shouldn't arouse me, yet somehow does. Christ, how she makes that petulant look sexy is beyond me, and don't even get me started on her yoga pants and T-shirt with *Save the Bees* emblazoned across the front. She always was an activist for any kind of wildlife at risk. "It was all fueled up, ready and waiting for us this morning."

"Now why would I tie up Cason's plane when I have a perfectly good plane of my own?" I ask as she drops into the light tan leather bucket seat beside me and crosses her arms in a defensive move. She's either being very protective of herself, or she's trying to hide the way her lovely, lush nipples are poking against her thin, summery T-shirt, compliments of the cold air flowing in from the overhead vent. Or maybe they're hard for a different reason. I'm not sure, but either way my tongue would love to spend some serious time on her body, trying to find out.

Don't go there, Roman.

Jesus, the last thing I should be thinking about is Peyton's gorgeous curves, or how everything about her kept me wide-awake last night, my cock hard and needy as visions of her in my bed—my mouth and hands on her delicate skin, devouring every delectable inch of her—filled my thoughts.

Simply put, she used to be Cason's kid sister. Until she wasn't. Now, well, now she's all grown up, with big green eyes and that mess of curly red hair that drives me mad. It's all I can do not to grab a fistful, tug it until her mouth is poised open and kiss the living hell out of her.

Shit.

She goes quiet as we settle in, making a show of dragging a magazine from her big bag and dropping it on her lap as the plane makes its way down the runway. Her silence is a welcome reprieve. But I won't think, not even for one minute, that she'll be quiet for the whole flight. Last night over dinner, she raked me over the coals, nonstop. Christ, she grilled me on everything, and by the time I dropped her off at her condo, I sported more char marks than the porterhouse steak I'd ordered.

The hum of the engine at full throttle fills the cabin, and the second the plane levels off I settle back with my tablet, ready to do some reading and a bit of work on the long flight ahead of us. I blink at the stream of letters before me yet can't quite seem to focus. I shift and lift my head when I can feel Peyton's laser-sharp glare burning a hole in my forehead. Jesus, if this plane had an emergency eject seat, and she was near the button, I'd be catapulting through space—violently. Not that I blame her for hating me. It's what I need from her.

"What now?" I ask, and set my tablet on my lap, realizing just how tightly it was clenched in my hand. I stretch out my fingers to circulate my blood and brace myself for impact when Peyton uncurls her fingers from her magazine and sets it aside with a calmness that belies the fire in her eyes.

Never one to disappoint, she glares at me and asks, "Why are you doing this, anyway?" Her gaze narrows, like a bird of prey ready to move in for the kill. A burst of icy air from the overhead vent rustles her long curls and does little to cool the heat building inside me.

I pinch the bridge of my nose, desperate to keep this about business. "Would you like a drink?" I ask, needing one, two or maybe even ten before she begins her interrogation again.

"No, well, yes." She flips her palm over, a gesture I've gotten used to over the years. "But I want answers first." Her tenaciousness is something I've gotten used to as well. I can't say that I dislike her determination and conviction. She has a resolve few do and won't stop until she's satisfied.

Shit, don't think about all the ways you can satisfy her, Roman.

Dammit, I'm thinking about it.

"We've been over this, Peyton. I told you last night, numerous times. I'm helping out a friend. My *best* friend. End of story. I'm not sure what else you think this is."

"I know you and Cason go way back, but this… this is going above and beyond friendship, in my book."

"Not in mine."

"All right then," she says, and I prepare for a change in tactics. "But agreeing to this whole charade after…" She arches a brow without elaborating. Not that she needs to. We both know she's talking about the kiss I never should have initiated—then stalked off like a complete asshole afterward. The heated memory burns brightly in my brain and continues to taunt my dick.

I'll never forget that warm summer night in the Hamptons during a friend's wedding. I could have easily taken her upstairs to my hotel room, where we would have done depraved things to each other, things that my best friend never would have forgiven me for. Thank God someone from the wedding party bumped me from behind before we were spotted making out in the corner like a couple hormonal teens, and my one working brain cell kicked some sense back into my balls seconds before I threw her over my shoulder and carried her out of the ballroom—caveman style.

"I'm helping a friend out," I reiterate for the millionth time.

"I mean, I know you're getting paid. It just seems

a bit much," she adds, and pulls a tube of lipstick from her purse. She smacks her lips together and my gaze drops. How the hell am I going to make it through this plane ride when she does things like that? Her innocent sexuality is going to be the death of me. "The air is dry up here," she explains as she removes the cap and rolls out the lipstick.

"Yeah, dry," I agree. "And it's not about the money," I say. The truth is, I'm not getting paid—I'm a goddamn millionaire and don't need her or her brother's money—but it's best I let her believe I'm getting compensated. She can't wrap her brain around me doing this favor for Cason as it is.

Is this really all about Cason?

Hell yeah, it is. It has to be. I can't be doing this because I want to spend time with her. I'm not a goddamn masochist.

"I expected some unemployed college student desperate for money, not a...a grown man, who's practically Italian royalty at that, with a steady career." Her lips part and thin, as she layers the creamy pigment over her luscious mouth, and I swallow the groan of want threatening to crawl out of my throat. "Can you see why this confuses me, Roman?"

Sweet mother of God. After last night, I was hoping I'd never see that fuck-me-red color on her lips again.

Do not think about her luscious painted lips parting for your cock, dude.

Dammit, I'm thinking about it.

My dick stands up, clamoring for a front-row seat

as that welcome—or rather unwelcome—image plays out in my mind's eye. Yeah, no, it's welcome.

I swallow, and shift to hide my erection. "He's just always been there for me, okay?"

I went to Penn State to get away from my overbearing Italian family. New to America, and a fresh-faced kid on campus, the change of scenery was all a bit intimidating. Cason was there though, my friend, my roommate, the guy who took me under his wing and brought me into his tribe. A guy who'd been kicked around his entire life, he knew firsthand what it was like to be excluded and made sure every damn newbie felt wanted. After college, I chose to live in New York and took the position of head web developer when Cason created Hard Wear—an online clothing business that caters to men.

"My family is in Sicily, remember?" I say, playing the ace that had been in my pocket.

"Yeah, I know."

"Malta is just a short ferry ride away, and this is a way for me to go visit them. I haven't been home since—"

My insides go cold as I let my words fall off, but she gets it. I haven't been home since my ex up and left weeks before my wedding. It's been two years, and my sisters still call to check on me—far too much. I tell them I'm fine, and I am, yet they remain intrusive, overbearing, and are always butting into my life—which is why I'm better off in New York where they can't stalk me on a daily basis.

I love them. I truly do, but I'm a grown man who

can make his own decisions. I scoff at that. I'm not even sure getting engaged had been my idea to begin with. One day I'm dating and the next there was talk of a wedding, and I'm pretty sure it was my mother who put Grandmother's ring on my ex's finger—not that it stayed there for any length of time.

"Roman, I'm sorry," she says, her voice thick and sincere. "I don't think I ever told you that." She reaches out and puts her hand on my knee. Her touch sizzles through my body and caresses my cock. I glance down, and suddenly, as if she just realized she was touching me, she snatches her hand back like I might have just given her leprosy. She links her fingers together on her lap.

"Thank you," I say, a canned response even though I do appreciate her words. "It's fine." Her brows lift, her expression dubious, but the truth is, it's not like my ex broke my heart. When she refused to sign the prenup, it confirmed my suspicions. The women in my life want my name and my money; they don't necessarily want me.

"You'll be visiting them?" she asks.

"Yeah," I fib. Hell, I haven't even told them I'm going to Malta. They'd invade our villa within minutes, before we could even unpack. They'd shower Peyton with love, hugs and kisses, and completely smother us both. "But my main reason for this is to help you get the position. I won't let anything interfere with that."

She gives a slow shake of her head. "I'm just not sure you can pull this off," she says, like she's still looking for a way out of this insane arrangement her brother cooked up.

"I can pull it off," I say.

She crinkles up her nose, scrunching the cluster of freckles that have been holding me captive since she grew into a beautiful woman. "You literally just flinched when I touched you."

I give a casual shrug. "You took me by surprise."

"What if I touch you in public? If you react like that people will know we're pretending. We have to present a happy, loving couple." She pushes back into her seat and lets loose a frustrated sigh. Her head falls back, her eyes unfocused on the overhead lighting. "They say the marriage restriction in hiring single female teachers has been lifted, but behind the scenes it's still practiced." The frustration in her voice is palpable and wraps around my chest like a tight belt. "They won't hire an unwed woman, Roman," she adds, her frown deepening.

I lean toward her, my stomach on fire at the unfairness in the world. She wants this job, and goddammit I'll help her burst through that glass ceiling and do whatever it takes for her to get it. No one, and I mean no one, deserves to have their dreams realized more than this woman does.

"That's not fair," I say, my tone just dark enough to have her gaze flying to mine. What, is she surprised that I agree with her?

"You're right. It's not."

"You should get the job on your own merit," I say. "You're smart, one of the smartest women I know.

You're dedicated, and kind, and let me tell you, I've never met any woman wanting to give back to a society that was so cruel to her. If they can't see your value, that's on them." She goes quiet, so quiet worry weaves its way through my body. Shit, maybe I shouldn't have been so blunt when reminding her of her past. "Peyton?"

She blinks, the sound of her swallowing breaking the silence. "Thank you."

I wave my finger back and forth between the two of us. "As for you touching me and me not flinching, I guess we'll have to practice," I say.

"Are you suggesting…" Mimicking my motion, she waves her hand back and forth, her words falling off as her dark lashes fall slowly over alarmed eyes.

"What I'm saying is we'll have to figure out a way not to react when touching each other." Not going to happen. "What did you think I was saying?"

"That." She nods. "That's what I thought you were suggesting. How do we go about that?"

"I'm not sure."

"We'd better figure it out, don't you think? To-morrow we'll be meeting my boss and the other teachers and the person I'm in competition with for the full-time position."

As she rambles, I study her mouth. The woman is sweet and sexy and so goddamn lush, but her never-ending questions and underlying accusations make me want to tie her up and busy her mouth in many other ways. Dirty ways. Delicious ways. Ways that would undoubtedly shock this sweet, young girl and have her pleading for mercy.

Seriously, you wouldn't believe what I'd do, the lengths I'd go to, to see those lush red lips parted, begging me for…anything. It's almost frightening and I have to fight it down with every fiber of my being. I redirect my thoughts to get my damn erection under control. Once my dick is marshalled into submission, I stand and reach over her head.

She flinches and presses herself into the leather seat. "What are you doing?" she asks. But holy Jesus I don't miss the breathlessness in her voice or the way her skin flushed from my closeness. Yeah, okay, it's true, the pull between us is insane, like so far off the charts, it's a nuclear explosion waiting to happen.

But it's not going to happen.

Cason didn't just take me under his wing in college. He's my best friend, the guy who had my back all through college, the guy who took a chance and hired me for a crucial position in his fledgling company and he was there to pick up the pieces when I finally faced the fact that women don't want me for me, they want to marry into my family. Honesty is important and my ex's betrayal gutted me.

Hypocrite much?

Okay, yeah, it's true. I screwed up with Peyton last summer. I can blame it on the romantic atmosphere, the consumption of champagne, and if I try really hard, I can blame it on heartbreak. But the simple truth is this: I wanted Peyton. I wanted her like a drowning man wants a life raft, a thirsty man wants a drink, peanut butter wants jelly.

Yeah. It's bad.

It's really bad.

And now? Well, and now I have to spend the next few weeks in Malta pretending to be her husband, and not exercise any of the rights that go with that.

I adjust the overhead vent. "I'm turning the air off. You're shivering."

"Oh, thanks."

Back in my seat, my gaze seeks out hers and I say, "Seems you need to work on not reacting, too."

"What are you talking about?"

"You damn near jumped out of your shoes when you thought I was about to touch you, Peyton."

Her green eyes are stormy, like the warm Mediterranean Sea stirred up during a squall. "You took me by surprise is all," she says, throwing my words back at me. But we're both smart enough to know what's going on here.

I grin. "Yeah, okay."

"You say that like you don't believe me," she shoots back, and weariness fills my bones. I'm done bickering and answering questions. I reach into my pocket and pull out a small velvet box. Her eyes widen and her hand goes to her chest.

"What…what is that?"

I open the box and present a ring. She gasps, her startled gaze flying to mine. "Roman?"

"This is why I was late last night. I was having issues getting this from my safety deposit box. There was some kind of mix-up."

She shakes her head. "I don't understand."

"What's not to understand? If we're going to pretend we're married, we have to cover all bases. Presenting you with my grandmother's ring is the first base."

Don't think of first base, Roman.

I'm thinking of first base.

My gaze drops, my mind back on her lush breasts.

"I don't know what to say."

"Say yes," I respond with a grin, wanting to lighten things up a bit. She frowns, and I don't miss the way she inches back. "What?"

"I don't want to wear your grandmother's ring."

I nod, a measure of disappointment gathering in my gut. For some reason, I thought Peyton might have reacted differently than my ex, that she'd respect and appreciate tradition. "It's a family custom... I just thought." She closes her hand over mine just as I'm about to snap the box shut.

"You don't understand, Roman. It's weird for me to wear the ring you gave your ex. I don't feel right about it."

My throat thickens and I give a humorless laugh. "It wasn't on her finger very long, Peyton. She said it was old and not her style. She wanted something newer, something shinier."

Her eyes widen. "Was she out of her mind?"

I actually think I was the one who was out of his mind for getting swept up in the proposal, for allowing my family to make decisions for me. I'll never allow that to happen again.

I take the ring from the box and hold it out to her. She lets me slip it on her finger, and for the briefest of seconds this feels all too real. I'd be wise to remember it's not, and she's completely off-limits.

"I'm committed to this, Peyton. You *will* be teaching children English," I say. "The full-time position is as good as yours. I promise, and I never break my promises."

"No, you just go around breaking hearts," she mumbles so low under her breath I'm not sure I heard her correctly.

"What?"

She nibbles on her bottom lip and after a few false starts she finally says, "We never did talk about that night, Roman."

My insides go dark as I push back into my seat. "Nothing to talk about. It was a mistake. I had too much to drink," I lie. I don't want to be a prick. I don't want to hurt her—again. But I can't tell her I'd lost all control of myself and was sure if I didn't have a taste of her, right that very second, I'd combust. I don't want to lead her on or let her think there could be more between us. I never want to let Cason down, and I broke the bro code once. I'm not about to lose my control and do it again. Nothing short of a brain tumor stealing my ability to think with clarity could make me kiss her a second time.

"Now what was that you said last night about us working the kinks out?"

Ah, shit, now why the hell did I say that?

"Details," she says quickly. "We need to work out the details."

"Isn't that what I said?" I ask to cover my slip, because no way, no damn way on the face of this earth am I going to think about Peyton and kink in the same sentence ever again.

Goddammit, I'm thinking about it.

"No," she says quietly, breathlessly, heat coloring her cheeks. "It's not what you said."

"It's what I meant to say." I push from my seat. "Now how about that drink?"

Unless, of course, she does want to talk about kink.

CHAPTER THREE

Peyton

I WAKE TO find a set of intense brown eyes watching me carefully. I stiffen and blink, glancing around as memories infiltrate my brain, and that's when I realize I'm on Roman's plane and we've just landed in Malta. Excitement wells up inside me as I reach for my phone and check the time. It's nearing midnight local time, six hours later than New York.

"Did you get any sleep?" I ask Roman as he finger-combs his dark hair, not that any of it is out of place. No, Roman Bianchi is always put together, and as I look at him, I wonder what it would take to rattle the man and shatter his hard-earned control.

"Just a bit." He shoves his tablet into his leather briefcase and smooths his hands over his button-down shirt and dress pants. "It was hard with all your snoring, though."

What the hell? I stare at him. My God, his delivery was so deadpan, I almost think he's telling the truth, either that or the long trip gave him a sense of humor. I open my mouth to come back with some smart-ass comment when the door to the cockpit opens. I turn to find two men stretching their limbs as they step into the cabin.

"Roman," the pilot says, his gaze sliding to me. He gives a curt nod. "I hope you enjoyed the flight."

"It was a great flight, thank you," I say.

Roman steps up to address the two men and I turn my attention to my belongings. I shove my magazine into my bag, and the ring on my left finger sparkles beneath the overhead lighting. I stand up straight, my heart jumping a little bit as I take a moment to admire the gorgeous diamond and gold band.

How could his ex-fiancée not want to wear something so precious? I can't blame Roman for being off women after getting his heart broken. Something twists deep inside me. That had to have been a horrible experience for him and I profoundly hate that he's resigned himself to the idea of spending his life alone. Then again, who am I to judge?

I flinch as Roman slides his big hand around my back, his warm scent filling my senses. Yeah, it's true. I'm really going to have to work on my reactions and figure out a way to *not* like his touch so much.

"All set?" he asks, his voice low and groggy… sleepy and sexy.

"I'm ready." I frown and reach into my purse. "I have the name of a cab company here. I'm supposed to call when we land."

He snatches his briefcase from the floor. "It's been taken care of."

"You arranged a cab?"

With his hand on the small of my back again—jeez, I wish I didn't really like that so much—he guides me to the door. "Something like that."

"Well, you either did or you didn't, Roman."

"You know, it was so peaceful when you were sleeping." I open my mouth, ready to tell him where he can shove his peace, but he smirks and adds, "Until you started snoring, of course."

Hell, who is this man? I'm not sure, but I have to say, I love this unusual playful side of him. Although I'm not about to tell him that.

"I do not snore," I mumble, hiding a smile, the warm night air falling over me as I begin my descent down the metal staircase. Our luggage is delivered to us from the baggage compartment, and Roman picks up both suitcases. I packed pretty light, assuming I'd pick up a few local dresses and accessories. I want to fit into the community as much as I can.

He leads me inside the airport, which is much bigger than I envisioned but fairly quiet this time of night. We move through customs and less than an hour later, we're standing on the sidewalk and I'm searching for our cab when a stretch limo pulls up in front of us.

Roman opens the back door as the driver greets us and sets our luggage in the trunk. "Nice car," I say, as I slide in. "A taxi would have done just fine."

He takes an exaggerated breath and lets it out

slowly as he slides in beside me. "Elias is our driver for the next month," he explains. "Anywhere you need to go, he'll take you."

I blink once, then twice, my sleeping brain taking a minute to understand. "I don't need a driver, Roman," I say, and take in his strong profile as he buckles himself into his seat. The driver, or rather, Elias catches my eye in the rearview mirror and gives me a smile before he pulls onto the road. I lean forward to give him the address to the small villa I rented. Roman touches my arm to stop me.

"What?" I ask.

"He knows where we're going."

"How could he? I never told him. I never even told you."

"He knows where we're going, Peyton."

My gaze goes from Roman, to Elias, back to Roman. "Wait, what's going on?"

He settles in his seat and stretches out his long legs. "I've made other arrangements for us."

"You can't do that."

"It's already done."

I glare at him, but he turns and glances out the window.

"You're a bully, Roman."

"Call me whatever you want." All business, like he's sitting in a boardroom, assigning orders to his staff, he reaches for a water bottle, uncaps it and hands it to me. "Your brother asked me to look out for you, and that's what I plan to do. He told me where you booked, and I didn't like the area, so I found us something more suitable, and it's closer to your work."

I take a long pull from the bottle and hand it back. "I can take care of myself." I lick a bead of water from my bottom lip. "I'm not a child."

He inhales sharply and tears his gaze away from my mouth. "Oh, I know. Believe me, I know." He tips the bottle to his lips and I watch his Adam's apple bob as he finishes it.

"What's that supposed to mean?" I ask.

He shakes his head. "Nothing."

"It's not nothing, Roman. You said it, so it's something."

"Can we just drive to the villa in peace, Peyton? I'm exhausted."

"No, I want to know what you meant, and I don't snore, I—"

"We're on the same page here, Peyton. A team." His gaze drops to mine, focuses on my mouth again, when he asks, "Do you have to question everything I do?"

"When it comes to you, I—"

Before I realize what's happening, he cups my chin, drags me closer, and presses his lips to mine. Sweet baby Jesus. My protest dies a sudden death on my tongue, and as much as I hate this man, I sink into his kiss as it stirs a need inside me. His warm lips move over mine, commanding, possessive, un-wavering and…antagonistic. Nevertheless, I moan into his mouth, my hand gripping the front of his dress shirt. He breaks the kiss and I just sit there, perfectly still, my mouth still poised open. He inches back and cold air moves in between us, snapping some sense back into me.

I swipe my mouth with the back of my hand, his alluring taste lingering as I glare at him. "Why did you do that?"

"Did you hate it?" My mind doesn't seem to want to work as his deep voice trickles through me, caressing all the parts he stirred awake with that fierce kiss. "Well, did you?"

He can't for one minute think I hated it. Not after the way I moaned. "Yes," I state flatly, and lift my chin a notch.

"Good, then every time you start yelling at me, or argue or give me a hard time, I'm going to kiss you."

"Like hell you—" He gives me a warning glare and my mouth slams shut. Although, and I hate to admit it, there is a part of me that wants to be defiant, just to push his buttons...just to get him to kiss me again.

Stupid jerk.

"I hate you," I mumble under my breath, sounding like a ridiculous, petulant child.

"Good."

Good?

Really?

He wants me to hate him?

"I wasn't yelling," I mumble. It's true, I wasn't, but I can't deny that I was beginning to annoy myself with all the questions.

We drive in silence, the heated tension between

us enough to fog the window. After a short drive, we pull up in front of a building and I peer out at it. The place is pitch-black, and I can't see much other than it has two stories and a rooftop.

"This is it?" I ask.

"Yes, let's get settled. It's been a long day."

I had very little sleep on the plane, most of it interrupted with unsolicited dreams of the man beside me, but as I take in the place, a new kind of energy sizzles through me. I doubt I'll fall asleep tonight, but that's not unusual. I wrap my arms around my body as I climb from the car, and Elias retrieves our luggage. Roman speaks to him for a moment and we head toward our villa.

"Where exactly are we?" I ask in a low voice, not wanting to wake anyone in the neighborhood.

"We're in Upper Gardens. It's a quiet community in St. Julian's, and very close to all amenities."

"How far are we from the school?"

"Walking distance," he says, his voice low, matching mine. He punches in a code to the door and pushes it open.

The night air is warm, but my body is chilled. It's always chilled, even more so when I'm in new situations or going on little to no sleep. I remember as a child lying wide-awake in bed for hours on end, my body arctic cold as I waited for the knock on the door to come—it always came—telling me it was time to go to a different foster home. I step closer to Roman and try to absorb his body warmth, but the cold remains.

"If the school is walking distance, why do I need a driver at my disposal?" I ask.

He mumbles something about me talking too much under his breath and I'm about to ask even more questions when he flicks on the lights and my words fall off. I glance around the spacious villa, beautifully decorated in black, chrome and white. The kitchen is sleek and modern, the living area lush and inviting. All the clean lines of its open concept give it an airy feel, and I like it. A lot.

I drop my purse and Roman stands at the door as I enter the place, taking it all in. I check the fridge and cupboards to find them fully stocked. After cataloging the main level, I hurry up the stairs to find two gorgeous bedrooms, floor-to-ceiling windows giving a clear view of the water, and a lovely contemporary shared bathroom in between the rooms. The place is absolutely breathtaking—and completely out of my budget.

I hurry back downstairs and find Roman locking up behind us. "Not so fast," I say. "We can't stay."

He turns to face me, and his eyes are half-lidded, tired from the long day. "You don't like it?"

"Of course I like it. What's not to like?"

"Then what's the problem?"

I raise a brow and give him a look that suggests he's dense. "Roman, I'm a teacher. I can't afford this kind of luxury." My brother might be a multimillionaire, but that doesn't mean I don't pay my own way in life. I pride myself on my financial independence. Cason put me through college but I insisted on working part-time to provide for incidentals, even though he didn't want me to.

"It's covered, Peyton," he says flatly.

"Why would you do this?" He hesitates, like he's not sure how to answer. A second later he closes his hand over mine. His touch is so soft, so achingly tender, my stomach takes flight. His eyes narrow.

"You're still cold," he states.

I pull my hand away. "I'm fine." He angles his head like he doesn't believe me, but I don't give him the chance to say anything. "I can't believe you rented this place without even asking me, and had it stocked full of supplies."

"I just wanted you in a safe place, close to your school, and the kitchen is stocked because we need to eat."

"Roman, I—"

He captures my hand and when he pulls me close, my body meshing with his, I can't for the life of me remember what it was I was going to say. His head dips and I hold my breath. Is he going to kiss me again?

Do I want that?

Oh God, I do.

"Before you say another word," he begins, his voice an octave lower, "come with me."

Giving me little choice in the matter, he ushers me up the stairs. We don't stop on the bedroom level. Instead we go up another set of stairs and he pushes open a heavy door. It takes me a second to realize we're now outside.

"Oh my God," I say when I see the breathtaking view from the rooftop. It's even better than from the second-floor bedroom. I turn and take in the long stretch of pool and crisp white outdoor furniture, shadowed beneath a pergola. I breathe in as the warm wind blows by, carrying the fresh scent of flowers with it. "It's gorgeous."

"I thought you might like the view."

"You mean you thought it might shut me up," I say, but I'm losing the will to fight. This is all too much for me, but it was incredibly sweet of him.

"Peyton," he says, and spins me around until I'm facing him, our bodies flush. He rubs his hands up and down my arms to warm me. Awareness flitters through me, and I can't seem to ignore it. "Maybe this isn't about you," he says. "Maybe it's about me. Maybe I just wanted to stay somewhere nice, something that suits my needs and lifestyle more."

He's selling it, but I'm not buying. I don't for one second believe this is about him. He might be a man used to luxuries, but everything in me, every ounce of women's intuition I possess, says he picked this place for *me* because *I'd* like it—and that confuses the hell out of me. One minute he's kissing me and laughing in my face, the next he's flying me here on his Learjet, putting a gorgeous ring on my finger and swearing he'll do whatever it takes to help me get this job.

This isn't about you, Peyton.

It's about my brother and their bond, and I'd be wise to remember that. Air leaves my lungs in a hiss, much like a leaky balloon deflating. What? Did I want this to be about me? No, I don't even like this guy.

"It's not a big deal, okay?" he says, but it's kind of a big deal for me.

"I don't want you to pay my way, Roman." The truth is, while I appreciate him wanting me to live in comfort—because he has some obligation to my brother—I don't want to rely on anyone. Outside of my brother, I can't ever let myself get used to someone else caring for me. Self-preservation has taught me to rely only on my small family of two. I just can't set myself up for that kind of heartache. I don't think I could survive being chewed up and spit out again—especially not by this man.

His head dips and those dark eyes of his narrow on me. His smile is slow and sincere. My stomach tightens as the hardness in his dark eyes melts, reminding me of a steaming mug of hot chocolate on a cold winter's night—the kind of warmth that comes close to thawing the chill in my bones, but never quite succeeds.

"Okay," he says. "You can pay me back."

I nod and my tightly strung muscles relax, slightly. "Good."

"Can we go to bed now?"

CHAPTER FOUR

Roman

PEYTON'S GREEN EYES widen at my slip and I quickly backtrack. "I mean, we should get some sleep. It's been a long day. Tomorrow will be busy for you. You have to meet the children, the teachers and the school's principal, and we need to be ready to make a good impression." *Okay, Roman, you can stop rambling any time now, and while you're at it stop picturing Peyton naked.*

"True," she says, and pushes her hair from her face to expose the pink flush on her cheeks. "Sleep is a good idea. Which room do you want?" she asks as we head inside. She starts down the narrow stairs and I follow behind.

"Why don't you take the master suite," I say, the room I normally take when I come to Malta to unwind. If I told her I owned this place, that my family owns many villas on Malta, it might set off another argument, and I'd have to quiet her with a kiss, which can't happen again. Her brother is my best friend.

That doesn't stop my dick from hardening at the thought of kissing her a second time today. "I'm fine in the smaller room."

She nods and glances at me over her shoulder, her jaw set, a stubbornness about her. "I do plan to pay you back, Roman."

I smile, liking that about her. Not her stubborn streak—that's just plain annoying—but I like that she's a girl who wants to pay her own way through life, even when she doesn't have to. She's always refusing her brother's financial help, and this is my villa—already bought and paid for.

"I know you do," I say quietly.

"I just…it might take a while."

"Or we could find another form of payment," I say, and when she reaches the landing her gaze flies to mine. No doubt she's thinking I'm talking sexual favors here. I'm not. I want her to want me regardless of what I do for her. Wait, no, I don't want her to want me. What am I thinking?

Dammit.

"Such as?"

"You could cook for me." I rub my stomach as I remember Cason's amazing seafood pasta. "If you cook anything like your brother, then that's all the payment I need."

"I'm a good cook," she says, and folds her arms across her body, a small quiver going through her. I make a mental note to adjust the air-conditioning. "I actually enjoy being in the kitchen."

"I hate it."

She glances down and a small smile touches her lips, like she's remembering happier times. "Cason and I did a lot of cooking together." She chuckles lightly. "I used to wear swimming goggles when I cut up onions. That always cracked him up."

I laugh. "Really?"

"Yeah." She rolls her eyes. "I was a weirdo. You don't have to say it."

"Nah, not a weirdo. That's genius-level intellect, my friend."

She chuckles and it curls around me, warms my soul. I like seeing her smile. I'd love to see her do it more often, but the world has not given this sweet girl much to smile about over the years.

She puts her hand on me and gives me a little shove. "You don't have to be a smart-ass."

"I'm serious, and you're the smart-ass, not me." I join her on the landing and throw an arm around her shoulders, nudging her chin with my fist. "No, I'm the one who's older and wiser, so you're going to have to trust me on that."

Her body tightens beneath my arm, and that's when I realize just how close I've pulled her, just how nicely her body fits with mine.

"I… I don't really trust too many people, Roman," she admits, a heaviness overtaking her as her eyes narrow, and I could kick myself. I didn't mean to dredge up demons from her past.

I give her a comforting squeeze before I pull my arm back. "I know. I don't either," I say, not wanting her to feel alone in this. "Not anymore, anyway."

She shakes her head, a bit of the tightness in her muscles gone. "I guess that's one thing we have in common."

"What a pair we make. You'll cook for me, then?"

She waves one hand around the long hallway. "You're here in Malta, away from your work, your friends and your beloved New York, helping me get a job. Cooking is the least I could do, don't you think?"

"It's a nice break from reality for a while and for the record, none of this is a hardship, Peyton." Nope, not a hardship at all. But that's not to say it's not *hard*, and when I say hard, I'm talking about my dick, of course.

She laughs. "Funny, Carly said something like that to me yesterday. She also told me I should be exercising my marital rights, pretend marriage or not." As soon as the words leave her mouth, her eyes widen. "I didn't mean… I wasn't suggesting we should do that." She gives a fast shake of her head. "That was before I even knew it was you, anyway."

"You mean you considered it before you knew it was me."

"No," she blurts out, a little too quickly. With the tip of her finger she pokes my chest and I wish to God she'd stop touching me. "Now that I do know, that's not happening. Ever."

"Yeah, we're not going to do that," I agree. I'm only going to think about doing it, repeatedly, while using my hand.

She exhales, and that's when I realize how weary

she looks. She pushes her hair from her face. "I don't even know why I said it."

"You're tired," I say, giving her an out.

"You're right. So why do you hate cooking?" she asks, redirecting the conversation. "You're Italian. Aren't all Italians supposed to be great cooks? Or is that a cliché?"

I laugh. "I grew up with five older sisters, Peyton. I couldn't get near the kitchen. Not that I wanted to. I was busy with sports anyway."

She nods, and a small, little-girl-lost smile touches her mouth. "That must have been so nice, Roman. I love my brother, dearly, but I always kind of wanted a sister, too. There was this one place…" Her voice falls off and a deep sadness invades her eyes. My gut twists, and it's all I can do not to pull her into my arms. She shakes herself out of her reverie and says, "Anyway, all those sisters. It must have been awesome."

"Are you kidding me?" I ask as she inches toward the bigger bedroom, stopping outside the door. "I had to set my alarm for three in the morning just to get some bathroom time."

She laughs. A sweet melodic sound that strokes my dick. "That does sound horrible," she says.

"Don't even get me started on the makeup and hair products. Everywhere, Peyton. Everywhere. In my cereal, on my soap, on my clothes. Do you have any idea how many girls accused me of cheating on them?"

Her brow arches playfully. "A lot, huh?"

"Well, I wouldn't say a lot." I grin. "A few, maybe."

She lifts herself up to her full height and squares her shoulders. "Well, you'll be happy to know, I'm not high-maintenance. I promise no hair on your soap, in your cereal or on your clothes."

What about in my bed?

Nope. Nope. Don't go there.

Before I can think better of it, I reach out and run a long strand of her silky soft hair through my fingers. My knuckles brush her cheek, and her chest rises with her fast intake of breath. "It's okay, I've gotten used to it over the years." I laugh as I think about that. "I think you'd really like my sisters."

"Really?"

I nod. "Yeah, you're kind of annoying like they are." Her mouth drops open and she whacks my chest. I snatch her hand before she can pull it back. "Kidding," I say, and brush my thumb over her wrist.

She shakes her head. "I do talk a lot sometimes, I know," she says.

"I don't hate it, Peyton." My gaze drops to her mouth. Damn, so sweet and succulent, it's all I can do not to dip my head for another taste while I think about sinking myself inside her. Kissing her in the limo was a bad idea. I have no idea what came over me. Maybe I should get checked for a brain tumor. I swore to God, I was never, ever going to put my mouth on her again. Yeah, I can blame it on her incessant chatter, but I think it had more to do with watching her sleep, hearing her soft breathing sounds and even softer murmurs. The type of noises I'd imagine she'd make between the sheets—while I was on top of her. "Not like you hated that kiss," I taunt.

Her lips pucker, like she'd just eaten something sour. "Yeah, I really hated that."

"Do you hate a lot of things?" I tease. "Besides me, I mean?"

"No, I reserve most of it for you," she jokes in return, a sly little grin on her face.

"I figured." I let my hand fall. "I guess I should let you get to sleep." I'm about to leave when her hand on my arm stops me.

"Roman."

I swallow as the softness in her voice seeps through me and zaps my balls. "Yeah."

"Your sisters." She leans against the wall, like she's not in a hurry to end our banter. "They're all older?"

I pause, and take in her big green eyes. She knows they are. I told her they were. Just a minute ago, and on the plane when we were going over the logistics of our fake marriage. She blinks up at me, and my gut tightens as realization dawns. She wants to talk, wants to hear more about my big family because she never had one of her own.

"Yeah, they're all older," I say quietly. She nods and smiles. "Do you…want a family?" I ask, even though Cason told me his sister was anti-marriage.

Her soft smile falls and she looks at me like I must be an idiot. It's one of the nicer looks she's given me tonight. "Hell no. I never plan on getting married, Roman."

"Another thing we have in common," I tell her.

"I guess so." Her eyes narrow and she looks past my shoulders, like her thoughts are a million miles away. "I learned early on that I'm no Cinderella and Prince Charming doesn't exist," she says, like all life's curveballs haven't bothered her at all. Maybe they haven't—and maybe I was born yesterday. One thing is for certain, she's a fighter, a woman who goes after what she wants. That's damn admirable if you ask me.

"Your sisters," she says, bringing the conversation back to me.

"You'd really like them, Peyton."

"I bet I would."

I wince as I think about that. "Not that you're ever going to meet them."

The light in her eyes fades and her smile tumbles. My heart follows suit. Shit, I keep saying the wrong things tonight.

"No, of course not," she says. "I wasn't suggesting… I didn't think."

"It's just that—"

"No. I don't want to meet them," she says quickly, and I study her face, not sure I believe her. "We're just here pretending. No need for me to meet them and give them the wrong idea."

"Peyton, if they got wind of us—"

"Yeah, right, I get it." She waves her hand. "Anyway, it's late. We better get some sleep." She steps into her bedroom, effectively cutting off my explanation. "Oh, wait, my suitcase."

"I'll grab it," I say, my pulse pounding against my throat as I make my way down the stairs. She might be hell-bent on remaining unattached, but if anyone needs a family it's her. No way can I let my sisters think I'm married, though. I can't even imagine what they'd do. Yeah, maybe I can imagine. All five of them would invade the villa and all their interfering wouldn't be good for Peyton or her job. Christ, we'd probably end up married for real, before either of us realized it, and neither one of us wants that.

I double-check the lock on the door, grab our bags and head back upstairs. I rap quietly on her door, and when I hear the water running in the bathroom that adjoins our rooms, I open her bedroom door and set her bag inside. With sleep pulling at me, I head to the other room and stretch out my tight muscles.

I unbutton my shirt and toss it onto a chair. As I walk to the window to take in the view, I tug my zipper down and kick off my pants. The bed calls to me, but a swim on the rooftop pool might be a great way to stretch my tight muscles. The shower shuts off and a few minutes later, footsteps on the floor reach my ears.

Dressed in my boxers that can easily double as a bathing trunk, I quietly leave the room and pad softly to the rooftop. I walk to the deep end of the pool and dive in; the water is cold and refreshing against my hot skin, but does little to snuff the heat deep inside me. I honestly don't know how I'm going to be around my best friend's kid sister and keep my hands to myself. Shit, I never should have kissed her.

It won't happen again. Cason's trust is too important to me. I spend the next fifteen minutes gliding through the pool, working to exhaust my mind so I'll be able to shut down and get some sleep.

I resurface in the shallow end, wipe my hand over my face and jerk back when I spot a figure standing at the pool's edge. "Shit," I say, my gaze lifting higher to see that it's Peyton.

"Sorry," she says, and even though I don't want to—yeah, okay, maybe I do—I let my gaze roam over her, taking pleasure in the tiny pair of sleep shorts that showcase her long sleek legs, and tank top that does little to hide her lush breasts. If she moved just right, I'd get a lovely view of her nipple. Good God, am I fourteen? My dick is sure acting like it as it twitches and urges me to go for it. I sink lower into the water. She folds her arms over her body and hugs herself, cutting off my exploration.

"I wasn't expecting anyone to be standing there," I say.

"I knocked on your bedroom door and you didn't answer. I heard a noise up here and figured I'd find you."

"You found me."

She scrunches her face up, her body wound tight, and I know her well enough to recognize when she's unsure about something. She has a lot of tells, much like her brother. Unease worms its way through me as she shifts from one foot to the other.

I narrow my gaze. "What's wrong?"

"I just…this is going to sound ridiculous." She

backs up a bit and drops her arms, a cascade of auburn hair falling over her breasts as she glances down.

"Hey, what is it?" I ask, and as my arousal morphs into worry, I step from the pool. Water drips from my body and puddles at my feet as her gaze drops to take in my near nakedness.

"Wow," she says under her breath, and damn, the fact that she likes what she sees isn't helping my hands-off situation at all. Tonight, however, under the covers, it's going to be all hand on dick.

"Peyton," I say, and her head lifts, a dazed look in her eyes. "What's wrong?"

She swallows, briefly closes her eyes, and when she opens them again she stares uncomfortably at the majestic view in the distance. "I just wanted to ask you if it was okay if I left the bathroom light on, and the door leading to my bedroom cracked. It's an adjoining bathroom, so I wanted to make sure you were okay with that." Her look is almost sheepish when she adds, "It's a strange place and all, and if I have to get up in the middle of the night…" Her words fall off and my stomach sinks. This isn't about strange places and needing to go to the bathroom at night. It's about Peyton not liking the dark. Sweet little Peyton who was tossed around in the system, oftentimes getting separated from her brother, is afraid of the dark, and that's so sad. My heart squeezes so tight I could damn near sob. Goddamn I hate how cruel the world was to her. I hate how cruel I was to her, but I need her to hate me.

"I don't mind at all," I say around a lump in my throat.

"Okay, thanks."

She stands there for a moment. "You should put a shirt on. You look cold. Pants, too." I follow her eyes down to see the bulge my boxers are doing a piss-poor job of hiding.

"I'm fine," I say, even though I'm far from it. "You're the one who's always cold."

She glances around and I stare at her ass when she walks up to a cabinet beneath the pergola and opens it. She goes up on her toes, stretching out her long, sexy legs, and visions of me taking her from behind hit like a punch and nearly knock the wind out of me.

"Jackpot," she says, and pulls out a big white towel. "At least wrap yourself in this before you freeze to death."

"I'm not cold," I say again.

Ignoring me, she shakes it out and our hands touch as she tries to throw it over my shoulders. Warmth, need and lust hit at the same time, and a growl crawls out of my throat as I envision my hands on her body, removing those sexy shorts and burying my mouth between her soft thighs.

"Shit," I murmur under my breath, and put the towel around her quivering shoulders instead. I tug her to me, offering the warmth of my body and anything else she might like.

Get it together, dude.

"Roman," she says as she swipes her tongue over her bottom lip. "What…what are you doing?"

My head dips, my lips inches from hers. I want to kiss her. Jesus, there are a lot of things I want to do with her. I breathe her in, let her sweet, flowery aroma feed the hunger building inside me.

"I'm not the one who is cold and wet," she says with a huff.

Oh God, Roman. Don't think about her being wet.

"You need to put the towel around you, not me," she continues.

"Peyton," I growl as she tries to shrug the towel off.

"What?"

"Leave it."

"Leave what?"

"Just…stop, okay," I say, my voice thick with lust.

"Stop what?"

"Stop talking," I say, the push and pull between us arousing me more. "You know what will happen if you don't."

"I am not going to stop—" Her protest dies on her lips and my words slowly register in her brain. Yeah, that's right, Peyton, you either shut up or I'll shut you up.

"Roman," she murmurs, her gaze moving over my face. A beat passes between us, and then a change comes over her. Her body relaxes, her throaty little moan letting me know exactly what she's thinking— what she wants. Oh, hell no! She steps closer, crowding me. "What if I don't want to stop?" she challenges.

Jesus Christ, is she really going there? She knows I can't—won't. I clench down on my jaw, hard enough to break bone, and work to fight the need racing through my blood. I can't let her get the upper hand here. If I do, I just might give her what we both want.

"Aren't you going to answer me?" She presses against me and her breath comes out a little quicker when my hard cock rubs against her stomach.

Summoning every ounce of control I have, I grip her shoulders and move her an inch back, welcoming the rush of cooler air falling over me. Her green eyes darken, turn venomous. She gives a humorless laugh and I put more distance between us before she kicks me in the shins.

"Typical Roman."

I grip my hair and tug. "What the hell is that supposed to mean?"

"Always starting something you can't finish," she shoots back.

"I can finish."

"Doesn't seem to me that you can." She's throwing me a challenge and I'll be damned if I don't want to pick it up.

Back the hell down, dude.

"If you weren't Cason's kid sister—"

"What does that have to do with anything?"

"He's my best friend, which means you're off-limits."

She goes quiet, her gaze latched on mine. "Do you know what I like about you, Roman?"

"What?" I ask.

"Nothing," she says, and a bark of laughter climbs out of my throat as I stand there staring at her back as she heads toward the stairs, an extra little shake in her sweet ass that teases my dick.

"Good," I say.

She glances at me over her shoulders. "You like that, though, don't you?"

"Yeah. I do," I say, my voice a husky murmur.

"You want me to hate you."

"I need you to hate me, Peyton. If you didn't, I'd bend you right over that table and bury myself inside you." She goes still, deathly still. I guess I got her attention now. "Would you hate that?" I ask.

A beat of silence, and then another. "Yes, I'd hate that," she finally says, the big fat lie hovering in the air, taking up space between us.

"Good."

CHAPTER FIVE

Peyton

I'D BEND YOU *right over that table and bury myself inside you.*

Okay, I might hate him—or not—but yeah, I seriously want him to follow through with that threat, which is probably why I spent all of last night tossing and turning between the sheets, imagining that dirty scenario playing out in real time.

No man has ever talked to me like that before. Is it shameful that I liked the deliciously filthy description of what he wanted to do to me, that it fueled all my darkest fantasies? Maybe, but I don't really care about that. Maybe it's the fresh Mediterranean air stirring a desire in me, or maybe I want to explore our kiss, expand upon it. I really don't know, but I'm as surprised as Roman that I suddenly want to get dirty with this man, want to be shameless and wide open to experience what I've never experienced before.

Go for it, Peyton.

At least now I know what's going on with him. There's an insane pull between us but he has some misguided loyalty to my brother where I'm concerned. I'm a grown woman for God's sake, and who I choose to sleep with is my business. It's about to become Roman's business, too. Oh yeah, he's about to learn firsthand that Cason has no say in my sex life.

The sound of Roman moving in the bathroom reaches my ears, and I kick my blankets off, my mind visualizing him stripping down to jump in the shower, his hard body hot and naked beneath the stream of water. Sweet baby Jesus, last night, the sight of him in the boxer shorts—the soft cotton the only thing separating my mouth from his very generous bulge—well…let's just say that eyeful awakened every nerve in my body. I've seen naked before, but not that kind of naked. He was all hard muscles and testosterone—the view completely hypnotizing—and it was a quick reminder that I haven't been touched in a long time, and never by anyone like him.

I slide from my bed, and through the crack in the bathroom door, I catch sight of Roman in the shower, his large body obscured in the steamy glass. What a shame. That thought makes me chuckle. Honest to God, I don't even know who I am with him. I'm not the type of girl to go lusting after a guy; heck, I haven't even wanted a man's hands on me since college—not that any guys were fighting to go out with me, either.

And why have you been flying solo, Peyton?

Oh, maybe because I've been hung up on Roman

for far too long, and it's definitely time to do something about it. I'm not looking for a future, but why shouldn't I exercise my marital rights while we're pretending? What would it hurt? Neither one of us wants anything more. We both know where the other stands, so why not have a bit of fun?

Why not, indeed?

I hang up a few of my dresses and putter around, a plan forming, taking shape in my mind. I bite back a grin as I think about my next move and all the ways I can press his buttons—sexually. Oh, this is going to be fun and the poor guy isn't going to know what hit him.

The water turns off, and his footsteps slap on the tile floor. I hum to draw his attention. His movements still behind me, and I bend to get the last of the things from my bag, purposely aiming my ass toward him. My sleep shorts lift, exposing the swell of my ass, and excitement skitters through me when I hear a low rumble, the deep sound reminding me of a wild animal's hungry growl. I stand and turn, blinking innocently at the man peering at me through the door that has been left ajar. For the first time in my life, I'm suddenly glad I'm afraid of the dark.

"Good morning," I say, trying to sound casual as he stands there, in nothing but a towel knotted around his hips. My nipples swell, and I don't bother to hide them as he grips the doorknob, his eyes dark, fierce like an animal about to take down its prey. "Don't bother closing it," I say. "I'm going to jump in the shower behind you. Do you mind if I soap up with your body wash? I forgot to bring some."

"Peyton," he grumbles, his voice low and dark as his attention strays from my face and falls to my peaked nipples.

I put my hands on the small of my back and push my hips forward, like I'm stretching out my tight muscles. "Yes?"

"About last night. What I said," he begins, sounding rattled, unsure. He grabs a fistful of hair as he waves his other hand between the two of us. "We just can't act on this, okay?"

"This. What do you mean by this?" I ask, feigning innocence as the bathroom door widens to give me a better view of his body. Lord, talk about a big yummy snack. Everything about the man is hard. Every damn inch of him delicious, and there are an awful lot of inches. I resist the urge to throw my hands up and shout out a cheer.

"You know what I'm talking about," he growls through clenched teeth, a good indication that he's wound as tightly as I am. Damned if I don't like that.

Sexual tension arcs between us, sizzles in the air like a live current, as I say, "Just so you know, my sex life is my business, not my brother's. If I wanted to sleep with you, or bend over so you could bury yourself inside me, the choice would be mine to make."

His throat works as he swallows. "Don't you think I have a say in it, too?"

"Yes, of course. I'm just saying. I'm a grown

woman, Roman, or haven't you noticed?" I stretch out a little more and his eyes darken.

"I've noticed."

"What I do with my body is up to me." I sink down onto the edge of my unmade bed, and by small degrees I inch my knees open. A welcome invitation he's fully aware of judging by the clenching of his muscles. "The fact is you want me to hate you, and I do, and that creates a huge problem."

"Yeah, huge," he mumbles, and I resist the urge to see if he's currently sporting anything huge.

"Pretending to like each other, or even touch each other in public, will be a hard task."

"Yeah, hard," he says, and I bite my bottom lip as I fake a repulsed shiver.

"I'm just thinking about the difficulties we're going to face."

"Oh, is *that* what you're thinking about?"

"I can't even imagine how much I'd hate it if you touched me. If you put your hand here," I say, and lightly run my finger up my inner thigh, "it would be horrible. The thoughts of you using your tongue." I crinkle up my face. "That would be worse, I'm sure."

"Peyton," he says, his nostrils flaring, his control fraying around the edges. "Don't."

"Don't what?" I bite back a smile as his rough voice caresses my body, the air in the room vibrating with the tension arcing between us. He stands before me, his chest rising and falling rapidly, as he battles an internal war, one I intend to win. My flesh tightens as I lightly stroke myself, a light feathery caress that stirs the restless desire in me.

"Just don't."

"Don't what?" I ask again. "Don't imagine how awful it would be to have your hands on me, your mouth between my legs, devouring me, you mean?"

"Fuck." His voice is deep, tight, revealing the lust he's trying to keep in check.

"Right, and *fucking*." I roll my eyes as my heart-beat speeds up. "My God, don't even get me started on imagining how much I'd hate that."

He stares at me, his pupils dilating, each breath harsher than the one before. "Peyton," he says again.

"Yes?"

"Maybe…" He begins and stops. He scrubs his chin, agony all over his face.

"Go on…" I encourage, and his gaze drops, watches my fingers dip under the fabric of my shorts. A little whimper catches in my throat as I widen my legs even more to tease him. Tempt him.

As I take in the strength and power of the man before me, a tortured sound rumbles from the depths of his throat and his laser focus centers on the hot spot between my legs. "Maybe you don't have to imagine it?"

Yes!

"Excuse me?" I say as I study the bead of water dripping down his chest, disappearing into his towel. My throat dries. My God, the man is perfect, and judging by the bulge in that towel, he wants me every bit as much as I want him, and I damn well plan to do my best to make it happen.

Like an animal free of its tether—untamed and feral—he shoves my door open. It hits the wall with a thud as he steps into my room, and pleasure gathers in a knot deep between my thighs as his presence overwhelms the space, making me feel small and delicate beneath his glare. But his size doesn't intimidate me. No, it actually empowers me, makes me a little more brazen.

I lift my chin, unafraid. "What exactly are you suggesting?" I ask, my voice laced with need. As he stares at me, another thought hits. What if he starts something, only to laugh and walk away? Do I have it in me to survive his rejection twice?

"Why don't we see just how much you're going to hate me touching you." He cocks his head. "I told you I was committed to this charade, and it's clear we're going to have to know what we're dealing with if we want to pull off a fake marriage."

"An experiment then. Hmm, I think—" My words fall off when he closes the distance between us, pulls me to my feet and grabs a fistful of my hair.

Heat courses through me as he tugs, none too gently. I breathe in his freshly showered skin as his head dips, his lips close to mine. His gaze moves over my face, and his rapid-fire breathing washes over my flesh as his lips twist.

"Do you hate this?" he asks.

"Yes, I hate it," I say, my voice deep and raspy from arousal.

Kiss me, already.

His big hands grip my sides and slide upward, his touch like fire to my skin. He stretches out his thumbs and brushes them over my nipples, effectively shutting down my brain. I moan and his resulting grin arouses me even more.

"Do you hate this, Peyton?" he asks, his voice a bit shaky. Maybe he's not as in control as he seems. Do I, Peyton Harrison, his best friend's kid sister, have the ability to rattle his composure and lance his self-control?

Let's see if I do.

"Yes, I hate it," I say, and arch into him.

"I can tell." His thumbs tease my tight buds, his touch flowing through me, teasing the needy spot between my legs. One hand slides up my leg and he grips my hip, his touch taunting the cleft between my thighs. His fingers bite into my skin, a rough touch that feels far more sensual than a gentle one.

"How about this?" he asks, and plants his mouth on mine. His kiss is hard, deeply brutal and bruising. Everything about it sends a sharp spike of need through me. I moan into his mouth and my hands slip around his big body, taking pleasure in the heat of his skin. His tongue plunders, tasting the depths of my mouth as he rubs himself against my stomach. My God, I love what I do to him.

He tears his mouth from mine and cups my breast. "What about this, Peyton?" he asks as he weighs my aching breast in his hand. "Do you hate this?" My voice disappears on me, so I moan instead. He cups my other breast and kneads me in his palms. "Moan for me. Show me how much you hate it."

My head falls back and I moan louder. It spurs him on. He dips a hand into my shorts, and with the rough pad of his finger, he circles my clit. "I bet you hate this, too." I gasp as he strokes me, his finger slick and wet from my arousal as it thrums against my clit. "What about here, Peyton?" He inches a finger inside me, to the second knuckle, and goes completely still when my sex clenches around him. "I bet you'd hate it more if I tossed you onto that bed and put my cock in here instead of my finger."

"Ohmigod," I cry out, his rough touch and crass words doing the craziest things to me.

"Would you?" he asks, his finger still unmoving inside me, like it's some kind of cruel punishment. I try to buck forward, try to drive him in deeper, damn near ready to lose my mind, but he grips my hips and holds me still, a knowing grin on his face.

"I would totally hate it," I say.

"How much?" he asks.

"I guess I don't really know. I guess you might have to do it before I can put a measurement on it."

"Hell," he growls, his mouth skimming my body as he sinks to his knees. He grips the elastic on my cotton sleep shorts and drags them down, just enough to expose my sex. He inhales me deeply, then exhales and my muscles contract as his hot, shuddering breath strokes my clit. He stares at my sex with heat and hunger, and he wets his lips as he parts me with his finger.

"Jesus Christ, Peyton." Tortured eyes glance up at me. "So damn perfect," he says, and I vibrate beneath his admiration. "This sweet little pussy…" He shakes his head as he strokes along the length of me. I practically orgasm and when he glances up at me again, it's clear he knows how desperate I am for it. "Have you been touched before?"

"Barely."

"Why?" he asks.

Oh, because you're the only man I ever really wanted to touch me. "The truth is, Roman, my one and only time was with a sloppy college boy who didn't know his way around my body." I take in Roman's dark eyes and everything tells me he's a man who knows just how to stroke all the spots that will bring me pleasure. "Guys never really paid attention to me, and that was okay by me because I didn't really want to be touched after that experience," I add honestly. It's true—guys didn't want me and I didn't want to be touched, unless it was by this man. I keep that bit of information to myself.

His eyes lock on mine. "You want me to touch you?"

"Yes."

"To see how much you hate it?"

"Uh-huh."

"I'll touch you, Peyton." His fingers sweep over my damp curls. "I'll touch this sweet little pussy until you're screaming my name in orgasm, but I have a condition."

"What?" I ask as he moves his finger a tiny inch.

I whimper and put my hands on his shoulder as my flesh tightens.

"I don't want you to just tell me how much you hate it. I want you to show me, too."

Fire licks through me. The man wants me to open up for him, bloom under his touch. "I can do that," I say.

"Good girl," he says, and I'm rewarded with the rest of his finger. He slides it all the way into my body, and I whimper.

"One more thing, and we need to make this clear."

"What?" I ask, pretty sure I'd agree to running through fire naked to get him to keep going.

"This is all I can give you."

"Trust me, Roman. I don't want more. No kids or family for me. I am not a girl you have to worry about," I say, eager to settle his worries. I am not going down any road—or aisle—with him, and don't want anything in return.

I try to widen my legs, but my shorts hug them tightly together, and damned if that doesn't come with its own excitement. As lust floods my body, something niggles at me. "I need one thing from you," I whimper.

"Just one." He ever so lightly moves his finger inside me, tease that he is.

"Maybe more," I say, my body on hyperdrive, but we're about to cross a line that neither of us can come back from. Yes, I'm seducing him. In the end, however, I don't want to be with him if it's something he'll never forgive himself for. "Promise me this. No regrets, Roman."

"Peyton." His hot breath washes over my tingling flesh. "I've struggled enough. Keeping my distance from you has been pure torture." My pulse jumps at the admission. An agonized groan catches in his throat. "I can't do it anymore," he says, his control snapping like a tightwire.

"Can't?"

"Don't want to."

"I don't want you to, either," I say, and touch his face. "Okay, no regrets. After I sign the contract, we go back to the way things were. A clean slate, okay?"

"Deal."

"You know, though. You know what I think I'd really hate," I say.

"No, what?"

"I would probably really hate it if you shoved me to my knees and put your cock in my mouth."

"Sweet hell," he grumbles under his breath. "We're going to find out, right after I devour this barely touched pussy of yours and watch you hate every damn second of it."

Yes, please.

He slides his wet tongue over me, and I let loose a loud moan, my fingers digging into his shoulder. "Oh, yeah," I murmur. "I hate that so much."

His chuckle races over my skin, and my entire body quivers. I move my hips to ride his tongue and this time he lets me. His thick, slick finger slides in and out of me, and I shut my eyes as pleasure dances along my nerve endings.

He flattens his tongue and swipes it over my clit, long leisurely strokes, every movement unhurried, like he has all the time in the world to simply give pleasure. I whimper and move and grind against his mouth. I'm shameless, I know. But goddammit, the man has a magical tongue. A second finger joins the first, stretching me in the most glorious ways. I moan in response, showing him just how much I hate it.

He draws my clit into his mouth. "Ooh," I say, a hard tremble working its way through my body. I run my hands through his hair, tug on it as he slides his fingers in and out of me. I lose myself in the sensations, so damn wet and slick as he penetrates me, pounding a little harder, I struggle to hang on, never wanting this moment to end.

With his fingers still inside me, he tugs my shorts down and nudges me backward until I hit the bed. He manipulates my body, moving me around easily until I'm on the mattress, my legs spread wide, my body his for the taking.

"Do you hate this?" he asks, his fingers soaked as he pulls them out.

"God, yes," I cry out.

"Take your top off," he demands in a soft voice. "Let me see your tits."

I quiver at his bluntness and remove my shirt. My pink nipples are hard, and he adjusts his hand to apply his palm to my clit as he lifts his head to take one hard bud into his mouth.

"Roman," I cry out as his fingers resume their pounding and he sucks on me. My muscles clench around his fingers, the glorious things he's doing to me shutting down my brain until all I can do is feel: his fingers pounding, his palm rubbing and his mouth devouring my nipple. I call his name again and judging by the way his muscles clench, it's easy to tell he likes the sound of it on my lips. "I hate this," I say, and he bites down on my nipple, pain and pleasure mingle, bleed into one, and I lift my hips, sensations zeroing in on my sex as my body explodes.

Dizzy, I close my eyes, hyperaware of the way my body is responding. I hold his mouth to my breast, crazed and breathless as I continue to spasm around his fingers, my hot juices slicking down my thighs. Heat spreads through me, my stimulated flesh tingling as I lose myself in the release.

"God, yes," I say, and he goes back between my legs, his tongue a soft caress on my pussy as he laps me up, long, hungry licks that warn he, too, is about to come apart. I put my hands on his shoulders, move my pussy against his face, and once he's had his fill of me, he leans back on his heels. I gasp when I see the unchecked need shimmering in his dark eyes, hot, needy...savage.

Lord have mercy.

Unnerved, my body shakes and I take a wheezing breath. This man is going to wreck me, use me like I'm a sacrificial offering, a pawn in a game I can't win, and leave me strung out like an addict when we're done. More importantly, I'm going to let him.

Without a word he stands and I wet my lips as he unknots his towel, exposing his beautiful body as the cotton sails to the floor. I take in the gorgeous length of him, thick and heavy and throbbing to be touched. Need flutters through me and I almost climax again.

"I wonder how much I'll hate your big cock in my mouth," I say shakily, and sound vibrates in his throat as he briefly closes his eyes, a tremor moving through him.

"On your knees, Peyton."

I drop and put my knees on the towel. I brace my hands on my thighs and open my mouth for him.

"Have you done this before?" he asks.

"Are you asking if I've ever sucked your cock before?" I say.

"Hell, Peyton. Do you always have to be a smart-ass?" I grin. The truth is, there's a storm going on inside me, and I hide behind humor. His face softens. "Peyton, do you want this?"

"I've never sucked your cock before, or any cock," I say. "But I want this."

He tugs my bottom lip between his fingers and slides his thumb into my mouth. "Suck," he says, and I do. His resulting growl is a good indication that he likes what I'm doing. A thrill goes through me. He yanks his thumb from my mouth and wraps his palm around himself.

"Hell," he growls when I moan. "That is so hot," he murmurs, and strokes himself. His cock hovers near my mouth as he fists himself, long hard strokes that show me what he likes. "Spread your legs. I want to see your pussy," he says.

Hands still on my knees, I widen my legs, and he strokes himself from base to tip as his hot gaze caresses every inch of me. "Do you hate what you see?" I tease.

"Yeah, I can't stand it." A couple long strokes over his cock and then, "Open your mouth."

I whimper and do as he says. Putting my hands on his thighs, I wait for him to feed his hard length down my throat.

"You want this in your mouth, Peyton?"

"Yes," I say.

His eyes squeeze shut for a brief second, and it's easy to tell he's fighting for his control. "Are you going to hate it?"

I swallow as his lids flicker open and he stares down at me. "I am," I say.

"What else do you think you'll hate?" he asks, circling and teasing my mouth to open more.

"I'll probably hate spreading my legs wide for you and letting you put this hard cock in my pussy." Lord, I've never said anything quite so dirty before. It almost brings a giggle to my throat.

"Are you going to hate me wrecking you?" he asks, his voice thick, heavy with need.

"Uh-huh," I say as he pulses against my mouth, reducing me to a hot, quivering mess dying to taste him. His hips power forward, his body flexing, and he finally offers me an inch. I moan around his length and he grabs my hair, his fingers bunching in my curls.

"That's it," he groans.

I tighten my lips to suck, sealing them around his bulging veins. While I've never done this before, one thing is for certain, I hate it. Yeah, I hate it so goddamn much I want to take him even deeper. I want him to spurt down my throat. I want to taste every drop of his release, knowing it was me who made him this hard, this aroused.

I grip him in my hand, feasting on him like it's my goddamn job, and his breathing is so ragged and rough, his male scent that much sharper as he fights release.

"Enough," he says, and I whimper when he pulls from my mouth. "Get on that bed and spread your legs. Let's see how much you'll hate it when I'm inside you."

My legs are so rubbery, it's all I can do to stand up, get myself on the bed and spread my legs wide. He growls as he lets his gaze roam the length of me. Then he walks backward and my heart lurches. My God, has he changed his mind? Is he going to leave me like this and walk away laughing?

I go up on my elbows, my skin hot and flushed and achy for his touch. "Roman?" I say.

"Don't move. You stay just like that, Peyton. I'm going to get a condom, then I'm going to fuck the hell out of you once and for all. Will you hate that?"

"Yeah, over the years," I begin, so breathless it's a

bit hard to talk, "when I touched myself, and thought about you inside me, I hated it."

"You've thought about my cock a lot, huh?" he asks as he tugs on it.

"A time or two."

"You rubbed that sweet pussy while you thought about it?"

"Uh-huh."

"Did you come on your finger, Peyton?"

"I did." I slide my hand down my body, rub my breasts and go lower to swipe the soft pad of my finger over my clit. "I would get so wet."

"I like how wet you get."

"That's what you do to me," I admit.

"This is what you do to me," he says, and glances at his cock. "I imagined this so many times in my mind. There are so many ways I want to take you."

"I bet I'll hate them all."

He grins. "Yeah."

"Roman."

"Hmm," he says as I continue to touch myself.

"Condom."

"Right." He moans and I slick my finger over my clit as he disappears. A second later, he's on the bed, ripping into the wrapper and sheathing himself. He falls over me, heavy and strong, and captures my lips. He kisses me hard, claiming my mouth in a frenzied rush. I put my legs around him and lift.

He breaks the kiss and buries his mouth in the hollow of my neck, tasting my skin as he probes my slick opening.

"Please, fuck me," I cry out, and he pistons forward. A gasp catches in my throat as he rams into me, seating himself high and going perfectly still. His cock stretches my body, hits places, deep places I never knew existed. His head lifts and he stares down at me.

"Worst damn thing I ever felt," he says, and begins to move his hips, creating need and friction in my core. I wrap my arms around him to hang on, but it's no use. I'm free-falling without a net and if the landing doesn't kill me, it will ruin me forever. It's frightening. Exhilarating.

"Roman," I say. "I want… I want."

"What do you want?"

"I don't know."

"You want it like this, baby?" he asks, picking up the pace, hard blunt strokes that force the air from my lungs.

"Yes." Thank God he knows what I need even when I don't.

His big hands grip my shoulders, and he presses hot, openmouthed kisses to my neck and chest. His body shifts, the angle forcing him in deeper.

"My God," I cry out as he hits my cervix. He pounds against me, stimulating, rubbing, penetrating so deeply, hitting me at just the right angle, a full-body orgasm rips through me. I open my mouth but no words come when a deep shudder sends waves of pleasure from the top of my head to the tips of my toes.

He goes still inside me and curses under his breath as I shatter around him. "Jesus, Peyton," he says as

I ride the high and bask in each and every glorious pulse. So, this is what sex is like? Damn, I'd have been having it every single day if I knew it was this good. Then again, I'm sure it wouldn't be like this with anyone other than Roman—and the truth of the matter is, what this man does to me, it's a bit frightening.

He moves again, and my body tightens around him. "You got me there," he says, and slides out, only to jerk forward and fill me again. "Right there."

I scratch my nails along his back, scoring his flesh, like I'm marking him as mine, and he pulses inside me. He finds my mouth again for a deep, bruising kiss as he gives in to the pleasure and comes high inside me. His heart pounds against my chest, his body slick, hot and spasming as he collapses on top of me. He kisses my damp flesh again. His rough tongue trailing along my shoulder, as his one hand goes to my face. He cups my cheek and his head lifts, the tenderness in his gaze a complete contrast to our frenzied sex.

"Peyton," he says, and I struggle to get my breath.

"Yeah."

"Fuck."

I laugh at that, loving that I reduced this man to a quivering mess. "Yeah, we just did."

He chuckles against my flesh and shakes his head. "Did you hate it?"

"I've never hated anything more," I say.

"We'll see about that."

CHAPTER SIX

Roman

I CANNOT BELIEVE I just had sex with my best friend's kid sister. Not only that, I owned her, took everything she was giving and gave it back to her just as hard, maybe even harder. The truth is, her sweet, barely touched body came alive under my greedy hands, and I swear to God, knowing I was the one who could do that to her… Let's just say it rocked my world, and I've never come so hard in my entire life. She might have given me everything, and I damn well took it, but it was Peyton who held all the power, in a fundamental way.

I cast her a glance as we walk down the sidewalk, the early-morning sun beating down on us, but the warm rays have nothing to do with the glow on her face. No, I'm the reason her cheeks are flushed with heat. I take in her light blue dress, perfect for the classroom, and smooth my hand over my tie. Peyton's look is more casual than mine, but I'm comfortable in a suit and tie—my usual business attire. I don't need it for my job, but I grew up always having to look my best in public.

As people hurry by, heading to their workplaces, she hums under her breath, and I wish she'd stop. Now every time I hear that sound on her lips, it will take me back to her bedroom. We shouldn't have done that. No, I should have been stronger. An uncomfortable pressure builds in my chest. Christ. If her brother ever found out…

He can't find out.

He won't.

No regrets, Roman.

"Peyton, about Cason, I—"

She puts her hand up to stop me. "First, I know how important he is to you and I'm not going to let anything happen to your relationship. Second, what I do with my body and who I sleep with is not his business," she says, and my shoulders relax.

I'm an honest guy. Shit, I pride myself on it, and I'm a complete and utter asshole for A, sleeping with Peyton, and B, keeping it from Cason. I guess in the end, the fact that neither of us wants more, that we will go back to a clean slate when we're done here, means Cason never really has to know. Never has to know the guy he trusted with his sister, the guy he could always count on, betrayed the hell out of him.

Shit.

"You ready for this?" I ask, and her smile is a bit shaky when she lifts her head to me. A small shiver goes through her despite the warmth in the air.

"Yeah, I think so."

"You're cold."

"Probably just from nerves."

I frown down at her. "You always seem a little bit cold, Peyton."

She shrugs and I put my arm around her and draw her body close.

"Look at that, you didn't even flinch," I tease, wanting to ease her tension. This job is important to her. Being there for young minds, making them all feel important, loved and cherished—all the things she'd never felt, from anyone but Cason, growing up—is her life's goal.

She chuckles. "I guess it's a good thing we had that little experiment, then."

"That's what we're calling it, is it?" My gaze goes to her lush mouth. She opened that mouth for me this morning, the sweet sight more welcoming than a hard rain after a summer's drought. Christ, she took me so deep into her throat. Deeper than I would've ever expected her to take me, and how is it that oral sex with a woman who'd never given it before completely eclipsed every experience from my past? I wanted to come down her throat, fill her mouth with every last drop, but I needed to be inside her. Needed her snug sex muscles to milk my release more than I needed my next breath.

Dark lashes fall slowly over emerald eyes, and her look is demure, coy. "Yes. That's what we're calling it."

Shit, I love this teasing side of her. But two can play that game. "Fine, but I'd prefer if you didn't use the word *little* when you're referring to sex with me."

Her jaw drops open and her gorgeous green eyes go wide. "Did the humorless Roman Bianchi just crack a joke?" She reaches up and puts her hand on my forehead. "Are you sick, running a fever... delirious?"

I shove her hand away. "All right, smart-ass."

She grins at me, but her nervousness about her first day seems to have ebbed, and for that I'm grateful. We cross the street when the light turns and both go silent. After a long while she speaks.

"Roman," she says quietly, so quietly I almost miss it.

"Yes."

She shades the sun from her eyes and glances down the street. I follow the direction and spot the school in the near distance. "Thanks for this," she says.

"My pleasure," I say, and mean every word of it. This girl nccds a brcak, and I'm happy to give it to her. "Like I said, it's a nice reprieve from reality." With my arm still around her, I give a comforting squeeze. "We got this."

"Yeah, I think we do."

"Cason told me a bit about the job. He said you were in competition for the full-time position. How is that all working?" She breaks from my arm and sneezes into the crook of her elbow. I frown when she turns back to me, take in the red in her eyes. "Are you getting sick?" Maybe that's why she always seems to be shivering.

"I think it's actually allergies."

"Allergic to Malta?"

"Probably the different foliage they have here."

"Do you have any meds for that?"

"I'm sure it will pass," she says, and offers me a smile. "Back to your question. The full-time teacher left for maternity and made the decision not to come back. I'm one of two candidates hired for the month of June. I'm not sure who the other person is. We both work in the classroom until the end of the school year, and whoever 'fits' the best will be offered the full-time position in September."

"Why Malta?"

"The opportunity presented itself. I want to offer something to the children, expand their horizons. I feel like I can give back more in a place like this."

"Does it have to be Malta?"

"No, but these jobs aren't easy to come by and I want to be in a community in need, know what I mean?"

"I do."

A woman and her young son, who looks to be about three, stroll down the sidewalk, and I catch the loving way Peyton watches them, her lips curving at the corners. For a girl who doesn't want a family, or kids—doesn't believe in Cinderella or Prince Charming—she sure has a longing smile on her face. Maybe that's why she became a teacher—maybe all the children help fill the hollowed-out holes in her life.

"And you have to be married?"

The small family passes and her chest expands as she takes in a deep breath and lets it out ever so slowly. "Technically the marriage bar has been lifted, but it's practiced behind the scenes here. I don't like to deceive anyone, Roman, but I couldn't take a chance. I'm hoping once they see me in action with the kids, my marital status will no longer matter."

"I get it, but it's all ridiculous. It's the twenty-first century, for Christ's sake."

She shrugs. "I know, but this job means everything to me. Which is why—"

"Which is why I'm your husband." My body stiffens at the words. Wow, why the hell did that come out so easily, sound so right?

"Fake husband," she corrects.

"Isn't that what I said?"

"No."

"I meant to."

"Yeah, I know."

Children file into the school and it brings a smile to her face.

"You really like kids, huh?"

She laughs, but it's forced, and a gust of breeze blows her hair from her shoulders. "When they're someone else's kids, I do."

I nudge her. "I bet you'll love being an aunt."

She goes still, her eyes wide with excitement. "Wait, do you know something about Cason and Londyn that I don't?"

"I hardly think I'd be the first to know. I just mean, I'm sure they'll have kids at some point."

Her big smile wraps around me. "I guess I never thought about being an aunt before." She blinks up at me. "Do any of your sisters have kids?"

"Yeah, and I'm a shitty uncle."

Her face twists, a dubious smile. "I doubt that."

"I try to be a good uncle. I really do. But whenever I visit, it's like the Spanish Inquisition and children are thrust into my arms. I feel like if I touch one, I'll get infected."

Her laugh fills my soul with happiness. "Infected. Like they're a disease?"

"No, maybe the word is addicted, or hooked." I shake my head. "What I'm trying to say—"

"What you're trying to say is having kids is the norm, and people can't understand those like us who are child-free by choice."

"Isn't that what I said?"

She laughs and whacks me. "Oh yeah, that's exactly what you said. But no, I get it, and isn't that just another thing we have in common?"

I give her a teasing wink. "It's safe to say we recently discovered quite a few things we have in common," I say, my cock twitching in remembrance as a sexy pink blush colors her cheeks. Jesus, I want her again. Want to bury my face between her legs and taste her sweetness as I bring her to orgasm. I capture her hand, and without even thinking bring it to my mouth and press a kiss to her fingers. As soon as I do, we find ourselves at the school, the doors swinging open. Peyton turns, and I let our hands drop but continue to hold hers.

"You must be Peyton Harrison," a gentleman in his late fifties, dressed in a light gray suit, says.

Her smile widens and she takes his outstretched hand. "I am, and you must be Mr. Galea."

"Please, call me Andrew."

"It's so great to finally meet you, Andrew." She lets go of my hand and waves it toward me, palm up, as she introduces me to the man I can only assume is the principal. "This is my husband, Roman Bianchi."

Andrew frowns, and I stiffen. I have no idea why I feel like I'm back in grade school getting caught in a lie. Maybe because I *am* in the middle of a whopper of a lie. But it's for a greater purpose in an unfair situation, making it justifiable in my mind. Sleeping with Peyton and lying to Cason about it, however, no greater purpose involved there, and not at all justifiable. Then again, I won't have to lie to his face, because he won't ask if I'm sleeping with his sister. He trusts me like that. Like Cason, I'm a guy who prides himself on the truth, too. But this is my best friend's kid sister, and I'd do anything for him. Okay, who the hell am I kidding? This is Peyton, and I'd do anything for *her*. Even let her seduce me into her bed.

"Roman Bianchi," the man says, and my breath stalls as my name sticks on his tongue, like he's trying to figure out where he'd heard it before. Shit, maybe we should have made up a fake last name. "Do you have a sister named Aurora?"

"Actually, yeah, I do," I say, and reach for Peyton's hand again when her eyes widen.

"My goodness, I had no idea I was in the presence of royalty," he says.

I hold my hands up to stop him. "The Bianchis are an old family, but we have no titles to our name. And please, I like to keep a low profile."

"Yes, I always heard that about you." His gaze goes from me to Peyton, and he must be remembering my failed engagement.

"We've kept things quiet," I say. "You can imagine why."

He nods, his blue eyes thoughtful. "Of course. I must tell you, though, your sister and my old college friend Lorenzo Costa are husband and wife."

Worry cuts like a sharp blade. "You went to college with Lorenzo? What a small world," I say, hoping to make light of it.

"Small indeed," he agrees, and my stomach is so damn tight with worry, I give Peyton's hand another fast squeeze. Shit, this is not good. If word gets out…

"Do you talk with Lorenzo very often?" I ask around the knot in my throat. Christ, I'm here to help Peyton, not screw everything up for her.

"No, it's been a while. I must give him a call soon. Catch up."

"Like I mentioned, I do appreciate my privacy." I roll my eyes playfully. "If you know my sisters, I'd never get a moment's peace if they knew I was here."

He laughs like he does indeed know my family. "They are all lovely women and I'm a younger brother in a big family, too, so I fully understand what it's like to have intrusive sisters." He claps his hands together and turns to Peyton, and I relax a bit hoping we just dodged a bullet. "How about a tour, and then I'll take you in to meet the staff before introducing you to your new students?"

"That sounds lovely," Peyton says, the hitch in her voice noticeable only to me, and only because I know this woman. I give a little nod to let her know I got this, that everything will be okay. Her big eyes scan my face, and she relaxes slightly with my reassurance. Jesus, this girl trusts me, and I better be able to back it up and make sure I don't mess this up.

We walk through the colorful halls and children's laughter reaches our ears. "Richard is already here," he says.

"Richard?" Peyton asks.

He shakes his head. "My apologies. Richard is the other teacher. An American, like you. He, too, is vying for the full-time position. His darling wife is with him. They've been here for over an hour." I glance at my watch. "He's eager to get started, I guess," Andrew adds. "I bet you will all hit it off."

I want to ask why he's holding a ridiculous competition in the first place. Peyton is clearly the best candidate and I don't even have to meet Richard, the eager beaver, to know it.

As if reading my mind, Andrew turns to me. "This is a much-coveted position, and while Richard and Peyton were top candidates, it's important to us to see them in their role."

I wrap my arm around Peyton. "I'm sure you'll be extraordinarily impressed. She impresses me every day."

"How did you two meet?" he asks.

"Roman and my brother are best friends. They met in college, Penn State. Perhaps you know my brother, Cason Harrison. He's the creator of Hard Wear, quality fashion for men, and Soft Wear, quality fashion for women."

Andrew's eyes widen. "I have heard of that app. I believe my wife uses it."

Peyton turns from us, sneezing into her arm again. "Sorry, allergies," she explains as she fishes a tissue from her purse. Andrew gives us the grand tour and we end in the teachers' lounge. He introduces us and everyone greets us with smiles and open arms, until he presents Richard and his wife, Paula, both of whom I instantly dislike. Oh, they're smiling, but I grew up surrounded by fake, and know it when I see it.

"If you'll excuse me for a moment," Andrew says and disappears, leaving us with Richard and his wife.

"I'm looking forward to getting to know you both better," Richard says. "Where are you residing for the month?"

For the month?

Okay, now that shit just pisses me off. He's acting like he's already got the job and Peyton might as well not get too settled.

"Not far," I say, when his gaze lands on me. I work to keep my cool and add, "In this community."

Paula flashes me a saccharine smile. "Looks like we're neighbors. We must socialize." She puts her hand on her husband's chest. "In the evenings of course. Throughout the day, I'll be home tending to the house and supporting my husband." Her eyes turn to me. "And you, Roman? What will you be doing when your wife is at work?"

I move closer to my *wife* and anchor her body to mine. As the protector in me roars to life, I fight the instinct to stand in between her and these assholes. Peyton is tough on the outside and has the ability to handle this guy and his wife. It's what's underneath her bravado that worries me, the flare of some deeper emotion she keeps tucked deep, protected by an impenetrable and unscalable wall.

"I'll be home supporting my wife, too," I say, remaining on my best behavior as my fingers curl.

"Like a house husband?" Paula presses manicured nails to her chest and lets out a mocking laugh, stoking the anger in me. "How adorable."

"So nontraditional," Richard, and when I say Richard, I mean asshole, pipes in.

"You don't want to stay home and have a family, Peyton?" Paula asks.

When Peyton's face pales, a muscle twitches beneath my eye and I open my mouth, not about to let anyone belittle her or question her choices, but she puts her hand on my arm.

"I'm not saying that. I'm saying I'm an independent woman," Peyton says. "My choices are my own, as are yours, and I hope we've come to the point where women have stopped shaming each other for their choices. We can have a family whether we work or stay home. I mean it is the twenty-first century after all."

Atta girl!

I glare at Paula as she lifts her chin. "Yes, of

course," she says. "I guess I'll always be that old-fashioned girl. Not that there is anything wrong with what you're doing," she says, her voice sweet, but the malicious glare tells a different story. "We just prefer to do things differently. That's how it is in the Ozarks, where we come from, our values are much like they are here in Malta. Very different from New York, obviously."

Two elderly ladies step into the lounge and I shake my head as Paula and her husband dismiss us and turn to charm them. I rub the knot from the back of my neck, hardly able to believe people like that still exist in this world. Then again, maybe that's exactly what they're looking for in Malta. Old time-y values. Peyton, however, has more values in her pinkie finger than almost anyone and while there is nothing wrong with staying home, no one and I mean no one should shame a woman for wanting a career. Peyton's choices are hers, and hers alone—and that comes to her sexuality, too. As that epiphany hits me like the slap of a teacher's ruler, it occurs to me she's right about a lot of things she said to me, mainly that she can sleep with whoever she wants to sleep with while she's here—as long as it's me.

Christ.

I love her brother dearly but all of a sudden I can't help but think maybe someone ought to tell him Peyton is a grown woman and her decisions are her own.

Andrew steps back into the lounge and claps his hands.

"Before I introduce you to your students, who are

ready and excited to meet you, I would like to extend an invitation to you all, a get-to-know-one-another dinner at my home tonight."

"We'd love to," Richard says quickly. Peyton, however, casts me a quick glance.

I appreciate the check-in; it's what most married couples would do. Making decisions together is something I watched my folks and my married siblings do over the years. I can't help but wonder if her reaction was because she's playing the part or she doesn't want to ask too much from me. But I'm here for her. This woman is beautiful and selfless, and became a teacher to give back and make sure every child feels cherished. Whatever she needs from me, she gets.

"Sounds great to me," I say, and the smile that splits her lips is enough to destroy any man. My heart tumbles a little in my chest, and I give a big swallow.

You're here to help her, dude, maybe engage in a few marital benefits, and nothing else.

"It's settled then. Let's go say hello to your students."

I put my hands on her shoulders. "Wish me luck," she says.

"You don't need it. You've got this, Peyton." I bend and press my lips to hers. I brush her mouth lightly, and at first the public display of affection startles her. Within seconds, she warms to my touch, to the show I'm putting on—or at least I'm trying to convince myself it's all for show and simply for our small audience. Peyton's mouth lingers beneath mine, like she's in no hurry to pull away, and

I slowly break free and pull myself up to my full height. Paula, clearly one never to be outdone, goes up on her toes and kisses her husband.

I put my mouth close to Peyton's ear and a quiver goes through her. "I'll be at home, waiting for you," I say. She nods, but the surprised yet appreciative look that comes over her face is a fast reminder that outside of her brother, this woman has never been able to count on anyone. I want her to be able to count on me.

Peyton casts a quick glance over her shoulder and I give her a little "you got this" nod as Andrew leads them from the room. It warms my heart and reminds me there really is still a lot of good in this world. Her brother must be so proud of the woman she's become. He just needs to realize she is a woman and not a small, parentless child he has to protect due to a neglectful grandmother, followed by years in the system.

Speaking of siblings.

My phone pings in my pocket and I don't have to check it to know it's my sister, Aurora. I gave them all personalized rings. I toy with the phone and fight down a burst of unease as Peyton and Richard follow the principal out the door. I hope Andrew didn't excuse himself so he could put a call in to his old college buddy—my sister's husband. Shit, if word of this gets out, all Peyton's hard work, hopes and dreams will go down the toilet. I can't let that happen.

I'm about to leave when Paula lifts her head, her eyes narrow. "I can't quite figure it out, but you look so familiar. Have we met before?"

CHAPTER SEVEN

Peyton

I SIT AT the front of the class and my insides are aflutter as all the little ones pack up their belongings and get ready to head home. My day was amazing. Meeting such wonderful children all eager to learn a new language. I'm in a different country yet deep inside, I feel oddly connected to it, like it's where I belong. Strange, I know, considering I've never belonged anywhere before.

Throughout the day I had to dig deep to recall my years of Italian studies. Maybe I should ask Roman to speak to me in his mother tongue to keep me on top of my game. I pack my briefcase and wave to the children as they file from the classroom. I'm about to follow behind but instead roam around the classroom, a small smile on my face as I take in the artwork we did today.

"All set?" a voice asks from behind and I turn, startled. My wide eyes narrow, and my heart misses a small beat when I find my "husband" standing there, looking so casual and relaxed, so sweet and sexy at the same time, I can't help but second-guess what I'm getting myself into with him.

"You startled me."

I quiver under his steely gaze and the air around us vibrates when he says, "Payback for sneaking up on me last night in the pool."

"First, I wasn't sneaking up on you," I say as his eyes visually caress me. "And second, I had no idea you were the vengeful type."

"I can be vengeful," he says, and saunters toward me, his hands shoved into the pockets of his khaki pants. His clothes are casual this afternoon, but no less devastating. Breathless—it's the only way to describe what his presence does to me.

I inhale shallowly as my body buzzes to life. "That polo looks amazing on you," I say. Heat floods my body as my gaze falls to take in the way *he* makes the shirt look good, not the other way around. I can only assume he wore a suit this morning to help make a good impression, and I truly appreciate his attention to detail—inside the bedroom and out.

He steps up to me, slides one hand around my body and with no finesse pulls me to him. Our bodies collide, and as he inhales, filling his lungs with my scent, I shiver under his touch. "Is that right?" he asks, splaying the hand on my back, his fingers lightly brushing the swell of my backside. Ripples of sensual pleasure move through me, and my little fluttering breath gives away my arousal. His grin is knowing when he says, "You know what I think would look even better on me?"

His sexy smile rattles me even more. "What?" I ask; the brown in his eyes deepens, a telltale sign of the lust building inside him. "Me?"

He laughs. "You took the word right out of my mouth," he answers, his voice raspy and fractured. Once again I can't help but think he's not as in control as he seems. I'm not sure why but it secretly thrills me when this man becomes unhinged.

I brush my thumb over his bottom lip and press my breasts into his chest. "Well, now that this mouth of yours is empty maybe we can fill it with something else."

His cock instantly hardens against my leg, and he gives an almost resigned shake of his head. "I can't believe you said that."

"You mean you can't believe *I* said it before *you* said it." I laugh and poke his chest. "You were thinking it. Don't even try to deny it."

"Not trying," he says with a cocky grin. The more time we spend together, the more playful he becomes. Before this trip, he kept that side of himself locked up tight. I guess humiliation in the past—he was dumped just before his wedding—forced him to keep his guard in place, and perhaps he doesn't feel the need to protect himself with me after we both made it clear where we stood. I get that he's still worried about his friendship with Cason, but I'm not a girl to kiss and tell. Heck, up until this morning, and the time he ravished my mouth at the wedding, I wasn't even a girl who kissed, period. Damned if I haven't been missing out, though. Then again, it's not like I'd want another man's lips on mine. No, and right there, that fact alone, could very well lead to a problem.

No regrets, Peyton.

I push that thought from my mind as he glances over his shoulder. His grin is mischievous, playful when he turns back to me, his eyes zeroing in on my mouth. His hips move, pressing against me, conveying all his needs. Desire twists inside me as I ache to lose myself in him a second time.

"Want to shut the door?" he asks, his voice a rough whisper that glides over my flesh and hints at things to come. Intimate things. Dirty things. I'd be lying if I said I wasn't excited by the prospect.

"No," I blurt out, and he cocks his head, his brow raised, his tanned skin glistening in the rays of sun streaming in through the big windows. I lean into him, soak in his warmth. The scent of his skin, clean soap infused with testosterone, swirls around me. "Well, yeah, of course I want you to shut the door." That brings a smile to his face. "But I'm not about to jeopardize this job."

His demeanor changes and he steps back, putting a measure of distance between us, and I instantly miss the connection. "Right. Sorry about that." He taps his head and winks at me. "Loss of blood there for a second."

"Don't be sorry." I sidle back up to him, put my hands on his chest, loving his strong heartbeat beneath my palm. "I kind of like that I can do this to you."

"Ah, something you *like*," he says, a slow nod of his head. "That's different."

I run my finger along his cheek, the bristles on his late-afternoon shadow rough against my flesh. How would it feel between my legs? "Let's hurry home. I'll show you what else I like doing to you."

He frowns. "Don't we have to go to Andrew's for dinner?"

I glance at the clock. "If we hurry, we—"

He snatches my hand and ushers me out the class-room door before I can even finish my sentence. Hand in hand, like two lovestruck teenagers, we laugh and hurry outside the school. I sneeze again when we pass by the same purple flowers.

He casts me a quick glance, and beneath the lust I spot genuine concern. "Allergies?" I nod, and he slows his steps when I become a bit breathless. "Tell me about your day," he says, his brow furrowed, real interest on his face. "Did you enjoy it as much as you thought you would?"

"It was so much fun. The kids are all wonderful." He grins at me and I talk endlessly, as I sometimes do, as we continue to make our way back home. We reach the villa and I'm winded from my incessant chatter. "I'm sorry," I say.

"For what?" Roman pushes the door open and gestures for me to enter.

"I talked nonstop and never even asked how your day was." I frown and his mouth drops to my lips, stoking my need for him as I push past him. "That was thoughtless of me."

"There's nothing thoughtless about you, Peyton." His voice is almost tortured as he says that, like it's something he can't quite comprehend, like it scares him a bit. Inside he shuts the door and pushes me against it. "And if you really want to know about my day, let's just say we're about to get to the highlight reel."

"Does the highlight reel have anything to do with me?" I slide my arms around his neck and take pleasure in his strength and sureness. The man is a powerhouse, and while I feel small in his arms, I also feel cherished.

"It has everything to do with you. Don't you realize you're the star of the show?" He runs his thumb over my bottom lip, and warm sensations grip me. "This mouth. I've been thinking about it all day." His nostrils flare and my nipples tighten with arousal. "I'm going to destroy it." I suck in a breath, his filthy words derailing my ability to think. He inches closer, his lips a breath away from mine, and I'm about to open for him, welcome his ravishing tongue inside, when my nose tingles.

"What…what if I'm getting a cold?"

His eyes are glazed, completely enraptured with my mouth, a hungry wolf about to feast on a lamb, when he says, "I thought you said it was just allergies."

"Can we take a chance?" I rake my hand through his hair and make a mess of it. The mussed-up look works for him. Then again, any look works for him. "I don't want you to get sick." Why the hell am I trying to talk him out of this when I want him to strip me bare and make a complete and utter mess of me?

He laughs, but it's more like a tortured growl and my body burns in response. "You think a cold is going to keep me from claiming this sweet mouth?" Oh God, I shouldn't like how he wants to claim me. I shouldn't like it at all. But I do.

He presses his body against mine, and his cock is so hard, I'm pretty sure the entire marine corps couldn't stop him from touching me. "I don't want to get you sick."

Just shut up already, Peyton.

"Yeah, I know. You're sweet like that." His demeanor changes, and in the blink of an eye the wild animal vanishes, the hunger receding, giving way to a soft smile as he pulls me from the door. "Come on," he says, the tenderness in his tone like a gentle caress over my skin, and I work to ignore the strange possessive tug on my emotions.

This is just sex, Peyton.

"Where?"

He leads me into the kitchen, and on the counter I see every kind of allergy medication known to mankind. "What did you do?"

He gives a casual shrug, like it's nothing, but it's not nothing to me. "I didn't know what kind you took."

I pick up box after box after box. "You have enough here to obliterate allergies from mankind."

"Just need to obliterate them from you," he says.

My heart thumps, my insides going to mush.

It's just sex, Peyton.

Why then, when he does stuff like this, does it feel like so much more?

"Roman," I say. I'm so touched by his thoughtfulness, it's hard to push the words out.

"I told you I was committed, Peyton. You're going to get this job and you're not going to be taken out by allergies."

I fight a stupid tear and my chaotic emotions scramble in all directions, every sentiment I've locked up over the years trying to crawl over the jagged-edged wall I erected early on in life. But there are too many moving parts, racing at a speed I'm not accustomed to, scattering before I can lasso them back in. I swallow, a silly attempt to rein them all in, but I can't let him see how much his random act of kindness has touched me or have him thinking I'm going to fall for him because of one thoughtful gesture.

Oh, but it's been more than one, Peyton.

"It's just…"

He puts his hand around my neck and spreads his fingers, lust once again returning to his eyes. "Maybe I had ulterior motives," he says, bringing this back to what's really between us—sex—and I'm grateful for that. No need to mistake the physical for the emotional. A person can attend to your basic needs—shelter, food, water…allergy medication—but that doesn't mean they care deeply about you. A lesson learned at a young age taught me that, and I'm not about to forget it now. I can't.

"Ulterior motives, huh?" I pop a pill from a bubble pack as he pours me a glass of water.

"Maybe I need you healthy so we can experiment more, see what else you hate—or what you like." I grin. This morning I put all my best efforts forth to seduce this man, but now that we've broken the seal—or rather removed our clothes and gone at each other like wild animals during mating season—this man is all in. He hands me the glass and I take the pill. I swipe my tongue over my lip, and much as I expected, a small moan escapes his throat.

"What was that you said about filling your empty mouth?" I ask, and arch a brow.

His grin is crooked. "I believe that is what *you* said."

I feign innocence and back up toward the stairs. "Me? I can't believe you would accuse me of saying something like that, Roman."

"Where do you think you're going?" he growls when I reach the stairs.

"I don't think I should be around anyone who would accuse me of saying something so…dirty."

"Get back here, Peyton."

I rush up the steps and his footsteps pound on the kitchen floor.

I glance over my shoulder. "Not until you tell the truth."

"Peyton," he says, his warning voice churning with passion.

"Admit it was you who said it."

"Calling me a liar, are you?" he grumbles, his deep, thick voice curling through me and teasing the needy little cleft aching for his attention.

"If the name fits."

As his long legs carry him up the stairs fast, and

he begins to close the gap, I bypass the bedrooms and go straight for the rooftop. He's hot on my heels and I can't stop laughing when I reach the top step, kicking my shoes off and tearing at my dress the whole way. I'm in nothing but my bra and panties when I reach the pool, and without bothering to remove them I dive in.

I swim to the shallow end, and when I surface, Roman is right there, his clothes soaked, and a bubble of joy wells up inside me. I can't remember the last time I had fun like this, or laughed this hard. Honestly, for the first time, I feel like the weight of the world isn't on my shoulders and I can just be... me. I'm guessing it's because we both know where the other stands.

Where exactly is it you stand, Peyton?

I shut down that inner voice—I cannot fall for him—as his arms slide around my waist. In a move that is less than gentle, he anchors me to his solid body, and I register every delicious detail of his hardness.

"Want to know what fits?" he asks, the lust in his eyes heating the surrounding water and pushing the chill from my bones until I'm almost warm.

"What?" I ask, breathless. He puts one hand between my legs and pushes my panties to the side. A thick finger presses inside me, and my breath hitches. God, that feels good.

"My cock, right here. That's what fits." His mouth finds mine for a mind-numbing kiss and I quake as he begins to finger me. His thumb slides up, stroking my cleft, increasing the sensations, and I quiver at the sweet agony.

He tears his mouth from mine and puts it to my ear. "Want to know something else?"

"Yeah."

"I don't take too kindly to being called a liar." His hands slide down my back and he splays his fingers over my ass. He kneads my flesh, his hands full of ownership as he tugs, to widen my cheeks, and a cold rush of water stimulates all my sensitive nerve endings.

"Say it again, and I'll own this ass," he growls.

"Oh God, yes," I cry out without thinking, and his soft chuckle curls around me.

"Oh, you *like* that, do you?"

"I…don't know," I say. "My guess is I'd hate it."

His growl of laughter vibrates in the air, ripples through the water, and I move my hips, try to work his finger around inside me.

"Yeah, I can tell how much you'd hate it." He slowly pushes his finger in deeper. "Maybe I'll have to find another way to punish you." He bites his bottom lip, his shoulder muscles flexing beneath my fingers, and my sex clenches, desperate for him to take the ache away. "Maybe I'll put you on the side of the pool, spread you wide, shove my fingers inside you and give you a good hard licking."

I close my eyes as the sensations and image pull me under, and I don't dare say a word for fear he'll change his mind. As I revel in all the things he's threatening to do to me, a strong palm cups my face.

"Look at me, Peyton," he says, and my lids lift. The intensity in his eyes is as frightening as it is exciting. His hand leaves my cheek, a slow exploration downward, his fingers sliding between my breasts, his hot gaze following behind. A second later my bra is gone, and his look is ravenous as he lifts me, taking one nipple between his teeth. His lips close over my bud, hungry, demanding, and I arch into him, loving this feral side that takes without asking. I've never wanted to open myself, give myself up like this before. But it's a game we're playing and I can't forget it.

The water moves around me, and that's when I realize he's walking me to the edge, his deep growl rumbling through my body. He settles my bottom on the stone decking. Strong fingers grip my thighs and spread my legs. Need zings through my body and my throat instantly dries.

His mouth finds mine for a ravenous kiss and my entire body heats, a small moan catching in my throat. He pushes himself against my leg, and with my panties pushed to the side, he works magic with his fingers and I grow impossibly slicker. I thrust my pelvis, demanding more.

"Have you thought about me today? Thought about all the things I was going to do to you?"

"Uh-huh," I say as he pushes a finger into me, and pulls it out, his concentration deep, like he's working out some mathematical computation.

"Yes. Have you been thinking of me?" I ask in return. He slides his finger into his mouth, and for whatever reason watching him lick my slick arousal from his finger is like a goddamn aphrodisiac. Pressure builds inside me, and I tremble and pant.

"Roman," I murmur, my gaze focused on his mouth.

He pulls his finger from his mouth and pins me with a glare, his hard body holding me in place, trapping me beneath him. "What, you want a taste?" He leans into me, his soft lips on mine, but his tongue, oh there's nothing soft about that as it roughly invades my mouth, wars with my own tongue, like a king about to conquer an army and claim the bounty.

I'm the bounty.

His mouth slides from mine, stopping to tease my nipple between his teeth in his quest for the treasure between my legs. I've never felt like it was a prized possession, something to be worshipped, until this morning. He growls around a hard nub, tugs at it, and pain and pleasure tangle for dominance.

I lean back on my arms, brace myself as he feasts on me. My nipple pops from his mouth, and he licks a path downward until he finds what he's looking for. His growl of pleasure wraps around me, and my skin tightens as the late-day sun shines on my body, sizzling the water on my exposed flesh, but I can't think about that. No, I can't think about anything other than his tongue and the lashes he's giving my clit, a brutal punishment so intense it ignites every nerve ending and pulls a cry from my throat.

"My God, Roman," I say, impatience in my voice

as I lift, bucking against his face as his tongue swirls through my slick heat doing delicious things to me.

He growls and holds my hips, better positioning me as he feasts, his mouth ravishing my pussy, hungry little laps that drive me insane. His fingers tease, delve deep, slick in and out of my channel, but then he changes tactics and scrapes his teeth over my engorged cleft. Small tremors grip me as he spears deeper inside me, pounds into my flesh, hot, dirty plunges that possess my body, and tease the building pressure.

I sit up and grip his hair to hold on. My senses explode, my body jerking in reaction to the intense pleasure. The man is wrecking me, and my struggle to hang on splinters, breaking me in two. Air leaves my lungs, and my words are nothing but a pleading whimper when I say, "I'm going to come." Oh God, am I ever going to come. So hard, I'm going to shatter in the most profound ways, ways there are no coming back from.

I throw my head back and my muscles convulse around him, shock waves rocketing through me as he nudges me over the edge until I'm flying. Flying and falling, living and dying all wrapped into one as the man frees my body in a way no one ever has before, in a way I've never been able to achieve solo.

I'm panting by the time he stops, but dark eyes meet mine, and giving me no reprieve, he tears my panties from my hips and pulls me back into the water. With my legs around him he backs up until he's sitting on the steps, water lapping at his ankles.

He tugs his pants down, just enough to free his cock, and pulls me toward him. "Ride my cock, Peyton," he demands. I widen my legs to straddle him and he growls as I reposition.

His crown presses against my opening, and delirious with need, he grips me and tugs me firmly down. I gasp as he fills me, and lean forward and lay my forehead on his shoulder, trying to catch my breath.

"I want you to ride me," he growls into my ear. "I want to watch myself slide in and out of you."

I savor the dirty, delicious way he wants me, the way he couldn't even get his pants off before he had me on top of him.

"Look at what you're doing to me," he demands, his eyes dark and feral as I tear my gaze away and look between our bodies. I lift, and his erection is wet and slick as he slides out of me.

"So hot," I say, my muscles rippling.

"Jesus, I feel you." His body tenses as my thigh muscles burn. He grips my hips and manipulates my body to take the strain from my legs. He's so damn strong he lifts me easily and pulls down until his steely length fills every inch of me. "Do you hate how hard you make me?" he hisses through clenched teeth.

"I hate it," I cry out. "I hate your cock. Hate the way you fill me up. Hate when I shatter around you."

"Keep riding me, Peyton." My nails dig into his shoulder, but he doesn't so much as wince. "I want you to make me come."

Oh God, it's crazy how much I love it when he

talks dirty. I let him move me, twist me to the way he needs me, and he lifts his hips, powering into me. My body flushes hot, and I reach between us to stroke my clit.

"Yeah, just like that." His nostrils flare, his lips part, and he thickens even more inside me. I'm so damn wet, his rapid thrusting picking up the pace until the friction is unbearable, control a thing of the past.

I briefly close my eyes, fearing I'm losing my damn grip on reality as this man drives into me, his fingers biting into my hips. Tomorrow I'll have little bruises and the thought thrills me. He jerks me up, then pulls me down again, so goddamn hard, he hits my cervix, and draws another full-body release out of me.

"Roman," I cry out, and practically collapse on top of him. My body shakes, a hard quiver, so powerful and intense, it leaves me trembling, on the brink of tears. Soothing hands drift up from my hips to wrap around me.

"I got you," he says, and my heart squeezes at the tenderness in his voice. I move my body as he cradles me, rotate my hips around his thick cock, wanting more, wanting everything as a new, almost frightening kind of hunger takes hold. "Take what you need, Peyton," he says, like he can see into my soul, understand I'm still that small frightened girl who asked for nothing. My throat squeezes tight, my hair falling forward as I lean into him. "Take everything you need," he says, his voice rusty and harsh, thick with an emotion I can't identify.

I rock against him, knowing I'll never truly have

what I need, not from him or any other man. My breasts rub against his face, and I lift, only to slowly sink back down. His hands move to my face and he cups my cheeks, bringing my mouth to his. He groans into my mouth, and I swallow his moans as he lets go, giving in to the need gripping his body. I struggle to breathe with each hard pulse inside me.

"I feel you," I murmur, the pleasure so intense as his release sears my insides and stimulates all my nerve endings, and I come again. "Oh my God, Roman," I breathe into his mouth.

"I know, Peyton, I know," he moans, and peppers kisses to my nose and cheeks and chin. "Jesus, I know," he says. I inch back to take in the darkness in his eyes, the need he's desperately trying to hide. Or maybe I'm imagining it. I've wanted for so long to be wanted and needed, maybe my mind is playing tricks on me and the sex is messing with my perception of reality. He cups the back of my head and brings my face to his shoulder. His hand strokes down my hair, his touch so soft and gentle, my stupid heart misses a beat. Once again, I let my mind wander, live in a fairy-tale world where Roman and I could be more. Is that what I want? I bask in it for a second, until his worried voice breaks the spell.

"Shit, we just made a big mistake."

CHAPTER EIGHT

Roman

I LIFT HER from my lap, and we both collapse on the warm decking. The warm late-day sun disappears behind a heavy cloud, darkening the rooftop—not to mention my mood. Talk about a colossal mistake. What the hell is wrong with me? What was I thinking? Oh, maybe I *wasn't* thinking—not with the head on my shoulders—because I simply couldn't get inside this sweet girl fast enough, but goddammit she deserves better from me.

"Roman?" Peyton's eyes are wide when they search mine, seeking answers, and the fear I see there is like a punch to the gut. Christ, I'm not even sure she's breathing.

"I didn't—" I begin, but stop when the worry in her eyes deepens, triggering a pang of unease deep inside me. I push the hair from her face. Shit, what is going through her mind? "I didn't use a condom," I tell her. "I completely forgot, and I'm so damn sorry."

She nods and the breath she'd been holding leaves

her lungs in a whoosh. "Is that all?" she finally says, and I put my hand on her shoulder, her muscles relaxing under my touch. *Is that all? That's her reaction? What the hell? I thought she'd be as upset as I am,* but she seems to be okay with it. What am I missing here, or more importantly, what the hell did she think I was going to say? What could be worse than not using a condom, especially when we have no future?

I brush my thumb over her skin. "What did you think I meant?"

"Nothing," she says quickly, and averts her gaze, but I'm not having any of that. I want openness and honesty between us. I cup her chin and bring her focus back to me. That's when I see it, right there in the depths of her eyes. This sweet vulnerable girl puts a big smile on for the world but underneath it all, she's still lost, still vulnerable, still thinks she's unlikable…unlovable.

"Did you think I meant me sleeping with you again was a mistake?" I ask, wrapping the question in a soft voice.

"I guess, maybe."

"Because of my relationship with Cason?" Yeah, he'd give me a beating if he ever found out—hate me for the rest of my life, likely—but she said she'd keep our secret and I trust her.

"Well…no. This isn't about Cason."

"Then what?"

She shakes my hand from her chin and turns from me, her long auburn curls falling over her chest. "Can we not talk about this?"

I take a curl between my fingers, rub softly. "I want to talk about it, Peyton. We're friends." Honestly if anyone can use a true friend, someone she can trust implicitly, it's Peyton. "More than friends right now, actually," I tease, hoping it brings a smile to her face.

"Look," she says, her dark tone cutting into my thoughts. "It's no big deal. I just thought you changed your mind about all this."

"Because I no longer wanted you?"

Shit, right there. Right there, all over her face, lies my answer.

She tries for a casual shrug, but fails miserably. "I just thought you'd changed your mind."

My God, her screwed-up childhood really did a number on her. I probably didn't help when I kissed her and walked away, leaving her to believe she wasn't likable. I just hadn't wanted to betray her brother.

Doesn't matter, I never should have started something I couldn't finish. Not with Peyton. If I could kick my own ass I would. What I can do now, however, is show her she's everything any man would want, and more. I roll toward her, my body pressing against her leg.

"I like being with you, Peyton." I brush my hand over her cheek. "I like *you*."

She grins and glances down past my waist. "I can tell."

I chuckle at that. Sure, I'm physically attracted to her, but I like her. She's a kind, caring and giving woman. I haven't come across many of those in my life, besides my family. I thought my ex was all those things, but look how that turned out. I hope someday Peyton finds a guy who can give her the family she says she doesn't want, because I get the sense that she's just too frightened to put herself out there, afraid that she's not enough, afraid of getting close, of getting hurt…again.

"You know, for years I kept you at a distance, but you were right when you said it's your body, yours to do with as you wish, and who you sleep with is none of Cason's business." The truth is Cason is completely overprotective of her. I can understand that, though. It was just the two of them against the world. Everything about Peyton, from her big green eyes to the way she tries to hide her vulnerabilities, brings out the protector in me, too. I'd like to put her in a bubble and keep her sheltered from a world that has been cruel to her. Of course, she'd introduce her foot to my nuts if I tried. She's a grown woman and mistakes or not, her decisions regarding her life and her body are hers.

"Coming around to my way of thinking, are you?"

"When you're right, you're right," I say, and trail my finger down her arm. "But we should have used a condom." My gaze narrows in on her. "I'm clean, but neither one of us wants a family, right?" I say, my gaze roaming her face. Will she agree with me, or finally admit that she wants more from life? I used to want a family. I used to want a lot of things, but

I gave up the idea when I realized women value my status over me.

"That's right, we don't, and it's okay. I'm on the Pill. It regulates my cycle."

A ridiculous laugh bubbles up inside me and spills from my mouth.

Peyton's brows arch. "What, does it make you uncomfortable to talk about a woman's menstruation cycle?"

"Hell no, it's just..." I shake my head. "This... us... I never in a million years pictured this..." I wave my hand back and forth between our bodies. "Correction, I've pictured this, a thousand different ways, but I never thought we'd be having sex, on a rooftop no less, forgetting condoms and talking about your cycle." I flop onto my back, a grin tugging at my mouth. I like the openness and honesty between us. A little too much, actually.

Careful, Roman.

"You didn't stand a chance, Roman," she says, a playful tone in her voice.

"Oh?" I angle my head to see her green eyes glistening with mischief.

She blows on her knuckles and brushes them over her chest. "I go after what I want, and I wanted you."

Liking that far too much, I roll on top of her and she squeals when I grab her hands and put them over her head. "You're a tease, you know that." I brush my lips over hers as I begin to harden again.

"You say that like it's a bad thing," she says, and

lifts her hips to grind against my swelling member. My God, I can't get enough of this woman.

"I think we have another problem." I press my lips to hers when she arches a questioning brow. "I want to fuck you again."

Her eyes dim with desire. "Pretty sure that's not a problem."

"It is when we have to be at your boss's house."

Her lids fly open. "Ohmigod, you're right. We need to get moving."

I roll off her, stand and pull her to her feet. Our bodies mesh, and she smiles up at me. "Thanks for saying that about my body being mine. I'm glad you see it that way and can finally understand why I get so frustrated with Cason."

"Doesn't mean he's not going to kill me, though."

She frowns and glances at my chest, her finger rolling around my nipple. "Yeah, I know he will. Are you regretting this, Roman? Are you sorry I seduced you?"

"Hell no," I blurt out, and it brings a smile to her face. "I was fighting a losing battle with you, and I want to be honest. I tried to tell myself that coming here with you was all for Cason. That was a lie."

"It was?" she asks, a small hitch in her voice.

"I wanted to be around you. I didn't plan for anything to happen between us, but I just wanted to be around you." A garbled laugh catches in my throat. "I must be some kind of masochist, huh?" She smiles and I put my hands on her shoulders to display just how serious I am when I glance down at her and continue with, "I also really wanted to help you, Peyton. What you want, well, if it's important to you, then it's important to me, too." She's important to me. She always has been.

Sometimes I think I didn't stop the engagement, went through with the wedding prep, because this girl could never be mine, and it was a way to make that clear—to myself. Even though the engagement failed, Peyton and I still can't have a real relationship. We want different things and her brother would disown both of us. She needs her brother more than life itself. I need him, too. The most important thing, though, is for nothing to ruin what they have. I'd never forgive myself if I came between brother and sister.

I swallow. Hard. "I don't want any kind of trouble with Cason, Peyton."

She goes up on her toes and gives me a soft kiss. "You won't. He never needs to know about this. It's not his business, anyway."

"Yeah, I know," I say, but that doesn't help with the guilt spreading through me. I give her a nudge, setting her in motion toward the stairs. As I gather our clothes, I realize there's something she needs to know. "You said you were only with one guy in college, but it's not because guys weren't attracted to you."

"What makes you say that?"

"Well, one, you're the most beautiful woman I've ever set eyes on, and two, your brother was well-known on campus. The guys all sort of knew not to mess with you."

Stark naked, her hand goes to her hip and her mouth drops open. Could she be any more adorable? "You have got to be kidding me."

"Nope, sorry." I give her a sheepish look. "Your brother would have killed anyone who got too close."

Her green eyes flare with anger. "I'm going to kill him."

I drag her to me. "Hey, you can't tell him I told you."

"How can I keep that in?"

"Please."

"Fine, Roman. I'll keep the secret." She rolls her eyes at me and I smile. I like having secrets with Peyton. "Let's go get ready."

Forty-five minutes later, Elias is dropping us off at Andrew's house. "See, we needed a car after all," I tell her.

"You don't always have to be right about everything, you know," she says, and playfully elbows me in the gut. We walk up the cobblestoned walkway, and she wraps her arms around herself and shivers as the night air falls over us. I put my arm around her to warm her and as we approach the door, it swings wide open and a very attractive lady with short dark hair and dark eyes greets us.

"You must be Peyton and Roman. Right on time." Her smile is warm and inviting as she takes our hands and gives a welcoming squeeze. "I'm Sofia, Andrew's wife. We're so glad you could join us tonight. Richard and Paula are already here." Her lips thin and her light laugh wraps around me. "I didn't have time to do my hair," she says, and even though she's still smiling, I sense the tension beneath. "Please excuse the mess of it."

"Your hair looks fine," Peyton says, and points to her own. "Look what the humidity is doing to mine."

Sofia laughs, steps back and waves her arms. "Come in, please."

She leads us through her gorgeous home and Peyton glances at the pictures on the wall. "Are these your children?" she asks.

A look of longing comes over Sofia's face. "Yes, twins. They're both studying in England."

"How nice."

"Not for me," she says with a laugh, and Peyton grins.

Understanding and warmth dance in Peyton's eyes. "You miss them."

"I do, terribly," she says, and gives Peyton a wink. "Someday you'll understand that."

"Yes, I suppose so," Peyton says, playing the part of my wife as the two share a bonding moment. Laughter comes from the deck.

"Sounds like the party has started without us," Sofia says, her voice a bit tight, and Peyton casts me a quick glance, her eyes telegraphing a secret message. I nod slightly. Yeah, I get it. Sofia doesn't appear to be a fan of her early-bird guests.

We step out onto the back deck, and I glance out at the Mediterranean Sea, which is right on their doorstep. "Nice place you have here," I say.

Sofia smiles at me. "Thank you. Let me fix you a

drink." She angles her head. "Let me guess, a scotch drinker."

I chuckle. "How did you know?"

"A woman knows these things," she says. "Peyton, how about you?"

"Wine girl."

"Ah, I knew there was a reason I liked you," Sofia jokes, and Andrew stands to greet us.

"Great to see you both again," he says, and gestures to the empty chairs around the table. We greet Richard and Paula, who are both sipping on some kind of cocktail, and Sofia comes back with our drinks and sits at the other end of the table, opposite her husband. She turns to glance at Peyton.

"How was your first day?" Sofia asks, and before Peyton can say a word, Paula jumps in to explain how much her husband loved meeting the children, and how they all loved him in return. I resist the urge to roll my eyes. We all listen quietly, politely of course, since most of us around the table have manners. I reach out and put my hand on Peyton's leg to give it a squeeze. The look on her face suggests she wants to give a hard eye roll, and I grin back.

When Paula finally stops talking, Sofia turns to Peyton. "How about you, Peyton?"

"It was enjoyable. I really liked—"

Paula gasps and we all go quiet. "You're Roman Bianchi," she blurts out.

"That's right," I say, and roll the ice around in my glass.

Paula taps her husband's arm repeatedly. "Richard, Richard, this is Roman Bianchi. Remember we read about him in the paper. He's from a family of Italian elites. His ex-fiancée left him before their grand wedding. There was a whole spread done on him."

I shift, uncomfortable as she rudely narrates the horrible articles splashed in the trash magazines.

"I remember," Richard says, and I don't like the gleam in his eyes as his gaze goes from me to Peyton, back to me. "You went into hiding for a while."

"I wasn't hiding." Both Andrew and Sofia go quiet, clearly uncomfortable by the direction Richard is taking this conversation. "I was in New York working."

"New York's most eligible bachelor." He laughs lightly, but it belies the vindictive look in his eyes. "I believe I recall you saying something about being a bachelor for life?"

I put my arm around Peyton and her body is stiff. I laugh and take a drink of my scotch, playing it off. "You can't tell me you believe everything you read in the paper, now can you, Richard?"

"No," he says, and pushes back in his chair to mimic my relaxed posture. "You're right about that." He focuses in on Peyton's ring. "Tell me, how long have you two been married?"

"Six months," we both say quickly, maybe too quickly.

"Newlyweds," Sofia says. "How romantic."

"A big wedding, with all your family?" Richard asks.

"No, we wanted a private wedding. I love my family, but they can be overbearing at times, so we just sneaked off. I'm sure they'll want to throw us a party when we go to Sicily to see them."

"I'm looking forward to meeting them all," Peyton says.

Richard's mouth drops open. "You've never met them then?"

"It all happened rather fast," I explain. "They'll meet her soon enough and fall for her as hard as I have."

"Malta is such a great place to spend your first year together," Sofia says, and waves her hand toward the sea. "I grew up here of course, but Andrew is from Italy, and we honeymooned right here on this island. It's where we're happiest." She points to a strip of beach in the distance. "We actually exchanged vows right there, all our family and friends in attendance."

"Perfect place," Peyton says, a longing in her eyes that she can't hide from me. She doesn't want a family my ass, and as far as big weddings, there was a point in this girl's life where she wanted to be Cinderella. I'm sure of it.

"Where did you get married?" Sofia asks.

Peyton coils her hair around one finger. "Oh, we just had a civil ceremony in Manhattan."

Sofia's eyes go wide. "Oh, my, I can't believe Roman's family let him get away with that."

I grin; obviously her husband told her who I was and the two know my history and that of my overbearing family.

"This is such a great island to raise a family," Paula says, and puts her hand over her stomach, giving her husband a small grin like they might have a secret.

Sofia beams. "Great indeed. My kids had a wonderful childhood here with the beach so close."

Paula gazes at her husband. "We would love to raise our family here, too," she says. "Of course, we're very traditional, and I'll be staying home to raise them, just like my mother did. That's how children end up with good old-fashioned values." She picks up her glass and eyes Peyton over the rim. "Did your mom stay home, Peyton?"

Holy shit. Is this woman for real?

"Actually, I lost my parents when I was young," Peyton says.

"Oh, so sorry to hear that, dear," Sofia says, and I shift uncomfortably. Something tells me Paula has done her homework on the competition and is using Peyton's childhood to her advantage. Every protective instinct I possess kicks into high gear.

"Do you plan to have children, Peyton?" Paula asks.

"Of course, someday," she says, a small waver in her voice that I don't miss.

I take her hand and bring it to my mouth and give it a kiss. "We plan to have plenty of children," I say.

"Will you continue to work?" Paula waves her hand. "I mean, if maternity leave is in your future, what would happen to the students?"

"I'm sure I can figure out a way to help pick up the slack," I blurt out without thinking.

Paula laughs. "You mean you'll help out in the classroom? What qualifications do you have?"

"I might not have a degree in education, but I speak numerous languages." What am I saying? I know nothing about teaching children, but if it means helping Peyton, I'd probably stand on my head and spit nickels for their entertainment.

"How unorthodox," Paula says.

"Andrew," I say, shifting the direction of the conversation. "Do the children have computer access?"

He steeples his fingers and lets his index fingers bounce off his lips. "We have a small lab, not enough for every student of course. They all must take turns."

"I'd be happy to volunteer my time and teach basic coding skills."

Andrew's eyes widen. "We could never ask that much of you."

"You're not asking. I'm volunteering, and I'd love to help."

A wide smile splits Andrew's lips as Peyton looks at me, her mouth agape. "That's a generous offer, Roman, and I'd love to discuss this in depth with you. Right now, I must get the barbecue going."

"I'll get the salads from the kitchen," Sofia says, and takes a look at our glasses. "And it looks like we could all use a refill on our drinks."

Richard jumps up. "I'd be happy to help with the barbecue. I'm sort of known for my barbecue skills back home."

I scoff silently. I'm sure he's known for a lot of things back home.

"I'll help you in the kitchen," Paula announces, and stands.

"No, please sit and enjoy your drink," Sofia says, a little too quickly.

Refusing to take no for an answer, Paula smooths her hand over her skirt and follows Sofia inside.

The women disappear inside, and as Richard brags about his skills, I lean into Peyton. "What the hell?"

"Wow…just wow."

"You don't like them either, huh?"

She frowns. "Do you think she's right? Do you think my values are going to stand in the way of me getting this job?"

"Your values are just fine, and your heart is in the right place, but we're going to have to be very careful. If we're not…"

I let my words fall off. Shit, maybe I wasn't the right guy for this job. I thought I could blend in when in fact, I could be the one to ruin her dream job. But the thought of any other guy pretending with her, touching her, kissing her, exercising marital rights with her…well, that just doesn't sit well with me. Not anymore, anyway.

I am so screwed.

CHAPTER NINE

Peyton

"YOU DON'T HAVE to walk me to work every morning, you know," I say, secretly liking his strong, solid presence beside me, not to mention the way he holds my hand, swinging it a little as we stroll. For the last week, he's insisted on walking me to work, and I always put up a fight, simply because I like pressing his buttons.

He groans and pinches the bridge of his nose. "Haven't we been over this?"

"Yes, but—"

"Jesus, girl, are you forgetting what happens when you argue with me?"

"Maybe I want you to kiss me." I lift my chin an inch. "Right here in the street."

"Fine." He grabs me by the waist and tugs me to him. His warm lips find mine, and I sink into the sensations as he ravishes my mouth. His growls reverberate through me, and I wrap my arms around him, loving how I can rattle him like this. He breaks free, leaving me breathless. "Just for the record, you don't have to give me a hard time every time you want a kiss."

"A hard time, huh?" I tease, and press against him.

"Cut it out. I do not need the mother of all boners right now. Not when you have to get to school, and I can't push you to your knees and enjoy this sweet mouth of yours."

Heat races through me and he gives a playful grin, knowing how much I like it when he talks dirty. "Was that payback for rubbing up against you?" He looks away and whistles innocently. It brings a laugh to my lips. "You're going to pay for that."

"Can't wait." He gives my ass a smack. "Now come on before you're late. We don't want to give Paula and Richard any more ammunition."

My shoes tap on the sidewalk as we head toward the school. "He's actually been pretty nice this week."

His hand tightens around mine. "You've heard the saying, keep your enemies close, right?"

"Yeah."

"Don't trust him, Peyton."

"I won't." We both go quiet for a second, lost in our own thoughts. I break it by asking, "When do you think you're going to visit with your family?"

He frowns. "Soon. I've been busy with some work for Hard Wear and haven't really had a chance."

"You did tell me that was one of the reasons you wanted to come here with me, yet you don't seem to be in any hurry to visit them."

"I know. It's true. I just...don't want them to know what's going on here, with you and me."

I crinkle my nose, a part of me wondering if they really would like me, or would they think I'm not good enough for their brother. Could that be why Roman really doesn't want them to know? On some level does he think the unwanted girl with no parents wouldn't fit in with his family?

"I hate for you to be so close and not see them, though," I say.

"It's fine, Peyton. When this is all over, and you're the new full-time teacher—and we're officially over—I'll visit them. They never have to know about any of this."

"I've always wanted to visit Italy," I say, putting a little cheer in my voice to hide the unease welling up inside me as I think about him leaving here, disappearing from my life—like so many others have before. "Not that I'm saying I want to go with you or anything," I quickly clarify.

He studies my face, opens his mouth and closes it a couple times. Finally, he says, "Are you going to pretend we broke up after you sign the contract, or pretend I was needed back in New York and carry on with the charade that we're married? We never really talked about that."

Even though I get the sense that's not what he really wanted to ask, I say, "If you have no intentions of ever getting married, I guess continuing to pretend is an option, isn't it?"

"I might not want to get married, Peyton, but I'm still a guy," he teases with a wink.

Yeah, I get it. Pretending we're still married means he can't be seen out with other women. Okay, so why does the idea of him being with another woman bother me so much? Then again, do I really have to ask myself that question? "How about we cross that bridge when we get to it," I say as I try to wipe the visual of him in bed with another woman from my mind. "Right now, let's just focus on me being the best candidate."

We stop in front of the school and he turns to me. "Tonight, let's get out. Go sightseeing, go to a restaurant. I'll make us a reservation for somewhere nice."

"That sounds like fun." I go up on my toes to kiss him. "Just so you know, you don't have to walk me home from work today. I'm a big girl. I can find my own way."

"Okay, I'll probably be too busy today, anyway."

Disappointment settles in my stomach. Damn, I was only kidding. I was hoping he was going to fight me on the matter. I smile to cover the ridiculous turmoil careering through me, settling around the vicinity of my heart.

The first bell inside the school rings and I reach for the door. "See you later."

I hurry inside and head to the staff room to grab a coffee before the second bell rings. I make it quickly and reach my classroom as the children start filing in. On my desk there's a little pink box.

I open it to find a gorgeous cupcake with pink

icing inside. I glance at the note, with my name on it. Paula made me a cupcake? I might not believe in Cinderella, but Snow White and the poison apple, that's a different story. Just then Richard pokes his head into the door, a big smile on his face.

"I see you found your surprise."

"How lovely of Paula," I say.

Anita, the math teacher in the class across the hall, peeks in. "I'm saving mine for break, although I was tempted to call it breakfast dessert and dive in."

Richard laughs at her and I mentally kick myself for believing the worst of Paula. She's obviously just trying to win the staff over with sweets.

"Saving it, huh?" Richard says with a laugh. "Then how did you get that blue icing on your nose?"

We all laugh and Anita, good sport that she is, quickly wipes it away. "Well, I didn't eat the whole thing," she says, a sheepish look on her face. "I only had a nibble, and it was delicious." She glances at my box. "What color icing did you get."

"Pink," I say.

"She made a different color for everyone. Based on your auras," Richard says.

I don't really believe in such things, but I do appreciate the effort. "Tell Paula thanks," I say when the second bell rings and they head to their respective classrooms. As I watch them go, Roman's words of warning jingle in the back of my brain.

All the lovely little children sit at their desks, their hair combed neatly, their faces scrubbed and shiny.

"Okay, class," I say, and pull a package of cards

from my bag. "We are going to learn animal names in English." I hold the picture up of a llama making a funny face, and the kids chuckle.

Before I know it, the bell signaling the end of the day rings, and the kids pack up their desks. My heart is so full as I watch them file from the classroom, and without even thinking I press my hand to my stomach. Not because I'm wondering what it would be like to have a child of my own, but because it's suddenly very grumbly.

I take a sip from my water bottle and put it back into my bag. My stomach growls a bit louder and I swallow uneasily.

"Hey."

My heart leaps at the sound of Roman's voice in my doorway. "What are you doing here? I thought you had work to do."

He jerks his thumb over his shoulder and he has a teasing grin on his face when he says, "If you don't want me—"

"I want you," I say.

He steps up to me and pulls me to his body and I slide my arms around his neck. "Yeah, I can tell," he says playfully.

"How about we go home and I get you naked."

My body warms at the idea as I say, "What time is our dinner reservation?"

He puts his mouth close to my ear. "The only thing I'm hungry for is you."

A thrill goes through me. "What a coincidence,

because the only thing I want to put in my mouth is you."

His breathing changes. "Jesus, girl. Keep that up and I'll bend you over this desk." He inches back and his brow furrows.

"What?" I ask.

"Are you okay? You actually look a bit pale." He touches my forehead. "No fever, but you're kind of cold and clammy."

"I'm always cold," I say, brushing it off, but he's right, I'm not actually feeling great.

"Not like this, Peyton."

"My stomach is a little funny, actually," I say. "It just started. Maybe I'm coming down with something."

"Let's get you home."

Home.

I like the idea of Roman, me and…home. I've always lived in houses, never homes, and I'd be wise not to think this time is any different. When he leaves, I leave the villa. I'll have to find something permanent for myself, something I can afford.

He leads me outside, and I wince as the sun shines down on me, the contents in my stomach churning. Roman keeps casting me quick glances, like he's worried I'm going to go down for the count. I'm a little worried about that, too.

I pick up the pace and he hurries along with me. By the time we reach the villa, I'm in a full-blown sweat and whatever is in my stomach wants out.

"Roman," I say, and grab his sleeve. "I'm not feeling good."

He scoops me up and hurries upstairs to the bathroom. "Are you going to vomit?"

"No." Oh God, this is so embarrassing. "Please leave."

"Peyton, I don't want to leave you." He stands over me as I grip my stomach. "I think you need my help."

"Roman, please, you need to leave right now," I blurt out, never more embarrassed in my life. "Trust me on this."

He hesitates, but the pleading look in my eyes must have convinced him. He steps into the smaller bedroom and closes the door behind him.

"Go downstairs," I yell, mortified. "I need to die in peace."

"Call out if you need me," he says as I hurry out of my clothes and drop down onto the commode, my entire life flashing before my eyes. "This cannot be happening," I cry as pain rips across my abdomen.

Sounds of Roman moving about in the kitchen, and possibly cooking something, reach my ears, although the thoughts of food turn my stomach even more.

After a long while, I wash up and Roman raps on the door. "You okay in there?"

"I'm going to our bed to die," I say.

"Can I come help?"

"Yeah," I say. I swallow against a dry throat as my weak legs carry me to the bed Roman and I have been sharing for the past week.

I collapse onto the mattress, and Roman enters from the hall. The concern in his eyes wraps around me like a blanket. He sits down next to me and pulls the cover over my now-freezing body.

"Do you think it's the flu?"

"I don't know. I have severe pains in my stomach."

"Maybe it was something you ate."

I run through everything I put in my stomach. "We had the same big breakfast, and you're not sick."

"What about lunch?"

"I was so full from breakfast, I skipped lunch."

"Same." He presses his hand to my forehead. "Do you think you can drink something?"

"Yeah, I'm really thirsty."

"I'll be right back." I close my eyes, and a minute later Roman is back with a tall glass of ice water.

"Can you sit up a bit?" He helps me up and I sip the water, praying to God it doesn't go through me and thinking it will, judging by the way my stomach is protesting.

"It came on so fast," I say.

He helps me lie back down and lightly brushes my hair from my face. "Are you tired?"

"A little bit."

"Do you want me to leave you to sleep?"

Before I realize what I'm doing, I reach out and take his hand. "Do you think you could stay for a minute?"

"Of course."

"Tell me about your day," I say, as if we're an old

married couple sharing stories like it's the most natural thing in the world for us to be doing.

"I did some work and talked to Cason. He called to see how things were going."

"I've been meaning to call him." I swallow as another wave of pain rips across my abdomen.

"I told him things were going good."

I groan. "They were. Right up until today. I mean they still are but…ugh, whatever this is, it's not good."

Concerned eyes rake over my face. "Do you want me to call a doctor?"

"I haven't had a chance to find one here yet."

"I could take you to Emergency, or I could call my sister Maria," he says. "Her husband is an emergency room doctor. He might be able to diagnose you over the phone."

"Then they'd know you were here."

"I think your health is more important than that, Peyton." He lightly brushes his hand over my forehead, and it feels good. "I can deal with their interfering if it means helping you."

"Keep doing that," I say as his hand soothes me. "The warmth of your hand feels good." He disappears for a second, coming back with a damp cloth. He lightly presses it to my flesh and it instantly makes me feel better. "That's good." I sigh. "Don't call anyone, though. I think it's just something I ate."

"I'm not sure, Peyton. We ate the same things and I'm fine."

"I'm sure it's just a bug. Promise me you won't

call." I don't want to bring the wrath of his family down on him, and he's spilled enough lies for me already. I'm not about to put him in a position where he has to lie to his family, too.

He dabs my head a few more times, sets the cloth down and fixes the blanket around me when an almost violent cold shiver moves through me. "Okay, if that's what you want." I don't miss the reluctance in his voice, but I don't think I need to go so far as to seek medical help.

"Roman."

"Yeah."

"Thanks for helping me," I say. Honestly, I'm so not used to counting on anyone, and he has gone above and beyond in so many ways. He's so kind, and so giving, and honestly that's just going to mess me up more when we go back to a clean slate. "I wish it wasn't you, though. I wish it wasn't you here with me," I murmur.

His shoulders tighten, and the wounded look on his face hurts my heart. "Why would you say that? I thought we'd become friends."

I pick up a pillow and put it over my face. "It's not that. We are friends, it's just… It's so embarrassing for you to see me like this," I say, my voice muffled. He takes the pillow away and sets it beside me, and the understanding and compassion in his eyes eases the mortification inside me.

"Don't be," he says softly. "I had older sisters, remember? They embarrassed me all the time. Someday I'll tell you about all the terrible things they did to their baby brother."

"Tell me now," I say, wanting him to stay longer. I like his calm, steady presence. I like…him.

His mouth twists like he's in pain, and I shouldn't laugh but he looks so adorable right now. "Fine, remember I told you how much they liked to be in the kitchen."

"I do," I say, and snuggle closer to him, to bask in his strength and intimate familiarity. My lids fall shut, and I relax to the sound of his deep voice.

He laughs and the rumble soothes me. "This is really horrible but when I was around five, my sister Lucy, who is a year older than me, had this Easy-Bake Oven. She made a chocolate brownie but didn't have any icing sugar. She made up this weird concoction of yogurt and regular sugar, and I think she put some mud in there for color." I open one eye and chuckle when he scrunches up his nose. "Of course, she talked me into trying it first. It was pretty bad."

"Oh, how horrible." I take in the small smile touching the corner of his mouth. "You're smiling."

He scrubs his face. "Yeah. I guess I miss Lucy. We were the closest. We did everything together."

"Like Cason and I did."

"If I ever had kids, I'd want a dozen so they could all have one another. I complain, but goddammit, Peyton. They do mean the world to me."

As he shares something very touching, very private with me, my heart thumps a bit faster. "I thought you didn't want children."

"I don't." He blinks a couple times, like he's trying to get his head on straight. "Isn't that what I said?"

"It's something you said before. Not what you just said."

"Oh, it's what I meant to say." He picks the cloth back up and dabs my forehead. "Just for the record, Peyton, you'd be an amazing mother."

"What makes you say that?"

"The kindness and compassion you have for kids."

"When have you ever seen me with kids? Hey," I say when a guilty look crosses his face. "What did you do?"

He gives a slow shake of his head. "Even sick, you're questioning me."

"When you look like the damn cat who swallowed the canary, yeah I'm going to question you."

"I was out for a stroll today, just to get some fresh air. I saw you in the schoolyard with the kids."

"You're a creeper, Roman," I murmur, and snuggle in tighter.

"I just wanted to make sure everything was going okay and you were happy."

I chuckle. "Still a creeper." My stomach squeezes, but this time it's from happiness. I like the thought of him checking up on me, just to make sure I'm okay and happy. "You're sweet," I say without thinking.

"Keep that to yourself. I have a reputation to uphold." He laughs softly. "Close your eyes and sleep."

I do as he says. A second later his warm lips are on my forehead and a soft sigh escapes my throat.

Don't fall for him, Peyton.

If I put that on repeat in my brain, will it sink in?

As his warmth and closeness cocoon me, his steady, even breathing sounds soothe me. I'm seconds from drifting off when a horrible thought occurs to me. My lids fling open.

"I did eat something different."

CHAPTER TEN

Roman

"YES, LUCY, I'M FINE. Working away as usual." I pinch the bridge of my nose as my lovely sister grills me about my love life, or lack thereof, on the other end of the phone.

"Why do you sound like you're close? Typically your calls from New York don't come in this clearly," she asks.

"I'm just…outside," I say, not a lie. Peyton had been up half the night with stomach cramps and slept through her alarm this morning. I shut it off. She's in no shape to go in to work, and when my phone rang, I ran to the rooftop to answer it, not wanting to wake her.

"You sound tired."

"I am tired." I spent the better part of the night worrying about Peyton and debating on calling a doctor, not to mention refreshing her water to keep her hydrated after every trip to the bathroom. There wasn't much time for sleep. I yawn, and something niggles in the back of my brain. I reach for it, and when I'm finally able to grasp it, I blurt out, "Wait, why wouldn't you expect me to sound tired? You're calling in the middle of the night." At least in New York it's the middle of the night. A long pause takes up space between us, like she's trying to figure out a way to tell me, and worry zings through me. "Lucy, is something wrong?"

"It's Mamma. She worries about you being all alone. She's not getting any younger, Roman. You need to find yourself a wife and settle down." I open my mouth, ready to blurt out that I did, just to ease my mother's worries. I stop myself before I do. While that might make my mother happy, it would bring a whole lot of trouble to this situation Peyton and I are in.

"Can you please tell her she has nothing to worry about? I'm happy, and life is good." I smile. Despite Peyton not feeling well, this last week has been good—probably the best week I've had in a long time, or ever. Yeah, being with Peyton has been fun, and I can't remember the last time I had fun or felt this alive. But in a few short weeks, after she signs the contract and I say I have to head back to New York for work, we erase this time from our memories and go back to a clean slate.

Why the hell does that idea bother me so much?

"That's why you called? To tell me our mother has been worried?" I glance at the gorgeous sea cliffs in the distance; a colorful blue bird chirps as it takes flight. "You're not telling me anything I don't know, so why the call in the middle of the night, Luce…"

"What was that?" Lucy asks.

"What was what?"

"If it's the middle of the night there, why do I hear a bird chirping?"

Shit.

"Sound machine," I say quickly. "Helps me sleep." Wow, aren't the lies just rolling off my tongue lately.

"I though you said you were outside?"

Crap.

"I'm back inside now."

"Sounded like a blue rock thrush."

"How would I know what it is? You're the bird-watcher, not me."

"It's the national bird of Malta. Don't you remember when we were kids, we used to chase them when we vacationed on the beach?"

"Vaguely," I say, my stomach twisting. "What I remember most is you making me eat mud. I'm going back to sleep."

Her chuckle fills the space between us. "No, wait. I called because I couldn't wait to tell you something."

I lean against the glass rail and let the sun warm my face. "What's up?"

"You're going to be an uncle again."

My heart squeezes tight. My God, the baby Bianchi sister is going to have a baby. How is that possible? "I'm so happy for you, Luce…" I can just picture the big smile on my sister's face. She was the youngest girl, and I came after her. The two of us were closer than any of us and Jesus, I really miss her. My heart thumps a little harder.

"I wanted to tell you before the others, that's why I called in the middle of the night. Sorry if I woke you."

My throat tightens. "Don't be sorry," I say, and cradle my phone. "I'm glad I was your first call."

"Roman."

"Yeah?"

"Miss you, bro." My heart squeezes tight. "Can you come home soon?"

"Yeah, I'll see you soon, Luce…" I think about next weekend. Maybe I can sneak off to Italy for a quick visit with my family.

"Love you," she says.

I spin when I hear movement behind me, and turn to find a pale Peyton watching me, her big green eyes wide and glassy. How much did she hear? Will she be upset that I'm planning a trip sooner rather than later, and leaving her behind, after admitting how much she'd love to visit Italy? She's been left behind enough, and yesterday I got the sense she'd like to go, but under the circumstances what choice do I have?

"I have to go. I'll see what I can do about visiting," I say, my voice thick with emotion. "Talk to you later, and love back." I end the call and shove my phone into my pocket. I examine Peyton's pale face. Honest to God, if that cupcake Richard gave her was tainted, he's going to have some explaining to do—to my fist.

"Hey," I say, and sink down in front of her. I press my hand to her forehead. "How are you feeling?"

"I spent time on a farm one summer," she begins. "My foster family had an orchard." I eye her. Jesus, is she delirious? I wait for her to continue, to see where she's going with this. She swallows and practically peels her dry tongue from the roof of her mouth.

"Okay," I say. "And…"

"They had this tractor." She lifts her arms and widens them, sounding a bit loopy and tired. "It was huge. It tilled the ground or something." She uses her fingers and opens and closes them like she's plowing the soil. "Anyway, I feel like that tractor ran me over, then backed up to finish the job."

I can't help but laugh at her description and it brings a small smile to her face. "I'm so sorry, Peyton."

"Not your fault." She takes a breath of fresh morning air and groans. "I need to get ready for school." She stands on wobbly legs. I jump up and catch her, scooping her into my arms.

"The only place you're going is back to bed."

She tries to wiggle from my arms. "No, I have to get to work."

"I already called Andrew. I'm going to be in the computer lab with the kids today."

Her mouth drops open. "Roman, I can't ask that of you."

"You're not. I'm happy to shape young minds, and maybe I'll have a hand in producing the next Bill Gates or Steve Jobs."

"Andrew agreed?"

I set her into the chair under the pergola and drop down in front of her. "He's pretty excited about it, actually."

She frowns. "Ohmigod, now I'm going to be in competition with you, too."

"Hardly. If you want to know the truth—" I stop to feign a shiver "—I'm scared shitless."

A little chuckle rumbles in her throat. "Why?"

"Kids, they kind of scare me. They can be evil little beings, you know. One time when I was in high school, my young nephew thought it would be funny to put blue dye on my toothbrush. It was my senior year and I was going on a date with this girl I was crazy about. Let's just say it was my one and only date with her."

"Why did he do that?"

I shrug. "I actually think my sisters put him up to it."

"Are you kidding me?"

"They passed it off as an April Fool's joke but deep down I think they were trying to sabotage my date."

She frowns and puts her hand on my cheek. She doesn't feel as clammy as she did last night. "That wasn't very nice," she says, siding with me, and I like that. Couples need to stick together, no matter what. Not that we're a real couple, but Peyton would undoubtedly be a ride-or-die kind of girl when it came to relationships. If she were open to one, that is.

"Sisters." I push her curls from her face. She's a hot mess and never looked cuter.

"They must have had a reason." She eyes me, curiosity all over her flushed face. "What did you do to them?"

"Me!" I exclaim, indignation in my tone as my head rears back in shock. "I'll have you know I was a saint, Peyton. A damn saint."

She laughs at that and the sweet sound goes through me.

"A *damn* saint? Yeah, and I'm Mother Teresa." Long lashes blink over tired green eyes. "Seriously, why did they do it?"

"I think it was because they didn't like the girl I was going out with. They all thought she wasn't good enough for me."

"Wow, tough crowd."

"Right— now do you see what I mean about butting into my life?"

"Yeah, I guess, and I bet they'd hit it off with Cason. He's always up in my business."

"You really do know how it feels."

"Something else we have in common," she says, and glances down, her brow furrowed. Her head lifts and her eyes are brimming with questions when she looks back up at me.

"What?"

"Did they like your ex-fiancée?"

"Yeah, they did. I think at that point in my life they were anxious for me to settle down and have a family. They either missed the signs or she fooled everyone."

"Fooled everyone?"

"Never mind. It's not important."

I'm about to stand when her hand on mine stops me. "Roman, if it's important to you, it's important to me." She pastes on a smile. "I am your wife."

I am your wife.

Shit. Shit. Shit.

I really shouldn't like the sound of that so much.

"She didn't want me for me, Peyton," I say, and go quiet as her eyes narrow, her brain absorbing that information. "She wanted my name and all that came with it."

"I didn't know. I'm sorry."

"I'm not," I say without thinking. The truth of the matter is, I was sorry to find out my worth to women, but deep down, I think I might have felt a measure of relief when she called off the wedding.

And why is that, Roman?

Oh, because she wasn't Peyton.

Well, shit.

She goes thoughtful for a moment. "Do you… think they'd like me?"

"Yeah, of course." I lightly nudge her on the chin. "I told you that already."

"Yeah, I know, but I'm probably not the kind of girl they'd like to see you with."

I stare at her long and hard. "Why would you say that?"

She rolls her eyes. "Come on, Roman. I hardly come from the right background."

"Why would you think that matters?"

"Are you seriously asking me that?"

"You think pedigree matters to my family?"

"Oh, it matters, Roman. When you're on my side of the tracks, it matters. I'm judged all the time. You have no idea what that's like."

Her words pierce my skin and I stand abruptly. "Is that what you think?" Jesus Christ, I'm judged all the time, too. I'm judged because I was born with a silver spoon, she's judged because she wasn't.

"No, I don't mean that." She squeezes her eyes shut, hurts from her childhood written all over her face. "Things aren't coming out right." Her glassy eyes meet mine. "If that came out as an insult, I didn't mean it. I think you're a really great guy."

"You won't for long." She gasps when I pick her up and carry her back to bed. "You're staying here for the rest of the day."

She wiggles and tries to protest as I cover her. "I don't feel right about this, Roman."

"Stop," I say, and pin her down. Her breath catches and I grin. "Oh, do you hate me restraining you right now?"

"Yes, you're such a bully."

I laugh at that. "Yeah, I am, aren't I?" I brush her hair from her forehead, everything in me softening. "I want to take care of you, okay?"

"Roman—"

A growl rumbles in my throat. "It's okay, Peyton.

It's okay to let someone else help." I dip my head and cup her face. "I'm not going to hurt you. I promise. Can you trust me on that?"

She swallows and water fills her eyes as she glances away. My heart nearly shatters. This sweet girl hasn't been able to count on anyone but her brother, for fear of being cast away like she was nothing more than yesterday's newspaper.

Goddammit, I want to be the person she can count on.

"Yes," she says.

"Good. I'm going to the school today. End of discussion."

"Bully," she murmurs under her breath.

"What's that?" I ask, a warning in my tone.

"Nothing." She pulls the blanket over her head and whispers, "Bully." Her chuckle wraps around me and I shake my head. This girl is killing me.

"You're going to pay for that."

"I know," she mumbles, more chuckles.

"Get some rest, Peyton."

I'm about to leave the room when she flings the covers off. "Roman."

I hover in the doorway. "Yeah?"

"Who are you going to see soon?" She flips her hands over, palms up. "It's not my business and you can tell me that. It's just when I walked onto the rooftop, I overheard you." Her eyes blink rapidly, and one thing I've come to learn about her is when she's upset about something, she rambles on. Another thing we have in common. "If you have someone here you want to see, some girlfriend or something—"

"It was Lucy," I say.

The apprehension on her face morphs into a smile. "Oh, your sister." Relief visible, she adds, "Easy-Bake Oven."

I laugh at that. "Yeah, she's the one, and I think I'm going to call her that from now on." I step back into the room. "She's pregnant. She wanted me to be the first to know."

Peyton closes one hand over her heart. "That is so nice."

"She wants to see me."

She smiles up at me, a longing on her face. "You should go see her."

"Yeah, I think I will." Before I can stop myself, I blurt out. "Will you come?"

What the ever-loving hell am I doing?

"I…" She grips her blankets, squeezes them in her hand. Her expression is troubled when she says, "I don't think that's a good idea."

Her words hit like a punch to the gut. Not good, Roman. Not good at all. Nothing good can come from introducing her to the family. I'd have to lie and tell them we were married, or let them in on the charade—they wouldn't be happy about that, and the fewer people who know, the better. Despite all that, I still want my family to meet her, and that's all kinds of messed up.

"Maybe I won't go."

"It's okay if you do," she says, smiling up at me, but the sadness on her face tears at my heart.

"I'll think about it." I'm about to step away but turn back and say, "Jealousy looks good on you, by the way."

Her eyes widen and her mouth falls open. "Excuse me?"

"When you thought I was talking to a girlfriend or something…"

"I was not jealous. I was curious. I'm very curious by nature, in case you didn't know." She folds her arms and lifts her chin an inch. "I was being nice, Roman."

"I like when you're nice," I say, and let my gaze drop to her mouth. The energy in the room changes, vibrates with the heat between us. "For the record I like when you're *not* nice, too." That remark gets me a pillow across the face.

I laugh and walk back to her. "That's quite a throw you have there. Little League?"

"The end of the school year fair is coming up. There'll be a dunk tank. I signed you up for it." She lifts her arms and flexes. "I've been warming up my pitching arm."

My God, she is so adorable. "Do you hate me, Peyton?"

"Yes," she says with a grin.

"Let's just hope all the evil little humans in the classroom don't feel the same way, otherwise they'll eat me alive."

She grabs my arm. "Roman."

"Yeah."

"They're going to love you."

"Right, what's not to love?" I joke. She rolls her eyes hard enough to give me a headache and I chuckle, despite the windstorm sweeping through my gut. The one person I want to love me doesn't. We're playing a game, having sex and having fun, but when push comes to shove, she's built a wall around her heart—something else we have in common—and her brother would disown us both if he ever found out. How could we ever be together after this?

More importantly, how could we ever be apart?

CHAPTER ELEVEN

Peyton

THE WARM SUN seeps in through the crack in the curtains and falls over my body, stirring me awake. My lids open and it takes me a second to remember where I am. My entire body tingles, my stomach full of butterflies, as I remember my morning conversation with Roman and that adorable smirk that crossed his face before he left me to sleep. When he teased me, saying he likes me nice and *not* so nice, his expression was filled with pure adoration and playfulness. Honestly, I love the way he looks at me. Roman Bianchi is so sweet, funny and playful—completely sensitive to my needs—how is a girl not supposed to fall for him?

Oh boy.

I can't go there. No way, no how can I go and fall for a guy who is completely off relationships. I'm off them, too, but that still doesn't change the fact that I'm crazy about Roman, always have been, and nothing good can come from that.

I push my blankets off and pad to the bathroom. I reach for the light, only to realize it's on. It's been on since Roman put me to bed last night, leaving the light on and the door cracked. My heart thumps a little harder in my chest and my throat is a gritty mess when I swallow.

God, where is my self-preservation when I need it most?

I step into the bathroom and gasp at my reflection in the mirror. Holy, I'm surprised the man didn't run back to New York. I cringe at the dark smudges under my eyes, and at the mess of hair on my head that would make Carrot Top look like a fashion model. I hurry into a warm shower and wash the remnants of the flu, or whatever this bug was, away. I can't for one second think Richard or his wife would stoop so low to put something in a cupcake to knock me on my ass—or rather the commode. We're adults, not devious children, right? I've dealt with enough of them in my childhood, and thought adulthood would be different. Maybe I'm wrong. Roman seems to think so.

Once clean, I dress and head downstairs to find a loaf of bread and a mug with a tea bag in it on the countertop. I pick up the note he left, and my throat tightens as I read his perfect penmanship.

Try to eat something and text if you need me. See you soon. I'll make us dinner, but it might not be edible!

A strange ache, deep in my chest, right around the vicinity of my heart, tugs at me. I drop down into the kitchen chair, note clutched between my fingers. I read it again and again, yet no matter how hard I try, I can't stop that wall around my heart from fracturing. My phone pings and I jump. I fish it from the bottom of my purse, and a stupid smile tugs up the corners of my mouth as I read the message.

Hope you're feeling better. I'm still alive. The evil little humans haven't taken me out yet.

I hold the phone close and laugh, a new kind of lightness in me as I text back.

Feeling much better. I'm up to making dinner no problem. Whatever I had has passed.

I stare at the phone and three dots appear, only to disappear. I guess he changed his mind on whatever it was he was going to say. I shoot a text off to Cason to let him know things are going well and set my phone down. My stomach growls and I make some toast and tea, appreciating Roman leaving this all out for me. After I eat, I glance around, suddenly bored with myself. I'm usually on the go, having a million things to do, and I actually have no idea how to relax.

Well, I have some idea…

But Roman is at work, so I'm left to my own devices. Maybe I'll head to the school and creep on him the way he creeped on me. I scoop up my purse and head out into the sunshine. Face tipped to the sun, I stand on the porch for a second. I truly love it here in Malta, and I haven't even really explored it yet. Something about the place gives me a sense of peace, of home. Would it be the same if I weren't here with Roman?

I'm too afraid to answer that.

I walk along the sidewalk leading to the school and pass joggers, and mothers pushing their children in strollers, and elderly people out for a walk. I'm not sure I ever remember my heart being so full.

As I approach the school, laughter reaches my ears, and I check my phone to see it's afternoon break at the playground. I walk around the school, spot Roman and cover my mouth to stifle a chuckle. The kids are pulling him in all directions. I lean against the brick building, a huge smile on my face as I watch him join them in a game of basketball, where evidently, it's him against the entire classroom.

"Hey, not fair," he calls out, when one of the kids distracts him so the other can get the ball. They all laugh, obviously loving how they're able to get the better of him. I stand there a few more minutes, and my smile falls as a flash of sadness envelops me. The man has been hurt in the past, has sworn off marriage and children. It's a shame, really. He's having the time of his life with them right now and it's clear he'd be a remarkable father. Dammit, I hate that past hurts have forced him to guard his emotions. Maybe it's time he let go of the past and move on to the future. My throat tightens. Yeah, I'm one to talk.

I fold my arms and hug myself as a cool chill moves through me. The sun is shining on my body, but the cold is always there, right below the surface. I'm about to push off the wall when I catch a shadow on the ground. I turn to find Richard coming toward me. I stand up a bit straighter.

"Late start to your day, isn't it?" he calls out, his loud voice grabbing my attention. He checks his watch and closes the distance between us.

"I was ill."

He raises his eyebrow and looks me over, like he's judging me. "You seem fine now." He finishes his perusal and I square my shoulders.

"I am now, but I was ill all night." I narrow my eyes as I remember Roman asking if Richard could be behind my illness. "I think it might have been something I ate. Maybe the cupcake."

Richard's head rears back, and he glares at me. "Are you suggesting my wife did something to your cupcake?"

"I'm not—" I say.

"I can't believe you would accuse her of something so vile… How dare you…"

"I never accused her of anything," I say, as my stomach clenches. Yeah, I'm beginning to believe more and more that Paula did something underhanded to keep me from the classroom, and with the way he's defending her, he's completely unaware.

I stare up at him. Even though I saw the worst side of many people growing up and trust no one, I still can't quite wrap my brain around the idea that Paula would go to such lengths to knock out the competition. Unease grips my throat. What else would she do to ensure he won the full-time position?

He rocks on his feet for a few seconds, and while I turn to take in Roman's solid presence on the playground, I can feel Richard's eyes drilling into me. "Where exactly did you say you and Roman were married?" he asks. My gaze flies back to his. His tone might be deceptively innocent, but every intuition I possess tells me there is nothing innocent about the abrupt change in conversation. This man is on a fishing expedition, although from the smug look on his face, he might have already reeled in a big one.

I tamp down the anxiety threatening to rise. "Oh, it was just a small ceremony at city hall in Manhattan," I say, and try not to shift or look uncomfortable as the lie spills from my mouth. "Why do you ask?" I take a deep breath, not sure I want to hear the answer.

He goes quiet, leaving my mind to call on every worst case scenario, and after a long pause he says, "I was just wondering, because Paula said there are no records that you two were married in NY State."

"Why on earth would she look that up?" I ask, almost afraid of the answer. "Is she that bored at home?"

He purses his lips and my gaze goes to Roman, who is now standing perfectly still, watching the two of us. Richard looks back to me. "Why don't you answer the question?"

"You didn't ask one, and I'm sure it's just a filing mistake. I'll look into it." The school bell rings. "If you'll excuse me," I say, ending our discussion as I walk away. I head toward Roman, who is standing still on the basketball court, his eyes dark and deep, locked on mine as I saunter toward him.

I keep my steps even and measured, resisting the urge to run, not only to put distance between Richard and me, but because of the need to be close to Roman, to revel in the way his strength always wraps around me. I step up to him, and as he lightly runs his fingers down my arm, he dips his head, positioning his mouth inches from mine. Being close like this, his strong hands on my body, has a way of soothing my worries—making me think things will be all right. But not everything will turn out all right, and I can't think about the loss that's going to slice through me when this man goes back to New York.

"What are you doing here?" he asks, his voice low and steeped in concern.

"I feel 100 percent better." I crinkle my nose. "And I was bored." Okay, maybe *bored* isn't the right term. Maybe *lonely* is a better way to put it. Without his big presence in the villa, it was just a big open space. Stark. Empty. Lonesome. That's insane, considering I love alone time.

He frowns and rubs his hands up and down my arms to chase away the goose bumps. "Did you think I couldn't handle this?"

"Well, you did say you were terrified," I say with a laugh. "But I can see you have everything under control."

"The kids are great."

"Honestly, I just needed a breath of fresh air." *Needed to see you.* "The kids seemed so happy to have you here."

"Not true. They were all asking for you."

My heart flips and my gaze rakes over his irresistible face. My God, what have I gotten myself into here? "Really?"

"Really." Concerned eyes move over my face. "You do look a lot better."

I laugh at that. "After last night. My God, I couldn't have looked worse today had I tried."

"Not true. You were adorable."

"You, my friend," I say, and poke his chest, "have become an awesome liar."

He frowns at that. "I don't lie, Peyton. Well, except for this pretend marriage, but we're fighting an unfair system and had no choice." He looks past my shoulders. "What did asshole want?"

Unwanted thoughts of Richard push back the warmth in Roman's touch, leaving room for dread to invade and spread through my blood. A hard quiver goes through me. "He asked about our wedding, and where we got married. Paula's been doing some digging. I think they know something, Roman."

"They don't know anything." He clenches his jaw and his muscles ripple. "They're just trying to rattle you."

"I never let on, but I think he succeeded." I shake my head, guilt eating at me. "This was a bad idea. I shouldn't have dragged you into this mess."

"It's fine." He shakes his head, takes a deep breath

and lets it out fast. "Maybe we should just get married for real," he blurts out.

My entire body goes stiff. Holy, that flu must have affected my hearing, because no way did he just say we should get married for real. "What did you just say?"

"Maybe we should have a ceremony here, something small. We could play it off that we decided to renew our vows on the beach."

"Are you serious?" Maybe I'm still in bed, lost in fever and having a bad dream.

But the thoughts of being with Roman, coming home to him every night, the two of us sharing hopes, goals, the good and bad, is not a bad dream at all. It's a fairy tale and I don't believe in them. I need to keep myself grounded in reality. It's the only way I won't get hurt.

"You still there?" he asks, his gaze roaming my face. "You went somewhere else for a second." He frowns. "I'm not so sure you're over this flu just yet."

"I am. I'm fine. You just took me by surprise."

"I can tell." He laughs, pulls me to him and after all the kids file back inside, he presses a kiss to my forehead. "You can stop looking at me like I just grew another head, Peyton."

"I'm not going to ask you to go through with a ceremony, Roman. You've done enough already, and I know how you feel about marriage."

"You're one to talk," he says, his voice low and intimate. His eyes narrow, like he's waiting for a counterargument. But I have none.

"When you're right, you're right. Not denying that I'm a bachelorette for life, but you've already gone above and beyond for me." I glance over my shoulder. "I'd better get inside. The second bell just sounded. I can take over now."

"Nice way to change the subject," he says with a snicker. "We'll talk about it tonight, then." He inches back. "And *I'm* finishing the day off with the kids. You go home and rest."

"Home is boring."

Without you.

"Go for a swim, and if you really are feeling better, why don't you do a search on restaurants, and we'll go out to eat tonight and do some sightseeing."

"I'd love that."

He kisses my forehead, takes a fast glance around and gives my backside a little whack. "Go."

I yelp. "Are you sure?"

"Positive. I'm actually having fun teaching these kids how to code. They really seem to enjoy it."

"Okay, if you're sure. I'll head back and find a nice place to eat tonight."

We walk back to the school, our bodies close, our knuckles brushing, and it's insane how much I miss his touch, his closeness, when he disappears inside. My phone pings and I welcome the distraction.

I smile when I see the call is coming from Carly. I quickly slide my finger across the screen. "Hey, Carly, I've been meaning to call you."

"Uh-huh. You get married and forget all about

your best friend," she teases, her voice light and full of laughter.

"Very funny. I've been crazy busy."

"Doing what? Playing house with New York High Society's Most Eligible Italian? The man is unbelievably hot. The pictures in the paper don't do him justice."

"I don't think of him that way." Her laugh of disbelief nearly deafens me. "Okay fine, he's hot."

"Oh my God," she says.

"What?" I ask.

"You slept with him."

I glance over my shoulder. I'm not sure why. Maybe I expect Richard to be leaning in to hear the call. I lower my voice and say, "So what if I did?"

"Peyton," she screeches. "That is awesome."

"Yeah, it kind of was, or is…because we're still doing it."

"Tell me everything."

I laugh. "Let's just say, it's possible he's ruined me for every other man."

"Is he, you know?"

I frown and saunter down the sidewalk, sneezing as I pass the foliage I seem to be allergic to. "No, I don't know."

"Is he big?" she blurts out, and I cover my mouth.

"I'm not telling you that."

"Like hell you're not, and actually you don't have to. I already know he is. I can tell by your voice."

"Going all Freud on me again, are you? How are things back there?"

"Same," she says. "But I want to hear about you."

"Things are going really good." A mortified sound crawls out of my throat. "You're not going to believe this, though…" I begin and for the next ten minutes, as I make my way back to the villa, I fill her in on where I'm living, how Roman took care of me last night and jumped in to help out with the students.

"Wow, what a guy. He almost sounds too good to be true."

"I know, right? But he's my brother's best friend and said he'd do whatever it took to help me get this job." She goes quiet, too quiet, and my stomach squeezes as I press in the code to open the front door. "What?" I ask.

"You like him."

"Yeah, he's okay," I say as need wells up inside me. Honest to God, I do like him, a lot. I always have. But I swore long ago I'd never give anyone the power to hurt me. Is that what I'm doing here? Have I given Roman the power to hurt me?

My entire body tenses, and the toast I washed down with tea threatens to make a second appearance.

"How does he feel about you, Peyton?" she asks, her voice changing as she goes into professional mode.

"I'm not a patient, Carly. Please don't analyze this. We're just two consenting adults, having a little fun while we pretend to be married."

"I just don't want to see you hurt."

I step inside the villa, and the cool air-conditioning

falls over me, although I'm not sure that's the reason I'm shivering. "I'm a big girl. I know what I'm doing."

I don't.

Not even a little bit.

"Okay, my morning break is over. I have a patient waiting. Call me soon."

"Will do."

I end the call and fight off the unease circling my stomach. I grab my laptop and do a search on restaurants. I find one not too far, make a reservation and head upstairs to get ready. I want to look nice for Roman tonight. I find my prettiest dress, spend a long time on my hair and makeup, and when I finally emerge from the room, Roman is coming in through the front door.

I hurry down the stairs and his gaze lifts to take me in. The heat in his eyes is like a visual caress over the tingling spot between my legs. My God, the man is addictive.

He drops his briefcase and stalks toward me. "You look beautiful." He slides his arm around me, and like a damn caveman drags me to him.

"Have I ever told you how much I like when you touch me like this, all rough and hungry and impatient?"

His lips quirk. "You didn't need to. But we have a problem."

I stiffen. "Does it have something to do with Richard?"

"No," he says, and I relax into his touch. "It has

something to do with me wanting you naked so I can put my dick in you."

I laugh.

"Not a laughing matter, Peyton," he growls, and rubs his growing erection against my stomach.

"No, not a laughing matter at all," I say, my voice husky as his lips find mine. "And I suppose we have a few minutes," I say, stepping back. He reaches for me, but I dodge him.

"What are you doing?"

"I was thinking. We do have about a half hour before our reservation, and if you're fast—"

"I can be fast," he says, and I bite my lip to stop my chuckle as my entire body heats up.

I move to the back of the sofa. "I guess if we need to do this quickly, it's a good thing I don't have any panties on to get in my way."

Raw need shimmers around him like an aura. "You're kidding me."

"Would I kid about something like that?" I lean over the sofa and lift my dress, exposing my body to him.

"Shit, Peyton. I'll take over your job every day if it means I get to come home to this."

I laugh. "Roman?"

I glance at him over my shoulder and my body quakes as he licks his lips, his eyes zeroing in on my sex as I spread my legs. "Yeah?"

"I believe you said something about bending me over a table and burying yourself inside me." The sound of his zipper releasing curls around me. "This isn't a table but…" I swallow as his crown breaches my wet sex, and my fingers curl into the fabric of the sofa as he powers into me. "Oh my God."

He pumps and grips my hips for leverage, burying himself to the hilt. I love the way he loves my body, the impatience in his touch like he can't get enough of me, like he can't get deep enough. I know the feeling.

"Jesus, girl, why are you so hot and wet?"

"Maybe because I was thinking about you thrusting into me like this all day."

He pants and grunts, his hot breath on my flesh as he slams into me. "Were you home touching yourself, wishing it was my cock inside you?"

"I wanted to, but I wanted to save my orgasm for you."

"You want to come, Peyton. You want to come for me?"

"Uh-huh," is all I can manage to say as he rides me, fast and hard, blunt strokes meant to get the job done. There's no choreographed moves with this man, no time for the finesse this afternoon. No, he's here on a mission, his sole focus on getting us both off. Damned if I don't like that.

I'm so slick and aroused, he slides in and out of me smoothly, the skin-on-skin friction creating an even deeper intimacy between us. After the night we forgot to use a condom, there was no sense going back.

"Yes," he groans, his body all muscle and power as he takes me hard and fast. He slides a hand around me and touches me where I need it most. I jerk against his probing fingers, and a groan tumbles from my throat. "You like that, babe? You like when I take you from behind like this?"

"Yessss," I hiss.

"Tonight, when we go out, you're going to sit there all sweet and prim but we'll both know you'll still be feeling me inside you."

"Roman," I cry out, and he leans in and digs his teeth into my neck. The second he does, I feel myself lose all control, chanting his name over and over as I come.

"Oh shit," he moans against my flesh, and his hands go back to my hips. With each hard thrust we work toward his orgasm now, and I move with him, my sex muscles clenching and unclenching around his hardness. His breath catches, his fingers bruise my hips, and I let loose a cry as he fills me with his hot release. He pulses inside me, his muscles hard against my soft flesh as he rides out the bliss. As I revel in the pleasure coursing through me, he falls over my back.

"Peyton, Jesus," he says as he pants against my flesh. "I loved coming home to this," he adds, and nibbles my ear.

"I loved it, too," I say, my heart hitching, warning me to be careful here, not to let this man into sealed-off places, even though it's too late for that. I'm in big trouble here.

CHAPTER TWELVE

Roman

I GLANCE AROUND the cozy Italian restaurant in the middle of downtown St. Julian's. "You picked my favorite restaurant, you know."

Peyton lifts her head from the menu and her smile slays me. "Really?"

"It's almost like you know me."

She cocks her head. "I know some things."

I lean toward her and lightly rub my fingers over her wrist. "I know things, too."

Her smile is warm and her eyes are steeped in desire when she asks, "Did you spend a lot of time in Malta?"

"When we were kids, we vacationed here. My family owns property."

Her jaw drops open. "The villa. It's yours, isn't it?"

"Yeah."

"Why didn't you tell me?" she asks.

I let loose an exasperated sigh. "You really have to ask that?"

"Yes."

"You would have argued with me." I stretch my legs out beneath the table. "You always argue with me."

"No, I don't."

"Yeah, you do."

She lifts her chin. "I don't argue about everything."

Grinning, I lean back into my chair.

"What?"

"You're arguing about not arguing with me."

She laughs. "Okay, I'll give you that. Seriously, I didn't know you spent time here, or owned property, and I appreciate you letting me use your villa, but I still plan to pay you for helping me out."

I arch a brow at her. "You think I'm going to let you do that?"

She glares at me, those lush lips pinched into a fine line. "Roman…"

"It's not been a hardship, Peyton."

Her demeanor changes, softens. "Yeah, it's kind of been fun." She sets her left hand on the table and eyes the ring on her finger, and I don't miss that look of longing in her eyes.

The hostess leads two people to a table behind us, and I go quiet until they're seated. I lean toward Peyton, my words for her ears only. "Any more thoughts about what I suggested earlier?"

Her shoulders tighten. "You mean getting married?"

"I just don't think we should risk anyone finding out."

Is that why you're asking, Roman?

Is that the only reason you're pushing for this?

She frowns. "I know what you're saying. We've come this far, and Richard's wife is obviously the kind of woman to play dirty, to make sure her husband succeeds."

The server comes back to take our orders, and as I glance over the menu, I notice Peyton keeps looking beyond me, like she sees someone she knows. I casually look over my shoulder after handing the menu back.

"What's going on back there?" I ask.

"I'm not sure. Two girls over there keep looking at me and whispering back and forth."

"You know them?"

"No, maybe they know you."

I touch her hand. "Maybe, but I'm here with you tonight, and you're the only one I want to talk to."

I pull my hands back when the server comes with our bottle of wine. He pours some into my glass, I taste it and nod. Once he's gone, I say, "I'm glad you're feeling better. I was pretty worried about you."

Her smile is sweet, grateful. "Thanks for taking care of me all night. I'm just glad whatever it was passed."

"I had a talk with Richard."

She toys with the stem on her wineglass. "He told me you did."

"I don't trust that guy. I still think he was behind whatever made you ill."

She sets her napkin on the table. "I'm going to make a quick trip to the ladies' room. I'll be right back."

"I'll be right here."

I pull my phone from my pocket and check messages as I wait for her to return. There are a few from my sisters, and one from my team at Hard Wear. I read it quickly, but it's something I can deal with later. I put my phone away and pour another splash of wine into our glasses as the server returns with bread. The warm scent fills my senses. I look toward the hall leading to the washrooms. What is taking Peyton so long? A knot coils in my stomach. Jesus, I hope she's not sick again. I'm about to stand, go to her, when she comes from the hall, her face a little pale.

What the hell?

She hurries to her chair. "Are you okay?"

"Yeah, that girl who was staring followed me to the bathroom. She asked who I was to you. I told her you were my husband, and she said you were old friends."

I turn and see the woman coming from the bathroom, headed our way. Holy shit. Here comes trouble.

Anna's eyes go wide, and she holds her arms out to me, a big surprised smile on her face. I stand and bring her in for a hug.

"Anna, it's so nice to see you. It's been a long time."

"Too long, clearly," she says, her gaze going from me to Peyton, back to me again. "I saw you two earlier, and let me say, it comes as quite a surprise to find out you're married. Lucy never said a word to me about it."

My throat tightens. "It was a fast ceremony, and we've been keeping things quiet."

Her dark eyes narrow in on me, and my stomach twists. "Are you saying your family doesn't know?"

I smooth my hand over my tie. "We prefer to keep it that way, for now."

She laughs, but it holds no humor. "Oh, Roman, what kind of mess have you gotten yourself into?"

"No mess at all." I force a laugh. "You know my family. They wouldn't give the newlyweds a minute to themselves. We'll tell them when we're ready."

"Yes, I suppose you will," she says, and casts Peyton a glance. "It was lovely meeting you, Peyton. Let's see if you can keep his interest. He tires of relationships very easily. Prepare yourself." Before Peyton can respond, Anna flips her long black hair over her shoulder and saunters away.

I sit back down and blow out a breath. "Shit."

"This isn't good, is it?"

"No."

"What happened between you two?"

"We dated but we were teenagers. She's a friend of Lucy's and has chased me forever. I was never really that interested, but Lucy wanted me to take her out, so I did. It was brief, and I broke it off before she could think we were going somewhere with it. I'm pretty sure she was more interested in my family name than me."

"I think she hates you." She gives a low, slow whistle. "If looks could kill."

"I know." I rub the knot in the back of my neck, tension tightening my muscles. "Trouble is coming, Peyton."

"Trouble?"

"Trouble in the name of Aurora, Lucy, Maria, Emma and Bianca."

She leans toward me, clutching her napkin. "You think she's going to tell your sisters?"

"Is she on her phone?"

She looks over my shoulder and grimaces. "Yeah, looks like she's texting." I shake my head, my appetite gone as Peyton wrings her cloth napkin. "Want to get out of here?" Peyton asks.

"Only if you do."

"Why don't we get our food to go and eat at the park. Somewhere private?"

"Okay." I call the server over and tell him our change of plans. Ten minutes later we're walking the downtown streets and heading to the park for a picnic. My phone has been going off in my pocket for the last five minutes, but I just ignore it. I can't answer them until I figure out what it is I'm going to say. We grab a seat at a picnic table, and I hand Peyton her take-out container with her penne chicken.

I settle in beside her and I dig into my ravioli as she stabs a piece of pasta.

With her fork halfway to her mouth, Peyton says, "You're going to have to answer them, Roman."

"I know, but I'm going to need a full stomach for the wrath that is about to come down on me." She nods and my mind races as we eat in silence for a few more minutes. The sun dips lower in the sky, and the streetlights begin to flicker on.

"This food is delicious," Peyton says, breaking the quiet.

"I know, right? That's why it's my favorite."

She lifts her head when a family of four saunters by. A smile touches her mouth. "Your family has other properties here in Malta?"

I nod. "I have some really fond memories from my childhood here."

Her smile widens and she sets her fork down and pushes her container away. "That's so nice."

"Come on, let's walk." I gather up our trash and dump it into a nearby garbage can.

We head down the street, busy with tourists, and pass by all the lovely outdoor cafés. We stop by an alleyway and I gesture with a nod. "This is my old stomping grounds. Right there, that's where I lost my virginity," I tell her with a smirk.

Her brow arches. "Really?"

"Yup."

"Romantic."

I laugh at that. "I was seventeen."

Her arm slides through mine as we walk, and I'm

not even sure she realized she did it. Being together like this is just so natural for both of us. "Young."

I give her a wink and hold her tighter. "She was eighteen."

"Ooh, a cougar," she teases, and I laugh, leading her to the walkway along the bay. We stop and stare out at all the boats bobbing in the water. She inhales, breathing in the salty air, and lets it out slowly. "I love it here."

"I do, too," I say, and give her a little bump with my body.

"What made you stay in the States when you could have this every day?" she asks, and waves her arms around.

"I needed to be away from my family for a while." She looks down at her feet and my gut squeezes. Christ, this woman would do anything for a family and I spent years running away from mine. "Sometimes it's nice to go where you can be under the radar, you know," I add. "Somewhere where your every move isn't scrutinized."

She nods. "I can understand that."

"Yeah?"

"I'm under the radar. People don't really notice me." I go completely still as she continues to walk. The second she realizes I'm not beside her she turns. "What?"

I shake my head, taking pleasure in her thick, auburn hair, the warmth and honesty in her green eyes, and the way that sexy dress hugs all her curves.

"You have no idea how beautiful you are, do you?"

She shrugs at the comment. "You don't have to say that."

"When you walk into a room, all heads turn, Peyton. You don't even know."

She looks away to gaze out over the water. A visible shiver moves through her, and I close the distance. I shrug out of my jacket and drape it over her. "I spent so many years trying to be invisible, Roman."

My throat practically closes over as pain grips my heart. I put my arms around her and pull her in. I press a kiss to the top of her head. "I know."

"If I didn't cause any trouble, if they rarely saw me…" She goes quiet for a long time, and I just hold her quivering body to mine, tucking her safely beneath my arms so no one else can hurt her. "I…" Her voice hitches, and she adds, "I guess I figured if I was small and invisible, they wouldn't be so quick to get rid of me."

Jesus, I hate that her childhood was so damn brutal and her scars are still so raw. "No one is going to hurt you anymore, Peyton. I won't let them."

She puts her hand on my chest, and her eyes are watery when she lifts her gaze to mine. "My very own knight in shining armor," she says.

I chuckle. "I thought you didn't believe in fairy tales."

"I don't," she says so quietly, so softly I almost missed it. I hug her tighter when a hard quiver racks her body.

"We should get you home. You're freezing."

I make a move to go but she stops me. "We should end this, Roman. I don't want your sisters angry or hurt, and you've…you've helped enough."

"No," I say so forcefully, her eyes widen. "I'm seeing this through to the end. I told you that right from the beginning and I'm a man of my word."

Really, Roman. Is that the only reason you can't walk away from this?

"But your sisters—"

"I'll deal with them." I put my arm around her and we hurry back to the villa. Once inside I carry her shivering body up the stairs to the shower. "We need to warm you up." I peel the zipper down on her dress, and there is something so completely open and honest about this sweet, vulnerable woman as she stands there stark naked, gazing up at me, I could fucking sob. The world might not have wanted her, but I sure as hell do.

I'm in love with her. So lost in her, I'll never find my way out. Not that I want to. I might have been engaged, but this is the only woman who's ever truly mattered to my heart. I strip down and help her into the shower, ignoring my pinging phone for the time being. Right now, Peyton needs my attention.

I turn the water to hot and pull her under the rain showerhead.

"Mmm, that is nice," she says.

"Getting warm."

She laughs. "I don't think I've ever been warm in my life."

"Come here." I pull her back to my chest and soap

up my hands. I run the suds over her body, cupping her breasts as I clean her. She rests her head against my shoulder, and a warm, contented sigh escapes her mouth. I spin her and rinse her clean. Once done, I turn the water off and towel-dry us both before I wrap her in a clean one, and knot another one around my waist.

She yelps when I scoop her up and carry her to the bed, setting her down gently and crawling in beside her. She snuggles into me, her skin warm and fragrant. I lightly touch her arm, trail my hand lower. Her sexy moan wraps around me, and I part her legs to caress her sex.

"Sore?" I cringe. "I sort of went a little caveman on you earlier."

Her soft chuckle strokes my balls. "I loved it."

"I loved it, too."

I love you.

She widens her legs even more and the welcoming way this woman invites me into her body, giving herself to me entirely, is one hell of a mind fuck. I put my finger inside her and her eyes roll back.

"Hate that?"

"Hate it sooo much, Roman."

"Yeah, I can tell."

I move my finger in and out of her until she's dripping and so close to release, but I pull back, needing to be inside her when she comes. I roll on top of her and her smile is soft, her mood far more mellow tonight, despite the storm we're going to face tomorrow. But we'll cross that bridge when we come to it. Tonight, all I want to do is make love to this woman.

I piston forward and slide my cock into her. She wraps her legs around me and hugs so tight, I nearly come. "Jesus," I murmur, and push her hair from her face. "Do you have any idea what you do to me?"

"I have a little idea."

"Didn't we agree that you weren't to use the word *little* when we're talking about sex," I say, and a laugh bubbles out of her. I laugh with her, and it changes to a moan when she brings my mouth to hers for a deep kiss. She breaks it and cups my face.

"There's nothing little about you, Roman."

"That's better," I say, and move in and out of her.

"You have a very big…heart."

"Hey," I say, and she chuckles.

She wraps her arms and legs around me and pulls me closer, until every inch of flesh is meshed together. This. Right here. This is what I want. Peyton in my bed, and in my life. Tonight. Tomorrow.

Forever.

Her eyes are at half-mast as she gazes up at me, and I lose myself in her just a little more. Impossible, I know, but I have never in my life loved a woman the way I love her. I'm 100 percent positive the wrath of five will be at my door tomorrow, demanding answers. As I think about that, with Peyton coming underneath me, the answer to our dilemma comes to me in a flash.

Peyton doesn't want to get married. She's a sworn bachelorette. But what if we did go through with it, if I lived here with her, stayed in Malta, maybe she would warm to the idea of a real husband. As far as her brother is concerned, I'll have to deal with that when the situation arises. All I know is I'm crazy about this woman, who came from nothing and wants to give everything. She's nothing like my ex. She's never said or done anything to lead me to believe she's the type of girl who'd marry for title or position. I could never be with her if she was. I hug her tight, knowing what I need to do next. I just hope she doesn't get frightened and run the other way.

CHAPTER THIRTEEN

Peyton

VOICES—LOUD VOICES—pull me awake and I roll over to find the other side of the bed empty. I jackknife up and the blankets fall to expose my naked body. I scramble to pull them back up before someone comes busting in, and try to figure out what is being said, but everyone seems to be talking at once, and in Italian. My tired brain can't seem to keep up.

I quietly slip from the bed and pull on a T-shirt and pair of yoga pants. I make a quick trip to the bathroom to fix myself up the best I can, although there is nothing I can do to wipe the contented smile off my face. Yeah, one look at me, and whoever is downstairs is going to know I was up all night making love with Roman.

Making love.

While I love it fast and hard, his touch was a bit different last night. Tender, gentle, so profound it seeped under my skin and wrapped around my heart. Yeah, I know. Not good for a girl who's a sworn bachelorette. But I feel myself falling, despite everything.

I open my bedroom door, and as my fuzzy brain clears, I gasp and wrap my arms around myself, knowing exactly what's going on. My God, I can't go down there. How can I face his family, let lies spill from my lips? I'm about to slam my door shut, crawl under the covers and stay there until everyone leaves, but footsteps pound on the stairs.

Roman's dark eyes meet mine, but he doesn't seem upset at all. Maybe I'm mistaken. Maybe his family hasn't invaded, demanding answers.

"My family is here," he says, and leans against the doorjamb.

My heart sinks. "Are you okay?" I ask.

"They want to meet my bride."

My stomach tightens. "Roman, you shouldn't... we can't pull this off with your family."

"Just for a little while. We have to let them think we're married. The fewer people who know the truth, the better." He exhales loudly. "Believe me, none of them can keep a secret and we wouldn't want them accidently spilling the truth here."

"I guess you're right, but how are they going to feel when we have to end this?"

He goes thoughtful and puts one hand on my cheek. "How about we cross that bridge when we come to it?"

"I hope we don't have to jump off the bridge."

He laughs, a big, deep laugh that eases the tension inside me and brings a smile to my face. "I don't think it will come to that." He bends and gives me a soft kiss. "Come on, they're dying to meet you."

A jolt of unease freezes my legs. "I don't know." What if they don't like me? What if they try to break us up like they did when they put blue dye on his toothbrush?

It's not a real relationship anyway, Peyton.

"It's going to be fine," Roman says, reading the worry on my face. "They're going to love you and vice versa. I promise."

"Am I dressed okay, maybe I should—" His lips close over mine, swallowing the last of my worries. He inches back, takes my hand and leads me down the stairs. As we walk, the scent of waffles reaches my nose.

"Are they cooking?" I whisper.

"Of course. They said I was looking too thin and need more meat on my bones." He puts his mouth close to my ear. "The only thing I need on my bone is you."

I chuckle at that. For a guy who was worried sick about his family, and lives in a whole other country to keep them from meddling, he sure doesn't seem upset with them being here now. He actually seems... happy. But I'm out of my element here, and so not the type of girl they'd want to see their baby brother with. Roman says otherwise, but unlike them, I have no real heritage, no family outside of my brother. I've accepted my lot in life. My past made me the strong woman I am today, but I'm smart enough to know how things work in the real world.

I reach the bottom step and all eyes turn to me—all eyes that resemble Roman's. It's not hard to tell they're all family. "Oh God," I whisper under my breath, completely overwhelmed, but Roman puts a strong, supportive arm around me and pulls me to his side.

"Everyone, this is Peyton. Peyton, this is my family."

I give an awkward little wave. "Hi."

A beat of silence and then one sister spreads her arms. *"Bella!"*

She comes toward me and Roman says, "I should have warned you. They're all huggers."

Before I realize what's happening, I'm being passed around, each squeeze tighter than the last. The women touch my hair and face, and their praise wraps around me.

"Mia sorella," Lucy says when she gets a hold of me, and my heart pinches tight. I can't believe these women are so accepting, calling me their sister. I seek Roman out in the flurry, and he's leaning against the kitchen island, a huge smile on his face.

One of the sisters, I think it's Aurora, speaks quickly in Italian. I struggle to grasp what she's saying.

"English," Roman says, and she turns back to me.

She fists her hands. "I ought to give it to Roman for keeping you from us, *bella.*"

"I told you. We wanted time alone before we let you know," he explains. "We were going to tell you soon, isn't that right, Peyton?"

"Yes, that's right," I say, pushing the lie past a tight throat. Pretending to be married for a job at a school that practices unfair hiring rules is one thing, but straight-up lying to the people he's closest to doesn't sit well with me. Not even a little bit.

"I think the waffles are burning," Roman says.

Aurora leaves my side, and that's when I spot an elderly woman on the sofa, her purse clutched in her lap, a small smile on her face.

"You must be Roman's mother," I say, and move toward her.

She nods and pats the sofa. I sit beside her and she cups my face. She kisses both my cheeks and takes my hand in hers to examine the ring.

"It fits you perfectly," she says, and I'm not sure she's talking about the size of it.

"Thank you, Mrs. Bianchi."

"Phooey," she says with a wave of her hand, and everyone laughs. "You, my sweet *bella*, can call me Mamma."

I take a fast breath as tears pound behind my eyes and threaten to spill. This sweet woman wants to be my mamma. I nod, my throat so tight I can barely swallow. "Okay, Mamma," I say and Roman must pick up on the hitch in my voice because a second after those words leave my mouth he's there, right there, pulling me into his arms.

"You have an amazing family," I say as I turn to him.

"Yeah, I know."

"But we have a problem," he says quietly as dishes clang in the kitchen.

I blink up at him, but don't see worry in his eyes. "What problem?"

"Remember I told you they were interfering?"

I nod.

"We want a real wedding," his mother says, and pushes to her feet. She holds one finger up. "Only then will I forgive Roman for getting married behind my back."

I blink rapidly. "A real wedding? What do you mean?" I glance around, and realize four out of the five sisters are on their phones; the fifth is in the kitchen dishing up waffles. One sister is talking about flowers, one about a dress. My God, are they making wedding arrangements for us? "What's going on?"

"They want to see us exchange vows. It won't be a big ceremony. Just a small one with family."

"Roman…" I'm about to say no, he's done enough, but there's a part of me that just can't. I actually want this. I want this to be real with Roman, and…maybe, just maybe he wants it, too.

He puts his mouth to my ear, his warm breath sending shivers along my spine. "It will solve our problem with Richard, Peyton."

Or maybe not.

"Please say yes, Peyton," Lucy asks, and pulls me in for another hug. I take a breath, completely overwhelmed with all this.

Say no, Peyton.

No matter how much I might want this, I can't go through with it. I have to say no. I have to.

"What do you think?" Roman asks.

"Roman, do you—"

"I do," he says, and for a brief second it catches me off guard, like I might have actually just proposed to him and he might have just agreed. My stomach rolls, wanting so much for this to be real.

"Do you?" he asks, and the room goes silent—a huge task for this group, I'm sure.

I take in all the hopeful, expectant looks. I can't bear to disappoint them, even though going through with a ceremony, only to nullify the marriage later, will undoubtedly leave me scarred and emotionally wrecked. "I do," I say, and the girls all start clapping and jumping up and down and talking a mile a minute in Italian.

Okay, I need a minute alone here to get my head and my heart straightened out. But no, that's not about to happen. The next thing I know I'm being led to the rooftop, with *Mamma* beside me as all the sisters bring up plates of food.

They set plates at the table, and the first thing I do is go for a coffee. Hard to believe I agreed to marry Roman, and he agreed to marry me, all before my first cup. I can only hope it's strong. I catch the way Roman keeps watch over me as his sisters fuss and talk details.

"Yeah, sure," I say when Emma suggests we exchange nuptials on the beach near the family villa. Questions about flowers, dresses and food get thrown at me, and my gaze seeks out Roman's. He opens his mouth, no doubt to tell them to back off a bit, but I hold my hand up to stop him. His presence is solid, and I really like having him in my corner, but I've got this.

I've never had a big family, and I've never had sisters. This might not be real, and everyone is going to be devastated when Roman and I end this, but right now—even though my family comes from nothing, and they might disown me when they find out—I just want to bask in the love and warmth and exuberant energy they're displaying. Can it really hurt for me to enjoy these ladies while I can and pretend that I'm family, too?

Yeah, I'm pretty sure it can, but I'm in too deep to pull the plug now.

"For flowers, I don't want any of those local purple ones, they make me sneeze." Roman relaxes and pushes back in his seat.

"No purple flowers," Emma says, and we all laugh and dig in to our waffles.

"What about your family?" Maria asks. "Will they want to come for the nuptials?"

My heart jumps into my throat. What do I say, I'm a nobody with only one brother? I open my mouth and close it again, not sure what to tell them, when Roman pipes in.

"This one will be for my side of the family," Roman says, and while I'm glad he jumped in to help, I also can't resist thinking he might not want them to know who I really am. He's a great guy, but he had a very different upbringing than me, and there are certain expectations placed on him, certain things he must live up to—marrying beneath his status is probably something that would be discouraged. Then again, I could just be projecting my fears. Maybe the only one worried about it is me. But to answer her question, no, my family won't be coming. No need for Cason to be made aware of our wedding, when it's not a real one.

I barely take my last bite when Lucy snatches up my plate. "Okay, let's go," she says, her dark eyes brimming with excitement.

I take in her little baby bump and my heart misses a beat. It would be so much fun to be a part of this family, watch that baby grow and be there to spoil it. "Go where?"

"We have one week to pull off a wedding," she says.

"One week?" I blink numerous times and take in the bobbing heads. "Why one week?"

"We have duties to get back to," Aurora says.

"Wait, where are your children and husbands?" I was so caught up in the excitement, I never stopped to consider they had lives to return to, children needing their mothers, husbands needing their wives.

"Our babies are with our husbands and nannies," Maria says. "They'll come next Saturday for the wedding."

My gaze moves around the table and I plant one hand on my hip. "Why do I get the feeling this wedding was in progress before any of you arrived?"

Bianca gives me a sheepish look. So far she's been the quietest in the bunch. "Probably because the second Anna reached out to Lucy, we were packing and making arrangements."

"I didn't stand a chance, did I?" I ask, and Roman mumbles something like, *I told you so* under his breath and all I can do is laugh.

"Okay, let's go," Lucy says.

The next thing I know I'm in the shops, and we're picking out flowers and cake and food. With little time to find the perfect dress, I'll have to pick one from the rack, but I don't mind. I don't want to spend a lot, although so far I haven't spent anything. These women insist on purchasing everything, but I don't want them to waste a lot of money on me. They just wave me off every time I try to protest.

They march me into a bridal shop and even without an appointment we're made a priority. I suppose that's how it is when you come from money.

The sisters all take a seat on the sofa and pull me down with them. The clerk, Lucille, a gorgeous middle-aged woman with long dark hair and big brown eyes, asks me to describe my favorite dress, and I basically sit there with my mouth hanging open. How on earth would I know? I wasn't like other little girls, dreaming of their Prince Charming. No, I was sticking close to the walls trying to be invisible. There was no time for fairy tales in that cruel world I grew up in.

"I…don't know."

She takes my hands and pulls me to my feet.

"Let's have a look at your body shape." I stand there like a mannequin on display as she spins me around and everyone excitedly gives their opinion on what would look best on me.

"I don't need anything fancy," I say. "Just simple."

The clerk taps her chin, her brown eyes narrowing as she goes quiet, thoughtful. "I think I have the perfect dress," she announces, and the women all clap their hands, excitement on their faces, and I can't quite help but get swept up in it.

"Okay," I say, and let her lead me to a change room. I step inside and strip to my underwear and she comes in with a gorgeous white gown.

"I think this ball gown will be perfect for you."

My heart races a little faster in my chest as she removes it from the hanger and helps me into it. The second I see the dress on me, the silhouette perfect for my shape, I swallow hard and fight the barrage of emotions pushing tears into my eyes.

"I knew it," Lucille says, and clips it in a few places. "We have to do a few alterations, and we'll put you at the top of the list of course."

My throat squeezes tight, my legs a little wobbly. "That's so kind."

"Anything for the Bianchis." She stands back. "What do you think?"

"I love it," I whisper, my heart aching in my tight chest. "But I can't go with the first dress, can I? I mean, I've watched the shows and it takes girls forever to pick their dress, right?"

A wide smile splits her lips. "When it's the right one you know."

My pulse leaps. She's right. When it's the right one, you know. A surge of love wells up inside me. At the wedding last summer when Roman kissed me, it sealed the deal. For years I thought he was the right guy, but that kiss was electric, setting off a storm inside me that would forever ruin me for other men. Maybe deep down, he feels it, too, but is too afraid. A little bubble of hope wells up inside me. Is it possible that he wants this, too, and is using Richard as an excuse? I spin around and there is nothing I can do to wipe the ridiculous smile from my face. I've always tamped down hope, too afraid of disappointment—too used to disappointment—but this just all feels so right.

"Should we go show the others?" she asks.

I nod, my hair bouncing around my shoulders as we step out and she puts me on an elevated pedestal. I glance in the mirror, and I really do feel like Cinderella. Is it possible that fairy tales really do come true?

"Okay, turn around, dear," Lucille says.

I spin and everyone smiles with lots of oohs and ahhs. The way they're all looking at me makes me feel like I'm someone very special, even though I spent my whole life telling myself I wasn't.

"It's perfect," Mamma says. "She'll take it."

I laugh at that and Lucille looks at me. "Do you say yes to the dress?"

I take in all the expectant eyes and put my hands to my chest. "I say yes to the dress."

* * *

I glance around my empty classroom. Honestly, I can't believe the week I've had, or that it's Friday afternoon already—my wedding is less than twenty-four hours away. For the last week, when I went off to teach, Roman's family would forge forward to put the perfect wedding together for me.

I push to my feet, ready to head home to my new...family. I smile and resist the urge to pinch myself. Honest to God, I'm just afraid to let myself get too excited.

"Oh, I didn't see you there," I say, finding Richard in my doorway.

He puts his hands in his pockets. "The big day is tomorrow, huh?"

"Yes, we're renewing our vows for his family," I say, disliking the smirk on his face.

He gives a humorless laugh. "Renewing? You say that like you guys are already married."

"Yes, well, if you'll excuse me." He steps farther inside, blocking my escape. I try to go around him.

"You're lying," he says. "You were never married. This is all a farce, some sort of fake arrangement you have with Roman. Go ahead, admit it." He scoffs. "Not that any of it matters now, not with you both sealing the deal for real tomorrow."

I lift my chin an inch. "I don't owe you any explanation, Richard."

"No, but you owe me one," Andrew says, entering the room from the hall. Richard's smirk widens, as he turns and slinks out, leaving me alone with Andrew.

"Peyton?" Andrew says, his brow furrowed. "Is it true? You and Roman were never married?"

My stomach clenches so hard I'm sure I'm going to throw up. "It's…um…the marriage bar…" Good God, no matter how I put it, it's never going to look good for me.

"We don't have a marriage bar." He angles his head, his eyes narrowed, studying my face. "Not anymore."

"I realize that, but from my research, and those I've talked to, I heard it was still practiced." As more words stream out, I attempt to turn the oncoming tide with, "I just thought it would be okay. No big deal. Harmless lie."

"I see." He adjusts the collar on his shirt and stands a little straighter, exuding his authority. "You lied, then?"

"I don't really think—"

"Presenting yourself as married when you're not is a lie, Peyton," he says, his voice taking on a hard edge that shoots daggers of worry through my body.

"I just thought…" I take a breath and change tactics. I can't lose this job. I just can't. This has been my dream for so long and I've connected with the children. "I'm good at my job, Andrew. You can see that. Marriage was an obstacle and that was my only way to get around it, so I could show you how good I am at my job. I wanted you to judge me based on my merits, not my marital status."

"Being single is something I would have accepted. Lying, however… I'm afraid you don't have the morals for this job, Peyton." As he frowns and shakes his head, my heart goes into my throat. "If you'll please take all your things with you when you leave."

My knees nearly collapse as the room closes in on me. I grip my desk and I take a few quick breaths as air squeezes from my lungs. Is this really happening? I open my mouth to plead but he shakes his head to stop me.

"That will be all," he states, and disappears out the door.

"Ohmigod," I say, and fall back into my chair.

I just lost my job.

I sit there for a long time, trying to wrap my brain around this turn of events, until the hum of the lawn mower outside my window sets me into motion. I have to tell Roman and once I do, there will be no need for us to go through with the wedding.

With my life crumbling around me, I force one foot in front of the other and somehow make my way back to the villa. "Roman," I call out, my voice as shaky as my hands as I drop my purse. I race through the villa and go to the rooftop, but he's nowhere to be found. I run back downstairs to grab my phone from my purse, but papers on the kitchen island catch my attention. Maybe he left a note.

I run to the island and pick up the papers, and as soon as I realize what I'm holding I sink into the closest chair.

A prenup.

A level of separation between those who have and those who don't.

A piece of paper that reminds me who Roman is, and who I'm not.

Tears press against my eyes and bile punches in my throat. An almost hysterical laugh explodes from my mouth. I drop the papers onto the floor like they're disease-ridden and slowly back away. Yeah, I should have seen this coming. People like Roman and his family need to protect themselves from someone like me—a girl from the wrong side of the tracks who will never be good enough, never really be accepted or loved for who I am.

I never, ever should have let myself believe in fairy tales.

CHAPTER FOURTEEN

Roman

"Okay, I have to run. Peyton should be back at the villa by now," I say, and my sisters all take turns giving me a hug. I absolutely love the way they took Peyton under their wings, readily accepting her and showing her love and affection, just like I knew they would.

Before I leave the family villa, I take a look at the beach below, the perfect spot for us to exchange vows tomorrow. A seed of hope wells up inside me. It's all kind of surreal, really. I'm not sure I can quite wrap my brain around the fact that I'm marrying my best friend's sister. After my gold-digging ex walked out, refusing to sign the prenup as is tradition in our family, I closed my heart off. But things are different with Peyton. She's sweet and beautiful, open and honest, and yeah her brother is going to tear me a new one, but once he sees how serious I am about her, how much I love her—that this wasn't just about sex—I think we'll be able to bring him around to our side. It's better to ask for forgiveness than permission, right? Besides, he wants his sister happy, and I damn well plan to spend the rest of my life making her exactly that.

I step outside and hop in the car waiting for me. "How are you doing today, Elias?"

"Very well, Roman, and you seem quite happy yourself."

I smile. "Tomorrow is a big day for me," I say.

"To the villa?"

"Yes, thanks."

As we drive through the streets, my heart beats a little faster, I'm so anxious to get home and pull Peyton into my arms. Being away from her for any length of time practically kills me, and that just makes me laugh. I pull out my phone to see if she messaged me, and disappointment wells up inside me.

Man, I've got it bad.

I stare out the window and take in the scenery. I might have to travel to the States every now and then, but most of my work can be done here and meetings can be held online. If Peyton wants to stay in the villa we can do that, or if she wants to buy a new place, I'm open to that, too. Whatever she wants, she gets.

Elias stops the limo in front of my villa, and I thank him and rush up the steps. I punch in the code and step inside.

"Peyton," I call out. "You home?" I note that her purse isn't by the front door, but she could very well have taken it to our bedroom. I take the steps two at a time and find the bedroom empty. I go all the way to the rooftop, but she's nowhere to be found. Perhaps she hasn't returned from school yet. I shoot her off a text and when she doesn't answer, I head back outside and walk to her school. I try the front doors and find them locked. Strange.

I walk around the school, only to find it's closed for the weekend. I check my phone again, worry gnawing at my gut. Is it possible that she went to the family villa, expecting I'd still be there? I shoot a text off to Lucy.

Hey, Lucy, is Peyton with you guys?

No, why, what's up?

Oh, nothing, she's probably just doing a bit of last-minute shopping.

You sure everything is okay?

Perfectly fine.

I shove my phone back into my pocket, but something isn't right. I feel it deep in my gut. I hurry back to the villa and make my way through the place again, but Peyton is still missing. I step into the bedroom. Something is off. I walk around the bed and to the closet. I open it and my heart sinks into my stomach.

"What the hell?"

I hurry to the other bedroom, check the closet there, but her things are nowhere to be found. In the bathroom I find her cosmetics and toothbrush gone.

Peyton packed up her belongings and left? I take a breath to calm myself, working to figure out why she would have done this, and I almost laugh when it occurs to me she's probably staying at a hotel tonight. Tradition dictates the bride and groom don't see each other before the wedding. Still, why wouldn't she have mentioned it? Perhaps she left a note and I haven't seen it yet.

I head to the kitchen to check, and my foot kicks up papers. I snatch them up and realize it's the pre-nup I left on the counter this morning, every intention of discussing it with Peyton tonight. Why the hell is it on the floor? I falter backward a bit, my mind racing and slowing on the most logical explanation here.

Peyton found these papers and bailed.

I sink into the chair, unable to believe this. I pull my phone out again and send another text. When it goes unanswered, I dial her number, but it goes straight to voice mail. Has she blocked me? Worry sets in, and I pick up my phone and check flights out of Malta. There isn't one until tomorrow, so it's not like she's taken off today, unless she chartered a private flight.

Fuck me.

I drive my fingers through my hair and pace and continue to wait for her response. When my phone finally rings, my heart leaps—except it's my sister. "Hey," I say, sounding completely irritated.

"Ah, are you okay?" Lucy asks.

"I don't think so."

She lowers her voice. "What's up, Roman?"

"I think she's gone, Luce. I think she saw the prenup and changed her mind." I glance around the empty villa. It's stark and hollow without her in it.

"That doesn't sound like Peyton."

"I didn't think so, either, but her things are gone, and she's not answering my messages."

"Maybe she's staying somewhere else tonight."

"I thought that at first, but *all* her things are gone."

"That doesn't make sense." She goes quiet for a moment. "Could something have happened at school?"

I tug on my hair as it gets harder and harder to breathe. "I don't know." I swallow but there's nothing I can do to hide the panic in my voice.

"You know the principal, right? Why don't you give him a call?"

"Okay, good idea. Thanks, Luce."

"Let me know, okay?"

"Don't say anything to the others, please."

"You know I've got your back, Roman. I wouldn't have made you eat mud if I didn't love you."

That pulls a chuckle from me. "Later, Easy-Bake. Love back."

I find Andrew's number and call his place, but no one picks up. Determined to get to the bottom of matters and hoping I'm making a huge deal out of nothing, I call for Elias and get him to drive me to Andrew's home. I'm out of the car before it even comes to a complete stop, and I dash up the stairs. I pound on the door, and Andrew opens it, a frown on his face.

"If you're here to try to get Peyton's job back for her, you're wasting your time."

My heart stalls and I grab a hold of the rail, squeezing until my knuckles turn white. "What are you talking about?"

His eyes narrow on me, assessing my face. "She didn't tell you?"

"No, I can't find her."

He nods, like he understands that. "Now that she's out of a job, she's probably going back to the States."

"Why is she out of a job?" Jesus, what the hell happened today? "She's the best person for it, Andrew."

"Is she now?" He taps his finger on his chin and worry explodes inside me. "Do good people lie about being married, Roman?"

I suck in a fast breath. "Oh, shit."

"Yes, exactly."

"You know we're getting married tomorrow."

"It was never about the marriage, it was about the lying."

"Come on, Andrew, you have to give her another chance," I plead. "A marriage bar is ridiculous. You must know that."

"I'm sorry, Roman. The contract has already been signed by Richard."

My throat squeezes tight. "You're making a big mistake."

"If you'll excuse me, I'm in the middle of something."

He closes the door and I stand there staring at it for far too long. How the hell did he find out? It had to have been Richard, and while I'd like to track him down and introduce my fist to his face, right now it's Peyton I'm worried about. She needs me. Phone in hand I head back to the limo and shoot a text to Peyton, telling her I know about the job and we need to talk.

Three dots pop on the screen and I stop breathing, waiting for her words to come in, but when they do, my jaw drops.

Peyton: Thank you for your support. You're off the hook. Marriage is no longer needed.

"What the hell?" I say as my life crashes down around me. She's letting me off the hook? Doesn't she know how I feel? A groan catches in my throat. How could she know? I was too afraid to tell her, too afraid she'd bolt.

Goddammit, even though I never expressed what she meant to me, she had to know, right? Or have I been reading what's between us all wrong? I sit in the back of the limo and pull the prenup from my back pocket. My mind searches for answers. Was I only a means to an end with her? Now that she no longer needs me for the job, is she done with me, or did this prenup have something to do with her running away? My ex left because I asked her to sign one and she refused, and that lesson taught me she wanted what I had, that she never wanted me for me. Is the same thing going on with Peyton? Does she want my name and what's in my bank? I shake my head slowly, refusing to believe that for one single second. But while my heart says one thing, my brain reminds me of past hurts.

No, she's not like that.

I sit in stunned silence as Elias drives me back to my villa. I give him a generous tip and head inside. With a headache brewing I go upstairs and into the bathroom. I toss back a couple pills and plunk down onto the bed. I turn my head sideways, and that's when I see my grandmother's wedding ring, sitting beside the lamp.

I jackknife up and reach for my phone. Goddammit, I can't let this happen. I just can't. I walked away from her once and it nearly destroyed me. I know there is more between us; I felt it in her touches and kisses, felt it when we made love last night. So why did she run away? Is she afraid I'm going to hurt her?

There's only one person who can help me figure out what's going on, and it's time I come clean. I pull up my contacts and press Call. The phone rings, and I take a deep breath when Cason answers.

CHAPTER FIFTEEN

Peyton

"COME ON, WE'RE going out," Carly says.

I sink deeper into the comfy sofa and plant my feet on the coffee table. "Nope, I'm not going anywhere."

"Yes, you are."

I pick up the remote and flick through the stations. I haven't left my condo in two weeks, not since I lost my job—and the man I love—and hopped on a plane to come home. Someone raps on my door, and I sit up a little straighter, my heart missing a beat. I honestly have no idea why I would think it's Roman. We had fun, played house for a while, but now it's over. I'm sure he's glad he's off the hook for marriage.

God, I miss him.

But I had to leave. I couldn't go through with a sham of a marriage—one I wanted to be real—after seeing that prenup. Does he really think I'm like his ex, that I wanted to get my hands on his money? I swipe at a stupid tear that threatens to fall—I've cried enough. Why should I shed tears for a man who doesn't know me or trust me at all?

Oh, because no matter what, you still love him.

Carly pulls the door open and my sister-in-law Londyn takes one look at me and shakes her head.

"Go away," I say, and take a sip of wine.

"She's worse than I thought," Londyn says.

"Yeah, she's been in those pajamas so long, the second she takes them off they're going to run to the washing machine themselves."

"I'm right here," I blurt out. "I can hear you."

"Come on, we have a long day ahead of us," Londyn says.

I stroke my wineglass and twirl the red wine inside. "What are you talking about?"

Londyn stands over me. "You know you look a little bit like the Joker right now."

I arch a brow at her. "I remember when you used to be nice."

"You have red wine all over the corners of your mouth and on your pajamas."

"Wine is my precious," I say, lifting my nose an inch.

"Get up," she demands in that no-nonsense voice of hers.

I snort. "I remember when I used to like you."

"You still like me, now get up. Cason is getting his plane ready."

"For what?"

She gives an exasperated sigh. "Did you forget?"

"Apparently."

"We're going to Belize, for Gemma's bachelorette party." She plants one hand on her hip, clearly frustrated with me. I don't blame her, all this self-pity and arguing is getting on my nerves, too. If Roman were here, would he kiss me to stop me from arguing?

Stop thinking about him!

I crinkle my nose. "Isn't that like a month away?"

"You've been moping so long you don't even know what day of the week it is anymore." Londyn hastily takes my wine from me and pulls me to my feet.

"I don't want to go." I stand there like a petulant child and dig my feet in. "I don't even like her fiancé."

Londyn waves a warning finger at me. "Who she marries is not your call."

"Well, if it was, I think she should be marrying Josh Walker."

Londyn smiles. "Yeah, she used to use his services at Penn Pals. I remember. I thought those two would end up together."

That's when an idea hits. I think it's brilliant, of course, or it could just be the wine. "Maybe we should kidnap the bride."

"We are not kidnapping anyone. Gemma is a good friend," she says, her voice softer. "We all need to support her. Now come on."

I pout. "You don't play fair."

There's someone else I know who doesn't play fair, either.

God, will I ever get him out of my head?

"Gemma is counting on you," Londyn says.

Okay, okay, I know she's right. Gemma and I met at Penn State and I have been looking forward to her bachelorette. It came much faster than I thought, but then again, I have lost all track of time.

"Will there be wine?" I ask.

"Yes," both Carly and Londyn say at the same time.

"You don't have to yell." I saunter to the bathroom, take one look at myself in the mirror and cringe. I rub the corners of my mouth. Londyn was right. I am channeling the Joker. Carly and Londyn are whispering something in the other room, but the shower drowns out their voices when I turn it on. I scrub off with hot, soapy water and head to my room to pack a bag, only to find it's already packed for me.

"Who did this?"

"I did," Carly says, her arms crossed as she leans against the door.

"How did you know what I wanted to pack?" I'm about to open the duffel bag but she stops me.

"Don't."

I frown and narrow my eyes. "Why are you acting so weird?"

"I'm not acting weird," she says lightly as she brushes me off with a wave. "You just had too much wine."

I nod. "That's fair."

"Everything you need is in that bag. Trust me."

Trust me. Isn't that what Roman asked me to do once. Where was his trust in me?

I eye her. "If you're sure…"

"I'm sure."

Londyn stands by the open door. "Come on, we need to go now."

One hour later, I'm on my brother's plane, ready for the long four-hour flight to Belize. I yawn, and my muscles relax. It's been a long time since I've slept well. Whenever I close my eyes, visions of Roman dance in my mind. I swallow hard. Is he relieved I never went through with the marriage?

He said he'd do anything to help me get the job, but agreeing to marriage, or rather being the one to suggest it, seemed a little over-the-top. That alone, not even taking into account all the other things he did for me, is why I thought he might want more. Why I thought that this was not about my job, and more about the two of us and how great we were together? I guess I was wrong.

Were you, Peyton?

I recline my comfy seat, let my lids fall shut, and the next thing I know, Cason is shaking me awake.

"What?" I say groggily, and blink my eyes into focus. Both Carly and Londyn are gathering their things.

"We're here."

"That was fast."

Cason's eyes narrow on me and he pats my hand gently. "Everything is going to be okay, Peyton."

"What are you talking about?" I ask, knowing, deep in my heart, that nothing is ever going to be okay again. I've lost everything. Cason doesn't know the whole truth, though. I kept my promise and never said a thing about my relationship with Roman. He only knows I didn't get the position.

"You trust me, right?" he asks.

"Of course I do."

"Then you know everything I do is with your best interest in mind, right?"

"Cason, what are you talking about?" I shake my head to clear the rest of the sleep away. "You're freaking me out a little here."

"Promise me you won't be mad," he says, a softness in his voice, making it the tone he used with me when I was a frightened child.

Everything inside me stiffens. "About what?"

He casts Londyn a quick look and she nods. "We didn't really go to Belize."

I jump up and look out the window. "Where the hell are we?"

"Come on, I'll show you."

I quickly gather up my things and exit the plane. Once we're on the ground, I look at the airport, but still can't figure out where we are. It's not until we land in customs that I realize I'm in Italy.

Italy!

Where Roman's family lives.

Oh, hell no!

"I'm getting back on the plane," I blurt out.

Cason takes my hand and tugs. "You said you trusted me."

"Cason, why are we here?" I don't want to see Roman. We're done. But I can't tell him that because he never knew what we were doing behind closed doors.

"There is something I want to show you, then we can turn around and head right back to the States."

My stomach cramps. "I don't get it. What about the bachelorette party?"

He gives me an exasperated sigh. "Do you have to question everything?"

"Yes."

"Fine. I'll explain everything shortly. Right now, I need you to trust me."

With my stomach in tight knots, we go through customs and outside there is a limo waiting for us. We all pile in and I put my travel bag by my feet. I have no idea what my brother is up to. All I know is that I do trust him and if he wants to show me something, I'm not going to say no. If it has something to do with Roman—and how could it not—I'm going to kill him.

As we drive, a cold chill moves through me despite the warm temperatures outside, and I dig into my carry-on duffel bag to see if Carly packed me a sweater.

"What the heck?" I ask, when I pull pair after pair of sexy underwear from the bag. "You didn't pack me any clothes."

She looks away, avoiding my gaze, and once again I can't help but think she's acting strange. "I didn't think you were going to need them," she says.

"Why on earth wouldn't I need clothes for a bachelorette party?" I snort. "Then again, I guess we're not really going to Gemma's party. I still don't understand all the underwear, though."

"To answer your earlier question, Peyton," Cason says, "Londyn and Carly are here because we *are* going to a wedding. Just not Gemma's."

"Then I do need clothes." Maybe I'd better lay off the wine, because nothing is making sense. The car comes to a stop and we all climb out. I glance around at the big open field, which goes on as far as the eye can see. "Where are we? Whose wedding?"

I take a step forward and go completely still when I spot Roman cresting a hill, walking toward me. But he's not alone—behind him I spot his entire family.

My legs go weak and Cason puts his arm around me. "Cason..."

"You two need to talk."

I glare at him. "You were behind this?"

"Yes," he says, a calmness in his voice that does little to soothe me.

"Why?"

"All I ever wanted in my entire life was to make sure you were safe and loved, Peyton. But you're grown up now, and it's time to stand on your own two feet and make your own decisions. A conversation I shared with someone very wise opened my eyes to that."

I gasp. "Really?"

"Roman and I talked, for hours. Now it's your turn to talk to him. What happens next is up to you. He's a good man, Peyton. In fact, he's the best, and if there was ever a man I wanted in your life, it's him. I know you'll make the right choice."

"You don't understand."

"I think you're the one who doesn't understand."

He gives me a little nudge until my legs are moving and the next thing I know, Roman and I are standing alone in a wide expanse of field, our family and friends in the distance.

"What's going on, Roman?"

"I'm sorry about tricking you into coming."

I cross my arms. "Say whatever it is you have to say."

"We have a problem."

I try to keep my breathing steady, but his proximity is seriously messing with my body and brain. "What kind of problem?"

"You see, I hurt you, Peyton, after I swore I never would. But you have to know I didn't do it on purpose. I'd never do it on purpose." I blink up at him, and he continues with, "I love you, Peyton. I've always loved you. I never thought you could be mine, but now, well, I'm going to do everything in my power to make that happen."

My throat dries. "You…love me?"

He laughs and shakes his head. "Is that what I said?"

I stiffen. Oh God, did he not mean it? "Yes, that's what you just said."

His smile falls, his face completely sober, when he says, "Then that's what I meant." He takes my hand and when I see love and desire reflecting in his eyes, happiness wells up inside me.

Roman loves me!

Wait, why is he suddenly frowning?

"I'm sorry you lost your job."

Hurt tightens my heart, and I blink back the tears pounding behind my eyes. Richard's wife might have been out to get me fired unbeknownst to him, but at least he was good with the kids, and they loved him in return. Their well-being is important to me. "Thank you."

"Teaching kids English in another country is still your dream job, right?"

"It is. But I don't see that happening now."

"Look around." I glance around at the wide-open space and catch my brother's eye. He looks on with worry, and my heart thumps. He's done right by me my whole life, and I love him for it, but I'm a grown-up now who can stand on her own feet, make her own decisions. "This is where your new school is going to be built."

I falter a little, my pulse leaping in my neck. "What?"

"I bought this land, and it took weeks to get all the permits I needed. I would have come for you sooner, but I wanted to make sure everything was in place."

I raise my shaky hands to his face. "Roman, I can't believe you did this." Then again, maybe I can. He's been nothing but good to me, going above and beyond to help me out...because he *loves* me.

Roman loves me.

"I don't know what to say," I push out, my voice as shaky as my body.

"Say yes." He drops to his knees, pulls a box from his back pocket and opens it. Tears flood my eyes and spill when I see his grandmother's ring. "I love you, Peyton, with all my heart. I want you in my bed and in my life, I want you for the good times and the bad. I want to go on this journey called life with you by my side. I want to be equal partners, and I don't care about the prenup."

My head spins, my heart so full it's ready to burst, but with everything he's saying to me, everything coming at me so fast, my mind focuses on the last words out of his mouth. "Why don't you care about the prenup?"

"Because I know you're nothing like my ex, that you're the most giving person I know and you don't care about my name or money. You care about the person behind all those things—you care about me. The prenup is simply a tradition, something that has been in my family for generations. I never even really thought about how it would make you feel. I'm an idiot like that sometimes."

"You're not an idiot, Roman, and I didn't know it was tradition," I say, my heart pounding so hard, I'm a little light-headed. "When I saw it, I thought…"

"I know what you thought, and I'm sorry. I never meant to do anything that made you feel like that lost girl from your childhood. The one who was afraid she wasn't enough and would never be enough. I never meant for you to think I wanted you to sign the prenup because I didn't trust you. I do trust you, Peyton. You're everything to me and to my family. You're kind, sweet, giving and so goddamn lovable that when I found the villa empty—" he shakes his head, agony all over his face "—it broke my damn heart. At first, I couldn't understand it. I thought you were done with me, thought you were discarding me because you didn't need me to be your husband anymore. I jumped to conclusions because of past hurts, but then I recognized that's not something you would ever do. I called Cason and realized the prenup brought back past hurts for you, too."

"It did, and I'm sorry, too, Roman. You've been nothing but sweet and helpful, and you showed me I have value, made me feel important."

He once confessed that helping me was more about me and less about my brother. Everything in his touch and actions told me he cared. After reading the prenup, I didn't want to believe him anymore, and I expected him to hurt me like everyone else. Self-preservation and a childhood in the system does that to a person. But there was a part of me that always believed him…believed in him. I was just so afraid. But I don't have to be afraid anymore.

"The prenup… I don't know, it just reminded me that I should never let myself believe in fairy tales, because…"

"Because there's still a part of you that believes you're not enough. But you have to let that go. You're everything. You're more than everything." He takes a deep breath and lets it out slowly. "The truth is,

Peyton, you *can* take care of yourself, I know that, but all I want to do is protect you and give you the world." His throat makes a noise and he puts a hand on my face. "I don't want to live without you. Correction, I *can't* live without you."

"You can't?"

"No." Eyes full of love and sorrow study my face. My heart races and happy tears full of joy spill down my cheeks. "Can you let me do that?"

"All I ever wanted from you was your love, Roman. Those other things aren't important to me."

He smiles. "Is that your way of saying you love me?"

"Of course I love you," I blurt out. "I've always loved you. For as long as I can remember I loved you."

"Then say yes."

"No," I say, and he falls back onto his heels.

Fear and sadness invade his dark eyes. "No?"

"No, if it's tradition, then I want to sign the prenup. I didn't know that before. I thought it was about me, but it's not, it's about your family and tradition and I want to respect that."

He smiles, stands and pulls me to him. "Right there, Peyton. That's why I *don't* want you to sign it."

I take a big breath, about to answer him, then glance up to see our families. "Wait," I say. "Why is everyone here?"

"Because if you say yes, I want to get married this very second. All the arrangements have been made."

"Oh."

He chuckles. "Yeah, oh, and I'm not the only one out here holding my breath here, Peyton. My sisters can't wait until they can call you sister, Mamma can't wait to call you her new daughter, and I can't wait to call you my wife."

I put one hand on my hips and shake my head. "You just took it upon yourself to make arrangements without consulting me?"

"I just thought—"

I throw my hands out, palms up, and those watching must think we're fighting. "And never considered if I wanted it to be on a beach or a church, or a… I don't know, somewhere else," I say, totally pressing his buttons and wanting to frustrate him.

"This is where your school is going to be built, I thought you'd like—"

"What about where I want to live?"

"If you liked Malta, I thought you'd like—"

"You thought I'd like all of this, did you? Maybe I don't like any of this, Roman. Maybe I *hate* it."

I grin up at him and that's when he clues in to what I'm doing.

His smile is slow, sexy. "Do I have to kiss you to stop you from arguing with me?"

"Yes, Roman."

He pauses, his lips inches from mine, hope invading his eyes. "Wait, what are you saying yes to?"

"I'm saying yes to being your wife, to living here, to building a school here, a future here, and celebrating a wedding today with our families."

He runs his thumb over my cheek and I melt

into him. "Are you going to hate all those things, Peyton?"

My heart beats so fast, I'm sure I might faint, but if I do, this man will be there to take care of me, and more importantly I'm going to let him. "I'm going to hate every single one," I say.

"Good."

Cheers erupt behind us as he picks me up, puts his lips on mine and as his love and warmth wrap around my body and heart, he spins me, pushing the last chills from my body. I kiss him back, deeply, passionately, my flesh absorbing all his heat and love, and for the first time in my life something miraculous happens to my body.

It warms.

* * * * *

THE GREEK'S
FORBIDDEN
INNOCENT

ANNIE WEST

This story is for Helen Sibbritt.

CHAPTER ONE

'Take a deep breath, Carissa, and tell me slowly.' Mina held her friend's shoulders tight. 'And another.' She nodded encouragingly as Carissa's breathing grew more normal. 'That's better.'

While Carissa focused on her breathing, Mina's gaze searched for the source of her friend's distress. But there was nothing unusual in the entry to the other woman's apartment. No blood. No disarray. No intruder. Just a large pink suitcase.

Yet something was definitely wrong. Carissa, the most easygoing person she knew, had grabbed Mina before she could open the door to her own apartment and yanked her in next door. There was real fear in Carissa's china-blue eyes.

'Come and sit and tell me about it.'

'No!' Carissa shook her head and a cloud of golden curls spilled around her shoulders. 'There's no time. They'll be here soon. *But I don't want to go. I can't go.*' Tears filled her eyes as her voice wobbled. 'I want Pierre! But he's not here in Paris. He's abroad.'

That at least made sense. Pierre was Carissa's boyfriend.

'Don't fret. No one's going to make you go anywhere you don't want to.' Mina kept her voice calm, ushering her friend into the small sitting room and gently pushing her into a seat. Carissa's whole body shook and her face was stark white.

Mina had received enough bad news herself to recognise shock. Her mother had died when she was young and just five years ago, when she was seventeen, her father had died unexpectedly from a brain aneurism.

Memories stirred of that terrifying time, held hostage

in a palace coup after her father's funeral. Then her sister Ghizlan's sacrifice, forced to wed the coup leader, Huseyn, so he could become Sheikh. It seemed a lifetime away from Mina's life now in France.

'Tell me what's up so I can help.' Mina pulled a chair close and took Carissa's hands. Her face was, for the first time Mina could recall, bare of make-up and her shirt wasn't buttoned right. For Carissa this was a fashion catastrophe. More like Mina's usual look than her own.

Mina's frown deepened. 'Has someone hurt you?'

Her stomach clenched as she remembered the day of the coup, the drench of icy fear as a soldier manhandled her, stopping her escape with brutal efficiency. She recalled the adrenalin rush galvanising her to fight back. It was the first time anyone had laid a hand on her. The first time she'd become aware of the sheer, physical power men could exert over women. Until then, Mina's royal status had protected her.

Carissa was trusting and gentle, always looking for the best in people. If someone had taken advantage of her—

'No, it's nothing like that.'

Mina's shoulders sagged. Relief rushed through her. In the years they'd studied together at a prestigious Paris art school, and since, she'd never seen Carissa distraught like this.

'So who is coming? Where don't you want to go?'

Carissa's bottom lip quivered and she blinked hard.

'Alexei Katsaros is sending someone. They'll take me to his private island.' A shudder ran through her. 'But I don't want to go. I can't. Even when Dad told me about it, I never thought it would actually *happen*! You have to help me, Mina. Please.'

Mina's worry eased and with it her frantic heartbeat. Not a life-and-death situation, then. She knew who Alexei

Katsaros was. Who didn't? He was a megawealthy IT entrepreneur. Carissa's father was one of his executives.

'Is it an invitation to visit your father? I'm sure Pierre would spare you for a short vacation.'

Carissa shook her head. 'This isn't a vacation. It's an arranged marriage! Dad told me he hoped to organise it but I never thought he'd bring it off. Alexei Katsaros can have his pick of women.'

Mina said nothing. Carissa was extraordinarily pretty and sweet-natured. That, plus her innate desire to please, would appeal to lots of men.

'I can't go through with it, Mina.' Carissa's fingers bit into hers. 'I could never love a man like that, so hard and judgemental. He wants a trophy wife, who'll do what he wants when he wants. My father's told him I'm pretty and biddable and...' Her shoulders shook as the tears became sobs. 'I never thought it would come to this. It seemed impossible, laughable. But I don't have a choice. My father's *counting* on me.'

Mina frowned. Arranged marriages she knew about. If her father had lived he'd have organised one for her.

'I'm sure no one will force you into anything.' Unlike in Jeirut. Her sister had been forced into an unwanted marriage and Mina remembered feeling utterly helpless at being unable to prevent it. It had been a miracle when, against the odds, the pair later fell in love. The match had seemed doomed to end in misery. 'Your father will be there. If you explain—'

'But he's *not* there,' Carissa wailed. 'I don't know where he is. I can't contact him. And I can't say no to Mr Katsaros. Dad warned me there'd been some trouble at work. He didn't say what, but I think his job's on the line. He's hoping this marriage will smooth everything over.' Carissa clung to Mina's hands, her fingers curling into talons. 'But I could never marry such a hard man. He has a new woman every week. Besides, Pierre and I are in love. We're getting married.' A flicker of happiness transformed her teary features.

'You're getting married?' Mina stared. She shouldn't be surprised; the pair were besotted.

Carissa's smile died. 'We were planning to elope next weekend, when he's back from this business trip. Pierre says it will be easier to face his family with a fait accompli.'

Pierre rose in Mina's estimation. He was a lovely guy but he'd never stood up to his stiff-necked family who wanted him to marry someone from old French money.

'But I can't marry him if I'm forced to marry Alexei Katsaros!' Carissa's tears overflowed.

'Did Katsaros *say* he wanted to marry you?'

'As good as. He said my father had told him about me and he was anxious to meet. He believed we'd find a lot in common and that we had a future together.' Carissa bit her lip. 'I tried to fob him off but he didn't hear a word I said. He cut me off and said his staff would be here in an hour to collect me. What will I do?'

Mina frowned. She didn't like the sound of this. He might be rich but that didn't excuse rudeness or give him the right to order Carissa around.

'Tell me again exactly what your father told you.'

But as Carissa spoke, Mina's hope that her friend had overreacted dissolved. There'd recently been a rift between her father and his employer. After years of faithful service it seemed Katsaros might dump him. Mina couldn't approve of Mr Carter's plan to use Carissa to cement his position, but such things happened. Several of Mina's peers in Jeirut had been married to older men they barely knew to strengthen family or business links.

She gritted her teeth, watching Carissa's hands flutter as she related the one-sided conversation with Alexei Katsaros. He hadn't invited Carissa to his island hideaway but simply informed her of the travel arrangements. As if she were freight to be transported, not a woman with a life of her own.

Mina's temper rose like steam from a kettle.

She prized her freedom, appreciating how different her life was in Paris, away from a world where every major decision was made by the male head of her family. Western women accepted freedom as their right, not knowing how precious that was. And here was some billionaire bully, trying to snatch that from Carissa. With the help of her own father!

It wasn't right.

'And there's nothing I can do.' Carissa sniffled.

'Of course there is. They can't force you onto the plane. Or into marriage.'

'I can't not go. What about my father's job?' She hiccupped. 'But if I go, what about Pierre? His family will find a way to stop our wedding.'

Mina wanted to tell Carissa to grow a backbone and stand up for herself. But Carissa wasn't made that way. Besides, she cared for her father, though he'd got her into this mess. Plus it sounded, from other things she'd said, as if Mr Carter hadn't recovered from his wife's recent death. That might explain why he'd slipped up at work. A good employer would make allowances for grief. Mina suspected Alexei Katsaros was a domineering tyrant, considering no one but himself.

Irresistibly, her thoughts dragged back to those fraught days after her father's death. Her future and her sister's had hung in the balance, their fate determined by a man with little sympathy for their hopes and wishes.

Mina remembered the horror of being utterly powerless.

She refused to let Carissa become a chattel to buy her father out of trouble, or satisfy Katsaros's desire for a convenient, biddable wife.

'I've packed a bag. I can't reach my father, so I'll have to go. But it means leaving Pierre.' Carissa wrung her hands and Mina felt something snap inside.

Carissa was sweet but she had as much grit as a marshmallow. Between them, Katsaros and Carter could herd her into a marriage that would make her miserable for the rest of her life. Mina couldn't change her friend into a woman who'd look a thug in the eye and send him packing, or tell her father he couldn't marry her off to a stranger. But she *could* delay things long enough for Carissa and Pierre to marry. A few days, a week at most.

'How long before they collect you?'

Carissa's answer was drowned by a sharp rap on the door. She gasped and grabbed Mina's hands.

The last shred of doubt fled Mina's brain as she read her friend's terror and despair. Carissa was a pushover, but Mina wasn't.

She got to her feet.

'Still no sign of Carter, sir. He hasn't been home.'

Alexei's grip tightened on the phone and he ground his teeth in frustration. But he refrained from chewing out the head of his London office. It wasn't MacIntyre's fault Carter had done a bunk. Alexei should have acted sooner, but initially he hadn't wanted to believe Carter's guilt. The man had been at his side for years, the only person Alexei really trusted.

That was why his betrayal cut so deep. Trust came hard to Alexei. He'd seen his mother betrayed and cast aside, made into a victim and her life shortened, because she trusted too easily.

Alexei bore a lot of the blame. He'd been gullible, falling for his stepfather's charm, believing the man genuinely cared. He'd persuaded his mother to let the guy into their lives. Too late they discovered he'd only cultivated

Alexei to get to his mother and her dead husband's insurance payment.

No one could accuse Alexei of gullibility now.

That was what made it so remarkable that, despite his caution, he'd come to believe in Carter. It wasn't just his way with numbers. His almost uncanny knack for identifying problems and possible solutions. It was his reticence, his scrupulous separation of business and personal life. He'd been the perfect executive.

Until his double-dealing came to light.

Alexei felt that sucker punch of betrayal. Worse this time because he should have known better. He was no innocent kid.

'Keep me informed. Have the investigator check in daily.'

'Yes, sir. Of course, sir.'

Alexei ended the call and scraped a hand through his hair, telling himself he'd grown soft. He should have acted sooner. Now he had to play catch-up.

He swung round to pace, ignoring the turquoise water and white sand beyond the window. He didn't want to be in the Caribbean, no matter how restful his private retreat. He wanted to be wherever Carter was. The man's depredations had been deep. Not enough to destabilise Alexei's business but enough to send a ripple of disquiet through anyone savvy enough to discover Alexei had been duped.

Despite his policy of employing the best, most innovative people in the industry, Alexei Katsaros *was* his company as far as the market was concerned. He'd worked hard to establish one of the world's leading software companies and build a reputation as a canny entrepreneur. His nose for success was only rivalled by his company's groundbreaking IT solutions. News of his fallibility would crack that image and damage his company's position.

Damn Carter. Where was he hiding?

Alexei slammed to a halt as he heard a vehicle through the open window.

At last. The ace up his sleeve.

Alexei breathed deep, easing cramped lungs, assuring himself that now, *finally*, he had the upper hand.

He crossed to the window and watched as the four-wheel drive pulled up. The driver's door opened but before Henri could get out the front passenger door swung open and someone alighted.

Alexei's brow twitched into a frown. That couldn't be her. He waited for the rear door to open but it stayed steadfastly shut. Henri walked ponderously to the rear of the vehicle and pulled out a single suitcase of candy pink.

That was all. One suitcase and one passenger, though not the passenger he expected.

Alexei's frown became a scowl. The call from Paris had assured him that she'd been collected from her apartment and deposited on his jet. Yet surely this wasn't Carter's daughter. He'd expected a fashion tragic with mountains of luggage.

His gaze rested on the svelte figure of a woman who stood, hands on her hips and head back, surveying his home. Far from being addicted to high-end fashion as he'd been led to believe, she wasn't dressed in designer casuals for a tropical island holiday, but for…what? A yoga class? An artist's garret?

Understanding took root. *That* was it.

Carter, when he'd raised the preposterous idea of a match between Alexei and his daughter, had waxed voluble about the girl he'd never mentioned in years of employment. He'd wittered on about her beauty and charm, her sweet disposition and eagerness to please. And her aspirations to be an artist in between shopping. She lived in Paris, playing at an artistic career, no doubt funded by the money Carter had embezzled from Alexei.

Pain radiated from Alexei's jaw down his neck to his tight shoulders.

He yanked his thoughts from Carter's crimes to the man's daughter.

She took her pretensions seriously. Or perhaps the outfit was for his benefit, though surely it wasn't designed to please a man. Flat black shoes, black leggings and an oversized black T-shirt that gaped over one shoulder.

Definitely not Alexei's style. He preferred a woman who dressed like a woman.

Yet even as he dismissed Carissa Carter as not his type, his gaze lingered on the length of shapely legs silhouetted in black. Long legs, the sort of legs he'd enjoy wrapped around his waist during sex.

His gaze flicked higher, skimming her slight figure. He supposed, in the right gear, she'd be a perfect clothes horse, but personally he preferred a woman whose curves were more abundant.

Then the tilt of her head altered and he found himself face-to-face with her.

She was too far away for him to make out her features properly. Just good bone structure and dark hair pulled ruthlessly back into a bun. He had the impression of a wide, mobile mouth, but he wasn't paying attention. His thoughts were on the sudden throb pulsing through his belly.

It couldn't be attraction. Not for the daughter of a criminal. A woman whose lifestyle had probably fed her father's depredations. He had no proof Carissa Carter knew of her father's crimes, but she'd benefited. Maybe she'd been in on the scheme, eager to fund her easy life in Paris. Alexei couldn't trust her. He'd play the part of eager suitor, pretending he was in the market for a wife.

As if he needed a third party to find him a woman!

He stared back at her, expecting her to duck her head and pretend not to see him.

Instead she stood motionless, watching as if *he* were under the microscope. It was a curious feeling. Alexei was used to people inclining their heads in agreement or deference. Except women, who tended to stare.

Carissa's bold regard was something altogether different. It sent heat skittering down his spine, drawing every sense to hyperalert.

Finally, after she'd looked her fill, she turned to Henri. Alexei caught a flash of white teeth as she smiled but it was the coltish grace of her movements that held his attention. There was a fluidity to her supple body that reminded him of a Russian ballet dancer with whom he'd once shared a fiery affair. Alexei recalled not only the dancer's grace but her athleticism and body awareness that had taken sexual pleasure to a new level.

He watched Carissa Carter saunter towards his house. Shoulders back, head up, yet she didn't march. Instead that loose-limbed stroll was a symphony of sensual femininity.

For his benefit?

Of course.

His guest might play at being the bohemian artist, but if she was her father's daughter, she'd have her eye on the main game, getting Alexei's money.

For the first time since he'd learned of Carter's betrayal, Alexei smiled.

He didn't want the woman here, except as bait to draw her father. The fact she'd accepted his summons told him she'd sell herself into marriage with a man she didn't even know. Though she knew the size of his bank balance. That regularly featured in rich lists around the world.

It could be amusing watching her try to seduce him.

CHAPTER TWO

MINA KNEW ABOUT WEALTH. She'd been born royal. But her family riches and privilege were tied to duty, responsibility and service. The palace where she'd grown up had been the nerve centre for her country's administration.

This was pure sybaritic indulgence.

As if it wasn't enough to own a tropical island rimmed with beaches so white they looked like sugar frosting, Alexei Katsaros's home was the last word in luxury. The pool wrapped around the house so every room looked out on water. There was a bar actually in the pool too, so he and his guests wouldn't have to stir from the water to get a drink.

Four-poster daybeds were scattered around the pool, their gauzy hangings romantic and alluring. Her artist's eye appreciated the cushions in turquoise, teal and jade that reflected the vibrant shades of the tropical garden and the sea beyond. Then there were the sculptures in pale stone, which she glimpsed through the greenery. She itched to detour and investigate.

Forcibly she yanked her attention back to the house. The huge entry door stood open. Beside her, Henri waited for her to precede him.

Strange, this momentary hesitation.

All the way from Paris she'd been buoyed by indignation on Carissa's behalf. Now though, Mina knew an uncharacteristic moment of doubt. A wariness at odds with her practice of facing problems head-on.

Her impulsiveness, her father would have said.

Why? Mina wasn't overawed by Katsaros's wealth, or cowed by any threat he could make.

Yet for a moment, as her gaze locked on the big man watching her from inside, something unfamiliar quivered through her. Something starkly unsettling.

An inner voice urged her to flee while she had the chance.

Of course she lifted her chin and stared right back instead.

The bright bowl of azure sky above her seemed to drop lower, the air thickening as she drew a slow, steadying breath. Still, he held her gaze.

Her bloodstream fizzed, making her fingers and the soles of her feet tingle. For a second she wondered if she'd been hit by a bolt of lightning out of the clear sky, till reason told her that was impossible.

Deliberately she turned away, feigning interest in her surroundings. Yet the image imprinted on her retinas wasn't the white mansion with its picture windows, but the powerfully built man whose eyes locked on her. Everything about him, from his wide-set stance to that deep, muscled chest revealed by his open shirt, screamed strength.

Well, Mina was strong too. No bossy tycoon would intimidate her.

Nodding to Henri, she headed for the door.

She was greeted by Henri's wife, Marie, whose smiling eyes and lilting accent made Mina relax in spite of herself.

'Alexei is eager to meet you but perhaps you'd like to freshen up first?'

Mina smiled and shook her head. The flight by private jet had been far from onerous. 'Thank you, but no. I'm eager to meet my host.'

'How…charming.' The deep voice came from beyond Marie. Its cadence drew Mina's skin tight, as if someone dragged a length of rich velvet across it. A shimmer of heat flared low in her body and she had to work to keep her expression bland.

Slowly, so slowly she seemed to feel each muscle and joint move, she turned her head towards the shadows.

Never had Mina been more grateful for her royal upbringing. She'd spent seventeen years learning to look composed and calm, even if she'd never quite mastered regal. At twelve she'd sat on podiums listening to interminable speeches. At fifteen she'd held her own at royal dinners. Her polite interest expression could fool everyone but her sister.

Which meant the man watching her through narrowed eyes had no idea she felt as if someone had sliced the tendons at the backs of her legs.

Mina's knees shook for the merest instant before she stiffened them, but her cool smile remained steady. As for the sizzle in her blood, no one else knew about that.

She waited for him to frown and say she wasn't Carissa Carter. Yet he simply stared down at her from his superior height. Could it really be that he didn't know what Carissa looked like? That flaw in her plan had kept her awake on the flight from Europe. Yet, against the odds, it appeared he didn't. So sure of himself. Arrogant enough to expect everyone to obey his every whim. So unquestioning.

Mina let her mouth curve slightly. 'Mr Katsaros. How lovely to meet you at last.'

'At *last*, Ms Carter? You've been waiting to meet me? Surely your trip was admirably quick?' His hint of indolent surprise and the tilt of one slashing eyebrow gave him an air of smug superiority.

'Oh, it was.' Mina looked down and flicked lint from her sleeve. 'Admirably so. Why, I didn't even have time to check my diary for commitments that might clash before I was whisked away. Or to arrange for someone to keep an eye on my apartment.'

She let her brow pucker in a frown. 'I hope the fruit I bought doesn't spoil while I'm away. And the milk.' She let her smile widen. 'But I understand. I'm sure you're used to wanting something and having it happen immediately. No time to waste on boring niceties like invitations or queries about whether the dates suited me.'

Below his rumpled black hair grooves corrugated that wide brow. Mina raised her hand. 'Not that it matters. I know how terribly valuable your time is. After all, what could I *possibly* have scheduled that could be nearly as important?'

From behind her Mina heard a snuffle from Henri that sounded suspiciously like a stifled laugh. Then he excused himself, murmuring something about putting her luggage away and prudently followed his wife down a corridor.

Which left Mina alone with Alexei Katsaros.

He didn't even seem to notice Marie and Henri leave. All his attention was on Mina.

If she were in the mood to feel fear it would have swamped her now, for the man watched her with the hyperawareness of a hunter. Then there was the sheer size of him, not only tall but well-built, all muscled strength beneath those straight shoulders. She'd caught a glimpse of a well-developed chest and taut abdominals that confirmed this man did far more than sit behind a desk, making money. His thighs beneath the faded jeans were those of a skier or a horseman, honed hard and strong.

Without taking his eyes off her, he slowly finished buttoning his white shirt. Then he tucked it into his faded jeans with a casual insouciance utterly at odds with the speculative gleam in his dark eyes.

Mina's manufactured smile solidified as he took his time shoving the material down, his hand disappearing behind the denim. For reasons she couldn't fathom the sight of him dressing made her pulse quicken. Her palm prickled as if her own hand slid down that flat abdomen.

'I'm sorry, did my arrival wake you?' The snap in her

words betrayed her discomfort but Mina compensated for it by slowly taking stock of his tousled black hair and the dark shadow of beard growth across that solid jaw.

His hands fell to his sides and he stepped out of the shadows. The light hit sharply defined cheekbones, a well-shaped mouth and a stern blade of nose, down which he surveyed her. Mina was reminded of precious icons she'd seen. But whereas those old saints had looked flat and unreal, this man exuded raw energy and the glint in his dark eyes was anything but unworldly. Alexei Katsaros was too... physical for sainthood. With his imposing size and posture he could model for a cavalry officer from a previous century, supercilious and deadly in a bright uniform, with a sabre at his side.

Mina repressed the warm shiver that started at the base of her spine and threatened to crawl, vertebra by vertebra, up her back.

'You know you didn't wake me. We watched each other.' His voice was both rough and dangerously soothing.

Mina couldn't explain it but he made the simple words sound almost indecent. As if they'd been naked at the time, or as if she'd watched him doing something—

'So, you're concerned about your groceries, is that right?' One dark eyebrow rose and it took a second for Mina to follow the change of subject. She was still lost in a hazy daydream of Alexei Katsaros stripping his shirt away and reaching for the button on his jeans. 'I can have one of my staff deal with your apartment, Ms Carter, since I put you to such inconvenience.'

Mina wrenched her thoughts back to the man before her. The man whose satisfied smile told her he knew he'd unsettled her. Whose tone conveyed that she'd managed to needle him with her pointed comments about being dragged away.

'That's very kind, Mr Katsaros.' She blinked up at him,

mimicking Carissa, then thought better of it. She'd never batted her eyelashes in her life and wasn't about to start.

'Something in your eye, Ms Carter?' Not by a whisker did he betray a smile yet Mina knew he laughed at her.

To her surprise, Mina had to stifle a smirk of her own. He was right. She couldn't pull off such feminine wiles. She was better to stick at being herself.

'Sand, probably.' She blinked again. 'My own fault. I insisted on driving with the window down to enjoy the breeze.'

Carissa would have shrieked at the thought of her hair getting messed up, but Alexei Katsaros didn't know that. Mina would have to get by with pretending to be a Mina version of Carissa. Less fluttery and uncertain, less overtly feminine, less willing to be bullied.

'Thank you for the offer to take care of my apartment but I prefer not to have my home taken over by strangers. I'm sure you understand.'

He understood all right. His smugness fled as he registered that she referred to his staff who'd politely yet inexorably ushered her from Carissa's flat.

'My staff disturbed you? You felt threatened in some way?' His voice was sharp.

Had he really thought she'd be happy, herded by armed bodyguards?

Mina remembered Carissa's tears and frantic fear. How would she have coped, confronting those big men with cold eyes and suave suits?

They'd been impeccably solicitous but Mina read in them the same quality she'd seen in her father's royal guards. Beneath the polish were men trained to use force. If she'd refused to go, they'd have bundled her onto that private jet without a qualm.

'Oh, I didn't feel at all threatened by anyone else while I

was with them.' She paused, letting him absorb her words. Would he understand *they'd* been the threat?

His expression didn't alter.

Clearly he had no idea how frightening it was for a woman not used to close personal protection to have stony-faced men wearing shoulder holsters usher her into an anonymous vehicle.

Suddenly weary, Mina suppressed a sigh. What was the point? He wouldn't care even if he understood.

'Your staff were polite and incredibly...efficient. I'm sure no express parcel could have been delivered to your door more quickly.'

She looked away, letting her gaze rove the white marble foyer, taking in the carved Cycladic figurine in a niche on the far wall. Mina's pulse quickened with interest but she couldn't afford to be distracted. Slowly she turned back to her host, whose hands, she noticed, were bunched in fists at his sides.

He stepped forward and Mina's nape prickled. This close she realised those intent eyes were a stunning dark green, opaque and intriguing. She'd never seen the like. Momentarily she was mesmerised. Then she dragged her thoughts back to their conversation.

'I prefer to make my own arrangements, Mr Katsaros. I'm sure you understand.'

Alexei understood all right.

He was being taken to task by a woman who didn't know she was playing with fire. Or did she believe she could set her own rules because he contemplated marriage?

That had to be it. There was no other explanation.

He'd wondered if Carter's daughter was a spoiled princess. As far as he could tell, she'd lived for years off her father's, and by extension his own, largesse, while enjoying a dilettante's life.

Now he had his answer. Carissa Carter was used to getting her own way. Spoiled rotten, he had no doubt. Her father had led her to expect an advantageous match and she seemed sure it would happen.

Yet her words disturbed him. Had she really been frightened of his security staff? Alexei barely noticed them now, just considered them a normal part of life.

He stared down at the woman who continued to surprise him. It wasn't only her plain outfit, or the accent that wasn't quite as he'd heard it over the phone, but then there'd been interference on the line. He'd imagined someone more eager to ingratiate herself. More overtly charming.

Carissa Carter was more complex than he'd imagined.

She was confident yet not in the way of a woman used to trading on male admiration. She carried herself with an intrinsic elegance that, when she looked down that straight nose at him, bordered on condescension. That intrigued. As did the intelligence shining in those sherry-coloured eyes and in the snarky undercurrent of her conversation.

He'd imagined Carter's daughter more eminently dismissible. The man had said her nature was sweet rather than incisive and that she wasn't cut out for business. Alexei had assumed she was pretty but vacuous.

How wrong he'd been.

Nor was she as he'd expected her to look. He saw no resemblance to Carter in her dark hair, luminous eyes or expressive mouth. Her skin was golden, not pale, and she met his gaze with a direct curiosity that, at any other time, he'd appreciate.

It evoked a hungry gnawing in the pit of his belly, a reminder that, despite his preoccupation with her father, Alexei was a vigorous man with healthy appetites.

He drew a slow breath, marshalling his thoughts, and was fascinated to see that, despite her sugared verbal barbs, Carissa Carter wasn't immune to him after all. Her eyes tracked the rise of his chest, her pupils dilating as if mesmerised. Then she blinked and turned away, feigning indifference.

Satisfaction stirred. He'd disliked her jabs about the way he'd got her here, had even felt a stirring of remorse. Seeing that chink in her armour pleased him.

'How remiss of me to keep a guest standing in the foyer.' Alexei smiled and watched a tiny wrinkle appear above the bridge of her nose, as if she concentrated on not reacting. Fascinating.

'Won't you come in?' He stood aside and gestured for her to precede him into the main sitting room.

'Thank you.' She inclined her head in the slightest nod.

Alexei caught a hint of perfume as she passed. Another surprise. He'd expected some expensive designer scent but this was one he'd never encountered. Instead of florals or cloying sweetness, she'd chosen a fragrance that hinted at the exotic Near East. Alexei inhaled cinnamon and spice and a warm, earthy richness that made him think, bizarrely, of veiled temptresses in gauzy silks. He canted towards her.

Fortunately she didn't notice. She entered the sitting room with that leisurely, swaying stroll that spoke of casual confidence. As if she were accustomed to a billionaire's luxury lifestyle. But then, given her father's thievery...

He watched as she caught sight of the ancient sculpture against one wall. The torso of a young man, the musculature and veining of chest and arms superbly executed, the filmy fabric of his tunic the work of a master. She stiffened and drew a sharp breath. A second later she stood before the ruined masterpiece, her hand stretching momentarily towards it before dropping to her side.

'It's magnificent.' There was genuine awe in her words. Alexei recognised it. He felt the same way about the piece.

His mouth twisted. Despite all expectation he found Carissa Carter…refreshing. Perhaps it wouldn't be so tough pretending to be interested in her till her father arrived.

'It was discovered at the bottom of the sea.'

As if his words broke the spell of artistic appreciation, she spun around, that oversized black T-shirt swirling wide. What did she look like beneath it? The rest of her was slim and beautifully formed.

'You have a very nice home, Mr Katsaros.' Her voice appealed too. It was low and musical. Not high and breathy as he recalled it from the phone call. Though he'd probably taken her by surprise with his invitation.

Alexei's mouth tightened. She was right. It had been a demand, not an invitation. Carissa had made him sound brutish and that annoyed him. But the situation demanded a swift resolution. He didn't have time for niceties.

Her eyebrows arched when he didn't respond to her small talk.

'Call me Alexei.'

'Thank you, Alexei.' Her voice slowed on his name and he felt the oddest sensation, as if she'd reached out one slim hand and trailed it down his chest, right to his belly. Abdominal muscles clenched in response. 'Please, call me Carissa.'

'Carissa.' He tested the sibilant on his tongue and saw her eyes darken. The sight sent another ripple of awareness through him. She was definitely attracted. 'You have an interesting accent. Not the same as your father's.'

Intriguingly she stiffened as if he'd hit a weak point. It was the tiniest movement but unmistakeable to a man who'd spent so long studying the vulnerabilities of business opponents.

'My father's accent is English. But we moved around a lot when I was young. I suppose mine's a hybrid.'

Alexei watched the unblinking way she held his gaze and wondered what she hid.

'Yours is interesting too.' She spoke quickly, clearly wanting to divert his attention.

Alexei was interested to find that despite his fixation on locating and punishing her father, his curiosity about Carissa increased by the moment.

He gestured for her to take a seat and sank down onto a leather lounge, crossing his ankles and leaning back.

'Russian mother, Greek father, moved to London as a kid.' He shrugged. 'Like yours, my accent's a hybrid.' More like mongrel, he silently corrected. He'd spent too long living precariously in places where the predominant language was that of the violent gangs who ruled through intimidation.

Silently Carissa nodded and sat opposite him. In contrast to her casual clothes her posture was graceful. With that long, slender neck and perfect poise he was reminded again of a dancer sweeping into a low curtsey. He could picture a tiara on her smooth, dark hair and a sheaf of flowers in her arms.

'Tell me, Carissa, have you heard from your father?'

'He's not here?' Her expression flickered but too fast for him to read it.

'No, but I'm expecting him soon.' As soon as Ralph Carter heard his precious daughter was staying at Alexei's private island he'd hotfoot it here, hoping the marriage he'd suggested would save him from Alexei's wrath. If that didn't work, Alexei had the perfect hostage to lure him from hiding.

'I see.' She chewed the corner of her mouth and then, as if aware of his scrutiny, offered a small smile. 'That will be lovely.' Once more her direct look suggested she hid something. What?

'So you haven't heard from him?'

'No. He seems to have his phone switched off. Do you need to contact him urgently?'

Alexei fought impatience. His desire for retribution against the one person he'd actually *trusted* in decades hadn't eased. Fury curdled his gut. He couldn't believe he'd been foolish enough to let Carter con him.

'Not at all. In the meantime we can get to know each other better.' That prospect grew more enticing by the moment.

She shifted in her seat, her first overt sign of nervousness. Intrigued, Alexei took his time surveying her, his fingers tracing a lazy circle on the soft leather of his chair's arm.

'I want you to be happy here, Carissa. Let me know if there's anything you want.'

'That's very kind of you, Alexei. For that matter, very kind of you to let me holiday here in this glorious place.'

She'd changed her tune. Fifteen minutes ago she'd been complaining about his staff and the speed with which he'd brought her here. What had changed?

Every sense stirred. He scented not fear but caution, as if Carissa suddenly felt out of her depth. Not so sure of herself after all?

She wasn't his target; her father was. Yet that didn't stop a frisson of satisfaction at the suggestion Ms high and mighty Carter had second thoughts about her situation. If she was cast in the same mould as her father, it would do her no harm to learn she couldn't have everything her way. Especially if she'd spent the past few years living off money her father had stolen from Alexei.

'Oh, I don't consider it a kindness, given our special situation.'

She stilled. It looked as if she didn't even breathe. 'Our special situation?'

'Of course.' This time Alexei's smile was genuine. 'Since we're marrying.'

CHAPTER THREE

MINA'S MOUTH DRIED as she watched a slow smile transform Alexei's face. It wasn't a polite expression of friendship or amusement. It was a wide grin that she could only describe as dangerous.

More than that. *Hungry.* As if he wanted to sink those strong white teeth into her flesh.

She shivered as heat licked through her. Disgust, of course. She wasn't some dish served up to satisfy his appetite.

Yet, on the thought, Mina realised her response wasn't so simple. A shiver drew her breasts tight till her nipples beaded. Astonished, she realised she was torn between annoyance and excitement.

As if she *wanted* to satisfy Alexei Katsaros's animal appetites. And hers, as well.

The realisation had her fingers clawing the arms of her chair as she fought the urge to reel back. As much at her own confusing reaction as at his overtly *masculine* perusal. He surveyed her like a man who'd just bought a woman.

She despised him. Yet despite her outrage, Mina felt a thrill of anticipation.

By the time she'd conquered her shock, there was no sign of that feral hunger in his expression. Had she imagined it?

Mina wasn't an expert on sex but she'd had her share of admirers. Men whom she found it easy to resist. For some reason they were fine as friends, but when they wanted more, Mina didn't. Yet she knew what sexual interest looked like.

She couldn't see it in his face now.

'We've only just met.' Her tone was cool.

One dark eyebrow rose. 'It was your father's suggestion that we'd make a good match. He told me you'd agreed. Are you saying that's not the case?'

Mina swallowed, ignoring the sandpaper abrasion of her throat, and wondered how best to play for time. All the way here she'd told herself Carissa had been mistaken and that Alexei Katsaros couldn't want *marriage*. He didn't need to marry a stranger. He was rich, successful and good-looking.

Also impatient, determined and self-obsessed, if his idea of finding a wife was ordering her to his island and giving her no choice!

What had she landed herself in? Surely he hadn't brought her here for a wedding!

Shock jagged through her, stealing her breath. If so, then this masquerade would be over before it began. Mina forced herself to take a deep breath and think.

'He did mention a possible marriage, but…'

'But?'

'We don't know each other! I can't agree to marry someone I don't know.'

He said nothing, just crossed his arms, the movement drawing Mina's attention to the depth of his broad chest and the muscled power of his biceps. He was a man whose physical size and fitness could daunt a woman who wasn't strong enough to stand up for herself.

'So you're here to what? Get to know me?'

'Is that so unreasonable?' Mina jumped on the idea like a lifeline. 'We're talking about a lifetime commitment.'

The hint of a smile flickered at the corner of Alexei's mouth. 'That's a refreshingly…old-fashioned view.'

Mina let her eyebrows climb. 'Marriage is a serious commitment. Why enter into one if you don't plan to make it work?' She wasn't sure why she didn't simply shrug off his comment. But marriage, like the right to make her own decisions, was something she felt strongly about. Her mother had married her country's Sheikh not for love but because her family decreed it. It hadn't been a happy match.

'I see your point.' Alexei nodded.

'So you understand I need time to determine if a marriage would work. Surely you want that too.'

'To assess if we're *compatible*?' Alexei didn't move, nor did his expression alter, yet the quality of that stare flicked a warning switch. Adrenalin surged in Mina's blood. Heat consumed her as if he'd surveyed every inch of her body with that searing scrutiny, instead of merely holding her gaze.

How did he do that?

More important, why did she react so?

Mina wasn't oblivious to men but she'd never been swept off her feet, or into bed, by one. Her history made her cautious about ceding control to any man. Before his death, her father had mapped out her life, giving her no choice, even about the clothes she wore and the subjects she studied. Since leaving Jeirut for Paris she'd devoted herself single-mindedly to art, determined to carve a career in the field she loved. The guys who tried to sidetrack her into a relationship had never caused a ripple in her world.

Now it wasn't a ripple she felt but an earth tremor.

Mina wouldn't let that daunt her.

She lifted one hand negligently. 'Before we worry about *compatible* perhaps we should start with finding out if we'd survive the marriage without killing each other.'

Alexei gave a crack of laughter. 'Good point, Carissa.' The light dancing in his eyes made him look completely different. Like someone she wanted to know.

Mina stiffened.

The first time she'd seen Alexei Katsaros, something happened that had never happened before. Her certainty had wavered and with it her confidence. Mina couldn't abide the idea of being tentative around him, like some gullible, awed girl. It was easier to confront him. She suspected if he exerted himself to be nice it would be too easy to feel the force of his charm.

Now, abruptly, as she met his smiling look, the events of the last twelve hours took their toll.

Exhaustion slammed into Mina. Despite her determination not to back down before this man, she felt herself slump. Adrenalin had kept her going. Now that dissipated, leaving her overtired limbs shaky and her head swimming.

She had to get out of here before she made a mistake. Mina was too weary to guard her tongue and thinking straight became harder by the second. This man with the piercing green eyes would trip her up, especially since she wasn't practised at lying.

If he discovered the truth, all this would have been for nothing. Carissa needed time to get away with Pierre and cover her tracks.

'I'm sorry, you'll have to excuse me.' Mina lifted her hand to cover a yawn, only to discover the fake yawn was real. 'I'm suddenly very tired.'

'You didn't sleep on the flight?' He looked surprised.

Mina shook her head. She'd been ushered onto the private jet late in the evening for the overnight flight to the Caribbean. But despite the comfortable bed, she'd had too much going on in her head to sleep.

'It's been a very long day.' She glanced at her watch, trying to calculate the time difference but to her surprise, her mind was too foggy. Tiredness and stress took their toll. 'I've been awake more than twenty-four hours.' And yesterday had been a long day, even before Carissa had dragged her into this mess. Or, to be fair, since she'd thrust herself into it to protect her friend.

Time to regroup before she said something she shouldn't.

Mina pinned on a smile, the multipurpose one she reserved for royal meet and greets. She hadn't used it in years and it felt rusty. 'I'm sorry, Alexei, but I'll have to leave you for now.' She rose, surprised at the effort it took to stand tall. Her knees were unsteady, and for a second she swayed.

'Could you point me towards my room, please?'

He loomed before her, the beginnings of a frown creasing his forehead. 'You look pale.'

'I'm fine,' she lied. How many hours had it been since she'd eaten? She hadn't been in the mood for food on the plane, refuelling on coffee and lots of it, but now the caffeine had worn off and she felt as powerful as a dandelion in a strong wind. 'If you could show me the way?'

When Alexei didn't immediately answer, Mina swung round towards the entry, remembering Henri heading down a corridor from there.

As she turned, another wave of tiredness hit and her movements lost their usual precise control. Her foot caught the edge of the plush carpet.

She didn't trip or stagger, just paused, swaying as she caught her balance.

'I'll take you.' The deep voice came from beside her ear as, to her astonishment, Alexei bent and curled his arms around her back and legs. An instant later she was in the air. Or, more precisely, in his arms, pressed against a hot body that seemed to be all solid muscle.

Mina's breath stalled, then released on a shaky sigh at how extraordinary this felt. No one had ever held her like this. She registered conflicting feelings: shock, pleasure and an unexpected desire to burrow closer. As if Alexei were someone she trusted. Or desired.

'There's no need.' The words were crisp, at odds with the strange wobbly feeling in her middle. It was impossible to sit straighter and assert control when she lay in his arms, unable to get any purchase.

Alexei ignored her words, marching out of the room.

With each step Mina felt her body move against his in a swaying rhythm that was surprisingly appealing. In other circumstances...

In other circumstances this wouldn't happen, ever.

'Thank you for your consideration,' she said between barely open lips. 'But I prefer to walk.'

That made him pause. He angled his head to look down at her and Mina was bombarded with impressions. The hard perfection of his squared-off jaw. From this intriguing angle, it was a study in obstinate power. The soaring, proud cheekbones that spoke of ancient Slavic heritage. The flare of arrogant nostrils and the fly-away effect of his winged eyebrows. The steady pump of his heart against her ribs and the power of those iron-hard arms encircling her.

Something shivered to life in the pit of Mina's belly. Something that grew as she inhaled a tempting cedar-and-citrus aftershave that melded with the hot, salt scent of male skin. Her nostrils twitched appreciatively and the shiver amplified.

Astounded, Mina watched his eyes darken, the pupils dilating.

The world eclipsed to the dark mystery of that shadowy stare, heating her in all sorts of places.

When he spoke the sound vibrated from his chest into her body. She'd never experienced anything as intimate as his voice reverberating through her while his eyes devoured her.

'Relax. I'm not going to hurt you.'

Despite the certainty he wouldn't drop her, Mina couldn't ignore the inner voice screaming at her to get away. Being this close to Alexei Katsaros was perilous, whatever his stated intention.

'I prefer to walk. If you'll kindly put me down.' Tiredness vanished, replaced with quivering watchfulness.

'And have you trip and hurt yourself?' He shook his

head, his rumpled locks swinging free. 'I wouldn't forgive myself.'

His tone was admirably sincere yet Mina read the tiny creases at the corners of his mouth and knew he was enjoying himself. Could he feel her heart hammer? She hated being vulnerable to him.

Before she could read any more, he looked away and began walking down the hall, carrying her easily, as if he carted unwilling women around every day.

Maybe he did.

'Contrary to what you might have heard, Mr Katsaros, women are capable of thinking for themselves. We don't appreciate he-men making our decisions for us. I—'

'Is that what you think I am?' Annoyingly his pace didn't falter. 'What exactly does that mean?' His jaw jutted as he ruminated. 'Someone very masculine? Someone who sees an exhausted guest and looks after her so she doesn't hurt herself?'

Mina counted to ten. If she thought it would do any good, she'd struggle against his hold. But, though fit, she was no match for all that hard-packed muscle, especially given his superior size. He was well over six feet. If Alexei Katsaros didn't want to release her she couldn't make him. The knowledge infuriated her and she began stringing together curses in her own language that she couldn't say lest he wonder how she knew Arabic.

She forced her gaze away from that annoyingly superior chin, focusing on the play of light and shadow on the ceiling as they passed down the hall.

'After all,' he continued, 'as you pointed out so eloquently, it was my fault your trip was so…precipitate. If I'd been more conscious of your comfort I'd have organised for you to travel during the day, or ensured the bed on the plane was more comfortable. I'll have it replaced.'

'There's no need for that. The bed was quite comfortable.' Even to her ears her voice sounded thin. She held on to her temper by a tiny margin. All her life she'd been taught not to reveal anger. This time she dared not lose control because he'd see it as a victory.

'Then it's a wonder you didn't sleep. Perhaps—' she caught movement in her peripheral vision and turned to see him send a teasing look her way '—you couldn't sleep because you were excited about visiting me.'

Excited! About as excited as if she visited a zoo to see a rattlesnake. Mina sucked in a rough breath, then stilled as the movement made her more aware of Alexei's big hand on her ribs, close to her breast.

'Perhaps I didn't sleep because I was busy contacting people to reschedule things for the period I'll be away. Since I had no opportunity earlier.' She slanted him a frosty stare only to find that smile lurking around his mouth.

'Ah, yes, no doubt your agenda is full of priority appointments.' His expression didn't change but his tone revealed how unlikely he thought it.

Mina didn't bother to disabuse him. She might not run a multinational corporation, but nor was she idle. As well as the exhibition she was preparing for, she volunteered with disabled kids and at a nearby nursing home, doing art therapy. Plus, there was some admin work at a women's shelter, the latest design commission for the perfumery in Jeirut and another from a French company that had seen her perfume bottle designs and wanted something similar.

'Mr Katsaros.' Her patience was perilously close to failing. One more jibe and she'd forget her resolve. 'I really must—

'Alexei, remember?' His voice rumbled through her like an intimate caress. It was the final straw.

'Put. Me. Down.' Her voice rose from request to imperious command. 'Now!'

Mina caught a flash of white teeth, a glimpse of glinting eyes and suddenly the world fell away as she dropped from his arms.

'As you wish, Princess.' He spoke as she landed with a puff of expelled air on her back. She was on a bed, looking up into dark, laughing eyes. But Mina was too tired and stressed to be amused. She didn't appreciate being the butt of his jibes or his arrogant certainty that her life was of negligible importance.

Mina jackknifed to a sitting position, swiping a cushion off the bed with one hand and throwing it in the same, fluid movement. She had the satisfaction of seeing it hit him square on his superior chin.

'Be thankful that wasn't anything heavier. My aim is as good as any man's.' She heaved a breath that, to her horror, felt far too shaky. 'Now, if you'd have the decency to leave, I'd like to catch up on some much-needed sleep.'

Damn. Damn. Damn.

Alexei stalked away from the guest wing to the master suite.

What had got into him? Half an hour with Carissa Carter and he'd veered between anger, attraction, approval and amusement. And far too much of all of them. He always controlled his emotions; he wasn't undercut by them.

He hadn't expected to be impressed by Carter's precious princess. He'd been ready to write her off as a pampered bimbo who viewed the world through the prism of her greed for an easy life. Instead he'd discovered someone witty, incisive, challenging and sexy. Ridiculously sexy, given her defiantly unfeminine clothes.

On Carissa Carter even a baggy T-shirt and leggings made his hormones surge. And that mouth. She was sharptongued in a superior way that made him want to take her mouth and discover what sweetness lay beneath its cutting edge.

There was definitely sweetness. He'd been surprised, when he held her, at the fretful way her pulse raced. He'd been mesmerised by her contrary reactions as she pretended not to respond. Her breathing had quickened, her pupils dilated, and he'd read confusion beneath her scorn and defiance. Even her awe as she admired the sculpture in the sitting room had charmed him.

He'd lit from within at the feel of her, supple, streamlined and, he discovered, curved in the right places.

What would happen if he followed her down onto that bed? He couldn't remember the dark frenzy of desire ever being so immediate or urgent.

The very fact he'd thought about it was a concern. Did he really want an affair with Carter's daughter?

Logic demanded an unequivocal *no*. Instinct screamed *yes*.

Which was an excellent reason to pull back. Apart from the fact he didn't take advantage of vulnerable women.

Alexei rubbed a hand across his jaw as he entered his suite and crossed to the window to stand staring across the infinity pool to the sea beyond.

Guilt trickled down his spine. Bad enough that there'd been a kernel of truth in Carissa's accusation about how he'd got her here. It had solidified into a jagged shard of ice when he'd heard the hint of a wobble in her voice as she stared up at him from her bed. She'd been flushed and furious and he'd revelled in his power to rile her, till he'd heard the tiny crack in her façade of superiority. Suddenly it hadn't seemed amusing.

It hit him that he'd behaved like a kid pulling a girl's pigtails, desperate to get her attention any way he could.

Him, desperate?

Hardly. Certainly not for the likes of Carissa Carter.

Except she wasn't as he'd expected.

He scraped his hand across his chin, feeling the stubble

he hadn't bothered to shave. He shouldn't allow himself to be diverted by her. She was incidental to his plans.

But, pending Carter's arrival, there wasn't much he could do to bring those plans to fruition. Steps had been taken to contain the damage, and while Alexei checked in daily, working via computer and phone, his team was working hard.

Which gave him leisure to ponder his would-be bride.

Alexei's brow scrunched. Funny. He'd assumed Carissa would be eager to marry. Her father had come up with the idea, no doubt desperate to cement personal ties that would save him when his embezzlement came to light. The fact a woman in her mid-twenties was willing to go along with such a plan pointed to her being venal, marrying for money and position.

Too many women had tried to tie him down. Not for love, but as their ticket to wealth and privilege. Alexei didn't fool himself into believing they were attracted by his character or sense of humour. Some were drawn by his looks but money was the deciding factor.

Yet Carissa hadn't given an unequivocal yes.

Why? Did she believe if he had to work for what he wanted, he'd appreciate her more? Because men enjoyed the chase?

He huffed a breath. Maybe she had something there. If she'd walked in the door and promptly agreed with everything his interest wouldn't have been piqued.

Except by that delectable body, which he'd discovered was curvier than he'd first thought.

Except for her intelligence and sensitivity.

Alexei shoved his fists in his pockets and rocked back on his feet, annoyed. He'd been so caught up in the need to draw Carter out of hiding, he hadn't bothered researching the man's daughter.

He'd acted rashly, driven by fury that the one person he'd trusted since his mother died had betrayed him.

That was a slashing wound that wouldn't heal till Carter was made to pay. It overset Alexei's equilibrium, evoking unwanted feelings that interfered with his decision-making.

It wasn't so much the money, but the personal affront of betrayal. The cold slap of horror that he'd let himself be gulled into believing the man, *liking* him.

Carter had made a fool of him, conning him into giving his trust. Not just because of the man's work qualities. *But because Carter reminded him of his father.*

Like Alexei's father, Carter appeared taciturn to outsiders, but his features broke into smiles when he mentioned his family. Uncannily, Carter also had a mannerism, a tilt of the head, that echoed Alexei's precious memories of the father who'd died when Alexei was six.

Then there was his utter devotion to his spouse. There'd been no mistaking the man's devastation when his wife was diagnosed with a terminal illness. His stoic determination to do all he could for her had touched a chord with Alexei. Plus there was that unexpected weakness for silly puns and his scrupulous honesty, both hallmarks of his dad.

Alexei shook his head. Scrupulous honesty!

For years Alexei's motto had been trust no one. He and his mother had suffered because they'd been taken in by a conman. After his stepfather there'd been others, loan sharks, employers, landlords, vultures who'd preyed on his vulnerable mother, turning her life into a misery till finally loss and disappointment crushed her.

Alexei scraped a hand across his jaw, dragging himself back to the present. To the woman in one of the guest suites.

He'd acted instinctively, securing her to give him an edge. He should have ordered a dossier on her so he knew something about her before acting.

All he remembered from Carter's conversations was

that she lived in Paris, where she'd attended an exclusive art school. She loved fashion and shopping and wasn't cut out for a commercial career. Alexei had gained the impression of a pampered airhead pretending to be an artist. A blonde airhead, he remembered from the photo Carter had waved before him and which he hadn't bothered to take in.

So Carissa Carter had dyed her hair. That was one extra fact about her.

Alexei considered ordering a full report on her. But why bother?

She was here. Whatever Alexei wanted to know, he'd find out for himself. He'd enjoy the process.

CHAPTER FOUR

MINA STARED AT the bathroom's enormous, full-length mirror and suppressed a groan. She looked like a stranger.

Carissa had said pink calmed her and made her feel centred. It was proof of how stressed she'd been that she'd packed only for her favourite colour. Almost everything in the case was pink. Candy pink, flesh pink, cerise, rose madder and more.

Mina's mouth curled in an unwilling laugh as she surveyed herself. She wore a candy-pink skirt with matching strappy sandals and a pale pink top with a silver logo that incorporated a highly stylised Eiffel Tower and an open book. Carissa had designed it for an indie book festival in Paris, one of her first commissions.

Had Carissa really planned to wear these clothes to visit Alexei Katsaros? If so she'd clearly had the Caribbean's casual, sunny reputation in mind, rather than any desire to dress up.

Or was her friend savvier than Mina gave her credit for? Maybe this wardrobe was her secret weapon, to prove she wasn't cut out to be a billionaire's wife.

That stifled Mina's humour.

Carissa needed her help and Mina wasn't quite as sure now about her ability to deal with her host.

Especially in a skirt that rode high on her thighs and a top that was more fitted than anything she usually wore. Mina wasn't ashamed of her body, but she covered more of it than her friend did. Plus Carissa was shorter and smaller in the bust, so the top was a snug fit. As for the miniskirt...

Mina shrugged. She had more to worry about than how much bare leg she displayed. Her only clothes were what she'd worn on the plane and the ones Carissa had packed. Besides, she was on a tropical island. Alexei Katsaros would be used to guests wearing shorts or swimsuits. Or, given his reputation and the knowing gleam in those remarkable eyes, nothing at all.

How many beautiful women had he seduced here?

Mina blinked as she caught the direction of her thoughts. *That* wasn't her concern. Deftly she caught up her long hair, winding it round and up into a tight knot at the back of her head. She jabbed in a securing pin and turned away.

If Alexei dismissed her because of her clothes, or because she wasn't the biddable woman he'd imagined, all the better. Clearly he hadn't expected her to voice her opinions or have more than a couple of brain cells to rub together.

It would be better if he concentrated on running his multibillion-dollar empire than on her. It hadn't even occurred to him that getting to know the woman he planned to marry was a good idea.

Remarkable!

Unbelievable!

What sort of man thought like that?

One who didn't expect to be questioned.

Who expected everyone to bend to his wishes.

Mina put away the hairdryer she'd used and entered the palatial bedroom where she'd slept like the dead for hours.

Her gaze rested on the bed she'd remade after her nap. Inevitably the image that filled her mind was of looking up from there into that fabulously sculpted face, into eyes alight with mockery, and knowing that physically she was at his mercy. It had infuriated Mina, for she'd had no choice but to put up with his macho posturing and derision.

That still smarted. She drew taller, pushing her shoulders back, as she relived the scene and wished she still had the small jewelled dagger she'd worn as a ceremonial courtesy in Jeirut. It had been decorative but deadly, and Mina had insisted on knowing how to wield it. Would he have taken her more seriously if he'd known she was fully capable of looking after herself, no matter what the situation?

The idea conjured suitably satisfying images, but her smile faded as she faced the real source of her concern.

Her reaction to Alexei Katsaros.

It wasn't only fury she'd felt. He'd been *interesting*.

Lips twisting, Mina shook her head. He'd been fascinating. That combination of bold assurance and blatant sexuality would catch any woman's attention. Especially since physically his form was…pleasing. But add to that occasional glimpses of humour and penetrating understanding that punctured her initial estimate of a smug bully, and you had a man who left her unsettled.

Mina tried to tell herself the disorientation of tiredness had made her react to him. But innate honesty wouldn't let her pretend.

She had to face the truth.

She disliked Alexei Katsaros and his high-handed ways. He was exactly the sort of man to make her hackles rise. Yet he made her blood heat.

She was attracted to him.

The situation she'd rushed into for Carissa's sake became fraught with unseen snares, like the notorious patches of quicksand in the desert of her homeland.

She hadn't reckoned on anything like this when she'd blithely decided to help her friend. Dimly, she heard her father's voice in her head, the memory of his disapproval as he complained of her impulsive ways. She'd tried to make him proud, do her duty no matter how dull or out of tune with her own interests. But she'd been a source of frustration for him.

Face it, Mina. Nothing you did could satisfy your father. He didn't want a daughter who craved love, but an automaton who could be diplomatic on every occasion, no matter what the provocation.

She'd failed there, hadn't she?

Abruptly she spun on her foot and crossed to the glass doors that gave out onto a crystal pool and, beyond that, the tropical garden.

Mina's eyes were drawn to the profusion of flowers, cadmium yellow, pale ochre and magenta. She felt the old temptation to reach for her sketchpad. To find peace by losing herself in art.

Instead she simply stood a little longer, inhaling the fragrance of salt air and unfamiliar floral perfumes, then set her shoulders and turned away. She couldn't hide forever. It was time to face her host.

She found him on a deep, shaded veranda. Overhead, a fan rotated lazily and the combination of wicker furniture and wide, wooden floorboards hinted at gracious days gone by, though the sprawling villa was modern.

Alexei sat, feet up, on a lounger, typing into a tablet. His hair was ruffled as if he'd combed his fingers through it and his shirt was open again. Mina saw the dark smattering of hair on his sculpted pectorals and jerked her gaze away.

That tiny sizzle deep inside didn't bode well. She'd felt it before, when he carried her in his arms. Now just the sight of him set it off.

Frowning, Mina surveyed the garden, trying to control feelings she couldn't fully identify. On the other side of the pool, a sculpture caught her eye.

'You're awake. Excellent.' Reluctantly Mina turned, fixing a bland expression on her face. She'd known this would be difficult but she'd hoped her earlier response to him had more to do with fatigue than genuine attraction.

Fate was clearly laughing at her naivety.

Alexei set the tablet aside and swung his feet to the floor.

'Please don't get up on my account. You're working. I'll come back later.' She was only too happy to delay being alone with him.

'No, I've finished.' He gestured to the seats grouped around him and she had no choice but to take one.

Instead of a recliner, Mina selected an upright chair, conscious of the way her skirt rode even higher up her legs as she sat. Resisting the urge to tug her hem in a futile attempt to gain an extra few centimetres, she crossed her ankles and tucked her feet under her chair. She didn't look directly at her host but *felt* his gaze. It raked her from head to foot, then lifted again to linger on her legs and higher—

Mina swung her head up abruptly and met his enigmatic dark gaze.

Had she been wrong? She could have sworn he'd been ogling her. Or did her sensitivity about wearing Carissa's clothes make her imagine things? The way her breasts tingled—

'What would you like to drink?' As he spoke Marie rounded the corner of the veranda, as if in response to the summons of a silent bell.

'Something cold would be good.'

'Champagne? A cocktail? Gin and tonic?'

Mina glanced at her watch. Early afternoon. Obviously his usual guests indulged themselves. Mina, on the other hand, needed a clear head. Besides, she was in no mood to kick back and pretend this was a holiday. She felt too agitated around Alexei Katsaros.

'A juice would be lovely, thanks.' She smiled at Marie.

'Of course, ma'am. And I'll bring some food.'

Mina was about to protest that she wasn't hungry, then remembered she hadn't eaten in ages. She'd feel stronger after food. She'd better!

Marie turned to Alexei, a question on her face. In response he shook his head and gestured to a half-full jug of iced water. 'I'm fine.'

So he expected Mina to indulge while he stuck to cold water. Interesting. But then, he'd been working and he hadn't built a hugely successful corporation by drinking the day away. Mina shot a glance at that firm chin and those uncompromising features and guessed Alexei Katsaros was good at discipline and control. Then her gaze collided with his and the impact sent a silent shudder of reaction through her.

She suspected he was also excellent at letting go and indulging. There was a sensuality about that steady gaze that would unnerve her if she let it.

'I'm sorry I slept so long. I didn't—'

His raised hand cut her off. 'You needed the rest. I hope you slept well?' It was a simple question, the sort any host might make. Yet holding Alexei's gaze, feeling heat wash her skin, Mina tensed, conscious of undercurrents.

She took in his relaxed posture, the small smile, yet sensed concealment. One long finger drummed on the arm of his chair and there was an intensity about that stare...

'Thank you, yes. It's a very comfortable bed.'

And just like that, it hit her what this undercurrent was. Sexual attraction. Potent and perilous.

Mina blinked but kept her expression serene, despite the frenzied rush of shock. In her room she'd acknowledged the attraction, but the potency of her reaction unnerved her.

She'd been attracted to guys before. But this was a blast of lightning compared with the weak flicker of a single match. It was the mighty Khamsin wind that scoured the desert and shifted whole ridges of sand, compared with a gentle zephyr that merely rustled the leaves in a courtyard garden.

Mina sank back, forcing down shock, fear and excitement.

It was the excitement that worried her most. She'd always found it hard to resist adventure and challenge.

But not with this man. Not with a man who treated people like pawns on his personal chessboard. She'd be crazy to go there.

'I'm the one who should apologise.' His words snagged her attention. 'I'm sorry if I distressed you earlier, carrying you to your room.'

Mina felt again that powerful pulse of connection and refused to acknowledge it. Was he apologising for carrying her or because he'd recognised how close she'd come to losing command of herself? Please, not the latter!

She inclined her head. 'You were concerned for me. I understand.' It didn't excuse the deliberate way he'd goaded her, but there was no point going over that again. 'I have a favour to ask.'

'Ask away.' He sat forward and Mina sensed he'd been waiting for this.

'Can I borrow a vehicle? There are some things I need to buy.' Like underwear. Mina drew the line at wearing Carissa's lacy thongs.

'I'm afraid that's not possible.'

Mina's eyebrows lifted. Was he really so petty as to deny her transport? 'You don't trust me with your vehicle?' She'd learned to drive on unpaved mountain roads and desert dunes. She'd bet she could handle a four-wheel drive better than him.

'It's more the lack of shops that's the problem.'

'Lack of shops?'

'There aren't any. We get supplies by boat. It's not easy to indulge in retail therapy here.' He spread his hands and Mina caught the ghost of a smile. She recognised the same teasing amusement she'd seen when he'd provoked her. Had Carissa's reputation as a bargain shopaholic preceded her?

Her friend was always searching for second-hand items to transform.

What exactly did Alexei know of the woman he planned to marry? So far it seemed he expected her to be obedient, possibly unintelligent and good at spending money. It was a distorted picture of Mina's friend, and didn't recommend her as a wife.

Which begged the question, why marry her?

More and more, the idea of an arranged marriage between him and Carissa seemed odd.

'Carissa?'

'Sorry?' She blinked. She'd missed what he said.

'If you need hygiene products, talk to Marie. She also has a supply of suncream and spare hats for visitors.'

Mina's smile was perfunctory. She refused to feel embarrassed by his assumption. 'Thanks, but that's not what I had in mind.'

'Later in the week, when your father's here, we'll go to one of the larger islands and you can visit the boutiques.'

Didn't that sound like fun? Steadfastly Mina yanked her mind from the inevitable scene when her masquerade was uncovered. She hoped Carissa and Pierre were safely married by then.

'Surely I could take the boat before that? This afternoon perhaps?'

'You're that desperate?' Alexei angled his head as if to survey her better. His expression didn't alter, but the flare of his nostrils hinted at impatience. 'I'm afraid not. The boat's being repaired.' Mina opened her mouth, but before she could ask he added, 'It will be available again in a day or two. I'm sure you'll enjoy an outing to the boutiques after that. I'm assured they stock an excellent range.'

'I can't wait.' Mina manufactured a smile and sank back in her seat. She didn't need a high-end boutique that catered for the rich at play. But there was no point explaining that. For now she'd simply wash her underwear every night.

Inevitably her thoughts jagged back to her unmasking when Carissa's father arrived. Her stomach squeezed uncomfortably.

She could almost hear her own father's pained voice, telling her she'd been reckless and headstrong. That she shouldn't have dared to disrupt a father's plans for his daughter.

But how could she regret helping her friend? She couldn't sit and watch her forced into marriage.

Mina wasn't afraid of Alexei's reaction when he discovered the truth, or Mr Carter's. After all, what could they do to her? And it served them right for putting Carissa in such an invidious position. Yet now the first rush of indignation on her friend's behalf was fading, Mina wasn't looking forward to the moment of revelation. It would be uncomfortable at best, especially as she relied on Alexei's goodwill to get off the island. He was bound to be furious.

What would an angry Alexei Katsaros be like? Loud and belligerent, or icily condemning?

Mina could withstand anything he threw at her. That went without saying. Yet she found herself wishing she were back in Paris, busy working instead of playing this cat-and-mouse game.

Suddenly the lack of underwear seemed the least of her concerns.

CHAPTER FIVE

ALEXEI TRIED AND failed to read Carissa's expression. She seemed distracted, almost uninterested, as if her need to shop wasn't urgent after all. He couldn't get a handle on her. Every time she confirmed his estimation of her as shallow and opportunistic, she confounded him.

Marie served drinks and a substantial platter of food but Carissa barely touched the lavish spread.

'You'll be glad to see your father again.'

Her soft eyes widened as if in surprise, and Alexei felt his own narrow.

What was going on? Had father and daughter fallen out? Surely not. If it appeared Carissa was on the verge of securing a marriage with Alexei, her father would be eager to give the match his blessing.

'Of course.'

'It's been a while since you saw each other?'

'A while.' She shifted in her seat, crossing her legs. Despite his determination to ferret out her motivations, Alexei was distracted by the toned golden skin on display. The ploy of a woman bent on seduction? Why else would she wear a micro miniskirt and a tight top that so lovingly moulded her breasts?

Unwanted heat flared as he considered the generous bounty barely concealed by Carissa's new clothes. How had he thought her lacking in curves? She was slender yet definitely feminine. And those legs went on forever.

Yet when he dragged his gaze to her face, she was staring, not at him but towards the horizon, her brow knitted in thought.

Alexei experienced an odd sensation, a clamping in his

gut. It took a moment to realise it was pique. He wasn't used to being ignored by anyone, especially women.

Especially a woman who thought she was here to marry him.

Was Carissa so sure of herself that she didn't feel the need to pander to his ego?

She turned her head, her gaze meshing with his, and his blood pumped powerfully. How would it feel if she reached out and touched him? The notion quickened his pulse to a hard, heavy throb.

'Something's on your mind.' His voice was rough. 'What is it?'

She blinked, as if surprised at his words. For a second he almost believed he'd unsettled her, though that was unlikely. When she'd arrived she'd been very vocal. There'd been nothing reticent or uncertain about Carissa. He'd enjoyed their sparring. It was rare Alexei had someone confront him, much less take him to task for his actions.

Carissa seemed to gather herself. She sat higher, those slim shoulders forming a straight, uncompromising line that even after such a short acquaintance was familiar. Her jaw angled up and Alexei felt anticipation thrum.

'Why do you want an arranged marriage? Why not marry someone you know?'

Again she surprised him. He hadn't suspected Carter's daughter would look a gift horse in the mouth. But clearly Carissa was intelligent. Even if she craved his wealth, she wanted to understand his expectations.

'I haven't found anyone I want to marry.' That, at least, was true.

'But why arrange a marriage this way?'

'Are you trying to back out?' He sat forward, fascinated.

'No.' She paused. 'I just want to know more about you.'

'It seemed an efficient way of proceeding.'

'Efficient?' She tilted her head and recrossed her legs.

He heard the faint sibilant whisper of fabric on skin and fought to keep his eyes on her face. If she thought he'd be distracted by the obvious tactic she was mistaken, but that didn't prevent arousal clamping his groin.

'You make it sound as easy as ordering from a catalogue.' She gestured dismissively. 'Wanted, one female of reasonable appearance and education. Must have all her own teeth and be of child-bearing age.' She snapped the words out, and again Alexei heard that edge of disapproval. Yet instead of annoying him, it stirred a desire to provoke more of the same. Heat simmered in his blood at the idea of Carissa aroused to heightened emotion.

If he had to wait for her father to come out of hiding, he might as well enjoy himself.

'Why not? Look what it's brought me.' He let his gaze drop, trailing down her long, proud neck to her collarbone, the high curve of her breasts and lower.

Her fingers dug into the arms of her chair, the tendons in the backs of her hands tensing.

'And since you mention child-bearing...' He lifted his eyes to hers. They blazed back at him with a banked fury that might have made him pause in other circumstances. He didn't want Carissa calm and dismissive or, worse, distracted. He preferred her hot under the collar, concentrating on *him*. 'How do you feel about starting a family straight away?'

'That's why you want to marry? To have children?' Surprising how stunned she sounded. Surely the thought of kids must have occurred to her?

Alexei shrugged. 'Why else? When I have children I want them to have my name, to be part of a family unit. There's nothing else I can get from marriage that I can't have already.'

Alexei *did* want a family. Kids of his own. He'd spent years driven by the need to drag himself out of poverty and hadn't looked beyond securing success and financial security. Determination had kept him climbing to the top. But one day, yes, a family of his own...

He had a few precious memories of happy family life before his father died but he knew how lucky he was to have those. The miserable years after his mother remarried made him appreciate what he'd had so briefly. He'd like to recreate that with his own children.

When this debacle with Carter was over he'd think of finding a woman suitable to share his life. Someone who'd make a wonderful mother.

'There's nothing else you can get from marriage?' Carissa's mouth twisted superciliously. 'How about emotional intimacy? Trust? Love?'

'Love?' He frowned. 'You believe in love?'

Yet she was happy to sell herself into a marriage of convenience. The woman was a mass of contradictions.

Carissa hesitated. Her hands plucked at the arm of her chair. 'I believe it exists,' she said eventually.

'But you've never been in love.' It was a guess, but Alexei always backed his hunches. The idea intrigued, that a pretty woman in her mid-twenties had never fancied herself in love.

'Have *you*?' She raised one eyebrow.

'No.' People talked of love but it was rare.

His parents had married for love and he admitted the idea held allure. But look where it had left his mother. When Alexei's father died she'd been heartbroken. Even as a young child he'd understood that. She'd forced herself to go through the motions of life but she'd never been the same. Her sense of loss had been behind her disastrous second marriage. She'd admitted it to Alexei before she died and he'd had to bite back a howl of protest that she hadn't been alone. She'd had *him*. But clearly that hadn't been enough. *He* hadn't been enough.

Almost as bad, it turned out her other reason for remarrying was to provide Alexei with a father. Because of that she'd condemned them to life with that miserable excuse for a man.

Futile anger boiled in his belly. Alexei wouldn't let anyone make him weak the way his mother had been.

He'd triumphed over adversity and made himself a man his father would have been proud of. He had no intention of falling into some sentimental trap.

'So you don't expect to love the woman you marry.'

Carissa's cool tone cleaved his thoughts. She surveyed him with faint disapproval.

'If you're waiting for a declaration from me, Princess, you'll be disappointed.'

Predictably she didn't bat an eye. This woman had grit.

'What if you fall in love with someone else after you marry?'

'I can't imagine it happening.' Alexei saw her open her mouth to object and raised a hand. 'But if, after some time, we divorce, you needn't be concerned. The legal agreement will ensure you're recompensed.'

Her jaw inched even higher. 'And if your wife fell for someone else?'

Alexei met her challenging stare and felt a tiny beat of surprise. At the idea of the woman he married preferring another man. And at Carissa's determination to speak in the abstract. As if discussing some faceless woman instead of herself.

Why did she pretend lack of interest when she was here for marriage? Even now, staring along the length of that straight nose like a monarch surveying a vulgar yokel, she couldn't hide her awareness of him. Alexei read her shortened breathing, the pebbled nipples pressing invitingly against taut fabric. He understood, with the experience of a man who'd attracted women since his teens, that Carissa was anything but uninterested.

The knowledge sent a frisson down his spine, to circle his body and lodge in his groin.

Carissa Carter might be a necessary encumbrance for now but increasingly Alexei recognised a woman he'd enjoy knowing better.

Perhaps when his business with her father was resolved they might come to a mutually enjoyable arrangement.

'You want to bring children into a family where there's no love, just a...commercial agreement?' Carissa's tone jabbed through his pleasant imaginings. 'Don't you think that's selfish?'

Alexei frowned. 'Children need stability.' His own childhood was a case in point. 'They'd have the love of their parents, and a caring, settled environment. That's more than many kids ever have.'

He took in the flat line of her mouth and the opaque look in her eyes, and wondered what Carissa was thinking. Had his words struck a chord?

Yet she'd been one of the lucky ones. The Carters had been a tight-knit family. There'd been no mistaking Ralph Carter's devastation over his wife's death, or his concern for his daughter.

Alexei recalled the late-night conversation he'd had with Carter after his wife's death. Alexei had been leaving his office and been surprised to see the older man still in the building, though his glazed eyes had told their own story. Alexei had taken a seat, unable to walk past the man, reading the small, telltale signs of fiercely suppressed emotion.

In that moment Ralph Carter had reminded him of his father, who, while devoted to his family, closely guarded deep emotions. Alexei had known he was loved, not by words but by his father's actions.

That night Alexei had felt a bond to Carter, enough to unbend and admit he'd count himself lucky to have a marriage such as Carter had enjoyed. It had been a moment of unfamiliar, unguarded sentimentality that surprised him.

No wonder Carter's subsequent betrayal stuck in his craw. For the first time in his life Alexei had opened up about his most private desires, while trying to help the other man. He'd felt a brief moment of shared understanding. Then a couple of months later the guy had ripped him off, proving Alexei's trust had been totally misplaced.

Not only that. Carter remembered Alexei's admission that since he'd never have a love match, he'd settle for marriage based on respect and common goals. Carter had tried to exploit that. Last week, before his embezzlement was uncovered, he'd suggested Alexei consider marrying his daughter. He'd described her as beautiful, gentle and generous, if impractical at building a career.

Alexei gritted his teeth. Clearly she wasn't impractical enough to resist the lure of marriage to a billionaire.

'So, Carissa,' he drawled. 'You're not in favour of marriage without love, but here you are on my private island. Why?'

She curled her fingers into the arms of her chair, discomfited. Then she shrugged, the movement making those lush breasts jiggle. 'I didn't say I'm not in favour of it. But I like to know where I stand, hence my questions.'

Alexei sat forward. 'Where *do* you stand, Carissa? Do you want to marry me and have my babies?'

Strange how saying it jolted heat through his belly. At the thought of Carissa in his bed. He had no trouble imagining that lissom body beneath his or astride it or against the wall of the shower as he took her with the water streaming over them. As for her pregnant with his baby—Alexei was stunned by the heavy whump of desire that slammed into him.

Carissa Carter was lovely to look at but far from the most beautiful woman he'd met. She was mouthy and opinionated, avaricious enough to marry a stranger for money. Yet, after knowing her mere hours, Alexei wanted her in his bed.

Had his wits taken a hike?

She sat back in her seat, taking time to recross her legs. Was the seat uncomfortable, or was she nervous?

More likely she was employing the not-so-subtle means of drawing his attention to her stunning legs.

Did she think he'd be so mesmerised she could manipulate him when they negotiated a prenuptial agreement?

'The jury's still out, Alexei. Surely you don't expect me to make up my mind within a couple of hours of meeting you.'

He applauded her aplomb. Her answer was designed to buy her time, and improve her bargaining position, making him more eager to seal the deal. It worked. Though there was no marriage contract to seal, Alexei felt his interest quicken. He'd always found it hard to resist a challenge.

'What if I don't want to wait?'

Her dark eyebrows arched. 'Then perhaps I'm not the woman you need. I'm happy to return to Paris…' She let the words hang but shuffled forward in her seat as if ready to get up and go right then and there.

As if he'd let her go! She was his bargaining chip. The reason Ralph Carter would believe it safe to come out of hiding.

If Carter baulked at showing himself, there were other possibilities. The man doted on Carissa. All Alexei had to do was suggest he'd make the daughter pay for her father's sins, in his bed, since she didn't have money, and Carter would come running to her rescue.

'No. You'll stay here, where we can get to know each other better.'

Did he imagine she tensed? Then she shrugged and the illusion vanished. 'That sounds ideal. I'm sure neither of us want to make a mistake on such a significant…'

'Merger?'

Fascinated, Alexei watched the faintest tinge of pink colour her cheeks. Was she thinking, as he was, of their bodies merging in the most intimate of ways?

'Decision.' Carissa's voice was crisp. She reached out and took a bread stick from the platter, broke it in half and crunched.

Alexei suppressed a laugh and reached for a piece of Marie's fried chicken. The delicious aroma made him inhale appreciatively.

'I look forward to getting to know you better, Carissa. And as for the question of starting a family immediately—' her eyes locked on his '—we can negotiate.'

She inclined her head slightly, the picture of cool condescension.

Which made Alexei want to ruffle her composure all the more. The urge to reach out to her made his fingers tingle but he refused to follow through. No matter how enjoyable that would be, he needed to keep his eye on the main game.

It was almost a shame that this was all a front. He'd enjoy negotiating with Carissa over sex. Perhaps he *would* see if she was interested in an affair when this was over.

Except by then her father would be ruined and in prison. It was unlikely she'd want anything to do with Alexei after that.

Reluctantly Alexei decided the best thing for now was to keep things low-key. He'd treat her as a guest rather than a prospective bride. He didn't need the complications that would follow if he acted on this attraction.

'When you've finished eating, I'll show you around.'

Mina enjoyed Alexei's voice, she realised. Its deep, suede quality was compelling. Worse, it weakened her, as if he brushed her flesh with plush fur that invited her to arch against it. There was his accent too. His English was crisp enough to prove it wasn't his first language; he had rich, round vowels, and the occasional soft consonant gave his voice a seductive quality.

Or perhaps he did that deliberately. He'd been toying with her, occasionally flirting as they spoke.

To see how she responded? Or because that was the nature of the man?

All she knew for sure was that Carissa had had a lucky escape. She'd have been miserable with Alexei, a man who viewed finding a wife as a matter of efficiency, and no doubt the woman herself as a possession!

It would do him good to discover she wasn't a chattel to be acquired so easily.

'That sounds marvellous. But please, don't let me keep you from your work. I can find my own way.'

Mina selected a skewer of tropical fruit and settled further into her seat, taking her time. She wasn't going to jump to his bidding.

'And neglect you?' He shook his head and a lock of dark hair tumbled over his brow, making him look more like a beachcomber than a business tycoon.

Mina's gaze strayed towards his unbuttoned shirt and the display of taut, packed muscle. She tried not to stare but it became tougher by the second. Why didn't he do up his shirt? Did he think himself so sexy he had to flaunt himself? That she wouldn't be able to resist him?

The idea was laughable. Yet Mina admitted the sight of his powerful frame set tremors running deep inside her.

She'd seen plenty of men wearing less than he did. She'd drawn nudes, even sculpted them, yet this was different. *She* felt different as she slanted a look at all that unvarnished masculinity. Not like an artist with an eye for angle and perspective. But like a woman.

There was a curious buzz in her bloodstream and her breath seemed far too shallow. The feeling was somehow both enervating and exhilarating.

Mina met his remarkable eyes. Malachite or tourmaline? The green was as deep as a fathomless ocean and just as unreadable. Beautiful yet dangerous. Like ocean depths where an unwary diver might be lured to disaster.

Setting her jaw, she put down her food and stood up. She reminded herself she was pragmatic, not fanciful, despite her creative nature.

'I'd love a tour, if you have time.' Anything was better than sitting, trying not to ogle a man she didn't even like.

The tour proved fascinating. More so than she'd anticipated. Alexei showed her the main rooms in his sprawling villa. Big, airy spaces that invited you to relax. And despite the presence of some stunning pieces of art that made Mina desperate to return for a longer study, the place didn't feel ostentatious, like a rich man's showpiece. It was luxurious but, above all, comfortable. Mina could imagine living here.

Nor did Alexei insist on a detailed tour of every designer detail. A wave of the arm indicated the cinema. Another incorporated his private wing. Then guest suites, gym and so on. As they passed outside, Alexei swept up two broad-brimmed hats and passed her one.

'It's easy to get sunburned.'

Mina didn't argue. She had a healthy respect for the power of the sun. In her country everyone covered up to shelter from its rays. Casting him a glance, she realised he looked more like a beachcomber than ever. An incredibly fit, sexy beachcomber who clearly didn't spend all his time lolling in a hammock with a cold beer.

They passed through a lush garden, with more sculptures she promised herself she'd come back to. Then they were out on a white sand beach, where small waves shushed ashore with the regularity of a heartbeat. There were no footprints on the sand. No other houses, only water and the birds in the trees and the warmth of the sun on her body.

It was paradise.

Mina dragged in a deep breath, rich with the tang of the sea, and sighed. How long had it been since she'd spent time away from crowds and cars? Not since her last visit to Jeirut. There she'd been rejuvenated by the rough majesty of the arid mountains, the sparkling clean air with its unique fragrance and the quality of the light that was unlike anything else.

'This is glorious.'

'I think so. There aren't many places like it.'

'With no neighbours?' She scanned the opposite end of the beach, seeing only the rise of a headland covered in a tangle of green forest.

'Partly that. But the island itself is pretty unique. It was never cleared for farming so a lot of the natural forest is left. Its conservation value is tremendous, especially for several species of endangered birds.'

Mina swung around to discover Alexei surveying her rather than their surroundings. She wasn't used to being the centre of attention, not since she'd given up her royal duties in Jeirut and disappeared into her life in Paris. Yet it wasn't just the fact Alexei watched her, it was the intensity of his regard. As if *he* were the artist and she a model.

'What are your plans for the island?'

'Plans?'

Mina turned back to the stretch of white sand, imagining it lined with buildings and an oversized marina. 'Eco-tourism or some other sort of development?'

'You assume I'm going to develop it?' Something in his voice snagged her attention and she looked up at him. His gaze was shadowed by the brim of his hat and unreadable.

'You're a businessman. Anyone with commercial sense would see it has enormous money-making potential.'

'Is that what you see?' His voice dipped to a gravelly note that made her skin shiver.

Mina shook her head and tried to repress regret at the

thought of it transformed into a busy holiday resort. 'I can see it, yes.'

'But you don't approve.' Had he read her so easily?

She shrugged. 'Not all progress is an improvement.' Her gaze took in the forest and a flash of bright colour as some small bird curvetted into the blue sky before disappearing again into the green.

'I agree.'

Mina started and swung back. 'You do?'

'Why so surprised? Even businessmen can appreciate beauty when they see it.'

Not all businessmen. Mina had met enough, so wrapped up in building more wealth or power, who never considered the impact of their actions on others or the environment.

At fifteen she'd had a stand-up argument with her father about a development proposal for the foothills near the capital. The scheme would bring short-term jobs but most profits would go offshore and the environmental damage would be catastrophic. In the end the plan was modified. It was one of the few times her father had been swayed. A local company had won the contract in a compromise between development and conservation. Now that area attracted tourists, drawn by the natural beauty and nearby facilities.

'Carissa?'

'Sorry.' She blinked and focused, reading the lines around his mouth that spoke of disapproval. 'What did you say?'

'I asked what you have against businessmen.'

'Nothing.' Just selfish rich guys who expected others to dance to their tune. Yet the vibe she got now from Alexei was a million miles away from that.

That intrigued her. Standing with the ocean lapping near their feet and Alexei's dark gaze heavy as a touch, Mina felt something new shiver through her. More than sexual awareness. More than impatience and indignation. Something that spread warmth and niggled at her protective, no, her combative attitude.

'So you're not going to change the place?' It seemed too good to be true.

'Oh, there'll be changes.' He waved his hand in an encompassing gesture.

Disappointment was sour on Mina's tongue. Why had she allowed herself to think otherwise? 'Such as?'

'Some cabins near the landing strip for visiting scientists and a small research facility.' Mina looked up and caught his fleeting smile. 'That's all.'

He'd deliberately led her on, and she'd fallen for it, because she was primed to believe the worst of him. And he'd guessed. Yet instead of taking offence, he was amused.

She hated to admit it but Alexei Katsaros threw her off balance. He was arrogant and annoying but he was perceptive and had a lighter, warmer side. Plus he valued this pristine environment as it was.

'Truly?'

'Truly. I spent my teens in a crowded city. Believe me, I realise how special this place is.' A slow smile curled his mouth and Mina felt the same curl etch a scrawl of heat deep inside. 'Now, how about I show you the spot where the turtles come in to lay their eggs?'

Silently Mina nodded. Then, following his example, took off her sandals, her feet sinking into fine, damp sand.

Because of Carissa, Mina and Alexei Katsaros were on opposing sides. When he discovered her deception he'd be livid. She couldn't afford to let her guard down. Yet spending time learning about him could only be to her advantage and Carissa's, couldn't it?

An inner voice warned Mina she was playing with fire. She should make an excuse and go back to her room.

But Mina had always been fascinated by fire and playing safe had never seemed so unappealing.

CHAPTER SIX

MINA'S HAND MOVED swiftly over the sketchpad, but her thoughts focused on the role she played. She should end this farce now.

She wouldn't betray Carissa and leave her prey to Alexei. Yet, with each hour, Mina grew more desperate. After two days on his island, the atmosphere grew thicker, more intense. He'd kept his distance physically but that only accentuated her catastrophic response to him.

As if it had a mind of its own, her body woke in his presence. The symptoms were depressingly irrefutable. Budding nipples, a surge of heat that threatened to flood her cheeks and flickered like wildfire in her veins. Butterflies the size of circling vultures in her stomach and a heavy, pulsing throb between her legs.

Sexual interest.

She could view it clinically. The trouble was that when they were together Mina felt anything but clinical detachment.

Frowning, she stared at her less-than-impressive sketch, then shoved it over the spiral spine of her drawing book to start afresh.

To make matters worse was Carissa's news, received via text. The elopement was delayed. Pierre was still in the USA, finishing negotiations on the tricky deal that he hoped would cement his professional success. Despite Carissa's pleas he was determined to stick it out, saying their future hinged on it. Mina sympathised. If his family disowned him for making a marriage they didn't approve, one of the pair needed a steady income. Carissa was talented but only starting her commercial design business.

Which meant Mina was stuck here for at least a couple more days, pretending to be someone else. Pretending to be impervious to Alexei. The strain was unbearable.

No other man had got under her skin like this. Just the mellow sound of his rare laugh or the deliberately confrontational twitch of one black eyebrow and her pulse revved out of control. Fortunately he never got close enough to touch. Despite those daydreams where he touched her in the most delicious, disturbing ways.

Mina set her chin and tried to focus on her drawing. She had work to do. An exhibition to prepare for. She couldn't sit in the Caribbean twiddling her thumbs. She needed...

Her hand stilled. There *was* a way out. Why hadn't she seen it?

Probably because her head was too skewed by thoughts of Alexei Katsaros.

Mina had accepted Carissa's assumption that her father's job would suffer if the marriage fell through. But surely it *must* fall through. Once Carissa was married to Pierre there'd be no question of a match with Alexei.

Besides, though Alexei could be daunting and demanding, the last couple of days had revealed another side to him. His manner with Marie and Henri indicated a man far more approachable and likeable than she'd imagined. A man who didn't expect to be treated as a superior being because he paid their wages. A man who could be surprisingly considerate.

He wasn't the complete ogre Carissa had imagined.

If Carissa, or, more accurately, Mina, were to say she couldn't go through with an arranged marriage, he'd have to respect that.

Mina blinked down at the half-formed sketch as she ran through the scenario in her mind. All she needed to do was say she'd considered but decided against the match. She'd be free to return to Paris, her work and her routine.

Funny how the thought didn't fill her with relief or anticipation.

Instead, Mina felt a pang of regret at the idea of leaving the island. And Alexei.

Her pencil dropped to roll unchecked across the paper. Mina blinked as it described a half circle on the page.

Was she serious?

Alexei Katsaros?

She huffed out a fierce breath. But it did no good to tell herself she didn't like big, bold, bossy men whose dark eyes twinkled with amusement just when she was about to explode with indignation.

Because she did. She liked him too much. Though he made her weak in ways she never wanted. For weakness was an invitation for men to trample you. She'd seen it too often.

'You look annoyed. Trouble with your drawing?' The deep voice came from beside her and Mina jumped. It was as if she'd conjured Alexei out of thin air by thinking of him.

She turned, her gaze on a level with snug faded jeans. Mina's heart rapped out a new, frantic tattoo as she fought not to let her eyes linger on the outline of muscled thighs. Instead she tilted her head up and up, till finally she met his quizzical gaze.

A jolt, like the impact of an electrical current, drove down through her body. Her breath stalled and the blood coursed faster in her veins.

This wasn't right. She didn't want to feel this or anything like it for Alexei. Despite his occasional charm he was the sort to stomp all over a woman.

'It's not going well.' She dragged her gaze back to the sketchpad and flipped it closed. The black cover mocked her with its blankness. That was how her brain was when he got near, and her artistic ability. How could she finish her designs when all she could concentrate on was him?

Suddenly it was imperative she put an end to this farce.

Mina was on her feet before she had time to think about it. 'I need to talk with you.'

Alexei stood so close her nostrils quivered at that delicious tang of citrus and cedar with base notes of warm male. Mina wanted to step away but he'd notice. He noticed everything.

'Of course.' He gestured to the chairs grouped on the wide veranda. 'Shall we sit?'

Mina was too agitated to sit. 'Let's walk.' Now she'd decided on her course of action she wanted it done. With luck, in a few hours she'd be on her way to Paris. Fiercely she smothered a pang of disappointment at the idea.

He wasn't good for her. No man who distracted her this way could be.

'Of course.' He turned towards the path that led to the beach. When they reached the fine sand Mina tugged off Carissa's pink sandals and put them to one side. Alexei, she noticed, was already barefoot. She liked the shape of his feet, the strength and composition of bone, vein, heel and arch.

The next time she sculpted a male nude she'd search for a model with feet and hands like Alexei. There was something powerful and appealing about them.

Catching her thoughts, Mina closed her eyes in self-disgust.

'Carissa? What is it? Surely nothing too bad?' For once there was no challenge or humour in Alexei's tone. He sounded concerned. 'Are you okay?'

'Absolutely.' She wiped her face of expression. 'But I need to tell you something.'

'I'm all ears.'

He began walking along the beach, heading for the hard-packed sand near the water. Mina fell into step beside him, wondering how to proceed. In the end she decided a direct approach was best.

'I've been doing a lot of thinking, Alexei, and I can't marry you.'

For a heartbeat he said nothing. Then he turned his head to survey her, his easy stride never faltering.

'Can't? Is there some barrier I don't know about?'

Because, of course, it would never occur to him that she didn't *want* to marry him.

'I'm not ready for marriage. I'm just turning twenty-three.' Yet many of her peers in Jeirut were married with children.

'Whereas I'm past thirty.'

'It's not that.' As soon as she said it, Mina could have bitten her tongue. Predictably Alexei pounced on her comment.

'So what is it?' His tone was even, yet she fancied she caught something sharp behind the smooth cadence.

'It's not the right decision for me.' She should have known he'd probe. She should have taken time to get her excuse straight instead of grabbing the first opportunity to talk.

Alexei stopped and Mina was forced to halt. Reluctantly she turned and looked up at him. Behind his head, out to sea, dark storm clouds built, promising rain and relief from the sultry weather. For Mina, raised in a dry climate, the air felt heavy and close, almost claustrophobic. It made her edgy.

Or perhaps that was Alexei's sharp scrutiny. No trace now of the understanding, almost easygoing man she'd glimpsed lately.

'So it's not the age gap. What, then? The idea of having my children?'

Mina stood, mesmerised by the gleam in those stunning eyes. She felt something burgeon deep inside. Excitement.

A well of tenderness as she imagined a toddler with black hair and green eyes, its expression morphing from serious to mischievous. Alexei's child. And hers.

Her heart dipped and a vast tremor shuddered through her.

It was preposterous. She'd known the man mere days. She had no plans for kids anytime soon.

Yet what she felt at that deep, visceral level couldn't be denied.

'No, you want children, don't you, Mina?' Alexei's voice was a soft thread, drawing through her, making her suddenly, shockingly aware that he was right.

Marriage had never been her goal. She hadn't played brides or pretended her dolls were babies. She'd only had one doll, a gift from a neighbouring monarch that was too precious to play with. She'd assumed she'd missed out on the so-called maternal instinct.

Yet with the right partner, Mina could imagine motherhood being wonderful.

With the right partner.

Suddenly Mina felt completely, devastatingly out of her depth. All these years she'd known herself and what she wanted—the right to choose, the chance to be an artist. She'd worked hard and that work was beginning to pay off. Now, out of nowhere, this man made her feel and want things she'd never wanted before.

He undermined her certainties and her understanding of herself. And he'd done it in mere days!

Her breath clogged in her chest and she looked away. 'It doesn't matter. I've considered this carefully and I can't marry you.'

Silence. So complete even the birds in the trees seemed to stop singing. All Mina heard was the soft shush of waves.

'You'll have to give me more than that.'

'Pardon?' She swung around and met his steady look.

He didn't seem at all put out. Instead Alexei looked merely intrigued and perhaps…amused? No, that couldn't be.

'You'll have to give me a reason. Your father assured me you were interested. *You* led me to believe—'

'I led you to believe nothing!' *He* was the one who'd dragged her here. 'I'm telling you marriage is off the agenda.'

Relief buoyed her. How much easier to stand up to Alexei when he riled her than when he was likeable.

'I'm afraid I can't accept that. Not unless you give me a reason.'

'Can't accept?' Mina couldn't believe the gall of the man. Her hands found her hips and she gave him a laser stare that should have singed a few inches off his height but sadly seemed to have no impact on that oversized ego. 'Then how about this? I'm not attracted to you. If I'm going to play happy families with any man, I'd like there to be some chemistry between us.'

Her chest heaved and her chin tilted high as her gaze collided with his. Then he inclined his head and her breath came more easily. He'd got the message. See? It had been simple after all.

'I'll go and pack. I'm sure you'd rather—' Mina paused in the act of turning when a large hand wrapped around her arm.

'Not so fast, Princess.'

Alexei took in her startled expression, and the quick, convulsive swallow, the darted look at his hand on her arm—her warm, bare, silk-fleshed arm.

For two days he'd been careful not to touch her. Not even to brush against her, for his awareness of Carissa verged on the primal and he preferred to keep a cool head where the Carters were concerned. Especially as her father still proved elusive, despite the efforts of a top investigator to locate him.

Alexei breathed deep, scenting her, that tantalising aroma of exotic spice that made him want more. Far more than a single touch.

More than a provocative game of advance and retreat.

More than this brush-off.

The marriage arrangement was a sham, yet Carissa's dismissal rankled. Did she really believe she could simply turn her back on him?

'You want *chemistry*?' His voice hit a bass note and he felt her shiver. Her eyes widened and he caught a hint of vulnerability in that sherry-brown gaze. But then she lowered those long lashes, veiling her eyes before turning her head to survey his restraining hand. Her pointed stare and haughty expression were a silent demand that he release her.

Why silent? Because she didn't trust her voice? Alexei watched Carissa's pulse thrum at the base of her throat.

How could she say there was no chemistry when the air was charged with animal attraction?

He stepped close and still she didn't look up. Alexei frowned. She wasn't scared, was she? The bizarre thought hit out of nowhere, tangling his thoughts. It was contrary to everything he knew of her.

Carissa was proud, opinionated and brave, considering how most people bowed to his wishes. It wasn't as if she were inexperienced. Carter had mentioned a failed affair with a Frenchman.

No, it wasn't fear holding her still. He read the shallow rise and fall of her breasts, the rushing pulse.

'I can give you chemistry,' Alexei murmured. He put his hand beneath her chin and lifted it till she had no choice but to look at him. Her mouth was a mutinous line but her eyes… Her eyes glowed dark gold. Desire slammed into him.

She lifted a hand to his chest, pushing as she opened her lips, no doubt to protest. So Alexei stopped her with his mouth, muffling her words, drawing in her warm breath.

For a moment there was stillness as shock tore through him. Just this simple touch and he felt poised on the brink.

Then Alexei gave himself up to instinct and delved deep, cradling her head with one hand, shuffling his legs wider as he lashed his arm around her and fitted her in against him.

He'd known this would be good. How right he'd been.

She tasted like every desire made flesh, rich and tantalising. Different from any other woman yet somehow familiar. Alexei pressed harder, simultaneously demanding and coaxing a response till finally her tongue slipped against his, tentatively at first, almost shy.

This was unlike anything he could remember. A judder of pure need ripped through him. His hands tightened as she caressed him again, slowly, learning the taste and shape of his mouth. As if he were some new treat to be savoured.

That slow, cautious exploration was more arousing than anything he'd experienced in years. It was all he could do to stand there, letting her take her time, when every lick threatened to blow the back off his head. He shuddered and his groin tightened as if she'd reached out and taken his burgeoning erection in her hand rather than simply returned his kiss.

Alexei's breath expelled in a huff of satisfaction as her responses grew more voluptuous. Leaning in, he demanded more.

Their kiss became fervent. She trembled but there was nothing tentative about her caresses now. Her lips and tongue were bold and sensual, carnal and eager. Carissa had given up playing games. The honest hunger, the lack of pretence, fuelled Alexei's desire towards the point of no return.

At his chest her fingers dug into his shirt as if to stop him pulling back. He pushed closer, trying to assuage his body's demand for more. Carissa met him with demands of her own. Her slim body arched against him, her small, plump breasts thrusting up, her nipples hard and arousing as they scraped his torso.

A growl built at the back of Alexei's throat. A sound of satisfaction and need. She'd taken him from zero to a hundred in less time than a supercar on a circuit. His blood surged in his ears and his body clamoured for more.

Dropping both hands to her rump, he lifted her higher, inserting his thigh between hers. He was as taut and hot as newly worked metal. When she moved, rotating her hips, tilting her pelvis against him, Alexei wondered if he might shatter. His hands shook as he fought the impulse to strip her naked and take her here, on the sand.

Yet why hold back?

Despite that intriguing initial hesitation, Carissa was no innocent needing protection. Her kisses were the deep, drugging caresses of a woman ready for sex, and her body told its own story, of a highly sensual woman eager to mate.

He breathed deep through his nostrils, inhaling the scent of musk mingled with exotic spice and sea salt. There was no mistaking her arousal.

Alexei shuddered at what her undulating body did to his. He was more than hard. He was in pain. A pain that could only be assuaged by more, much more.

He lifted one hand, grazing it up her ribs to her breast, pulling back from her enough to close his hand over her.

Yes! Her breast filled his hand perfectly. Excitement flooded him as she arched further, thrusting herself into his palm. His erection throbbed against her softness and he heard her hiss of pleasure.

His qualms evaporated. Why wait? Why not?

Suddenly Alexei felt pressure on his chest. Two palms pushing at him. Carissa wriggling as if to get off his leg.

Her mouth broke from his and he heard her raw gasps. Still, he didn't relinquish his hold. He couldn't. His brain was locked onto the elemental need to mate. It wasn't what he'd intended when he kissed her but chemistry like this couldn't be ignored.

'No.'

At first the word didn't register as anything other than a sound. Then she said it again and he focused on her lips, red and slick from their kisses. Heat flooded his gut as he watched her mouth move and imagined her lips caressing his bare body.

He'd wanted Carissa before. From the moment she'd crossed his threshold and pretended to be unimpressed with him and his home. Her disdain had the perverse effect of sharpening his interest, especially when he had no trouble identifying the passion beneath it.

Now his need tested his control to the limit.

'Alexei, let me go!'

He frowned down into her beautiful face, seeing her mouth tighten, her jaw bunch, and her words filtered into his brain.

She couldn't be serious.

But she was. He caught what looked like desperation in the flicker of her eyes and immediately let her go. She stumbled back and he grabbed her by the elbows, holding her steady. She shook as if her legs wouldn't support her.

'Thank you.' Her eyes fixed on a point near his mouth and delicate colour washed her cheeks, highlighting her patrician features. Her hair had come undone, spilling a wash of dark silk across her shoulders. It had felt like gossamer in his hands. With the sun on it, it looked like some glossy, fabled treasure. Alexei wanted to catch it up in his hands.

He wanted to kiss her and feel again the triumphant moment when her yielding became a sensual demand.

Instead he released her and stepped back, disconcerted at the lingering strength of his desire. That was supposed to be a kiss to prove a point. Yet he felt he'd walked into an ambush. His gaze sharpened on Carissa but she looked just as poleaxed.

Yet as he watched, she regrouped. Her hands went to her hips and her chin rose. She drew a deep breath and Alexei's attention dropped to those proud, perfect breasts pouting against her pink T-shirt. His fingers twitched as he recalled the feel of her breasts. He wanted to discover if she tasted as good all over as her mouth did.

Inhaling sharply, Alexei took another step back and felt a rush of warm water around his bare feet as a tiny wave came ashore. He wished it were icy, and deep enough to wash away the erection still jutting against his jeans.

He wasn't in the habit of losing control. His mouth tightened.

'I'll go and pack.'

'Sorry?' He scowled down at her determined features.

Carissa made a vague gesture with one arm. 'I'd like to go home now.' Her gaze lifted briefly to his before skittering away again. 'If you can arrange the transport.'

Alexei shook his head, a harsh laugh grinding from his throat. 'You've got to be kidding. You're not still pretending we're not attracted.'

'I...' She chewed her lip.

'Because if you are, maybe I should kiss you again. Then when we're naked on the sand and I'm deep inside you, you can tell me how sexually incompatible we are.' His voice dropped to a husky cadence as he imagined it. 'One more kiss is all it would take, Princess. You know it and I know it.'

Her nostrils flared and her eyes flashed. Alexei loved

her passion. He wanted to reach out and touch it, bask in its heat.

'Nevertheless, I want to leave. I told you I won't marry you.'

Alexei shoved his hands into the pockets of his jeans as he surveyed his confusing guest. A woman who'd tampered with his peace since she arrived. Who'd distracted him more than was advisable when he still had to bring her father to book.

What game was she playing? Some elaborate sexual tease? Except it was clear she suffered as much as he from unfulfilled desire.

Impatience stormed through Alexei. At himself for being diverted. At Carter for not showing himself. At Carissa for making him feel like an out-of-control teenager instead of a mogul with the world at his feet.

'That's a shame, Princess. Because you're not going anywhere.'

CHAPTER SEVEN

MINA STARED UP into Alexei's set face—the haughty winged eyebrows, the set jaw, the calculation in those gem-bright eyes—and knew she'd blundered terribly.

How had she imagined leaving would be easy?

It would have been if you hadn't kissed him back. If you hadn't tried to climb onto him like some sex-starved nymphomaniac.

Her naivety was truly remarkable, she realised belatedly.

Not only was the attraction between them real, but Alexei was a man used to getting his way. Right now he wanted a bride. And since Mina had demonstrated how sexually compatible they were, he also wanted her, physically.

Excitement eddied deep inside at his possessiveness. It should annoy her. It *did*. And yet...

Heat flushed her throat and breasts as she recalled the weight of his erection. The way she'd ground herself against his thigh, trying to ease the desperate ache between her legs. The way one kiss had made her cast aside a lifetime's caution.

Maybe she was sex-starved after all. In twenty-two years she'd never felt anything like this compulsion. No man had come close to breaking her absorption in her art and arousing such fire.

'Don't call me Princess. I don't like it.'

Those expressive eyebrows lifted higher as if he were surprised she'd choose that to complain about. But the way Alexei said it in that deep, roughened voice cut too close to the real Mina.

In her youth she'd chafed at the title 'Princess,' for it encompassed all the restrictions placed on her life by her father and her birth. Yet it was indelibly, undeniably hers, something she could never erase, though she didn't use it.

Hearing it now, from this big bear of a man who smashed through all the layers of civilisation and control she'd built up over a lifetime, evoked an atavistic fear that he *knew* her as no one else did. That he recognised the real Mina. More, that the wild, reckless woman who'd lost her mind and her self-respect when he kissed her, *was* the real Mina.

Her jumbled thoughts were crazy, surely, yet she had to put at least an illusion of distance between them. Hearing him use her title, even if he didn't know how apt it was, made her feel he saw past her attempts to be indomitable.

Besides, the cynical way he said it made her shiver thinking of his retribution once he learned the truth.

'Then of course I won't call you that. Carissa.'

The name was a deliberate caress, the soft sibilant curling around her vital organs like a silken cord.

The terrible knowledge hit that Mina wanted to hear him say her real name like that. Not that it was nearly as musical. It was plain and ordinary, but the longing to hear it on his tongue was almost overpowering.

She folded her arms across her chest and stumbled back a step. He'd see that as proof of weakness but that wasn't as important as retaining her sanity.

What had he done to her?

How had a kiss tumbled her defences and addled her brain?

But it had been more than a kiss.

It had been momentous. Life-changing. Mina felt as if she'd woken from a dream to a new world where everything took on a sharp clarity. Where every sense was heightened and alert. Where light and shadow were more defined, colour brighter, feelings more vivid.

She hefted a deep breath, saw his eyes flicker on the movement and angled her chin.

Weakened she might be, but she was no pushover.

'I'm sorry if my response just now misled you, Alexei.' She faced his stare head-on, telling herself this was nothing compared to challenges she'd faced as a royal. Except then she'd been confident in her own abilities. Now, suddenly, she realised she wasn't as strong as she'd believed. This man made her feel unexpectedly weak. 'But I'm serious. I don't want marriage.'

He folded his arms over his chest, the movement mirroring her posture. Yet on him the gesture was challenging rather than self-protective. She watched his biceps bulge and tried not to remember the iron-hard strength of his embrace. His virile power had been part of the magic she'd felt in his arms.

'So what do you want? An affair?'

'No!' Mina heard the shock in her voice and gave up any hope of pretending to be insouciant. 'My response was…a mistake.'

'A mistake?'

'You're a very persuasive kisser.' She refused to look away, despite the heat warming her face. 'But I've decided I'm not ready to settle down and marry.'

Mina paused, waiting for him to respond but Alexei said nothing. 'I'm sorry to disappoint you. But it's better to know now than later.' She drew a slow breath, annoyance rising at his continued silence. 'In the circumstances I'd like to return to Paris.'

'That's not possible.'

'Not possible? Is there a problem with the plane?'

Alexei shook his head. 'I need you here until your father arrives.'

'Sorry?' Still dealing with shock at her physical response to Alexei, Mina found it hard to grasp his meaning.

'Have you heard from him recently?'

Mina frowned. 'Heard from him?'

'A phone call? Text or email?'

She shook her head.

That shadowy green gaze bored into her but now he didn't bother to hide his expression. It was sharp with disbelief. With distrust.

'It's true!' Mina had been thankful Carissa's father hadn't arrived, because it delayed the moment of her unmasking, giving her friend time to get away with Pierre. Now Mina's stomach sank and her skin tightened. She had a bad feeling that this situation was more complex and fraught than she'd suspected. What had she walked into?

'Then lend me your phone. I'll check the number I have for him. Clearly the one I've got is wrong. It's vital I contact him.'

Mina bit her lip. This conversation got odder and odder. But she could hardly refuse. 'I'll write it down for you.' She'd have to get it from Carissa.

'Hand over the phone, Carissa. That will do.'

There was something about the way he spoke, the air of ruthless command that sent warning cresting through her. Something was very wrong.

Drawing on years of royal training, she masked her tension. 'Of course. I'll go and get it now.'

She felt his suspicion like tiny pinpricks on her skin but eventually he inclined his head and relief juddered through her. For a moment she'd thought he'd insist on walking her back to her room.

Mina turned away, forcing herself not to run. But all the way to the house she felt shaky. From the sudden sense of foreboding when Carissa's father had been mentioned? Or from that kiss?

In her room she turned the latch to lock her door and sagged against it, knees wobbly with reaction. But she had no time to waste.

Seconds later she had the phone in her hand, punching

out Carissa's number. But her relief when her friend picked up was short-lived. Mina recognised the panic in Carissa's voice as she admitted she hadn't heard from her father. It wasn't like him to be out of contact so long. Worse, Pierre had rung again to confirm he wouldn't be back in Paris for two days. Could Mina hold out till then?

Mina pressed a hand to her forehead, her thoughts frantic. Two more days here wouldn't affect her work schedule too much. But did she really want to stay with Alexei Katsaros? Especially now the stakes seemed infinitely higher. What had started as a defiant plan to save her friend grew tangled and risky.

Then Carissa sniffed and said Mina should tell Alexei the truth. She'd done more than enough and it was time Carissa fought her own battles.

Mina was tempted to agree.

Except Carissa would be bulldozed by Alexei. She'd be cowed and if not browbeaten then emotionally blackmailed into doing what her father and Alexei wanted. Could Mina stand by and see that happen to her dear friend?

There was even a part of her that protested at the idea of Alexei with Carissa, not for Carissa's sake but Mina's.

Where had that come from?

Mina drew a steadying breath and thrust aside the wayward thought. She warned Carissa to move out of her apartment as a precaution, in case the masquerade came unstuck and Alexei came looking for her.

Then she ended the call and stared at the phone in her hand. If she was to play this role any longer she couldn't let Alexei see her call history or contacts. It would be obvious she wasn't Carissa.

Which meant refusing to hand over her phone.

Adrenalin rushed her bloodstream at the thought of Alexei discovering the truth. But there was no other option.

All she had to do was hold out for a couple more days.

A rap on her door made her stiffen.

'Carissa?'

Mina's heart thumped and she knew a craven desire to admit defeat. To open the door and tell him everything.

Except Carissa relied on her. Carissa, who'd been there when Mina was desperately homesick and convinced she'd never make it as an artist. Carissa, whose warm, gentle nature made her the best friend Mina had ever had. The only real friend, since all the people she'd mixed with in Jeirut had been hand-picked by her father.

Carissa didn't care about her royal status. She liked Mina for herself. She was genuine and caring and Mina refused to see her throw her happiness away for some moody tycoon.

Mina breathed deep and tiptoed to the glass door that led outside.

Behind her the door rattled. 'Carissa?'

The sound sent her catapulting into the garden, eyes on the path to the beach, her phone gripped in one clammy hand.

He wouldn't be happy. In fact, Alexei would be furious. The thought lent her speed, though of course there was no real escape. The best she could do was ensure he didn't discover she wasn't Carissa. It still amazed her that he hadn't bothered to check her photo. No one but the immigration official had bothered to view her passport.

Her stride slowed as she approached the beach. Did she really mean to—

A rhythmic thudding reached her ears. Louder than her pumping heart. Mina looked over her shoulder and saw Alexei covering the ground between them in long strides. For a second, a primitive thrill of fear engulfed her, freezing her limbs. But Mina was no cornered prey. Her hand tightened on the phone. Then she turned, hauling her arm back and letting go.

Alexei grabbed her arm a moment too late. She heard his rough breathing, felt the clamp of his fingers on her wrist and the heat of his massive frame behind her as the phone arced over the water and disappeared into the endless azure sea.

The die was cast.

With a sense of disbelief, Alexei watched the phone plummet into the sea.

He'd almost convinced himself that despite her contrariness Carissa was an innocent pawn in her father's scheme.

Because her kiss blew you away.

A kiss meant nothing. Logically he knew that, yet Alexei had been close to believing in her.

Because he'd wanted her since she stepped across his threshold. Her feisty attitude and subtle sexiness were a unique turn-on, especially combined with that indefinable sense of connection, as if behind the charades they played he knew her and she him. As if at a level so deep it defied logic, they understood each other.

When they'd kissed it was combustible. *He'd* been combustible.

She'd been far more than he expected. Responsive. Blatantly hungry for him, wildly passionate and yet, when he'd first tasted her he'd sensed a hesitance that felt almost like innocence.

Innocence! She was in cahoots with her thieving father. She was messing with his mind.

'You're so desperate that I don't contact your father?' He slid his free arm around her waist, holding her back against him in a travesty of the passionate embrace they'd shared on this very beach.

Now the passions he felt were fury and jarring disappointment. He'd actually wanted to believe in Carissa.

Because you want her in your bed. You'd begun to trust

her. Even now, knowing she's part of his scam, you can't turn off your hunger.

It was true. His arm around her middle wasn't lover-like and his grip on her wrist was unbreakable, yet his body reacted to the soft pressure of her rump against him, the underside of her breasts brushing his arm and the scent of her hair teasing his nostrils.

If anything, ire hiked his arousal higher. His sharpened senses picked up her ragged breathing and her quick, thrumming pulse and the tension of her muscles, as if she waited for him to slacken his hold so she could run.

There was nowhere she could go that he wouldn't find her.

Suddenly, their situation took on a whole new, delectable piquancy.

'I didn't want you prying into my private messages.' Her voice was choppy, and Alexei felt as well as heard her harsh breathing.

'Why's that, Carissa? Have you been sexting with your French boyfriend?'

Her hissed breath confirmed it. Alexei's constraining arm tightened. At the idea of her sharing erotic messages and images with another man?

Impossible.

Yet he felt a deep satisfaction that while she was on his island she'd have to devote all her attention to him. There'd be no other men in her life.

'You know about him?' Her voice was wary.

'Was he supposed to be a secret?' Of course he was. She'd even faked a show of tremulous innocence when her lips met his. Not that it had lasted.

'My messages are my affair. You have no right to pry. You're a bully.'

She yanked her arm, trying to free it. The movement was so violent it slammed her into even more intimate contact with Alexei's hardening body. Flame shot through him as she rubbed against his groin.

Carissa froze, her breath a shocked hiss. He felt the pulse at her wrist sprint out of control as if she only now realised how intimately close they stood.

'You think I care about seeing your nude photos? All I want is to bring your father out of hiding.'

'Hiding? What are you talking about?'

Alexei applauded her acting skills. She sounded confused rather than guilty. 'Spare me the dramatics. Only a woman desperate to hide the truth would pitch her phone. You're in this with your father.' He hadn't quite believed she'd do it, even as she drew her arm back in that perfect curve. 'You've just proved it.'

She was silent for so long he wondered if she were about to admit defeat till she said in a completely different tone, 'In what?'

Furious and sick of her lies, he spun her round, his hands on her narrow waist.

Yet, reading her expression, Alexei felt a splinter of doubt.

'What has he done?' Instead of avoiding his stare, she peered up at him, a tiny wrinkle between her eyebrows, her look searching.

Probably hoping to pretend that she didn't know.

'Embezzled a fortune. And that's just the funds he's stolen in the last couple of months. Who knows what the total is in the years he's worked for me?' Alexei spoke through clamped teeth, watching her eyes grow wide.

He'd thought his financial systems the best. The rigorous accounting and auditing processes were held up as the gold standard. But when the man who designed them was the one with his fingers in the till…

'You're sure?' Carissa looked the picture of shock. He felt a tremor pass through her and held her more firmly, telling himself he didn't want her pretending to faint. It wasn't dramatics he wanted but retribution.

'Absolutely. There's a complete audit underway. You can be sure it will uncover every cent he's stolen. Including the money that's supported your party lifestyle while you pretend to be an artist.'

The fact some of the stolen money had funded this woman's taste for idle self-gratification twisted the knife. Alexei had laboured hard for everything he possessed. It had been tough, especially scraping together capital to invest in his first innovative software package when he'd had no track record and only a mediocre education. He hadn't even had a permanent roof over his head.

Nothing had been handed to him. And he knew all about leeches who fattened themselves by living off the hard work of others.

Yet he'd allowed himself to be conned by Carter.

He stared down into soft brown eyes and knew they lied. His voice held bitter amusement. 'After this you'll have to work for a living like the rest of us. That will be a novel experience for you.'

Now Mina understood the rage flaring in that deep green gaze, the snap of his words and the harsh jut of his chin. It was like staring into the boiling heart of a volcano.

The raw quality of his emotion should unnerve her. Yet at the same time, that elemental ferocity drew her.

Was she mad?

Her father had always said she was reckless, yet there was something so vital about Alexei in this moment. Even as she warned herself to be careful, her artist's eye was busy cataloguing the changes in him, the way potent masculine anger imbued every sharp angle and bunched muscle.

Already his hold on her waist loosened. Was she ridiculously naive? Yet the vibe she picked up from Alexei was the same as she got from her brother-in-law, Huseyn. When he'd first appeared, Huseyn had been the enemy, storming in to snatch the kingdom and her sister in marriage. Big, abrupt and deliberately provoking, he'd nevertheless proved appearances wrong. He'd turned out to be a devoted family man and an unobtrusively kind brother-in-law, whose bark was worse than his bite, at least with those he cared for.

Was Alexei like him? Or did her instinct lie because she was attracted? And because she battled a compulsion to commit that sparking, urgent energy to paper? Mina wanted to capture his aura of power.

Almost as much as she wanted that energy focused on kissing her again.

She blinked. She couldn't take her safety for granted.

'Do you plan to hurt me because of him?' Mina had no idea if confronting Alexei directly was the right approach but she had to know.

His head reared back, a scowl settling on his forehead. 'I suppose you'll find it tough to work for a living instead of living off your father's ill-gotten gains. But I'd hardly call that hurting.'

'I mean, are you so angry you'll *hurt* me.'

She saw the moment her meaning registered. Alexei's instinctive recoil and the horror in his eyes.

His hands dropped to his sides. 'No! Of course not.'

'There's no *of course*. Some men do.'

Slowly he inclined his head, his breath expelling in a rush of warm air that feathered her hair. 'Not me. Not ever.'

Mina surveyed him steadily, wondering whether to believe him, and her instinct.

'I think you're wrong about the theft. I think it's a mistake. Maybe someone else stole the money and made it look like he did it.' What she knew of Carissa's father pointed to an honest man, though his idea of engineering an arranged marriage was bizarre. Maybe his recent bereavement had affected him more than Carissa feared.

Alexei shook his head. 'There's no doubt. It was definitely him.' He raised his eyebrows as if challenging her to prove otherwise.

'Well, if so, he didn't fritter it away funding parties in Paris.' Carissa's father had paid his daughter's art school tuition and now helped with part of her rent, but Carissa was talented and hardworking, supplementing her income from her art by waitressing and modelling. Even her shopping addiction for second-hand clothes was a source of income since she sold items she'd refurbished.

Alexei merely crossed his arms over his chest. He looked as unmoved and unmovable as the rocky outcrop at the far end of the beach.

Mina suppressed a sigh. What was the point of protesting Carissa's blamelessness? He'd never believe her. And, if he'd been ripped off so badly, who could blame him?

She slicked her tongue around her parched lips, feeling the rush of her pulse and the jitter of nerves still unsteady after that sprint to the beach, with Alexei at her heels. And Alexei holding her against him as if he'd never release her.

In fury, Mina reminded herself. Not desire. She was the one plagued by that. To Alexei she was a conniving thief, or as good as.

She shivered and looked away, out over the water where the dark clouds grew more threatening by the moment. The humid air felt heavy, sultry with ominous foreboding.

It was hard not to see it as a sign, a warning that Alexei had some revenge planned.

Of course! Abruptly she swung towards him. His gaze was already on her, sending sensation wrinkling down her backbone. Mina's mouth tightened. She had to stop *reacting* to him!

'Why am I here, Alexei? What do you really want?'

'Don't look so worried. Nothing's going to happen to you that you don't want.'

Mina took a second to digest that. It should have reassured except the dark speculation in his eyes and her answering tremor of awareness undermined certainty. As if their bodies spoke a different language. As if he expected her to *want* far more than was good for her.

Mina refused to go there. Bad enough to find her first stirrings of real desire were for a man who didn't trust or like her. Who was, to all intents and purposes, her enemy.

She crossed her arms, mirroring his posture. 'Why am I here, Alexei? And don't give me that line about wanting to marry. That's clearly a lie.'

One dark eyebrow slanted. 'You take offence at a lie?'

Mina was about to tell him she abhorred dishonesty as much as she did selfish men who manipulated women for their own ends. Then she remembered she was here under false pretences. For the best of reasons, but still...

'Spit it out, Alexei.'

His eyes held hers. 'You're bait, to draw your father out. Since he had the front to suggest I marry you, I figure when he learns you're here, he'll assume his theft hasn't been discovered or that I'm willing to come to some agreement with my soon-to-be father-in-law.' His disdainful tone and chilly stare told her how likely that was.

'And until he gets here?' She swallowed. Her throat was tight and she had a hard time projecting calm.

'Till then you're my trump card.' His lips curved in a smile she could only describe as dangerous. 'I'll keep you close.'

CHAPTER EIGHT

THE SOUND OF the wind finally distracted Mina. She looked up from the intricate design taking shape on her sketchpad and realised the noise she'd been vaguely aware of was the howl of a strong wind from the sea. The dark clouds had moved closer in the hours since her confrontation with Alexei and the light was lurid green.

The hairs on Mina's nape and arms lifted. She didn't know tropical weather, but that eerie light reminded her of the explosive storms that occasionally devastated the mountains of her homeland.

A crash made her jump. Mina put her drawing down and crossed to her bedroom window.

A sun umbrella had fallen, knocking over a wrought-iron chair. As she watched, a cushion tumbled past and came to rest against a gardenia hedge.

Mina opened the door and went out, feeling the whip of the wind. Another cushion floated in the pool. She concentrated on saving the rest, gathering them and dropping them inside her room.

As she turned around, a chair slid, screeching across the flagstones. Mina chewed her lip, looking beyond the garden to the taller trees, bending in the wind. If the storm worsened, unsecured furniture could be dangerous, especially in a house with so many big windows. As for that umbrella…

She was grappling with it, trying to close it against the force of the wind when she heard a voice behind her.

'Leave that to me.' Large hands took over, Alexei's shoulder nudging her out of the way. She watched the strain of bunching muscles and tendons in his arms as he fought to close it, then heard a grunt of satisfaction as he finally succeeded. 'You get inside. This will get worse before it gets better.' He was already lifting the long umbrella pole and marching away.

Mina frowned, staring as he disappeared around the corner of the house. What had she expected? Thanks for trying to help? She should have known better.

But as another chair careered across flagstones, she set her mouth, grabbed it and followed him.

Nearby, yet screened from the house, was a large garage. Inside, in addition to the four-wheel drive, she discovered a couple of jet skis, a windsurfer, canoes and Alexei, stacking the furled umbrella against a pile of outdoor furniture. He must have been working for some time, securing it all. Mina had been so busy working she hadn't noticed.

'Where's Henri?'

Alexei's head jerked up. He hadn't heard her approach over the noise of the wind. 'Gone with Marie to the larger island for supplies. But the storm's changed course, coming in faster than expected. They'll have to stay there till it blows over.'

Even in the gloom Mina could see the gleam of Alexei's steady stare. Did he expect her to panic at the idea of a powerful storm?

'What can I do?'

'Sorry?'

Behind her the door banged shut, leaving them in almost darkness. But not completely. Mina could make out his towering form, close now. The wide spread of his shoulders, the jut of his jaw as if he were still furious.

Mina didn't step back. To retreat would be to admit fear. She might be stuck here, an unwilling guest of an angry host who saw her as an avaricious plotter, but she refused to show anxiety. Even if there *was* something about Alexei Katsaros that made her breathing ragged and her pulse skip.

But it's not fear, is it?

It's desire.

Mina inhaled a breath redolent with the tang of citrus and Alexei, and strove to ignore the flurry in her belly.

'You said the storm's coming more quickly than expected and Henri's not here to help. What can I do to prepare?'

Alexei peered down at the slim figure before him, wishing it were light enough to read her expression.

It wasn't the first time she'd surprised him. When he'd rounded the house to find her struggling with the oversized umbrella his heart had almost stopped. Did she have any idea how dangerous that would have been, if the wind had ripped it out of her hold? How much damage it could do as a projectile?

'Get into the house and stay there.' He had enough to do without worrying for her safety. The wind was still rising.

For answer, she spun on her foot, headed for the door and yanked it open. Alexei saw her silhouetted against the light, long legs, short white shorts and a tight top that outlined a deliciously willowy body. He remembered the feel of her against him; the combination of taut flesh and enticing, feminine softness had been irresistible.

Then she strode towards the house.

Good riddance. Alexei had more to do and time was running out. Yet, as he carted more furniture to the garage, he found Mina marching towards him, carrying another chair. The wind had strengthened and her long dark hair whipped around her face.

'What are you doing? Get inside. Now!'

For answer she kept walking, would have passed him if he hadn't caught her arm.

Her haughty stare could have stripped bark from a tree. 'There isn't time to argue. Accept my help and do what you have to. What about shutters? I can't see any. How do we protect the windows?'

Alexei paused, surprised to discover she was serious. She planned to help him batten down for the storm. 'They're electric. They'll come down at the punch of a button.'

'Then shouldn't you go and punch that button before we lose power?'

She was right. Plus he wanted to double-check the backup generator.

Alexei considered picking her up bodily and carrying her inside. She'd be safe. But no doubt she'd race back out here as soon as his back was turned.

'Very well.' He cast a look at the trees bending in the wind and, behind them, the inky, threatening sky. 'But only five minutes more. The main entrance will be open. Come in that way.' He lowered his head to her level, watching her pupils dilate. 'No longer than five minutes. Got it?'

Silently she nodded.

But when the time was up, Carissa was nowhere to be seen. The wind was stronger now, the sound like a freight train approaching from a distance. They had to take shelter. They didn't have much time left. Fat drops of rain fell and a second later he faced a grey sheet of solid water.

His mouth tightened as he scanned the exterior of the house. All the furniture was shut away. The house was secure, storm shutters in place. But Carissa was nowhere to be found.

Alexei called her name but the wind tore the sound away. Anxiety nipping at him, he sped through the garden, drenched by the needling deluge.

He couldn't see her. Not near the pool or house. He ventured further into the garden, blinking to clear his vision. With each passing second tension coiled tighter, his pulse racing faster.

Alexei rounded a curve in a path to see something staggering towards him. The sight was so unexpected, the shape lurching drunkenly, that it took precious seconds to process what he saw. When he did, he stifled an oath and raced forward, anger vying with stupefaction.

A sculpture! She'd stayed out in *this* to save a sculpture.

Arms out, he grabbed the ungainly wooden shape as Carissa staggered against him, blown by the force of the gale.

'Leave it! It's not worth it.' He felt her flinch. Saw her eyes widen as he tugged it from her.

She clung on like a limpet, mouthing something he couldn't hear. 'Save…together.'

Alexei shook his head. 'Inside. Now!'

Whether she heard him over the wind's rising scream, Alexei didn't know. But her mouth set in a mulish line as she held on tight. They didn't have time to argue. The wind was still picking up speed. Soon the flying debris would be larger, more dangerous.

Hefting the sculpture more securely, Alexei grabbed her hand and started back down the path.

The way back took forever. The sodden ground was treacherous and the wind buffeted mercilessly. More than once he saved Carissa from falling when her foot skidded. Then, as they approached the house, the wind caught Alexei and the wildly rotating sculpture full force and almost plunged them into the pool. He would have dropped it there and then, except this time Carissa was dragging at his arm, holding him steady.

Cursing, Alexei regained his balance and lurched forward. His muscles strained at the effort of carrying the cumbersome sculpture that wanted to fly from his arms into the screeching wind.

Darkness. The slam of the door. Stillness after that riot of rushing air and hammering rain.

Alexei struggled to the control panel on the wall, jamming his elbow against the switch that brought down the final storm shutter. Another jab and light filled the foyer.

His breath came in rough gasps that tore his throat. Water sluiced down his face and he almost lost balance in the spreading pool of water as he bent to lower his ungainly burden.

Finally he straightened to stare at the convoluted collection of carved sails that still spun and shivered with the dying momentum of the wind. No wonder it had felt as if it might take off from his arms. It was designed to move in a breeze. Breeze, not a cyclone!

Alexei had bought it as a brilliant, evocative piece that paid homage to the centuries of seafarers who'd passed this way. Now, looking past the still-turning sails to the woman beyond, he wished he'd never seen it.

She could have been hurt. More than hurt.

The savage clench of his ribs around his organs wrapped fiery pain around Alexei's torso.

Mina was bent forward, hands on knees, dragging in desperate, gasping breaths. Her hair was a slick, dark curve that arrowed over her shoulder. Her nipples stood proud against the dark cherry pink of the top that plastered her breasts. Her slim legs glistened with water and there was a long red scratch on her shin.

'What. The. Hell. Were. You. Thinking?' He ground the words out.

Her eyes lifted. A second later Carissa straightened, abandoning her recuperative pose for that now-familiar haughty stance. Chin forward, slender neck stretched high, eyebrows slightly raised. She did obstinate condescension to perfection.

'Saving a wonderful work of art.' She reached into a back pocket of her shorts and produced a large screwdriver. That explained how she'd dislodged the sculpture from its plinth. She must have grabbed it from the garage.

'What on earth possessed you?'

Still not quite believing what she'd done, he watched as she turned away and put the screwdriver down on a side table. It landed with a clatter. There was a jagged tear at the hem of her T-shirt and another scratch down the back of one toned thigh.

Alexei felt something surge high inside. Something rough and sharp, scrabbling and clawing at his control. He clenched his jaw so tight he wondered if he'd ever unlock it.

A spasm shook him as he remembered the waving boughs, the lashing storm and thought of the lucky escape she'd had.

Carissa turned, eyes dark and wide in her too-pale face. 'We couldn't leave it there. It's a masterpiece.'

Alexei stared. He couldn't believe what he heard.

'You know it is.' Her voice was clipped. 'Otherwise you wouldn't have bought it.'

He knew all right. He wouldn't have paid the exorbitant amount he had for it otherwise. But that didn't matter.

'That was the single most stupid, irresponsible thing I've witnessed in years.' His voice lashed as he relived the sight of her, refusing to budge without her precious sculpture. 'I don't care about the money.'

She flinched, her face paling even more. 'Of course you don't! Obviously I was mistaken. You probably bought it because it had a big price tag to match your big ego.' She drew a breath that emphasised how shaky she was, despite her show of defiance. She looked proud and glorious and frighteningly vulnerable. And Alexei couldn't understand why the vein of fury ran so deep and strong within him.

It was a good thing they were on opposite sides of the room. Dimly he realised fear fed his anger. That terrible moment when he'd discovered her missing. Guilt that she could have died out there because he hadn't forced her inside earlier.

'It's not worth your life. Do you have any idea how dangerous it was out there?' Alexei heard his voice rise from a hoarse whisper to something close to a roar. 'Are you really that thoughtless? That unbelievably stupid?'

His loss of control stunned him. When had he ever been this angry? When he'd discovered her father's theft he'd been livid, determined to get justice. He'd felt personally betrayed, made a fool of by the one person he'd trusted in years. But he hadn't experienced this visceral level of dismay. This gut-scouring scrape of horror.

Carissa didn't flinch. She faced him with cool—almost *too* cool—composure.

Finally the echo of his words died. Outside the wind wailed, but in here there was nothing but the sound of heavy, uneven breaths and the tumble of rushing blood in his ears.

'If you'll excuse me, I have a cut I need to attend to, before I stain your floor.'

Carissa spun around and walked away down the dark corridor towards her suite. Belatedly he realised she was cradling one hand. And that she walked with the careful precision of someone marshalling their strength to stay upright.

The red mist edging Alexei's vision began to clear. The cyclonic rage eased. His brain kicked into gear, enough to suspect her superior bearing hid something other than disgust at his fury.

His gaze dropped to the floor. A spatter of dark droplets led down the corridor. The sight was a kick to the belly.

Her hand was bleeding and he hadn't noticed. He'd been too busy berating her.

Alexei slumped against the wall, palming his wet face, trying to scrub away the last vestiges of blinding fury.

He still reeled from the fact Carissa had pitched in to help secure the house, making herself useful as if she wasn't the spoiled, self-absorbed woman he'd pegged her as. Alexei had expected her to demand he spirit her off the island. Or that she'd cower in the house, frightened by the ferocity of the weather. He wouldn't have blamed her.

Carissa never did what he expected. *She* wasn't what he expected.

Now she made him feel as if *he* were in the wrong.

Residual anger made his heart pound his ribcage. Yet that didn't explain the unfamiliar, queasy feeling in his belly. It wasn't fear, not now she was safe.

Surely it wasn't guilt? She *had* risked her neck out there.

The woman was trouble.

Alexei straightened from the wall, circled around the sculpture that had caused this drama, and headed towards the light streaming from her suite. He needed to see how badly she was hurt.

Mina bit her lip and tried to stop shaking enough to tear open the box of sticking plasters she'd found in the bathroom. It dropped to the floor and she sagged against the wall, eyes closing.

She'd pick it up in a minute, when the shaking stopped.

She was so angry. But soon she'd be calm.

Except it wasn't simply anger that made her tremble from head to foot. Mina wiped her uninjured hand across her cheeks, scrubbing away the fresh trails of wetness that had nothing to do with the sodden hair dripping down her face.

There was a blockage in her throat, hot and sour, making it hard to swallow. A ball of emotion that refused to go away.

Stupid. Thoughtless.

The words circled again and again. She didn't know how to silence them.

Mina told herself she was in shock. The storm had been

terrifying. When she'd started out to save the sculpture, the wind hadn't been so bad and she'd been sure she'd have time. Then all hell had broken loose and she'd been stunned to realise danger was upon her, upon *them*. It was her fault Alexei had been out there too.

What if he'd been hurt trying to save her?

Her mouth crumpled and a sob seared her clogged throat.

Mina shook her head. She didn't cry. She never cried. Not even when her father died.

Stupid. Thoughtless.

She swallowed again and this time tasted tears.

The last time she'd seen her father they'd argued. She'd wanted to go to art school and he'd already enrolled her in university to major in economics. It was one of the rare times he'd lost his temper. Usually he was cool and distant. He expected his daughters to obey, to do whatever he expected, including acquiring appropriate qualifications to prove women in Jeirut could play a part in the country's modernisation.

There was no room for an artist in the royal family. Mina's value, like her sister Ghizlan's, lay in being *useful*.

Their father's focus was the country, not them. He'd never cuddled them or laughed with them. Never been close, let alone shown love. They were tools in his grand plans. Her mother had died when she was an infant so there was no one to argue on her behalf.

But at seventeen, Mina had believed she had a right to choose her career. Her father had put paid to that. He'd been brutally frank about her purpose in life. As a princess she'd be a model for Jeiruti women and have a key role in royal events. In time, she'd make a dynastic marriage to a man her father chose.

Mina was stupid, thoughtless and selfish to question his plans.

Two days later he'd dropped dead from a brain aneurism.

She'd never had a chance to mend the breach between them. She told herself it didn't matter because her father hadn't loved her, or she him. Yet regret lingered. Hearing those words again, whiplash sharp—

'Carissa? Are you all right?'

Mina's eyes popped open, horror enveloping her. She caught sight of herself in the mirror and groaned. Her eyes were pink and she couldn't stop her mouth quivering.

'Yes.'

The door rattled. 'Why have you locked the door?'

Mina sank her teeth into her bottom lip. She didn't need this. She didn't have the energy to face Alexei. She needed time to marshal her defences.

'Carissa?'

'I want privacy. Is that too much to ask?' Her shaking grew worse, not better. She wrapped her arms around herself, trying to hold in the ache. And the cold. She felt so cold.

'Open the door, Carissa. I need to make sure you're okay.'

Great. Another man who refused to take a woman's word or believe she could look after herself.

But Alexei thought her stupid, didn't he?

To her horror, fresh tears prickled her eyes and she blinked frantically. She felt…raw, unprotected, unable to summon the assurance she projected to keep people at a distance.

It was ridiculous. Words couldn't hurt her. Yet Alexei's expression as he'd spoken… The knowledge he'd been right—

'Open the door *now*, Carissa, or I'll break it down.'

'I said—'

'Now!' He didn't shout like before. But the low resonance of his voice convinced her more than any ranting threat.

Mina stumbled to the door and flicked the latch. It swung open and Alexei surged in, making her back up.

She refused to meet his eyes, turning instead to the packet she'd dropped on the floor. 'Since you're here—' she tugged in a swift breath and tried to sound nonchalant '—would you mind picking that up? My hands are a bit unsteady.' There was no way of hiding that so she might as well admit it.

Without waiting for a response Mina turned to the basin and ran water over the jagged cut in the fleshy part of her hand, cleaning away the dripping blood. Her grasp of the screwdriver had slipped on the last screw and dug into her flesh. Strange, she couldn't feel any pain.

'Here, let me.' A large hand took her elbow and Alexei pushed her down onto a chair beside the vast bath. His touch was surprisingly gentle. Mina opened her mouth to protest but found she didn't have the inclination. Her shoulders slumped as her energy ebbed.

Alexei wrapped a fluffy white hand towel around her hand. Mina frowned, thinking of blood on the pristine cloth, but said nothing. It was his towel.

He took her other hand and pressed it to the cloth to keep the pressure steady. Then he collected the packet she'd dropped plus a bottle from the cupboard and hunkered before her.

She was aware of his heat above all, like a furnace sending out warmth to tease her frozen body. But she refused to meet his eyes. Instead she concentrated on those hard, beautiful hands. They worked deftly.

'This will sting.' He unwrapped the towel and dabbed the wound. Mina felt the burn of antiseptic but didn't flinch.

'It doesn't look too deep.'

'No. Fortunately it drove along my hand instead of in.' If it had surely she wouldn't feel so calm. A major injury to her hand would be catastrophe.

Alexei's grip tightened for a second, then eased. Mina frowned, watching him work. A moment later it was all over.

'How does that feel?'

'Fine.' She flexed her hand, discovering she'd stopped shaking as he held her. 'Thank you.'

He didn't move. Beyond the thick shutters, Mina heard the rush of the wind driving against the building. It reminded her of the danger she'd put them both in.

Her heart thudded against her ribs as if trying to fly away on the storm. She drew in another breath, this time through her mouth, trying not to inhale Alexei's spicy scent. The storm seemed to have heightened it rather than washed it away.

'Carissa, I'm sorry. I—'

Mina surged up, stepping sideways, away from him. It felt wrong, hearing him apologise, when she'd been at fault.

It felt even more wrong, hearing him call her by someone else's name. She wanted *her* name on his lips. How crazy was that?

'No. Don't.' She swallowed. He rose and she fixed her eyes on his collarbone. 'I apologise. I was wrong to put you in danger by making you look for me.' She sucked in a shallow breath. 'You're right. A sculpture isn't as important as a person.' If he'd died because of her...

Reluctantly she lifted her eyes and met his deep green gaze. A thrill of recognition and awareness shot down her spine. Strangely, he didn't look angry any more.

'It *was* stupid of me. I thought I had more time. Obviously I underestimated the force and speed of the storm.'

'I applaud your desire to save the sculpture. Just not your timing.' His mouth flattened. 'I shouldn't have spoken the way I did. That was fear talking. But it was no excuse.'

'You were frightened?' Alexei had seemed so in control, so competent, it hadn't entered her mind he was frightened.

'I was frantic. You could have been badly hurt.'

His eyes locked on hers and Mina felt as if she were being pulled under by a jade-green sea, sucked into an undertow where, no matter how she struggled, she couldn't break free.

Or had she forgotten to struggle? She tried to rouse herself from this strange torpor but couldn't.

'I'm tougher than I look.'

Alexei inclined his head. 'So I'm learning. It took guts to do what you did.' His words astounded her.

'And stupidity.' She couldn't let it go.

Something shifted in his expression. 'You thought it important. That made it courageous.'

His words sowed a kernel of heat deep inside. Heat that glowed and spread as he stared down at her.

'Does that mean you don't despise me quite as much as before?' Better to remind them both that they were on opposing sides than be lulled into surrendering her guard any further.

'I don't despise you.' Alexei's voice was gruff as he lifted his hand to wipe the tear tracks from her cheeks. His touch ignited a terrible yearning. Mina had to fight to not lean closer.

'I find that hard to believe.' Mina moved back, breaking contact, injecting hauteur into her expression.

Alexei followed, hemming her in and planting a palm on the wall beside her head. 'You infuriate me. Intrigue me.' His voice dropped to a low note that resonated through her. 'Attract me.'

Mina's pulse thundered as she read the stark determination in his eyes. She struggled to hang on to anger but it slipped like precious water from her hands.

'That's impossible.' It had to be. Because she feared she didn't have the strength to remember they were enemies.

'Then perhaps you'll believe this.' Alexei leaned in and every emotion, every sensation Mina had tried not to feel, exploded into life.

CHAPTER NINE

THE TOUCH OF his lips on hers was gentle yet not tentative. As if he gave her time to adjust to the inevitable.

And it *did* feel inevitable.

As if she'd waited half her life for this. As if the kiss they'd shared on the sand hours ago had evoked a longing that, once roused, couldn't be assuaged or argued away by common sense.

Common sense?

Where was that as Mina curled her fingers around those hard, wet shoulders?

Where was it as his kiss deepened and Mina not only opened for him but slicked her tongue against his, curling, inviting, *demanding* more?

She'd learned a lot from their earlier kiss. It had blasted away the little she'd thought she knew about kissing. Her limited experience hadn't prepared her for Alexei's wholesale takeover of her senses.

He didn't even touch her, except for his lips and tongue, but that was enough to create a sensual storm. Mina was swept away, clinging to his shoulders for support and to prevent him pulling back.

She'd been the one to withdraw last time. His hand on her breast had broken the moment, terrifying her. Not because he'd overstepped the bounds. But because Mina had been overwhelmed by how much she'd wanted more. How reckless he made her.

Stupid. Thoughtless.

The words lost their sting as Alexei's heat swamped her and she felt his body all down hers. He angled his head for better access to her mouth and growled his appreciation as she sucked his tongue hard.

Had she ever heard such a sexy sound? It made her nipples pebble and heat blossom at the apex of her thighs where she felt an achy emptiness.

Mina might have an impulsive streak but in some things she was innately cautious. She'd never given herself to a man. Never been attracted enough to trust someone so intimately. Never been so swept away that it wasn't a matter of *if* but *when* she surrendered.

Alexei made her feel more than she'd thought possible. *That* scared her. He didn't.

Fingers still curled into his shoulder muscles, she turned her head, breaking the kiss. The sound of their ragged breathing filled the air.

'You don't really want me here.' Mina struggled to find an argument that would end this.

'But I need you here.' His words were hot on her sensitised skin, his mouth moving against her cheek in a caress that made her tremble.

'Only as bait to lure him.' She gasped the words, trying to catch her breath. Trying to find the strength to push Alexei away. If she had any self-respect, she'd stop this.

His fingers gripped her chin, inexorably turning her head. Alexei was so close she fell into that malachite gaze.

'He can go to hell. All I can think about is you.' Alexei frowned, his look almost savage, his breathing as uneven as Mina's. 'If you'd been seriously hurt out there…' He shook his head. 'You have no idea how I felt, thinking about that.'

Mina read the echo of her own stark emotions in Alexei's flared nostrils, tight jaw, grim line of mouth and shadowed eyes.

'Believe me, I know.' Mina couldn't hold back the words. 'When I thought about how I'd put you at risk I felt sick.' Alexei's hand softened against her face, palming her cheek, inviting her to turn her head into his touch. She did, luxuriating in the comfort of it, even as it sent a buzz of adrenalin ricocheting through her body. 'It's crazy. I don't even know you—'

'And you don't like me,' he added with a wry tilt of his mouth.

'I don't think this is about liking.' What she felt came from a deep, vital part of herself and it demanded honesty. She was beyond prevarication.

The hint of humour in his expression died. 'Carissa, I—'

'No!' She pressed her fingers to his mouth, desperate to stop his words. Mina couldn't bear for him to call her by her friend's name. Not when she trembled on the brink of something so huge. 'Don't say anything. No more words, please.'

There were lies enough between them. But what she felt, however unexpected, was real. More real than anything she'd felt for any other man.

It had to be just sex. It couldn't be anything more. Yet this felt as unstoppable as sunrise. As wondrous as a child's smile.

She could no more turn her back on this than she could stop the storm outside.

Even if she could, she didn't want to.

It was time.

Instead of smiling, Alexei's expression grew more serious. There was no triumph in his eyes, or greedy anticipation, just a steady regard that told her he felt the same.

Or was she impossibly naive, painting her own wash on circumstances?

Before she could decide, Alexei bent, slid an arm around her back and another behind her legs, and lifted her off the floor. Mina slipped her hands around his neck, torn between dismay at being hoisted high against his hard chest and quivering delight at how strong and sure he felt. How utterly feminine he made her feel.

She'd never ceded control to any man. Had resisted it, she now realised, after seeing so many acquaintances pushed into unwanted, arranged marriages. Her sister included. Now she discovered the delight of being with a man whose physical strength far surpassed hers. Surprisingly she didn't feel vulnerable but treasured.

He carried her out of the bathroom and Mina's pulse quickened as they approached her bed. But Alexei kept going, through the door and down the corridor that formed the spine of the house. Towards the master suite.

The hall was gloomy and the wind sounded like the malevolent howl of the desert djinns her nurse had told her about when she was little. Mina shivered.

'We're safe here.' Alexei must have sensed her thoughts. 'The main house is built to withstand worse than this.' He stopped walking and fixed her with that steady gaze. 'But if you prefer, we could sit this out in the basement storm shelter.'

He was giving her the opportunity to change her mind. One last chance at sanity.

For answer Mina slid her fingers into his wet hair and tugged his head down, pressing her lips to his. She slicked her tongue along his mouth till he opened. Alexei shuddered, then gathered her closer still, his hold so tight he crushed her breathless.

When, finally, he lifted his head, she couldn't hear the wind over the thunder of her blood and Alexei had lost that veneer of calm. She read naked hunger in his dark eyes.

Mina squirmed as arousal coursed through her, coalescing in a sensation like wax melting and softening between her legs.

Then Alexei was striding down the dim hall, eating up the distance to his room.

Fleetingly Mina wondered about mentioning her inexperience, but she shied from anything that might delay or even stop what lay ahead. Besides, instinct had worked fine so far.

Alexei lowered her feet to the floor and switched on a bedside lamp. Mina had an impression of space, of furnishings the colour of parchment with azure accents, then Alexei put his hands on her waist and she had eyes for nothing but him.

His black hair glistened, wet against his skull. Lamplight highlighted the severe, beautiful angle of his cheekbones and threw into relief the stern set of his nose.

Mina's gaze dropped to his mouth, so sensual and generous. Her heart dipped and she felt again the liquid rush of desire.

She swayed closer, grabbing his shirt. Of their own volition her fingers began undoing his buttons. Gone was the deft quickness of a woman who worked with her hands. She fumbled first one, then another, but Alexei didn't help, just stood, still as a breathing statue.

A breathing, hot statue of majestic proportions. Mina finally slid the final button free and pushed her hands between the open edges of his shirt. Damp heat, heavily moulded muscle, the crispness of chest hair, the quick throb of his powerful heartbeat.

A quiver ran through him as she slid her palms over his pectorals to his collarbone, pushing the shirt wide across his shoulders and down his arms. Alexei shrugged and it fell, leaving Mina in possession of a view that stole her breath.

She wanted to sculpt him. She wanted to run her hands over every contour and angle, from the heavy weight of muscle to the masculine symmetry of ribs and hips. She wanted to taste him, to see if he responded to her lips on his body.

'My turn.' Alexei caught her as she leaned closer. She was still processing his words when he tugged her T-shirt up. Obediently Mina lifted her arms and tossed it free.

His gaze dipped to her breasts. Mina felt her nipples harden and, realising her bra was probably transparent when wet, felt heat rise in her throat. Not from embarrassment, but from a cocktail of pride and daring at Alexei's expression. There was glazed heat in his eyes, while his tight mouth and flared nostrils spoke of immense control.

'Not pink?' His voice was hoarse, as if his throat had dried.

To her surprise Mina found herself pushing her shoulders back, inviting him to stare. Was this the same woman who never flaunted herself? Who found male attention more often a nuisance than anything else?

But this was different. With Alexei nothing was as it had been.

'No, not pink.' Her bra and matching knickers were of silk and cobweb lace in dark anthracite grey. The combination of bold colour and soft, exquisitely worked fabric was pure Mina, who'd never chosen a pastel in her life.

'I like it.' His mouth barely moved on the words. 'Take it off.' His voice was as harsh as the sanding block she used to finish a stone sculpture.

Suddenly his eyes were on hers, the cool green no longer cool. Mina felt a judder pass through her, something shared between them. Understanding. Desire. Desperation.

Not allowing time for second thoughts, Mina reached back and unclipped her bra. Her breasts swung free as she tugged it off. A flash of exaltation filled her as she watched Alexei's expression, his sudden swallow, the tension in his jaw.

Alexei might be more experienced, he might be bigger and stronger, but Mina had her own power.

Then a hard palm centred over her nipple, closing gently on her breast, squeezing with just the right amount of pressure, and Mina's self-satisfaction disintegrated.

Something zipped like lightning from her breast to her

womb, leaving a scorched trail. Her knees rocked and for a second she wondered if they'd hold her, till Alexei curled his arm around her waist and pulled her close. Her hips pressed the damp denim of his jeans.

Her breath was a choked moan and his mouth rucked up in a smile that looked as if it bordered on pain.

Still, he worked her breast and Mina felt something vital inside her give and break free. She leaned closer, desperate for more, overwhelmed at the escalating pace of desire.

Alexei pressed his mouth to the side of her neck, near the curve that opened to her shoulder. But instead of kissing, he grazed with his teeth, then nipped gently. Mina jumped as another electric charge passed through her, exacerbating the neediness low in her body. She wriggled against him, desperate for relief.

Her hands went to his jeans, flicking the button undone as if she'd done this so many times before. Then his zip, harder to open because of the erection straining the fabric. Finally she succeeded, inserting her hands between his hips and the fabric, drawing slowly down.

A shudder passed through him, his hold tightening, then the hot length of him sprang free to rest against her.

Mina moulded him with her hands, her touch inquisitive, wondering, testing the fascinating weight and surprising silk-over-steel sensation.

But not for long. Alexei captured her wrists, pulling them away. He muttered something under his breath and stepped back. But before she could protest he shucked his shoes and shoved his jeans down.

Mina had thought his upper body beautiful, his erection arresting. But those thighs, even the carved shape of his knees and, when he turned away from her, the bunch of muscled buttocks... She breathed deep and felt herself quiver and quicken. An artist's response to beauty melded with a woman's need. It was an irresistible combination.

When he turned back from the bedside table, he was rolling on a condom. It was the most erotic thing Mina had ever seen.

She wanted, how she wanted.

But suddenly she couldn't bring herself to move or touch. Her feet were welded to the floor and a curious weakness stole through her. Nerves? Now?

Alexei didn't smile as he flicked open the snap at the top of her shorts. His expression was serious as he tugged the zip down. Mina shifted but not from embarrassment or doubt. She found herself tilting her pelvis towards him, till he cupped her with that big hand and she felt pressure just where she needed it.

So good. She closed her eyes as they rolled back, which meant she didn't see him push the last of her clothes down her legs. When she opened them again he was crouched before her, undoing the tiny buckles on those flimsy pink sandals.

Mina's legs were so wobbly she put her hands on Alexei's shoulders as he slipped off her shoes, then freed her shorts and underwear.

She stood naked before him, primed and ready. Mina felt the moisture between her legs, knew it would help when they came together, yet still Alexei didn't rise. Instead he surprised her by leaning in, dipping his head to the soft curls above her thighs.

Obeying the silent pressure of his hands, Mina moved one leg wider. She heard a grunt of approval, then nothing but a roaring in her ears as he touched his tongue to her. More than touched. Dipped and swirled and probed.

Mina's fingers turned to talons, raking his shoulders. Her knees shook so much she'd have fallen if not for his grip. And then, suddenly, coaxed with a delicacy and precision that spoke of generous expertise, Mina exploded into rapture. Lights blurred behind closed lids, piercing pleasure filled her, so sweet it made her ache and throb, so shocking she felt as if the world collapsed in on itself.

Or maybe that was her. She was no longer standing, but lying on the bed and the soaring, intense orgasm kept going as Alexei pressed his hand where his mouth had been and kissed his way up her stomach and ribs to her breast.

Mina sucked in a desperate gasp. She'd died and gone to paradise. But surely she couldn't take any more delight.

Which proved how innocent she truly was. For Alexei proceeded to illustrate with ease exactly how much more she could enjoy.

Her senses blurred. The only constant was the heat of Alexei naked against her, the tender touch of those hard hands, his scent, sharp and addictive, and the taste of salty skin as she kissed his shoulder, chest, throat, wherever she could reach.

Finally, when she thought she'd go mad with desperation, he gave in to the urging of her hands and restless body and settled between her legs. Mina lifted her knees, wrapping her calves around his waist and linking her ankles. She was so ready, she wouldn't allow any more delay.

Alexei's hot eyes held hers as he tested her then, with one hard thrust, embedded himself deep within.

Mina's breath snared in her throat and for a shocking moment she couldn't get enough oxygen. She read Alexei's puzzlement in that furrowed brow and questioning eyes. But her attention was on her tight lungs and even tighter body. She felt pinned to the bed, fuller than she'd imagined possible. She couldn't move, couldn't possibly—

'Breathe. Slowly, sweetheart.' Alexei's voice infiltrated her stunned brain. His fingers trailed her cheek in a touch that was as delicate as a butterfly wing, so different from the invasive weight of his possession.

Belatedly Mina sucked in air. Relieved, she breathed in and out with him, watching his mouth, watching the flare of his nostrils and matching her efforts to his. Gradually her frantic pulse eased a fraction, the fog in her brain clearing.

Panic subsided and she felt her taut muscles soften. There was no pain. Simply surprise, a sensation that was neither good nor bad.

Alexei moved, beginning to pull back, and despite her reaction a moment before, Mina couldn't bear the thought of him leaving her. This might feel strange but she craved more. She tightened her legs around him, digging her fingers into his shoulders.

'Don't go.'

He shook his head, his wavy black hair flopping endearingly over his brow, making him appear younger, despite the lines of tension etching his features. 'Don't worry, sweetheart. I'm not going far.' Holding her gaze, he withdrew, then, at the last moment thrust forward.

'Oh.' Mina blinked, stunned at the fizz of appreciation his movement stirred.

His smile looked close to a grimace. 'Exactly.' He repeated the movement, this time with a little more force, and the fizz became of zap of arousal.

With each tilt of his hips, each surge towards her, Alexei kept his attention on her, reading her reaction in her expression. As she'd guessed, her body knew what to do, even if she didn't. Already she'd learned to tilt her pelvis to accommodate him. Yet Mina wanted to do more. She wanted to be as generous as he'd been. She wanted to see him lost to the world, floating in rapture.

'What can I do to make it better for you?'

His laugh was a harsh, grating sound. 'Nothing. It's already too good.'

Mina frowned, fighting the urge to acquiesce and simply enjoy the wonderful new sensations. Her knowledge was all theoretical but it gave her a few ideas.

The next time Alexei thrust, she didn't just grip him

with her thighs, but clenched her inner muscles too. She was rewarded with a hoarse gasp that bordered on a groan. Beads of sweat broke out on his brow and he shuddered.

Delighted, Mina tugged at his right hand, lifting it from the bed and clamping it over her breast. It stayed there, moulding and plucking and adding to her pleasure.

Another thrust, another squeeze and this time Mina had to swallow a gasp of delight. Her tactic worked, she could see it in Alexei's febrile, almost vacant stare and the way his fluid movements grew suddenly jerky.

Then he seemed to gather himself. His eyes focused on hers and his mouth opened. 'Car—'

No! Not another woman's name now.

In a flash she reached up and drew his head down, kissing him with all the desperate yearning he'd awakened. Mina sucked his tongue deep into her mouth, palming the back of his head, drawing him closer with her whole body.

Suddenly Alexei's control broke. Hard fingers dug into her buttock as he angled her body higher. He took over the kiss, driving into her mouth as he drove into her body, with a shocking, wonderful synchronicity that pushed her straight over the edge into spasms of ecstasy.

His body was steely hard, his movements convulsive, and the moan of release she swallowed sounded as if it had been drawn from the depths of his soul. Through it all they stayed locked together as one. Each explosion of sensation in one echoed in the other.

Finally, when the last shudders subsided to tiny tremors, Alexei broke their kiss and rolled onto his side, pulling her with him.

Struggling, Mina opened weighted eyelids. That sea of green engulfed her again and this time she didn't mind. She felt weightless and languorous and so very, very good.

No, it was more than that. It felt as if they were one. It

was remarkable, far more fantastic than she'd believed possible. Surely there was some magic involved that made this more than a mere physical act. It felt…momentous.

Slowly she smiled, though even that took too much energy. 'You were right. There's definitely chemistry.'

CHAPTER TEN

ALEXEI STARED INTO those beautiful, sleepy, sherry-brown eyes and didn't know whether to laugh or run for the hills.

Except running wasn't an option. Problems had to be confronted. And no matter how delightful she was in his bed, Carissa Carter was a problem with a capital *P*.

He should be annoyed she hadn't warned him she was a virgin. He should be worried that in her inexperience she could misread great sex for something more. He should be checking the storm shutters and weather warnings. And he definitely should be disposing of the condom.

Alexei stayed exactly where he was, surrounded by firm, silky heat. Her legs around his waist were a perfect fit. His eyes flickered shut as he replayed the moment when she'd gripped him hard, everywhere, and he'd been ready to explode like an untested kid.

Speaking of untested... He opened his eyes and focused on the dreamy smile still lingering on Carissa's lush, reddened mouth. He recalled the taste of her, the hungry, avid kiss that had sent him hurtling over the edge. It made him throb within her and he saw her eyes pop wide.

It surprised him too, the fact that there was a spark of life when he'd spilled himself so completely.

'Are you okay? Are you sore?'

Move. You need to leave her alone.

Yet he couldn't bring himself to do it yet. Not when she was so inviting, clinging as if she never wanted to let him go.

Alexei had never liked post-coital pillow talk. He kept a definite line between sex and friendship, not giving lovers the idea they might be in his life long-term. And still he couldn't bring himself to move.

She shook her head, her dark hair, still damp, sliding around her shoulders and onto the pillow. She wore not a trace of make-up and her only adornment was the pair of tiny, intricate gold earrings she'd worn since she arrived.

Yet she was one of the most alluring women he'd seen. Not a perfect beauty, but then the supposedly perfect beauties he'd known weren't either. The more time Alexei spent with Carissa, the more fascinated he was by the line of her cheekbones, her lush mouth and speaking eyes.

'No, I'm not sore.' She clenched her muscles, gripping him tight, and Alexei felt himself quicken. That should be impossible.

But he was learning to expect the unexpected with Carissa.

'Still, you should have told me I was your first.' The words filled him with a mix of feelings. Privilege. Triumph. And, he was stunned to discover, possessiveness. As if he wanted to lay claim to her.

Carissa shrugged, the movement dragging her breasts teasingly across his torso. Another shimmer of tension arrowed to his groin.

'Maybe. But I was afraid you might stop.'

Did she have any idea what her words did to him? How they encouraged the half-formed lascivious, proprietorial thoughts in his befuddled brain?

'It would have taken much more than that to stop me.' He tried to imagine pulling back and couldn't. As well he hadn't been put to the test. Alexei prided himself on mastery over his animal instincts. But with Carissa that untamed side came to the fore. He was tempted to see how far this gathering arousal could take him, take them.

Witnessing Carissa lose herself so totally, spread before

him like a delectable feast, had been better than anything he remembered for a long time.

Too long. He told himself it had been all work and no play recently. That was why the sex had seemed so preternaturally spectacular.

'But you enjoyed it.' It was couched as a statement but Alexei read the question in her eyes. It was a timely reminder that this was new to her. She had no reference point, no way of knowing that they'd shared something out of the ordinary.

How had that happened? Why had such a sensual woman remained celibate? Alexei had no doubt her responses were genuine, not feigned. She enjoyed sex as much as he did. Her patent enthusiasm had added spice to his pleasure.

Why end her virginity now, with him? Because, like him, she'd been unable to resist the elemental attraction that had sparked since she stepped over his threshold?

No, even before that. Alexei had felt it as she stood, arms akimbo, surveying his house. When she'd stared up at him with such arrogant confidence. He'd never experienced anything like it—so instantaneous and compulsive.

But the question remained, why end her virginity today?

Because it could be a useful negotiating tool?

The thought eddied like a circling shark.

Did she think to convince him to go easy on her father, despite his crime? His mouth tightened. Distrust was hard to shake when it was so ingrained.

'Oh, yes. I definitely enjoyed the sex, Carissa.'

Something passed across her features. Something he couldn't define, but it made heat score her cheeks. Instantly he wished he'd chosen his words more carefully. No matter what her ultimate motivation, she'd been generous with him and deserved the same. He prided himself on being a considerate lover. But even to him, the words had sounded harsh, almost dismissive.

With a stab of self-loathing he stroked her hair back from her face. 'Thank you, Carissa. It was wonderful. *You* were wonderful.'

It was true. What they'd shared was beyond anything he recalled. Was he so jaded it had taken sex with a virgin to turn him on?

No, the truth lay elsewhere. It was something about Carissa and the way she made him feel. She was different. Enticing and provoking and more besides. Alexei breathed deep, drawing in her evocative spice-and-cinnamon scent. He could easily become addicted to it. To her.

Lightly he grazed the base of her neck with his teeth. Carissa shivered and clutched at him.

Alexei closed his eyes, savouring her responsiveness and the prospect of more voluptuous pleasure. It would be a simple thing to coax her into more. As he thought it, he recognised the tightening in his groin. He could stay here and sate himself. She was willing. He felt it in the way she arched into him, and in her quickened heartbeat that throbbed against his chest.

Yet he couldn't do it.

He was the experienced one. He was the one who'd initiated this. It was up to him to act responsibly. To be considerate.

Dispose of the condom. Let her rest. All sensible, but it was difficult to make his body obey his brain.

With one last open-mouthed kiss on her satiny flesh, Alexei sighed and pulled back. He gritted his teeth, for in his semi-aroused state the friction was a powerful inducement to stay where he was. As were Carissa's limbs around his body.

'Must you go?'

He opened his eyes to find her watching him with an expression of such disappointment he knew he'd been right. Staying here, luxuriating in her sensuality would be a mistake. It would probably leave her aching. Plus it might convince her this was more than an act of simple physical intimacy. That she should expect more than he was willing to give.

Alexei grabbed her wrists from behind his neck and drew them down between their bodies. Her soft breasts and plum-coloured nipples brushed his hands, diverting him as erotic energy zapped through him.

He was crazy, denying himself. It was clear from her hitched breath and dilated eyes that Carissa wanted more.

But his conscience wouldn't let him stay. She'd change her mind if he made her chafed and sore.

'Be honest with me. Did I hurt you?'

She shook her head. 'No. It felt…odd but not painful.'

'Odd?' His brows drew together and she laughed, a rich chuckle that reminded him of melted chocolate and sunshine.

'Unusual. But good. Very, very good.' Her smile was two parts sultry seductress and one part carefree woman.

Alexei was intrigued by the latter. It struck him that he wanted to learn about that woman, discover what made her tick. He couldn't meld her in his mind with a conniving accomplice to theft he'd imagined.

'Good. That gives us something to aim for next time.'

Her smile lit her face. 'There'll be a next time?'

'Oh, yes.' Alexei wasn't strong enough to abstain permanently.

He lifted one of her hands and kissed it, starting on the back of her hand and working his way around her wrist, where her pulse fluttered wildly, to her palm. He licked it slowly, savouring, and watched her shiver.

'I want it to be soon,' she whispered. Her eyes were sultry and enticing. Alexei had to force himself to move away.

'As soon as you've rested.'

'I'm not tired!'

Was that a pout? Heaven help him—that mouth tempted him to forget good intentions.

'Perhaps *I* am.' It was a fabrication but better than telling her he acted for her own good. She hated any hint he had power over her. Except when he'd had her beneath him.

Her gaze shifted down his body and his erection stirred. 'You don't *look* tired.'

Alexei muffled a bark of laughter. She was right. He felt energised.

He should simply get up and leave her to rest, but that was beyond his powers. What he needed was a distraction. 'How's your hand?' He angled it to inspect the bandage.

'I can't feel any pain.'

Alexei darted a glance at her. It would probably hurt later when the endorphins faded. It was a nasty gash. But then, he'd realised as he treated her, she'd had a few accidents in the past.

He slid his thumb over the fine skin at the back of her hand, seeing two tiny scars, faded now. And on the palm some rougher patches, as if it had seen work instead of simply lotions and manicures.

Alexei turned her hand over again, considering the supple strength in those slim fingers, the lack of jewellery, the short nails.

Why hadn't he noticed? This wasn't the hand of a pampered socialite.

'What sort of art do you do?'

It was only because he held her that he noticed her flinch. It was momentary, so brief he almost thought he was mistaken. But now her hand was stiff, not relaxed. His curiosity deepened.

'All sorts of things. Drawing, oils, sculpting, even some pottery.'

His sixth sense stirred. She was being evasive. Why?

'Surely you specialise in one? Don't successful artists focus their energies?'

Mina read the acuteness in Alexei's gaze and wondered at his instinct for pinpointing vulnerability. It was as if he knew exactly what to ask to uncover the truth. Carissa was a successful graphic artist but Mina's expertise and passion lay in sculpture.

No wonder he was such a successful businessman with that uncannily accurate instinct. Or was it a fluke? Was she overreacting?

In the distance she heard the furious rush of the storm. It echoed the abrupt warning clamour surging within her.

Mina told herself it was just as well she was no longer crammed up so close against him he might feel her response to his words. Even so she was still desperate for his caresses, for more of the glory they'd shared. That had challenged her preconceptions about him and made her wonder if Alexei was someone more than simply a demanding tycoon, used to getting his way.

Or was that her bias? The virgin fixating on the man who'd introduced her to sex? Because what she'd experienced with Alexei had felt almost transcendental, as if they'd achieved a union that was unique and precious.

Her thoughts were in turmoil, her emotions all over the place. She was in danger of letting feelings cloud her judgement. But, oh, how she wanted to bask in what Alexei made her feel!

'Carissa?'

'Sorry. Yes, artists do tend to specialise.'

What harm was there, telling him about her work? Remarkably, this was the man who hadn't bothered to look at Carissa's photo before bringing her here. If he wasn't interested enough to do that, he wouldn't have checked out her work.

It was a startling reminder that, despite the intimacy of the moment, they were still opponents in a dangerous game. That left a sour tang on Mina's tongue and an ache in her middle.

It grew harder and harder to reconcile that imperious tycoon with the man lying naked beside her.

'And your specialty?'

Mina hesitated, then took the plunge. She was finding some success but it wasn't as if her work was well known. Soon, hopefully. 'I sculpt.'

'*Now* it makes sense.' His rueful smile made her heart hammer and warmth unfurl inside. It was as if they shared a private joke. Mina realised she wanted more of this. More of Alexei's warmth and understanding.

'Saving the sail sculpture? It's a masterpiece. I couldn't leave it.'

He nodded. 'Of course not. I see that now.' His tone held no rancour, just understanding. Why not? It was obvious the man loved sculpture too. The pieces scattered through his home were superb.

'I was working in Paris on ideas for something similar, but with stylised birds' wings that will move, propelled by the wind. It's far more difficult than you'd imagine.' If she could bring it off it would be perfect for Jeirut's first royal art exhibition. Mina had promised Ghizlan she'd contribute something special and she could imagine the piece at the Palace of the Winds.

'I'd like to see that.'

'I've got drawings…' Mina closed her mouth over her eager response as doubt welled. What else was in her current sketchbook? Anything that would give away her true identity?

'I'd be fascinated to see them.'

Slowly Mina nodded. She'd like to show him and hear his thoughts. She suspected his response would be informed but honest.

'I'll check to see if I have them with me,' she said finally. Mina looked away, hating the dishonesty of her situation. She had the strongest desire to strip away the lies. To know him properly and have him know her.

She wanted…more.

Except Carissa relied on her.

Mina swallowed, bitterness filling her mouth.

'Are you sure you're okay, Carissa?'

She suppressed a shiver. Even being called by her friend's name felt wrong.

'Of course.' Mina darted a glance towards him, but didn't quite meet his eyes. 'Maybe you're right. I think I need a rest after all.'

It was another lie. For Mina felt sparking with life and eager for more of Alexei's loving. What did that say about her? She'd known the man mere days!

She knew so little about him. Except that he felt deeply. That he abhorred cheats, was impatient yet surprisingly kind, determined, outrageous and used to getting his own way. That when he made love to her she felt as if she could fly and that everything in the world was bright and fresh. When she was with Alexei everything was more intense.

With him she had the strangest feeling she could be more herself than she could with anyone else. And that wasn't just about sex. The realisation was disquieting.

'I'll leave you to rest.' He rose and Mina had to clench her hands rather than reach out and draw him back.

She missed the warmth of Alexei's powerful body and the feeling of oneness. She wanted to see that smile in his eyes and bask in that wonderment again.

'Okay?' His hand brushed her cheek and delight coursed

through her. Such a simple gesture, yet it affected her profoundly.

When had she let anyone close? Mina had spent so long hoarding her emotions to herself, first as self-protection, then because she'd focused on achieving her dream. Only Carissa had suspected Mina's air of assurance and practicality masked innate loneliness.

Mina looked up into Alexei's alert green gaze and her chest pinched tight.

'Yes, I'm okay.' And she was. Despite the circumstances, despite the lies between them that she so wanted to obliterate. In this, she reminded herself, she had no choice...yet. But soon she'd be free to explain. 'Just tired.' And suddenly that too was true. Mina stifled a cracking yawn.

'Sleep then, lover. I'll be back later.'

Mina settled her head on the pillow and watched him go, hearing that *lover* as an echo that refused to die.

Tall, shoulders back, he sauntered towards the bathroom with the grace of an athlete utterly at home in his skin. What exercise did he do to keep so fit?

Her gaze traced the curving sweep of his spine, the tight bunch of his backside, the powerful, well-formed legs.

Mina wanted to sculpt him. Almost as much as she wanted to run her hands over all that warm, muscled flesh.

Her last thought before sleep took her was that she enjoyed being with Alexei Katsaros. Too much.

Alexei checked the house, the generator and the radio. The storm had hit quickly but was even now easing. The forecast predicted it would pass over soon.

Yet all the time he busied himself with what had to be done, his thoughts tracked back to Carissa. How she'd felt in his arms, in his bed, her body yielding and soft yet strong. Her slick heat driving him out of his mind. And those little growls of pleasure she gave. The memory sent a judder of longing through him.

Which was why he spent as much time as he could away from the bedroom. He knew next to nothing about virgins. There hadn't been many in the rough streets where he'd grown up. But common sense dictated he should let her sleep.

Yet an hour later he was back in his room, staring down at the woman who'd turned his life upside down in a mere couple of days. Unbelievable that it was such a short time. It felt as if she'd been in his world much longer.

He drew a steadying breath and shoved his hands in his pockets as he surveyed her, sprawled across his bed. In the lamplight her glossy, dark hair splayed around her shoulders and her lithe, gold-toned body was a masterpiece, more alluring than any work of art.

Alexei was surprised at the depth of his desire to possess her. Not just possess her body, as he fully intended to when she woke, but to claim this woman as… What? His mistress? Carter's daughter shouldn't be for him.

Yet, when he was with her, it wasn't her father's wrongdoing that came to mind. It was the tug of something else that drew him inexorably. Desire. Attraction. Curiosity. Appreciation that she gave as good as she got. And for her humour, her unpretentious attitude, the way she'd developed a bond of friendship with Marie and Henri so quickly.

So much about her intrigued.

She mumbled and rolled over. Alexei's thoughts frayed as he watched those tip-tilted breasts jiggle. The curve from breasts to narrow waist, then out to her hip was so sweet it stole his breath. One slim leg slid over the other, almost hiding that V of dark hair. The memory of their coupling, of her virginal tightness and shocked ecstasy, created a jolt of triumph so strong it flattened his good intentions. She'd been delectable, so charmingly enthusiastic.

Alexei's resolve disintegrated as a wave of need slammed into him. He'd done his best, he told himself as he reefed his shirt up. He really had, he assured himself as he reached for the box of condoms in the bedside table.

But he was a man, not a saint.

Minutes later he gathered her to him, his chest against her back, his legs curved into hers from behind, the burning heat of his groin hard against the sweet curve of her rump.

'Alexei?' She turned her head, her hair falling back against his chest, a sliding silk curtain that tickled and aroused.

'Yes?' He slid his hand around to cup her breast. Immediately her nipple puckered, hard against his palm. The tension in his lower body screwed another notch tighter.

'I'm glad you're here.' She sounded breathless.

'So am I.' He bumped his groin against her and felt her chuckle resonate through him. Her hand covered his, pressing down as she arched into his touch.

'Are we going to have sex again now?'

Her words sent a flurry of need rushing through him. 'If you're not sore.' If she was he'd have to be inventive. He was definitely up to that challenge.

'I'm not.' She turned, trying to roll towards him but Alexei held her where she was. 'Don't you want to be on top?'

The question reminded him how inexperienced she was. That he was the first man she'd been with. This time the surge of erotic excitement was so profound it threatened to blow the back off his skull. Or make him come before he was ready. Her soft, warm flesh against him was almost too good.

'There are other ways,' he murmured and bit her neck. She sighed and angled her head to give him better access. Alexei released her breast and arrowed his hand down past her ribs, her belly, to her hidden core. He found her slick and hot, unmistakeably ready. His erection throbbed needily and Carissa pushed back against him.

'Show me,' she demanded, fingers stroking along his arm, then back up, sending shivers across his flesh to coalesce at his nape and groin. He liked her bold acceptance of pleasure.

Alexei inserted one knee between hers, opening her legs a little. He nudged between her thighs, positioning himself.

'You don't have to do anything but, if you like, in a minute you can push back when I…'

His words died as he thrust forward, slowly at first. But then she wriggled, taking him deeper with a sexy little shimmy of her hips and Alexei found himself bucking hard and strong, as deep as he could go.

Behind his closed lids stars burst. So good. It felt so unbelievably good that it took a second to realise Carissa had gone rigid in his arms.

Was he too much? Had he hurt her? Heart pounding, Alexei began to withdraw, silently cursing. He should have taken more time, pleasured her more.

Her hand clamped the back of his upper thigh like a talon.

'Don't!'

'Carissa?' He frowned, disorientated by the contradiction of her sharp voice and the clench of her inner muscles that threatened to destroy the last vestiges of thought.

For answer she drove back against him, impaling herself. 'That feels…'

'What?' For the life of him he couldn't move away. His hand circled her hip, then crept up to her breast. Her breath caught. 'How does it feel?'

'Wonderful,' she whispered. 'So wonderful.'

And that, to Alexei's amazement, was all it took for him to feel the fierce rush of power as a climax tore through him. He barely had time to ease back and surge again, right to the heart of her, and hear her laugh of shocked pleasure. Then the madness was upon him, fire in his blood, a roaring shout of ecstasy and the hard pump of him spilling into her beautiful body.

It took a long time to come down from the high. Aftershocks rocked him, setting off Carissa's orgasm, which in turned drove him on a desperate, slowly diminishing cycle of delight.

Finally, what seemed a lifetime later, he slumped against her, head in the curve of her neck, arms encircling her as if to prevent her leaving. Dazed, Alexei realised he didn't have enough energy even to pull away and lie on his back. His body was locked with hers and there it would stay.

'I think…' Her words were so faint they were a shadow of sound.

'Yes?' Alexei struggled to focus.

'I think I could get addicted to this.'

His mouth curved against the satiny skin of her neck. He knew the feeling. Sex with Carissa Carter was either the best idea he'd ever had or the worst mistake of his life.

CHAPTER ELEVEN

MINA STRETCHED, BLINKING, and surfaced from one of the deepest sleeps of her life. She felt wonderful, apart from a little tenderness. When she recalled why she was tender, she smiled. So this was what all the fuss was about!

Being with Alexei was unlike anything she'd imagined. Better. Wonderful. She felt...different.

She rolled over to find the storm shutters open. Beyond the windows was the vivid blaze of green foliage, scarlet flowers and turquoise water. A songbird trilled and the hush of waves on sand proved yesterday's maelstrom was over.

How long had she slept? Long enough for Alexei to be up and about.

Cravenly she wished he hadn't gone. If she'd woken wrapped around him, she wouldn't have a chance to think. She'd be too busy exploring *him*. Carnal excitement filled her.

In his absence thoughts crammed her head, vying for supremacy over her feeling of contentment.

With a sigh she stuffed pillows behind her and sat up. The fine linen sheets felt heavy over her sensitised skin, grazing her nipples as she tucked the fabric under her arms. Making her remember last night in delicious detail.

If Alexei walked in now, she'd fling the sheet aside and indulge in her new favourite pastime. Sex.

Except, what they'd shared seemed much more than a mere physical coupling. It had felt...

Mina shook her head, her hair sliding around her shoulders. Whatever it had felt like, it had to stop.

She caught her lip between her teeth. It would be easy to tell herself she wasn't thinking straight after such mind-boggling pleasure but she couldn't escape her conscience. Responsibility, doing right, had been drummed into her from childhood.

Despite what her eager body urged, it wasn't right to sleep with Alexei while he believed her to be someone else!

A selfish part of her wanted to thrust that aside. After all, he'd given Carissa no choice. He deserved whatever he got for his high-handed actions. And yet... Even in so short a time, she knew he was far more complex than the bogeyman they'd made him into. For one thing, Carissa's father had stolen from him, on a large scale. Who wouldn't be irate in the circumstances? Alexei was a victim of crime and deserved sympathy, not more treachery.

Besides, this wasn't a question of Alexei's culpability but hers. This masquerade didn't sit well with Mina's conscience. True, she did it for the best reasons, but it was still a lie. It was one thing to be swept off her feet in heightened passion and not reveal the truth. It was another to share Alexei's bed while duping him. She'd feel cheap and tainted, prolonging that lie while they were physically intimate.

Mina hugged herself as a chill enveloped her. She wanted to be selfish and have more of what she'd had last night.

But she couldn't, not without telling Alexei who she was.

Her conscience urged her to find Alexei and reveal the truth. Surely he'd understand. He wouldn't insist on dragging Carissa into this.

Then she remembered his fury when he'd spoken of Carissa's father. That adamantine set of Alexei's jaw as he'd spoken of retribution. A chill spread through her like mountain frost. Mina hoped he'd change his mind but she couldn't guarantee it. There was a chance he'd go through with his plans for Carissa.

Nausea swirled in her stomach and bile rose in her throat at the idea of Alexei with Carissa. *Marrying* her.

She wanted to scream that it wasn't possible. He wouldn't do that, not now, he'd more or less admitted that had been a ploy to get her here. But there were no guarantees. Alexei was a powerful man used to getting what he wanted.

She couldn't risk it. Carissa had pleaded for another couple of days. If Mina revealed the truth now Alexei might still use her friend as a pawn. Mina hated to think it but she had to face facts.

Which left her lusting for a man she couldn't fully trust. Lying to a man she liked more than she'd expected. Yearning for—

Mina thrust aside the sheet and scrambled out of bed. Two things were clear. She couldn't tell Alexei who she was until she knew Carissa was safe with Pierre. And in the meantime, honour demanded Mina didn't sleep with Alexei again.

'Alexei?'

He looked up from the tray he was filling and saw her framed in the kitchen doorway. His heart did a crazy somersault.

She wore a miniskirt the colour of ripe watermelon and a sleeveless white shirt that tied at the waist, emphasising her slenderness. There was plenty of honey-toned skin on display but it was her hair, a dark cloud around her shoulders, and her glowing eyes, that captivated.

Heat scudded through him. Desire. Satisfaction.

He'd had her all night but that hadn't sated his need.

She was delectable. A mix of hesitant, innocent and wanton sensualist.

'You should have stayed in bed. I was bringing brunch.' Then Alexei registered the stiff way she held herself. 'Are you okay?' He was across the room in an instant, taking her hands. 'Tell me.' Uncharacteristically, Alexei felt anxious. He told himself women lost their virginities all the time.

She swallowed and his eyes tracked the movement, senses alert. Especially when he realised she hadn't yet looked directly at him.

As he thought it, she raised her eyes, her expression serious. His gut tightened.

'I realised I never told you I'm sorry about the theft. About…my father's actions.' She grimaced. 'I didn't really think about the impact on your business. Is it a complete disaster? Will the company recover?'

Days ago Alexei would have been astounded to feel relief at her words. Yet that was what flooded him. Carissa was okay; she wasn't hurt. Or having second thoughts.

He brushed his thumbs over her wrists. 'Thank you.' Strange how something as simple as her concern, and her apology, acted as a salve on the raw wound to his pride. Because he hadn't seen the betrayal coming. Because despite excellent systems, his enterprise had still been vulnerable. 'It's…manageable.'

The theft caused major problems but not enough to destabilise the company, if handled carefully.

'Manageable?' She tilted her head, trying to read him. 'Is that code? He hasn't bankrupted you, has he?' No missing her sharp note of worry.

Alexei felt her tremble, saw her features pale. For once Carissa's thoughts were easy to read. Horror and distress.

'No, nothing like that.' He squeezed her hands. 'The company wasn't that vulnerable.'

'Good.' She nodded. 'I'm glad.'

The words were simple but he knew her well enough to realise her sentiments were genuine. Had he really believed she'd connived with her father? Watching her now, it was hard to credit. Her concern and sincerity, clear in her eyes and taut body as well as her words, made a mockery of his doubts. She might not want to betray her father but she was innocent of his crimes.

Belatedly it hit him how difficult this had been for her.

'I've put you in a tough situation.' The words emerged without thinking. It was too late to regret his actions, especially since he couldn't regret having her here with him. But given his time over, Alexei would have taken a different approach.

Those brown eyes widened in shock. Then she lifted one shoulder. 'I've survived worse.'

She made light of it but suddenly Alexei couldn't. He felt wrong-footed. 'I acted rashly. For that I'm sorry. I assumed you knew about the theft.' When her eyes widened, he shook his head. 'My default position is not to trust anyone. I learned long ago it was safer than being disappointed.'

Even Alexei was surprised by the admission. He never explained himself. But in this case, he knew he owed her an apology.

Carissa's hands grasped his. 'Could we, maybe, put all that aside for a little?'

She looked so earnest he had to smile. Especially since, after giving an apology, Alexei wasn't quite sure where to go next. This was unfamiliar territory.

'With pleasure.' He brushed the fall of long hair off her shoulder and wrapped his other arm around her waist, tugging her close. 'I'm sure we can find something else to concentrate on.' He was leaning in to kiss her when a palm on his chest stopped him.

Carissa was staring at his collarbone, not his face. High colour flagged her cheeks.

'About that,' she said to his shirt. 'We need to take a raincheck.'

Alexei frowned. He couldn't believe it, especially as she arched sinuously against him. He could tell when a woman wanted him and Carissa did, without doubt. 'Sorry? You don't want to have sex with me?'

Her crack of laughter unlocked something tight that had

formed in his chest. She shook her head. 'You're so sure of yourself.'

'With good reason.' His hand wandered lower, to the hem of her miniskirt. She stiffened.

'The fact is, I can't. I...' She lifted her face and met his eyes with an unblinking stare. 'I've got my period.'

Disappointment seared him. It was so savage it felt like pain. Alexei opened his mouth to suggest there were ways they could, but seeing her blush deepen, recalling she'd been a virgin yesterday, he shut it again.

He dragged in a slow breath. 'I won't say I'm not disappointed. But I've survived worse.'

When she registered the echo of her own words, Carissa grinned. Suddenly she looked more like the vibrant, confident woman he knew. A weight he hadn't registered lifted from his chest. Alexei slung his arm around her shoulder and turned towards the tray he'd prepared.

'Things will seem brighter after we've eaten.'

If only food could cure sexual frustration. Because the next few days would surely test him to the limit.

'For someone who's never been on a boat you look right at home.' Alexei's voice stirred Mina from her reverie. She looked across the dinghy's bench seat to find him watching speculatively.

Three days ago his questioning stare would have made her wary, consumed with worry that he'd unmask her, for, unlike Carissa, she'd grown up in a desert kingdom with no experience of the sea. But a lot had changed. By mutual consent they didn't speak about business or revenge or the future. They existed totally in the present.

Their relationship was fragile. It could only last until the outside world intruded. But for the first time in her life it was enough just to *be*.

To be with him.

All her life, she'd strived to live up to others' expectations. First to meet her father's impossible demands. Then, finding a niche in the competitive art world, working harder than her peers to prove she hadn't achieved her initial success because of her connections.

Being with Alexei was like breathing fresh air after stale. Even though they weren't physically intimate since her lie about her period—the only way she could think of to keep him at arm's length—to her amazement he hadn't shown annoyance or frustration.

Alexei made her feel good about herself. Not because of her royal status, but because...

Because he genuinely liked her? The thought was tempting. But she couldn't afford to dwell on it. She adjusted her wide-brimmed hat.

'I'm adaptable,' she murmured, taking in the crystalline ocean and white beach. 'Besides, the view is fantastic.'

'It sure is.' Heat simmered in his dark jade stare and Mina felt the familiar tickle of awareness. It began in the soles of her feet, climbing up her legs to swirl and intensify between her thighs, then rise, via her breasts to her throat where her breath caught.

Every time Alexei watched her she felt that same drag of muscles, the quickening, the eagerness. The sensations grew stronger with each day they spent together.

Henri and Marie hadn't returned, their boat damaged in the storm, which had hit the main island badly. They could have returned by Alexei's helicopter but it was busy on relief work and Alexei and Mina were more than able to look after themselves while the others waited for repairs.

'When you invited me out on your boat I'd pictured a massive cruiser. But this suits you better.' Her gaze drifted over his open shirt, cotton shorts and strongly muscled legs. Her pulse revved pleasantly.

Alexei shrugged, his expression wickedly knowing. 'I

prefer something a little laid-back unless I have to entertain for business.'

'I can relate to that.' Mina extended one bare leg and wriggled her toes in the sunshine. How fabulous to be free of the formal clothes appropriate to the royal court. That was something she hadn't missed in France.

'You don't like dressing up?'

'I prefer comfort.' Carissa's clothes might not be her style, but at least they included shorts and summer skirts rather than evening gowns and high heels.

Alexei reached out and stroked his finger across the arch of her foot, then up to her ankle and calf.

Mina shivered. His touch evoked a memory of his loving. It had been days now and abstinence was tough, tougher than she'd imagined.

'I can imagine you in some glamorous outfit. You'd look spectacular.'

Mina smiled. The deep timbre of his voice told her he meant every word. 'Why, thank you. I'm sure you clean up pretty well too.' He'd look stunning in formal clothes. Her insides clenched just thinking about it.

She hesitated on the brink of suggesting they go out one night in the future, he in a tuxedo, she in something slinky and feminine. Except that would mean a date and that was impossible. Once the truth came out Mina wouldn't see him again.

A sudden tightness in her chest stole her breath.

This interlude was a snatched moment out of their real lives. Neither were interested in long-term relationships. Mina had a career to build. She couldn't afford distractions. And Alexei…

'What are you thinking?'

Mina became aware of Alexei's hand, warm on her knee, of his quizzical stare fixed on her face. Regret pierced her. She wanted what they shared to last longer than a few days.

Underlying regret was surprise that Alexei understood her well enough to read her expression. Mina had spent years keeping her emotions private. She was an expert. Discovering a man who saw beyond her projected calm and sensed her disquiet should make her feel vulnerable. Yet Mina felt a thrill of excitement that Alexei was so attuned to her emotions. As if she mattered.

What did he read in her face?

Surely not her foolish longing for what could never be.

'I'm thinking you should grab that fishing line. I saw it move.'

Alexei muttered something beneath his breath and grabbed the neglected reel.

It had surprised her that he hadn't produced sleek, professional-looking fishing rods. Yet these battered hand reels, like the unpretentious boat, seemed as right for Alexei as his architect-designed home and priceless art.

He was a man who couldn't be labelled and stuck in a box. She wanted to find out more, discover what made him tick. But she resisted the temptation to pry. It could lead to places she couldn't go.

'Have you got a fish?' She leaned forward, fascinated by his sudden alertness.

'Could be.' He held the line in one sinewy hand, his attention on the water.

Mina peered over the side but couldn't see anything.

Alexei felt the tug on the line and began to reel it in.

There'd be fresh fish for dinner. Not that there was any danger of starving. Marie's well-stocked kitchen would keep them till she came back with supplies.

Strangely the thought of having company, even Marie and Henri, who were friends as much as employees, didn't appeal. He wanted more time alone with Carissa.

When she wasn't driving him to distraction with sexual

frustration she was surprisingly restful company. She didn't pry or quiz him about his private life, yet Alexei had found himself talking far more than usual.

They'd discussed music and art and found more areas where their tastes overlapped than where they'd diverged. They'd discovered a shared passion for football, which made Alexei reassess his unconscious sexism. When, in the past, had he discussed sport with a lover? He'd assumed women weren't interested.

A chance comment about doing business across continents led to a discussion about the global economy and international trade. Alexei again realised he'd underestimated Carissa.

He felt ashamed that he'd been so shallow. Carissa was unique and she clearly hadn't been coached by her father. They'd veered into areas he knew were beyond Carter's expertise. Besides, Carissa had been distracted at the time, cooking. She'd got so caught up in their discussion she'd forgotten the food, till Alexei salvaged it.

She'd shrugged and admitted she wasn't much of a cook. Then she'd described her one attempt to bake a soufflé and the disastrous result. Carissa's laughter had wrapped around him like warm silk as her eyes lit at the memory.

Now she looked like an excited kid.

It hit Alexei that if she'd never been in a boat, she'd probably never caught a fish. The thought snagged.

His childhood had been short on fun experiences after his stepfather got his feet under their table. But Alexei had one precious memory of his father teaching him to fish.

He recalled the sun on his face and the breeze off the water, and the scent of baking as his mother laid out a picnic on a blanket. Alexei remembered walking to her, one hand in his dad's big, sure grasp and the other holding up the fish he'd caught. He'd been so proud, so secure, so innocent that he'd taken everything he had for granted.

It was his final happy memory before the dark days.

'Here.' He gave Carissa the line. 'You do it.'

The excitement in her eyes hit him like a shot of liquor.

'I can feel it!' She reeled in, carefully at first, then with more confidence. 'There it is!'

Silver flashed near the water's surface but it was Carissa, animated and happy, that captured his attention. Belatedly he grabbed a scoop net and secured the fish as she brought it in.

'It's on the small side, isn't it?'

He saw her gnaw her bottom lip. Her forehead creased as if she were unhappy. Carissa's frown deepened as the fish struggled. It seemed she had a soft heart.

'Not the biggest I've seen.' He paused, watching her. 'It's almost too small to keep.' It was a reasonable size, but Carissa was already nodding.

'Can we let it go? Give it a chance to grow? I read fish stocks are dropping because the population doesn't get a chance to reproduce.'

'*That's* why you want to let it go?'

'Well...' She shrugged. 'I liked the thrill of catching it but we're not desperate for food. I could make a salad and there's plenty of other stuff to cook.'

Alexei nodded and unhooked the fish, then put it over the side. A second later it wriggled out of his hand and away. Carissa's beaming grin as she watched was worth it.

'Thank you, Alexei.'

'No problem. Especially since you've offered to cook.' He paused and tilted his head to one side. 'I know. How about you make us a nice cheese soufflé?'

He ducked and grabbed her wrist as she swept off her sunhat and batted him with it. Then, catching her off balance, he dragged her onto his lap. The boat rocked wildly.

'That was a low blow. Just because I'm not a good cook.' She pouted but her eyes sparkled.

'But look what it got me. Who wants a fish when they can have a mermaid?'

Alexei slipped his hand behind her head and pulled out the pin securing her dark hair. He'd become adept at that. Carissa began the day by brushing her hair and securing it back from her face but Alexei preferred it loose.

His breath huffed out in satisfaction as he threaded the satiny locks through his fingers. Then he stroked lower, down her side to the couple of inches of warm, golden flesh showing between her pink shorts and cropped, polka-dotted shirt.

Carissa shivered and he saw the hard points of her nipples rise against the thin fabric. She stilled, looking up at him with a sultry, heavy-lidded look before she caught herself and tried to pull away. 'You know we can't—'

'I know. Kisses only.' Knowing she wanted him as much as he wanted her was strangely satisfying. Even though holding her and knowing he couldn't have her was an exercise in sexual frustration.

Alexei pulled her closer. He heard a splash but focused instead on that wide, delectable mouth.

'Alexei?' Carissa struggled to sit up. 'I think that was the net going over the side. Alexei?'

'Leave it.' He hauled her closer, hand splaying low on her hip. 'I've got more important things on my mind.'

Their gazes collided. A shower of sparks rained down, peppering his body with pinpricks of fire. Her expression changed and in one swift move she grabbed his shirt and tugged his face down to hers.

Alexei covered her lips with his and felt her open up. Despite the turmoil of thwarted lust, he had no desire to pull back. He couldn't recall ever feeling so…light, so unencumbered by life's burdens.

Since childhood he'd been focused on the need to survive, to succeed, to secure his place in the world. With previous lovers there'd always been a part of him that wasn't engaged. That focused on business or fending off unwanted expectations.

With Carissa, he simply enjoyed the moment. He felt just plain happy. It was a revelation.

CHAPTER TWELVE

'WHEN DID YOU know you wanted to be an artist?' Alexei watched as Carissa's sketch took shape. A couple of swift strokes and there was the outline of his hands. Another and the hint of a wrist appeared.

Watching her work, as he had these last days, left Alexei in no doubt Carissa really *was* an artist, not a spoiled daddy's girl playing at being something she wasn't.

She didn't look up. 'I never consciously decided. It's just me. I was always interested in art.'

'So your father organised for you to attend classes?'

Strange how the mention of Ralph Carter didn't make him feel that heavy twist in the gut it had before. The anger remained, and indignation, but not the seething sense of urgency. The investigator had a lead on Carter in Switzerland, but for once Alexei wasn't impatient to confront the man. That would come.

Alexei had other things to occupy him.

Carissa's brow knotted as she rubbed out a couple of lines and replaced them with others more to her liking.

'Sorry?'

'You had art lessons as a child?'

She snorted. 'I wish. I was self-taught till I went to art school. I'd have loved to have learned sooner. I couldn't even take art at high school. My father didn't approve.'

'He didn't?'

Carissa shook her head and a tendril of hair escaped her severely pulled-back hairstyle. It flirted over her collarbone as if inviting his attention to the tight white top clinging to her breasts.

Her clothes reminded him that she wasn't as Alexei

had first assumed. Instead of glamorous designer outfits from expensive shopping sprees, she favoured shorts and skirts, skimpy and incredibly sexy. And that black outfit, the leggings and loose T-shirt that didn't fit with the rest yet seemed right for a woman so obviously comfortable with her body and uninterested in primping.

Carissa didn't need fancy clothes to hold his attention. She was sexy, vehement, impulsive and had a mischievous sense of humour. She was full of energy and surprising depths.

And he wanted her more than he'd wanted anyone or anything in a long, long time. Perhaps ever.

Acknowledging it made something inside him still. As if the treadmill of his world, driving him on and on, paused, allowing him to take stock.

It was a strange sensation. As if he were an onlooker to his own life, his wants and needs.

And the result of that self-examination? The realisation that, after a lifetime of self-reliance, he wanted more. The laughter and sharing, the warmth of having someone special.

The revelation stopped Alexei's breath, crushed his lungs and made his heart thunder.

Share his life?

It shouldn't be a surprise. He had the example of his parents' loving partnership. Days ago he'd begun toying with the idea of finding someone to start a family with. But now the idea wasn't abstract. It wasn't a theoretical, faceless woman who came to mind.

It was one specific woman. One spirited, restful, infuriating, generous woman. A woman about whom he knew so little, yet felt he knew everything important.

Not that this was *love*.

Alexei wouldn't fall victim to sentimentality. But Carissa and he shared more than sex. They'd exercised abstinence for days and he grew more, rather than less, interested. This warmth, respect and liking could form the foundation of a solid relationship.

Instead of rejecting the idea, he felt a quiver of anticipation. It was like the moment he'd realised his first software innovation really worked. That it had the makings of a runaway commercial success. He was a loner but deep down he'd always wanted more than solitude.

Alexei waited for common sense to kick in and object that he'd known Carissa just a week.

It stayed silent.

And all the while the effervescence in his blood signalled he was onto a winning idea.

He always trusted his instincts.

He stared at Carissa, absorbed in her drawing. She never tried to charm or flatter. It was refreshing not to be fussed over, to be treated as an equal, or, Alexei realised with a silent huff of laughter, as an inanimate object to be sketched. But he knew one touch, one word, even a *look*, would have her burning for him. She was her own woman, but she was his too.

For the moment.

Did he really want more?

If so, what about her father? Alexei couldn't let Carter off the hook.

She'd want nothing to do with Alexei once he brought her father to justice. Yet she knew that was Alexei's goal and it hadn't deterred her.

'Why didn't your father encourage you to study art?' Maybe father and daughter weren't as close as he'd imagined.

'He wanted me to do something useful. Like *economics*.' Mina's tone echoed horror. 'It would have been a disaster!'

That didn't sound like the man who'd spoken indulgently about his artistic daughter. But Carter had said she wasn't suited to business. Perhaps he'd originally wanted her to follow in his shoes. As for Carissa not coping with economics, Alexei recalled their conversations and knew she had a better-than-average understanding.

'So you persuaded your parents to let you try art.'

Her hand stopped on the page, her knuckles tightening. Had he hit a nerve?

'I didn't ask. I just applied.' Slowly her hand moved again, though her strokes weren't as bold as before. She stopped and raised her head. Alexei's curiosity rose as he saw her flushed cheeks.

'How about you?' Her bright eyes snared his and awareness throbbed. How easily they struck sparks. 'How did you start in IT? Did you spend all your free time as a kid on the computer?'

'Hardly. We didn't have one.'

He read the question in her expression yet she didn't ask. She kept to their unspoken agreement not to pry.

Alexei was the one pushing the boundaries. His curiosity was insatiable. He had to decide if he wanted more than the time they had left till the showdown with her father.

He needed to know more about this woman who engaged his mind as well as his body. To do that he'd have to share things he never shared with anyone. He paused, considering.

'There wasn't money when I was growing up, and what little we had my stepfather spent on himself.'

'He sounds unlikeable.'

'You could say that.' Alexei's vital organs knotted. 'He targeted my mother for the insurance money she inherited when my father died. It wasn't a fortune but it would have paid for a roof over our heads and a decent education for me.'

Instead the money had gone on his stepfather's whims. A sports car that he crashed while drunk. A 'get rich quick' scheme that failed. Expensive clothes, 'business' expenses for unspecified enterprises that involved late-night entertaining.

'You didn't have a home or decent education?' He heard sympathy in Carissa's voice as she bent her head, concentrating on a new sketch. Of his hands clenched in fists rather than relaxed as before. There was something soothing, almost hypnotic about watching the lines appear on the page, seeing form appear out of what had seemed random scratchings.

Though she worked, he knew she focused on his words. There was a tension about her that hadn't been there earlier. But she didn't push. She gave him space, and a measure of privacy, avoiding his gaze.

'We had a roof for the first couple of years. Mum remortgaged the place to finance his spending but he ran through that soon enough. He lived off her for years but when the money went, so did he.'

Alexei raked a hand through his shaggy hair, then realised what he'd done.

'Sorry.' He dropped his hand, fisting it on his thigh like its mate.

'Don't worry.' Her upward look, with that fleeting smile, eased the old tension brewing inside. 'I'll sketch your hands however you hold them. I love them. I'm thinking of using them in a piece I want to do.'

Alexei scowled down at his tight hands. For reasons he couldn't define her words unsettled him. Love. She'd used the word casually, yet he'd experienced a pang of…could it be *yearning*?

It was easier, suddenly, to think about the past than the knotty issue of how she made him feel.

'He sounds despicable,' Carissa said, her quiet voice vibrating with rage. 'To target a woman. To *use* her. There are too many selfish people in the world.'

Alexei's stare sharpened. 'You sound like you've met some.' He'd imagined she'd led a cosseted life.

'A few.' Her mouth flattened and she flipped the page. 'Actually, can I move your hands?' Her eyes held his. Something passed between them that inexplicably loosened the tension in his shoulders.

'Sure.' He watched as she turned his hands so they lay, palms up and fingers cupped. Her own hands were narrow and warm. Alexei liked the brush of her fingers.

'You must have been relieved when your stepfather left.'

'Definitely. He was a difficult man at the best of times and, believe me, there weren't many of those.' Alexei remembered the sound of his mother's sharp cry, waking him in the night. The hard crack of a beefy hand against his jaw and the lash of a belt around his backside. 'But the trouble didn't end when he went.'

'It didn't?' She lifted her head.

Alexei shrugged. 'He'd somehow run up debts in my mother's name, and loan sharks have no sympathy for defaulters.' Even if the defaulter was a defeated, desperate woman struggling to make ends meet. 'My mother worked three jobs to keep us safe from the enforcers.' Was it any wonder she'd worked herself into an early grave?

Warm fingers clasped his. Carissa didn't say anything but the gentle pressure was wonderfully soothing. Not that he needed sympathy. He'd conquered his past long ago. Yet he didn't move, just let her fingers curl around his, enjoying the sense of connection.

'That doesn't explain your education.'

'Sorry?'

'You indicated your education was patchy. Surely school was free.'

Alexei added tenaciousness to Carissa's qualities.

'I missed school to earn money to help out.'

'How old were you?' Her brow scrunched.

'Eleven. Early teens.'

Carissa shook her head and covered his cheek with her palm. The gesture felt like balm. How long had it been since anyone had tried to soothe his hurts? No one had since his mother. 'Your mother must have been so worried about you.'

Surprise jabbed him. But of course Carissa understood his mother's concern. After they'd stopped sniping at each other, he'd quickly recognised empathy as one of her core traits.

'She was, but I had to do my bit for the family.' There it was again. Family. Until this week he hadn't let himself think about how it had felt to be part of something bigger than himself. To care and be cared for.

'Having a mother to love you. That's special.'

'At least you and I were lucky enough to know our mothers.'

He frowned, registering Carissa's brittle smile and wistful eyes. Did she miss her mother? It wasn't long ago she'd died. 'I'm sorry, Carissa. Sorry for your loss.'

'Thank you.' She blinked, her eyes bright. Then she pulled her arm away and sat back.

Mina had no memories of her mother. She'd told herself that didn't matter. Her older sister, Ghizlan, had been as good as any mother, making up for their father's distance.

Yet Alexei's words reopened a raw wound. One she'd refused for years to recognise. She felt it now, the sharp pain of loneliness, of being rejected by her father, abandoned by the mother who'd died.

Self-pity was pathetic. She had Ghizlan and she couldn't wish for a better sister. And Huseyn, her brother-in-law, was a sweetie beneath that incredibly gruff exterior. She had her little niece and nephew in Jeirut, and there was her friend Carissa.

But no one just for her.

Mina hated the direction of her thoughts. *Look at Alexei.* He'd lost his father young and had all sorts of trouble as a kid but he didn't give in to self-pity.

'So how *did* you start in IT?'

'A community youth centre.' Alexei shook his head. 'One of the staff was particularly persistent. I look back and realise how hard he worked even to get me to talk. But the place was heated and relatively safe so it appealed.'

'You weren't safe?' Silly to feel concern now. But Mina hated the idea of a young kid alone and scared.

Alexei shrugged. As usual, his shirt hung open over his broad chest and she watched the play of his muscles. It made her slightly dizzy. She wanted to plant her palm there, where his heart beat.

'It wasn't a good neighbourhood. There were gangs.' His tone was dismissive. 'And it didn't matter where we moved, the heavies collecting the money we owed always found us.'

We owed. Not his mother, or even his stepfather.

We.

Alexei had assumed responsibility for something that shouldn't have been his concern. He should have been running around a school playground without a care.

A lump rose in Mina's throat and she swallowed hard. Why was she so sentimental? Millions of children lived in harsh conditions they didn't deserve, some in her own country. She and Ghizlan were particularly active in supporting disadvantaged children. But why did Alexei's past hurts specifically unsettle her?

Because you care for him.

You care too much.

'They had an old computer. One of the guys taught me and I discovered an aptitude for it.'

'You make it sound easy. You don't go from being a kid

with a second-hand computer to launching a megasuccessful software and communications company.'

'True. But I won't bore you with a blow-by-blow description.'

Mina opened her mouth to protest. She was fascinated. She wanted to hear more about Alexei. Anything about him. But she sensed he'd had enough of the subject.

'How did they meet, your parents?'

His winged eyebrows lifted, giving him the look of a particularly rakish fallen angel, especially with that tousled hair threatening to flop over his forehead.

Fire ripped through her.

'Don't move a muscle.' She flipped a page and started drawing, trying to get the haughty angles, the stark beauty of spectacular cheekbones and determined jaw, the sensuality of his mouth.

As she worked, darting looks at him and then back to the paper, something changed. His expression grew less arrogant and more focused, the gleam in his eyes brighter. Mina became more than ever aware of Alexei's scent—cedar, citrus and male, with an undertone of musk. She inhaled deeply, her hand moving furiously across the paper. If Ghizlan could bottle that scent at her perfumery, the enterprise would make a fortune.

'Finished?' Those malachite eyes glinted more brightly than any faceted gem.

'Almost.' Mina read his impatience, sensed his arousal and strove for something to distract him. 'You didn't tell me how your parents met.'

'At the Olympics. He was an athlete and she was a physio travelling with the Russian team. They fell in love and eloped the day before the closing ceremony.'

'Wow! That's fast. They must have been head over heels.'

'They were. Completely and utterly in love. When my father died, my mother was devastated. It was almost too hard for her to go on.' His mouth twisted and Mina felt a thud of pain in her middle. 'That's why she remarried. She couldn't face the loneliness.'

Mina watched emotions play across Alexei's face. He looked angry, as if he blamed his mother. She'd made his life miserable with her rotten choice of second husband.

Yet things were rarely black and white. 'Maybe she wanted someone to take your father's place, for your sake. So you'd have a dad.'

The spasm of pain across his face lasted only a moment but it told her so much.

He felt guilty about his mother's choice?

And maybe for blaming her?

'How about you?' he asked. 'How did your parents meet?'

Mina felt a flutter in her chest. A battle between innate honesty and her need to cover for Carissa. Mina was increasingly uncomfortable with these lies. Surely Carissa was safe. The elopement was supposed to happen this weekend. She wanted so badly to blurt the truth but couldn't risk it.

Because you don't want this to end, do you? You want to stay here with Alexei and dream of impossible things.

She closed her sketchbook. She wouldn't give Carissa away, nor would she pretend to have lived Carissa's life.

'They didn't know each other before the engagement.'

'It was an arranged marriage?' He looked stunned.

'It's a tradition in my family.' Mina suppressed a pained smile. As far as she knew, her sister was the only woman in a long line of ancestors to find love in marriage. It wasn't something either of them had believed possible, having been bred as dynastic bargaining chips.

Now finding happiness with the man you loved, and who loved you, seemed incredibly alluring.

Mina put her sketchbook down, ignoring the drag of unhappiness. Her time with Alexei was limited. She refused to mar it. Instead she stood and stretched, forcing her attention away from *if onlys*.

'I've sat too long. I need exercise. How about another archery contest?' She'd been delighted to find it was a sport Alexei enjoyed, and one of the few she was proficient in, since it was Jeirut's national sport. 'Or a swim?' Her gaze turned towards the pristine beach. She'd had no qualms about using the brand-new swimsuit Carissa had packed. An errant thread of heat circled her womb at the thought of dispensing with the swimsuit and swimming naked with Alexei. If he knew the truth about her maybe they could...

Suddenly he was beside her. The fine hairs on her arms and neck prickled and her insides melted.

'If it's exercise you want—' his voice was an earthy growl that tumbled down her backbone and drew her belly tight '—I know just the thing.' His green eyes darkened and she swayed towards him.

Then, abruptly, he stepped back and groaned, shaking his head. 'You'll be the death of me yet.' But his lips curved in a smile as he reached for her hand. 'Come on, we need to work off some of this surplus energy.' He tugged her hand and she followed.

That was the problem. She was long past resisting Alexei. She wanted to be with him, all the time.

She was headed for disaster and couldn't pull back.

CHAPTER THIRTEEN

PHONE TO HIS EAR, Alexei sat back in his desk chair, grinning. Ralph Carter had been found in a casino in southern Switzerland. Either through cunning or sheer luck, he'd led the investigators a merry dance, but now there was no escape. Carter would face the consequences of his theft.

Satisfaction warmed Alexei.

Until Carissa's face swam in his mind. He recalled her sparkling eyes, the throaty husk of her voice as she cried his name in ecstasy, her decadently addictive mouth.

How would she react when he made her father pay for his crimes?

Doubt stirred Alexei's gut. He'd learned this week that she was anything but a selfish social butterfly. He admired her honest, generous spirit, even her obstinacy. This would hurt her.

He stiffened his resolve. She couldn't expect him to forget her father's crime. She knew it was coming. She hadn't asked for mercy on Carter's behalf. Though now Alexei considered that odd, surely.

Carissa was passionate and unafraid of ruffling his feathers, yet she'd never tried to intercede for her father.

As he listened to his PA, Alexei reached idly for Carissa's sketchbook and flipped it open. She'd left it by the pool and he'd brought it inside when he took this call. Clearly she'd forgotten it, focused instead on the fact it was her turn to cook.

Tomorrow Henri and Marie returned and the food would be restaurant quality again. But Alexei would far rather have another week alone with Carissa, sharing responsibility for chores, than any amount of exquisite dishes.

His insides twisted. Alexei told himself it was from eagerness to face Carter. Not concern as he anticipated Carissa's reaction.

'Excellent. See to those arrangements and we'll wrap this up.'

'There's one more thing.' His PA sounded unexpectedly tentative. 'A woman has been ringing, insisting she speak with you.'

Alexei frowned. He paid his PA an excellent salary. In return he didn't expect to be bothered by importunate strangers. Obviously this woman was out of the ordinary. 'And?'

'She gave her name as Carissa Carter.'

Arrested, Alexei sat straighter. 'Say that again.'

'She claims to be Carissa Carter, daughter of Ralph Carter.'

Alexei looked at the sketch before him. It was one he hadn't seen before and there was something incredibly intimate about it. Not just the fact that he was asleep on a sun lounger. He felt tenderness in the way Carissa had drawn the rumpled hair shadowing his forehead, and the lines of his mouth.

Was that really how she saw him?

A curious buzz started up in his ears.

'Obviously the woman is lying.'

'That's what I thought. But she gave enough detail to be very convincing.'

The fact his PA pressed the point was significant. She was not only loyal but intelligent. She must have good reason for pursuing this. 'Very well. Give me her number.'

Minutes later Alexei made the call.

'Hello? Carissa speaking.' Her voice was high and breathy and slightly familiar.

Alexei leaned forward, hand splayed on the desk, pulse quickening.

'Carissa Carter?'

'Yes, I... Who is this?' Her voice wobbled and Alexei felt the blood drain from his face. He recognised the voice now. It was the woman he'd spoken to a week ago. The woman he'd arranged to have collected in Paris. He'd assumed the line had distorted her voice because she sounded different in person.

He pinched the bridge of his nose with his thumb and forefinger. 'It's Alexei Katsaros.'

He heard a gasp, then a noise as if she'd dropped the phone. Adrenalin shot through him and his stomach lurched.

'Are...are you there?'

'I'm here. What do you want?' The person responsible for this elaborate hoax would pay. Alexei was in no mood for games.

'I rang to tell you I got married. I know my father led you to believe I was...available but he was wrong. A match between us isn't possible.' Her words were rushed, her breathing so uneven the words slurred together. 'I should have told you my plans sooner. I'm sorry. But I was too... That is, I wasn't thinking clearly when you rang. Pierre said I should have told you straight, and so did Mina, but I was too...' She hiccupped as if holding back a sob. 'I've tried and tried to call Mina but I can't reach her. Is she all right?'

Alexei's head spun. His pulse throbbed so hard it felt like a hammer against his temple.

He wanted to tell this stranger to quit wasting his time. But something stopped him. The suspicion this was no joke. That the impossible was about to become possible.

Twenty minutes later Alexei stared unseeingly across his desk, the phone silenced.

He'd got to the bottom of the situation all right. He'd taken some convincing, and more checking, but he was absolutely sure the woman on the phone was Carissa Carter.

He reeled at learning the truth. All this time he'd thought

his guest was his employee's daughter when she was Princess Mina of Jeirut, sister of the country's Queen. A rich royal who'd played the part of Carissa, duping him.

Making a fool of him.

Alexei imagined the field day the press would have with this. What impact would that have on his business? He screwed his eyes shut and tried to focus his scrambled brain on damage limitation.

But focus was impossible. It was all he could do to accept the preposterous truth. The two women had conned him. And he, so wrapped up in the pursuit of vengeance and the need to act decisively, had made it easy, not bothering to check details.

This wasn't business. It was far more personal. Briefly he acknowledged he'd made it so when he'd brought Carter's daughter to his private retreat. But his actions didn't sink to these depths of deception.

Alexei's gaze drifted to the abandoned sketchbook on his desk. He turned it over, opening it at the very beginning, to the images he hadn't viewed before. Why? Was he so desperate to believe, even now, that the woman in his kitchen was genuine? That the woman he'd come to care for was real, not some pretend persona adopted to dupe him?

Alexei stopped on the second page, on a series of intricate designs for a flask. They were exquisite. But it wasn't the design's beauty that caught his eye, it was the stylised calligraphy around the base. Calligraphy in Arabic. A talented artist could have copied the flowing script. Except there were also what looked like scribbled notes on the edge of the page in the same language.

Alexei turned the page. There was another bottle, again with scrawled notes in Arabic.

His mouth tightened. If he'd only taken the time to look, instead of being so caught up in that blaze of attraction for Carissa. For *Mina*, he corrected himself.

Despite Carissa Carter's breathless, half-defiant, half-apologetic explanations, Alexei knew they'd made a fool of him.

He looked down to see he'd again reached the page where she, *Mina*, had drawn him sleeping. With new eyes Alexei realised it wasn't tenderness revealed in the portrait. That wasn't vulnerability in his sleeping features but weakness. She'd been laughing at him.

She'd sashayed in, daring him to make a pass at her, teasing him till he didn't know which way was up. Pretending to be someone else, pretending to be honest and open and vulnerable. Had her virginity also been a lie?

Alexei shoved the book so hard it toppled off the desk as he surged to his feet and stalked to the window. It wasn't the view he saw. It was himself, laughing with... Mina. Telling Mina about his past, his stepfather, because he'd actually considered extending their relationship into something else.

Relationship!

He snorted. They had no relationship beyond sex and lies.

The sex he could cope with, but not the lies.

He'd been conned as a kid and that had brought disaster.

He'd trusted Carter, had actually liked him, believing he and the older man shared an understanding. Till Carter knifed him in the back and stole his money.

Now Alexei found himself tricked again. By a slip of a woman with big brown eyes and a devious mind. A woman who'd burrowed her way into his—

Alexei yanked his thoughts to safer ground. To the blaze of anger searing his gut.

She'd made him reconsider his single status. She'd made him think about babies and belonging and all the while...

He swore, a mix of Greek and Russian that was far more potent for cursing than English.

Only when he had himself under control did he turn towards the door.

* * *

Mina hummed as she took the casserole from the oven. The aromas were mouth-watering. This was the one meal she could cook well, a traditional spicy vegetable dish from her homeland. It had been worth the extra time and effort.

For once Mina would be able to present Alexei with something delicious. There was a spring in her step and a smile on her face as she crossed to put it on the counter.

Alexei never complained about her culinary efforts. Nor did she aim to become a domestic goddess. Yet there was something deeply satisfying about cooking something nice for your man.

Mina blinked, staring down at the fragrant meal in astonishment.

Your man. Where had that come from?

This was temporary. Alexei Katsaros wasn't her man and never would be. Yet some tremulous, defiant voice inside disagreed.

He *felt* like her man.

She *wanted* him to be hers.

Mina stumbled back against the big island bench and slumped there, her mind racing at the enormity of the revelation.

She crossed her arms over her chest as if she could contain the swelling sensation inside. The rising demand that she face the truth.

What she felt with Alexei was more profound than sexual attraction. She'd spent her time on the island studiously ignoring that, pretending this was animal magnetism and no more. Because the truth of what she felt was too enormous, too life-changing. Too preposterous.

She'd imagined herself immune to romance, to dreams of being with one special man. No one had come close to distracting her from her drive to make art. But Alexei did that, even though they hadn't had sex in days. No one had ever made her *feel*, made her want to be part of a couple.

Mina put her hand to her breastbone. Her heart pounded high and hard.

A noise on the other side of the room made her look up. Instantly the tightness in her chest eased, and something inside her soared.

Alexei stood in the doorway, one shoulder propped against the doorjamb, arms crossed over his chest in a way that accentuated the curves of well-developed biceps and pectorals.

Desire throbbed through her. And more, far more. When he was with her she no longer worried that she was out of her depth. With Alexei she felt utterly right. It should be crazy to feel this way after a mere week, but there was no avoiding her feelings.

Mina smiled, not bothering to hide her delight. 'Smells good, doesn't it?' She leaned over the dish, inhaling the aroma that reminded her of Jeirut. What would Alexei make of her homeland? She'd love to take him there. 'And I promise it's not charred or undercooked. I'll get the plates.'

'Surely you shouldn't be waiting on me, *Princess*.'

Mina's head jerked up as if yanked on a string. It wasn't just Alexei's words but his tone that shook her. She looked into that searing green gaze, registered the flaring nostrils and savagely flattened mouth. Her stomach plummeted.

He knew.

And he was livid.

Alexei watched the laughter and the blood drain from her face, leaving her features pale and proud.

In that moment his last hope that this was a mistake died. And with it the foolish desires he'd entertained.

He waited for her to show embarrassment or guilt. There would have been some satisfaction in that. He might even have listened to an explanation if she'd shown regret and shame.

Instead, she drew herself up, shoulders straight and pushed back. Her neck lengthened as her chin came up. The welcome in her eyes died, replaced with a hauteur Alexei recognised from her arrival on the island.

It was like watching an actress don another persona. Except instead of seeing a make-believe character, the woman confronting him with that cool stare and regal bearing *was* the real woman. A conniving, lying woman.

The enthusiastic, caring person he'd known was a chimera. She'd been created to hold his attention long enough to distract him from the fact he was being fooled. How much of her had been real? Any of it?

He slammed the lid on such thoughts. He refused to search for pitiful fragments of a woman who didn't exist beyond his imagination.

The anger that had been brewing since the phone calls bubbled over. 'You must be used to having servants scurrying to do everything.'

Her face changed even more, shutters coming down behind her eyes, making her unapproachable. No wonder he'd likened her to that Russian ballerina. Both could project regal hauteur fit for a queen.

But no blue-blooded princess would play a part for public entertainment like a dancer. How much had her role-playing been for personal entertainment? Had she laughed at how easily she'd fooled him?

A knife twisted in his chest.

'You're wrong, Alexei. I have no servants.'

Maybe it was the way she said his name, her voice husky and low, reminding him of her throaty purrs as she climaxed, that fuelled his ire to spilling point. More probably it was the unblinking gaze that revealed the barriers she erected between herself and the hoi polloi.

After all, despite his wealth, Alexei had spent most of his early years living in slums. Whereas she was descended from generations of royalty.

This was the woman he'd wanted in his bed, his home, his life. She'd laugh if she knew exactly how much of a fool she'd made him.

'Quit lying, Princess. The pretence is over.'

He spoke like a stranger. A looming, ice-cold stranger. Shock made Mina shuffle back a step.

If there was ever a time to call on those early lessons in self-control, this was it. This furious stranger wasn't her lover. She knew without question this man wouldn't respond to appeals for mercy or reason. He had no softer side.

Mina had known there'd be trouble when the truth emerged. But lately she'd convinced herself it wouldn't be so bad. Maybe she and Alexei might even laugh it off.

Only sheer willpower stifled the hysterical laughter bubbling inside. Again she'd been naive.

Desperately she wrapped herself tighter in that cloak of composure she'd learned to wear since childhood. The cloak she'd worn when facing her father's beetling regard, or the curious stares of the public. Both had been more concerned with the appearance of royalty than the real girl behind the façade.

'You're right.' She breathed deep. 'It's time for the truth.' With every hour she'd sunk deeper into that hazy world of self-deception, where Alexei cared for her as much as she did him.

'Past time.' He spoke through gritted teeth. 'You *are* Princess Mina of Jeirut, aren't you?' He said it as if it were a mark of shame rather than honour.

Wearily Mina nodded. 'I am.' She searched for what to say next, then surprised herself by blurting out, 'But it's true. I don't have servants. I look after myself.'

Why she insisted on telling him, she didn't know. His expression showed he wasn't interested. Yet it seemed important he understand she was an ordinary person despite her lineage.

'Is that a ploy for sympathy?' His eyebrows rose mockingly. 'Did you do this scam for money? Because you've spent your inheritance?' His words bit so deep it was a wonder they didn't leave marks. 'Are you looking for someone to fund your lifestyle?'

The insult wasn't camouflaged. Even someone as inexperienced as she could read the curl of his lip and the dismissive gaze flicking her from face to feet.

Something inside Mina shrivelled, like a delicate bloom blasted by the desert sun. The ache inside became a tearing pain but she wouldn't let it show. 'Don't be ridiculous. I—'

'Ridiculous?' He straightened from the doorjamb and prowled towards her, arms still crossed. He didn't stop till he was right in front of her, toe to toe.

Mina blinked and widened her stance, grounding herself rather than stepping back. He intimidated her. If she weren't shell-shocked by his reaction she'd probably be scared. But pride refused to let her reveal that.

'Of course it's ridiculous. I'm not after financial support.' How could he believe that? Did he think everyone was out for what they could get from him?

'Then what was this past week? Some social experiment for a cosseted princess to see how the other half lives? Was royal life so tame you wanted to spice it up with someone who grew up on the other side of the tracks?'

Horror stole her voice for precious seconds. 'You can't believe that!' It was a scratchy whisper.

'Why not?' He leaned close and Mina read nothing but contempt in his eyes.

'I'd hardly call a man with your power and finances anyone's idea of a bit of rough.' How dared he attack *her*? Yes, she was culpable. She'd lied and she hadn't been comfortable with it but she'd had good reason. 'Secondly, you need to take responsibility for what happened.'

'Me?' He had the nerve to look outraged.

'Who else?' Through the pain anger erupted. 'You put Carissa through hell. And I—'

'You what? You can't tell me this last week has been your idea of hell.' He leaned in and Mina inhaled the cedar-and-citrus scent that always made her senses tingle. To her horror she felt a softening between her thighs, as if, even facing Alexei's scorn, she wanted him.

She drew herself up, slowly reciting in her head the names of her five favourite sculptors, then another five, till she trusted her voice.

'I did what I did for my friend. You threatened to kidnap her.'

'I did no such thing. Her father offered her to me and I simply invited her here to—'

'Rubbish!' Mina's control frayed and she prodded her fingers into the solid muscle of his shoulder. '*You* started this when you decided to use Carissa for your own ends. Have you any idea how scared she was when she got your call?'

'Because she was in cahoots with her father.' If possible he looked even grimmer than before.

Mina shook her head. 'If you knew Carissa you'd know that was impossible. She can't tell a lie to save herself. She couldn't even think of an excuse to fob you off when you sent your goons to collect her.'

'But it wasn't Carissa who came, was it? It was you, lying through your teeth.'

'You expect me to apologise for that?' The nerve of the man stupefied her. 'I've known some manipulative men. Men who'd use a woman as a convenience as if she weren't a real person. But I thought they were dying out. Until I met you.'

Mina refused to think about the man she'd fallen for this past week. He'd either been a mirage invented by her yearning soul or a cruel joke.

'You brought this on yourself. Poor Carissa was beside herself, thinking her father would lose his job unless she agreed to come.'

Mina stepped back, not in retreat but so she could turn and march across the kitchen. She couldn't stay still, couldn't pretend to be calm. Not when everything had gone up in flames.

'Don't you walk away from me!' The growl came from just behind her and the hairs at her nape stood to attention.

'Or what?' She spun round and fixed her tormentor with a furious stare, barely able to believe how this confrontation had exploded. 'You'll lock me up? Hold me to ransom?'

'You're so sure your royal status exempts you from the consequences of your actions.'

'This has nothing to do with being royal.'

Alexei's eyes blazed. 'You deliberately connived to keep me from finding Carter. The man's a thief.'

'*All* I did—' she jammed her hands on her hips '—was buy time so my friend wouldn't be railroaded into marrying an arrogant jerk who treats people like disposable toys.' Mina drew a deep breath. 'Did you ever, once, stop to consider the collateral damage to other people from your actions?'

'Like you, I presume? You're claiming to be an injured party?' His contemptuous stare incinerated her last, frail hope. 'I'm no expert on Jeirut but I know it's very traditional. A royal princess who has casual flings would be frowned on. What's your plan? To claim I forced you into my bed when it comes out we've been alone for days?' His voice was a snarl, ripping through her stupid fantasies.

'How can you think such a thing?' Tears of indignation and pain needled the backs of her eyes.

His eyebrows lifted, the only sign of animation in a face turned mask-like.

'Then what? A kiss-and-tell story for the media? You'd get a small fortune for that, and revenge for your friend. But you'd wreck your reputation at home if it came out you had an affair.' He paused, his mouth tightening. 'Or am I to expect a demand from the King of Jeirut that I pay for the privilege of having despoiled your supposed virginal status?'

Mina flinched at his brutal accusations. How could he *think* such things? A yawning pit of hurt opened up inside.

'I see.' Abruptly Alexei's fury vanished, replaced by a look of weariness and bitter disillusionment. His voice turned flat. 'So that's it. You have your bit of fun and expect someone else to pay the price.'

Mina opened her mouth and shut it again. She was without words. How had she given her heart to a man who thought so little of her? For it was her heart she'd lost to Alexei, not just her innocence.

She pressed her hand to her middle, trying to hold in the lacerating anguish that felt as if her insides had crystallised to glass and shattered. She'd gone from heady delight to the depths of humiliation and pain so fast her head spun.

She needed to find words to make him understand. But what was the point? This wasn't her Alexei. This was a man who could believe the absolute worst of her. Her Alexei was nothing but a phantom.

'I'd like to leave the island now.' Her voice was stilted but she was beyond caring. 'I assume you can arrange that?'

'Nothing would give me greater pleasure.'

Mina turned to the door, unable to face his disdain any longer. 'Excellent. At least that's one thing we agree on.'

CHAPTER FOURTEEN

PARIS WASN'T FAR enough away.

Mina stared at the blinking light of her message bank and knew if she hit Play, Alexei's deep voice would fill the room. Worse, it would inveigle its way inside her, reinforcing the hollow ache she carried.

She knew because that was what had happened earlier. She'd come out of the shower and hadn't thought twice about checking her messages. Only to find herself fighting a rush of pain at the sound of that familiar voice. She'd slammed the phone down and deleted his message, unable to listen.

It didn't matter if he'd rung to berate her some more, or even to apologise for his sniping accusations. The fact was she *had* lied to him. But worse, she'd made the mistake of falling for the man.

Even if he called to say he was sorry he overreacted, which was about as likely as snowfall in the desert, it wouldn't be enough. Even if by some miracle he'd forgiven her and decided the sex between them was so good he wanted an affair, Mina knew she needed more.

She needed all or nothing.

Nothing was the only logical option.

Mina turned and paced. She needed space to think. Somewhere with no reminders of him.

A tattoo on the front door made her heart leap. It couldn't be. She didn't want it to be. Yet her hands shook as she opened it. Savage disappointment sliced through her at the sight of her best friend.

Mina really was desperate. And delusional. As if Alexei would turn up at her door!

'Carissa!'

Her friend enveloped her in a hug and a cloud of rose perfume. 'Are you okay? You look like hell.'

Mina managed a chuckle, despite the scratchy throat that made it hard to swallow. 'Lack of sleep. I'll be fine. But you look fabulous. Marriage agrees with you.'

Carissa grinned. She'd never looked prettier. Something tugged at Mina's heart but she refused to feel jealous that her friend had found happiness with the man she adored.

'It *is* wonderful. Pierre's the best. And I have you to thank. Without you stepping in—'

'I was glad to help.' Mina shut the door and led her towards the lounge room. But Carissa stopped her.

'I'm sorry, sweetie. I don't have time. Pierre and I are heading off to see his family. He's going to introduce me, so wish us luck.'

'They'll love you once they get to know you.' Mina pressed her hands. 'Give them a little time.'

Carissa nodded. 'That's what Pierre said. But I'm not sure and—' Her eyes rounded. 'How could I forget? Are you in trouble? That's what I came to ask.'

'Trouble?'

Carissa nodded. 'You must have got home very late last night. I didn't even know you were back. Then just now I was coming up the street when I saw those men. The ones who took you to Alexei Katsaros. They were coming out of our building and drove away in a big black car.'

'You're sure it was them?' Had she missed a knock on the door as she dried her hair?

Emotions stormed through Mina. Excitement vied with hope that she knew she had to crush. She and Alexei had no future.

'As if I'd forget.' Carissa shivered. 'I got a good look through the peephole the day they took you away. What do they want? Why are they here?'

'Probably checking I got home safely.' Maybe Alexei's conscience was troubling him and he wanted to make sure. Last night she'd refused an escort from the airport, insisting on finding her own way home.

'You're such a bad liar, Mina. I'll tell Pierre we can't go yet—'

'No. You have to go.' Her words were sharp, yet her mouth quivered. Reaction, she told herself. She'd barely slept. She needed time alone.

'Then what can I do to help?' Carissa put her arm around her and Mina had to fight the urge to weep on her shoulder.

Mina never ran from trouble but she felt too raw, too destroyed by the enormity of her feelings to cope. She needed to lick her wounds and recoup. 'Help me pack a bag. I'm going to Jeirut.'

The royal palace of Jeirut was imposing and warlike. Only the banners snapping in the wind alleviated its grimness. Perched on a high plateau, it commanded views of the city spread around it and the desert below.

Alexei followed a courtier through an oversized portal into a series of antechambers, each more magnificent than the last. But Alexei wasn't in the mood to be impressed. His mind was on the upcoming interview.

His one chance. The knowledge tightened his gut.

Finally he was led into an audience chamber with a forest of pillars around the perimeter. His gaze went to the golden throne and on it a tall, powerfully built man in white robes. His face was rugged, his nose uneven and eyes piercing. This man—Alexei knew, his pulse quickening in anticipation—made even the best negotiators nervous.

Introductions were made, complete with a scraping bow from Alexei's companion. Sheikh Huseyn, colloquially known as the Iron Hand, remained stony-faced. It was only when the doors closed behind the courtier and Alexei was alone with Mina's brother-in-law that the Sheikh raised one eyebrow in interrogation.

'You have a request?'

Alexei met that assessing stare with one of his own. 'I want to speak with your sister-in-law.' As if Sheikh Huseyn didn't already know that. As if Alexei hadn't been through this multiple times with officials.

'If you have something important to say, I can pass on a message. At present she's busy.'

Alexei wasn't deterred. He'd missed her in Paris but he *would* see her here. Mina might be furious and hurt but she wouldn't hide from him. She was too proud.

At least he hoped so. Unless he'd given her such a disgust of him that even her pride wasn't enough. He shoved the idea aside, refusing to countenance the idea of defeat.

'Thank you. But I prefer to speak with Mina.'

Sheikh Huseyn's eyes narrowed as if questioning his use of Mina's name.

'Why should I let you see her?' His even tone held an undercurrent of menace.

Instead of being abashed, Alexei stepped closer. Royalty or not, he refused to let the Sheikh stand in his way. 'Surely that's Mina's decision.'

The Sheikh didn't reply and as the silence lengthened, ice-cold sweat trickled down Alexei's spine.

'Are you saying Mina refuses to see me?' Nausea rolled through him. He tasted acid and recognised it as fear. Would Mina send him away without a chance?

'Why should she? What's your relationship?'

'That's between me and Mina.' Alexei's gaze followed the perimeter of the room. Did one of those doors lead to her? Frustration rose. The palace was enormous. If he made a break for it he had no hope of finding her before the royal guard stopped him.

'And if I make it my business?' The Sheikh rose and

stepped onto the floor. He moved with the ease of an athlete and, sizing him up, Alexei guessed they'd be well matched in a tussle.

'I can only repeat that my business is solely with Mina.'

'I am her King and head of her family.' Huseyn moved to stand toe to toe with Alexei. The air was redolent with latent danger. 'It's my role to protect her.'

Alexei met his eyes. 'I respect your desire to protect her, but Mina can manage her own concerns. I doubt she'd be impressed by anyone, even family, speaking on her behalf.'

A ripple of expression crossed the Sheikh's features, then, to Alexei's surprise, his face creased in a smile.

'You know Mina well.' He paused. 'What brings you to Jeirut? Surely not simply seeing my sister-in-law. Are you opening an office here? Or perhaps one of your youth centres. Such a laudable programme.'

Huseyn had done his homework. Alexei respected that. It was what he would have done. Due diligence was second nature.

Except that one vital time when he hadn't checked out Carissa Carter because he'd been determined to snaffle her quickly as bait. Technically that had been a grave error, but Alexei couldn't think of it in those terms since it had brought him Mina.

Elusive Mina. He stifled impatience with difficulty.

'I congratulate you, Highness. Not many know of my link to that initiative.' Alexei made sure of it. His community training and support scheme for disadvantaged teenagers wasn't done for kudos but to make a difference. Those kids didn't need their problems aired for public sympathy when Alexei could quietly provide the start-up money for programmes that eventually became self-funding.

'I make it my business to know about men who take an interest in my sister-in-law.'

Huseyn was toying with him. Mina had been a sexual

innocent until she'd come to him. Despite what he'd thought in the white-hot sear of anger.

'So, would you be interested in working in Jeirut?'

'It depends on the result of my discussion with Mina.' Alexei set his jaw. 'Is that the price for letting me see her?'

For a moment longer the Sheikh watched him through narrowed eyes. Then he nodded abruptly as if coming to a decision. 'You're not what I expected, Mr Katsaros.' He paused. 'Come, I'll take you to her.'

So he'd passed a test. Alexei should have felt relieved. Instead, as he followed Huseyn he felt more nervous than he could ever remember.

Perhaps that was why, when the Sheikh ushered him into a lavish chamber, it took Alexei a moment to recognise Mina. There were two women, both focused on a velvet-lined jew-ellery case open on a table. One he knew from his research as the beautiful Sheikha of Jeirut. The other... His breath stopped as she looked up and eyes of rich brown snared his.

Mina. One look and the ground shuddered beneath his feet. Yearning filled him.

Instead of the casual clothes he was accustomed to, she wore an evening dress of crimson with a square-cut neck-line that emphasised the purity of her slender throat and graceful posture. Her hair was up and a tiara of brilliant diamonds sparkled in that dark mass.

How had he ever imagined her to be Carissa Carter? She was every inch a princess.

She was the most stunning woman he'd ever beheld.

Alexei's heart battered his ribs as he fought not to cross the room and pull her close.

As he watched her mouth flattened into a straight line and her beautiful eyes clouded. The hurt he saw there tore his conscience and his hopes.

All his resolve, all his certainty he could set things right, were shaken to the core.

* * *

He looked the same. No, not the same. Bigger, sexier, more charismatic than she'd let herself remember.

Heat swamped Mina. Her quiver of awareness was proof that, if anything, memory had done Alexei Katsaros a disservice. The only change in him, apart from the suave suit, was that he looked hollow around the eyes. Tired from travel. She wouldn't allow herself to imagine their parting had interfered with his sleep.

She was the one cursed with wakeful nights.

She drew a deep breath, hands clenching. That was when she remembered the diamond necklace in her palm. She moved to put it in its box but her hand shook ridiculously. Fortunately Ghizlan reached out and scooped it from her.

Mina had been on tenterhooks all day, unable to settle, after Huseyn told her Alexei was coming. Ghizlan's insistence that she decide on some finery for an upcoming royal reception had been a welcome diversion that stopped her checking the time every two minutes.

Now she'd been caught all glammed up. Full-length silk rustled as she shifted. Diamond drops swung from her earlobes and she was conscious of the pins securing the heirloom tiara.

Her chin tilted as she took in Alexei's stare. So what if he had a problem with her royal status? She wasn't ashamed. She was what she was, as much at home in a formal gown as old jeans.

'Mina.' Alexei's voice was the same, a deep cadence that did crazy things to her self-control.

She drew a sustaining breath. 'Alexei.' Then she turned to her sister. 'Ghizlan, this is Mr Katsaros.'

'Mr Katsaros.' Contrary to her usual friendly manner, Ghizlan gave the tiniest nod, her expression a degree short of glacial.

Alexei didn't look fazed by the lack of welcome. 'Your Highness.' His eyes tracked back to Mina.

She'd arrived here unexpectedly, desperate for the comfort of her sister's presence. Like when she'd been a child. Ghizlan and Huseyn had, in their different ways, provided that comfort. Huseyn's expression now made it clear he'd intervene if Alexei upset Mina, and Ghizlan bristled with protectiveness. She'd guessed Alexei had caused the unhappiness Mina couldn't hide. Bless her, and Huseyn too, for closing ranks.

But this was Mina's battle.

'I'd like to speak to Alexei alone.' It was a lie. Facing him was torment. But this had to be done. One final conversation and their abortive relationship would be over. Pain crested to a point behind her ribs and Mina rubbed the spot, till Alexei tracked the movement. She dropped her hand.

Huseyn folded his arms. 'Anything he wishes to say can be said before your family.'

'But surely,' Alexei said, without taking his eyes from her, 'Mina has the right to privacy.'

Mina stifled the urge to roll her eyes. The air was thick with testosterone, the two very alpha males each determined to stand their ground.

'This won't take long.' Mina ignored the pang of regret she felt at that, and sent a pleading glance to Ghizlan. 'Then I'll come and join you.'

After a searching glance Ghizlan nodded. 'We'll finish this later.' Not just the choice of jewels, but, she made clear, a conversation about Alexei Katsaros.

Wearily Mina nodded. She owed Ghizlan an explanation even if it was a truncated version of the truth. For no matter how she'd tried, since arriving in Jeirut she hadn't been able to hide the fact that something was terribly wrong.

Her sister took Huseyn's arm. For a moment he stood, unmoving. Then he nodded. 'Very well. We'll be in my study.' His tone held a warning as if daring Alexei to step out of line.

'Your family is very protective,' he said when the door closed.

'They are.' Sometimes overprotective. But there was comfort in having family who cared.

'I'm glad. You deserve to have people who care.'

Surprised, she shot Alexei a wary glance and was snared by those green eyes she'd tried to avoid.

It was impossible to look away, no matter how she ordered herself to do so. It was as if he drew her to him, compelled her against her will.

No, not against her will. That was the problem. Despite everything, Mina couldn't eradicate her weakness for Alexei. All she could do was pretend it didn't exist. It *shouldn't* exist. They'd only been together for a week. Far too short a time to fall in love. What she felt was infatuation.

A lump rose in her throat as she fought to stifle her feelings. She felt so wretched, not like herself at all. Once she'd have lost herself in work no matter what was going on around her. Now work took second place to the pain she carried like a layer beneath her skin.

Mina propped her hands on the table, grateful for something to lean on. She hadn't thought he'd come. Whenever she thought of that last day his words burned her soul. She'd told herself he'd spoken in the heat of the moment. That he didn't really believe what he'd said. But maybe he had.

After days of thinking herself at her lowest possible ebb, Mina knew she'd finally hit rock bottom. Shame, outrage and, yes, sheer hurt, scraped every inch of her flesh, making it smart. She tore her gaze away, pretending to tidy the gems that blurred before her eyes.

'I know because you're standing there, unscathed, you didn't suggest to Huseyn that you owed him a fee for taking my virginity.' She spat the words out, hating their acid taste. 'So let me reiterate, once and for all, I don't need your wealth. Nor does my family. There's no fine to pay.'

In the old days it would have been called a bride price and the suitor would have been ushered into a hasty marriage. But Alexei was no suitor. He despised her.

Mina clasped her hands, projecting as much calm as she could when her heart pounded like the hoofs of a runaway stallion. 'So there's no reason for you to stay. I can arrange for you to be on the next flight out.'

'I didn't come for that, Mina.'

His voice didn't sound right. She was used to lazy cadences, the mellifluous sound of a man confident and at ease. Her senses quickened at that too-tight timbre, as if something squeezed his voice box. Till his meaning sank in.

There was only one other reason for Alexei to come.

Another scrape of pain, this time so deep Mina was surprised she didn't see blood.

She lifted her head and met his eyes. The shock of what she saw reverberated through her. He looked gaunt and strained where minutes ago he'd looked solid and strong. His olive complexion was a sickly grey that made his eyes look sunken.

The alteration was so profound she actually moved towards him, then stopped mid-step.

'If you've come to check if I'm pregnant, you can relax.' Her voice was harsh. 'Those condoms did the trick. No inconvenient accidents to worry about.'

To her surprise Alexei recoiled as if from the lash of a whip.

'Are you sure?' His voice held a husky quality that reminded her too much of his words of praise and encouragement when they'd made lo—when they'd had sex. 'I assumed your supposed period was a sham.'

Mina's fingers pressed tight together. 'Absolutely sure.' She'd been amazed to find herself fighting tears when

she arrived in Paris and discovered her period really had
started. She should have been relieved, she *was* relieved
there was no pregnancy to complicate things. Yet it had
been final confirmation that the fantasy was over.

'I'm sorry, Mina.'

She blinked and realised he'd closed the space between
them. Instantly she stiffened. 'Sorry there's no baby? I can't
believe that.'

'Sorry for *everything*.' He lifted both hands in a gesture
that was at once open and weary, as if he carried an impossibly heavy weight. 'If I could eradicate everything I said
that day I would. I'm *ashamed* of the accusations I threw
at you. That's why I came, to apologise.'

Mina stared, grappling to connect this desperate man
with the one she recognised. They were both Alexei, both
real, but this one, with the anguished eyes, was new.

'You were right, Mina. I need to take responsibility for
my actions. Instead I got wrapped up in my disappointment.'

'Disappointment?' At last she found her voice. 'It was
more than that. It was rage.'

He inclined his head, but paused as if gathering himself.
His mouth lifted in a bitter curve.

'You probably won't believe this, but I'm renowned for
never losing my cool, even when things go badly wrong,
even in highly pressured situations. I don't waste energy
on anger because I prefer to focus on fixing things and
moving on.'

Mina opened her mouth to argue when Alexei put up
his hand. 'Please, hear me out.' Reluctantly she nodded
and watched as he drew a breath that expanded his chest
mightily. He looked intimidatingly big and bold and heart-
breakingly desirable, yet his expression indicated a pain that
might even match her own. She didn't understand what he
wanted but she had to hear him out.

His hands dropped. 'As a kid I had a lot of anger, directed at my stepfather. Then at the people who harried my mother into an early grave. But I learned to control my feelings and focus on the future. It worked. Once I had that goal I had somewhere to channel my energies.'

Alexei waved an impatient hand. 'Sorry. Too much information.'

Mina was fascinated. But she was desperate to discover why he'd come. 'Get to the point, Alexei.'

A brief smile curled his lips but it wasn't reflected in his eyes. 'The point is I never lose control. Only twice. First when I discovered Ralph Carter had swindled the company and betrayed me.' His voice dropped to a sombre note. 'I'd trusted him, you see. The first person I'd actually trusted in...' He waved a dismissive hand again. 'Not that it matters.'

It mattered. It didn't take an expert to understand Alexei had major trust issues.

'Then, when I realised you weren't who you said, I lost it. Totally.' He shook his head and the lock of dark hair that had been combed back ruthlessly from his forehead tumbled over his brow, reminding her of the rumpled, gorgeous beachcomber she'd known in the Caribbean.

Brilliant green eyes focused on Mina. 'I told myself I was furious because you'd fooled me, that you and Carissa were laughing at me. I know now you weren't. But at the time all I could feel was hurt that I'd believed in you, *trusted* you and you'd betrayed that trust.'

There was that word again.

Alexei stood straighter. 'I lashed out because I cared for you, Mina. I wanted more from you than I'd ever wanted with anyone else. That's why I was furious. Because I hoped...' He stopped and she leaned forward, eager for more. 'As I said, it doesn't excuse my behaviour. You didn't deserve that and I apologise.'

Mina stared, trying to read his thoughts. She saw regret and shame. But what else?

'What did you hope, Alexei?' Her nerves were shredded, her heart racing.

Those stunning, familiar eyes locked on hers. 'I'd hoped we might have a future together.' His voice dropped. 'I'd even wondered how you felt about children.'

Mina gaped at him. 'But we'd only known each other a week.'

He shrugged, the usually fluid movement jerky. 'I trust my instinct. A week was long enough for me to feel things I've never felt before.'

'Things?' Her breath was a shallow draught of oxygen scented with warm male. Her brain froze.

Large hands took hers, their touch gentle yet compelling.

'Emotions. Not just desire but affection. Trust. Pride. Caring.' His eyes clouded. 'Not that you'd think so, the way I went for you when the truth came out.' His hands tightened on hers. 'The way I overreacted has nagged at me ever since.'

Mina watched him swallow. 'It made me realise the way I've stifled my emotions all these years isn't healthy. I'm determined to learn a better way to deal with my feelings. I need to make changes.'

Mina stared into Alexei's determined features, her emotions splintering in a dozen directions.

Wonder that he was here, baring his soul.

Sadness that his childhood experiences had affected him so profoundly.

Pride that he should confront his problems head-on and take action. Most men would run a mile from the idea of examining emotions and their own behaviour.

Regret that Alexei took all the blame when there'd been fault on both sides.

But above all excitement that he was here because he

cared for her. He'd wondered about the future…with her! Did he still wonder? Or was he here simply to explain? Surely he couldn't be so cruel.

'I'm sorry too, Alexei. I lied to you and I wasn't comfortable about it—'

'You were protecting your friend.' His hands squeezed hers. 'Loyalty like that is a wonderful thing.'

'Even if I acted impulsively?' Her eyebrows rose.

'If you hadn't, we wouldn't have met.'

The look he gave her, grave yet intense, turned her heart over. No man had looked at her that way. As if he spoke to *her*. Not the artist or the princess but the woman who sometimes struggled to find her way, who loved her life, yet made mistakes and sometimes doubted herself, like everyone else.

'You're not saying anything.' His hands tightened.

'We both overreacted.' Mina drew a shuddery breath as if she'd inhaled a field full of butterflies. 'I was so attracted to you but scared of what I felt.' Even though it was glorious it was far beyond her experience.

Was that why she'd given up so easily, scurrying away rather than forcing him to accept the truth? Because she was frightened of where such a relationship might lead? Because she was used to being alone, not trusting anyone to know her fully?

'Was? In the past?' His voice was harsh, cracking on the last word.

Mina stared into that proud, handsome face, drinking in the familiar features that could seem intimidating or playful and right now looked drawn with tension.

She tilted her face high, defying the cowardly impulse to lie. 'Am. Right now.' It felt like the bravest thing she'd ever done, admitting that.

Mina swallowed as he stroked the line of her jaw from ear to chin.

'Me, as well. I'm attracted and scared too.'

Her lips curved in an unsteady smile. 'Who are you and what have you done with Alexei Katsaros? He's not scared of anything.'

He shook his head. 'I'm scared of losing you. Scared I blew my chance.' His words made everything within her still.

'Your chance for an affair?' She had to ask, though she knew, deep inside, what he meant. She needed the words.

Alexei cupped her face in both hands, leaning in so his words feathered her mouth. 'My chance to build a future with you. I know it's too early. I know we barely know each other, but there's something about you, Mina, that I can't do without. I want you in my life and I'll do whatever I must to convince you to give me that chance.' He drew a deep breath and she felt his hands shake. 'I think I'm in love with you.'

His words resonated like the echo of a bell, the sound filling her with not just joy, but recognition.

'It's unsettling, isn't it?'

For a moment Alexei looked dumbfounded, as if he couldn't believe his ears. Then his face creased into a smile so broad it blinded. He released her hands and instead wrapped his arms around her, yanking her close so she was pressed against his hot, hard frame. It was heaven. Mina melted into him, her hands clutching, wearing a grin of her own.

Was this really happening?

'Unsettling in the best possible way.' He paused, his eyes locked on hers so Mina felt as if she were falling into a deep, bright sea. 'You mean that? You feel—'

'I've been falling in love with you since the day I reached your island and you made me furious and turned on at the same time.' Mina shook her head. 'I thought love was supposed to be all hearts and roses but you make me feel—' she struggled for words to convey at least some of her feelings '—*everything.*'

He nodded, his smile fading, eyes serious. 'Exactly. I want you even when we're arguing. Even when we don't agree. I want to make love to you all the time, but I also simply want to be with you, to share with you. To grow together.'

'Even though I live in Paris and you live—'

'I'm flexible. I can move.'

Mina's eyebrows shot up. He was a CEO with a business to run. She was the artist who could work almost anywhere. 'Even though I'm a princess?'

'You're not getting away from me that easily.' He lifted a hand to her hair and began to tug out the pins that secured it up. 'Besides, you look hot in a tiara.'

Mina saw a devilish glint in his eyes and sweet heat pierced her middle.

'Even though my best friend is Ralph Carter's daughter?'

Alexei shook his head. 'Stop trying to distract me. It won't work.'

'Distract you?'

Alexei's face lowered till his lips almost touched hers. 'I'm going to kiss you, Mina, till you stop throwing up objections. I'm going to kiss you till you agree to let me into your life so I can prove how good we'll be together.' All tension was gone from his face, replaced with a smug determination that made Mina want to laugh. For the first time today he looked like the man she'd fallen in love with.

For the first time since she left the Caribbean she felt happy.

'And if I don't agree?'

'Then, my sweet, sexy, Princess, I'll have to keep kissing you till you do.' There he was again, the confident tycoon with lurking humour in those slumberous eyes. But the tension humming through him, and the racing flick of the pulse at his temple, revealed Alexei took nothing for granted. He was still tense, waiting.

That, most of all, showed the change in him.

His lips brushed hers and Mina's knees went weak. Her arms tightened around his neck.

'If I agree, we need to take things slowly, get to know each other properly. We barely know each other.'

'I believe we know each other in the ways that count.' Alexei nuzzled the base of her throat and delight shuddered through her. 'But I won't rush you.'

'I should warn you, I'm no pushover.' Yet she arched against him.

Alexei lifted his head, his smile wickedly knowing. 'I'm counting on it. I'm here for the long haul.' Then he took her mouth with his and Mina entered a world of bliss.

Ages later she heard a man clear his throat. Huseyn. It had to be. But Alexei didn't react and Mina was too lost in a haze of delight to pull back.

Her brother-in-law wasn't used to being ignored. Would he march over and pull them apart? Then she heard Ghizlan murmur something and the door clicked shut.

Alexei pulled back enough to look down at her. The gleam in his eyes made her heart tumble. 'So, your family is tactful as well as protective? I like them better all the time.'

Mina dragged air into starved lungs. 'Don't think they'll make it easy for you. They'll give you the third degree about your life, goals and intentions.'

His smiling eyes held hers. 'I can't think of anything else I'd rather discuss.' He stepped back the tiniest fraction, unhooking one of her hands from his neck and bringing it to his lips. 'My intention is to be the man who'll make you happy. Always.'

EPILOGUE

A YEAR LATER, to the day, Alexei entered their Parisian home. Not the cramped place Mina had rented, but a spacious, high-ceilinged house with space for a studio. He smiled. That was where she'd be, working, even though there was barely time for him to shower and change before they headed to tonight's exhibition.

He ripped off the tie he'd worn for a press conference and tossed it over the back of a settee. His pulse quickened as he headed for the studio. Thinking of Mina filled him with a heady excitement he didn't think would ever fade.

But for once his sweetheart wasn't up to her elbows in clay or working with metal. The place was empty, save for the usual clutter. A half-finished piece stood near the window. Sketches were pinned to one wall near a scuffed workbench.

Alexei's eyes went to a small, familiar piece in bronze on a nearby table. A man's hands, *his* hands, cupped and holding the slim fingers of a woman. *Mina's*. Though he appeared to support her hands, their fingers were intertwined as if sharing strength. Sharing a bond.

Whenever he saw the piece, Alexei felt a thump in the region of his heart. An awareness of how lucky he was to have Mina. This year had been everything he could have hoped and it made him more determined to keep what he had.

Smiling, he put his hand to his pocket and turned towards the door, only to pull up short.

The woman he adored stood there, wearing a curiously unreadable expression and a stunning dress of flame red. Alexei's lungs expanded on an appreciative breath as he took in the tiny shoulder straps and flirty skirt that were an invitation to explore.

'Mina! You look stunning.' He imagined his hands skimming her taut thighs beneath the fabric. Heat circled his chest and drove straight to his groin.

'You don't look so bad yourself.' She crossed the room and kissed him. Alexei gathered her up, relishing the fire that ignited between them and the sweet sensation of coming home. Coming to Mina.

When he ended the kiss, he kept his arms around her. Her exotic spice and cinnamon scent was warm in his nostrils and he savoured how right this was.

'I heard from Carissa today.'

'Hmm?' He looked down into velvety eyes. She was smiling.

'She and Pierre are visiting Ralph in Jeirut. He's thriving and even picking up some of the language.'

Belatedly Alexei caught the thread of the conversation. Ralph Carter. In Jeirut.

Mina walked her fingers up Alexei's chest, making him wish she'd found him naked in the shower.

'It was a stroke of genius, getting him involved in your programme there.'

Alexei shook his head. 'It was as much your idea as mine. You suggested Jeirut.' Because the opportunities for gambling there were limited, so Ralph would have less temptation.

Alexei had revised his view of Ralph when he learned of his gambling addiction, a coping mechanism to deal with overwhelming grief at his wife's death.

After hearing of the older man's shame and desperate plan to pay back the money by gambling more, and his near suicidal despair when that failed, Alexei hadn't pressed charges. Prison wouldn't get his money back. Instead he'd co-opted Ralph into the initiative he and Sheikh Huseyn had begun to give unemployed youth the skills and confidence to start up innovative businesses.

After a rocky start, Ralph, with his financial expertise, pernickety attention to detail and genuine interest in his budding entrepreneurs, was a surprise hit. It helped them and gave him back a sense of purpose and self-respect.

'But you were the one who suggested including him.' Mina's fingers reached his chin and traced his jaw, teasing. 'You gave him a second chance. Not many people would do that.' The way she looked at him stirred Alexei's soul. His chest swelled.

'Everyone deserves a second chance, sweetheart.'

She smiled and Alexei felt the radiance of it all the way to the centre of his being. 'Which shows how right I was about you, Alexei Katsaros. You might be savvy and über-successful, but there's more to you than business.'

'Oh, much more.' He slid his hands down Mina's back, over that pertly rounded rump, and pulled her against him. That was better. Much better.

Mina wriggled and Alexei was tempted to forget their plans to attend a new exhibition. Except he had other plans too. A romantic dinner for two in one of the city's best restaurants as a prelude to something much more significant.

But looking into Mina's smiling face, Alexei knew it wasn't a picture-perfect setting that mattered. It was her. And how she felt. Suddenly he couldn't wait.

'Mina.' He swallowed, trying to eradicate the betraying husky edge to his voice. 'I have something for you.'

She blinked. 'That's a coincidence. I have something for you too. Over there—'

'Sweetheart.' Alexei turned her head back towards him and reached into his pocket. 'I've waited a whole year to give you time to be sure of me and what you feel. I'm in love with you, Mina. I want to spend my life with you.'

He'd spent hours thinking of how to say this, searching for something unique and memorable. But when he looked into

Mina's warm gaze, each carefully crafted word disintegrated and he was left with the bare truth. 'Will you marry me?'

He lifted his hand and showed her the ring he'd had made for her. A unique, modern piece of white gold and a square-cut ruby. Sparks shot off the facets as it trembled in the light.

Mina's hand closed around his and he realised they were both shaking. He heard a muffled gasp and saw her eyes were overbright.

'Mina? Sweetheart?'

She shook her head and smiled, her mouth a crumpled curve. 'That sounds like a wonderful plan. I love you too, darling. And yes, I want to be with you, always.'

Elation surged so high he felt ten feet tall. Alexei bent to kiss her but her fingertips on his lips stopped him. 'You don't want to see my gift?'

'Sorry?'

'My gift.' Mina reached over to a nearby table and picked up a small box. She flipped the lid and there were two matching wedding rings. 'I thought a year was time enough. I want you with all my heart, Alexei.' She laughed, the sound like liquid crystal, shining with promise. 'It seems we both had the same idea.'

'Because we're perfectly matched.' He spared an appreciative glance for the finely crafted wedding bands, then lifted her hand and slid the engagement ring onto her finger. Emotion threatened to overwhelm him.

'We definitely are.' She moved her fingers, admiring the ring. 'Thank you, Alexei. I never thought I could be so happy.'

'Nor did I.' He raised her hand to his lips and kissed it. 'And this is just the beginning.' Then he scooped her up and swung her round till the room rang with her delicious laughter. It was a sound he looked forward to hearing for the rest of his life.

* * * * *